FEDERAL PROTECTION AGENCY

BOOKS 4-6

BY EVIE RILEY

FEDERAL PROTECTION AGENCY

BOOKS 4-6

COPYRIGHT © 2022-2023

EVIE RILEY

SECOND EDITION

ISBN: 978-1-77357-701-2

PUBLISHED BY NAUGHTY NIGHTS PRESS LLC

COVER ART BY WILLSIN ROWE

FEDERAL PROTECTION AGENCY: BOOKS 4-6

Cooper

The right path can save a life...
Growing up in foster care, the only true friends Cooper Jones had were the black hat hackers at the community center. Now an analyst and hacker for Homeland Security, Coop prefers to be behind a computer to fight his battles. Recently scooped up by the Federal Protection Agency, he is a valuable asset to the team.

Noah

Letting go is truly the most powerful control of all.
Federal Prosecutor Noah Riley has had enough of what he feels is a failing justice system. He's watched one too many times as young victims are let down and the men who have caused them harm go free.

It's time for a change in his life, but he has no idea where to start.

Damien

It takes three to make life go right...
Private Investigator Damien Anderson can be sweet and kind but the moment anyone puts the people he loves at risk, he has no problem becoming lethal. Working with the Federal Protection Agency, Damien finds himself at a crossroads his past starts to catch up to him.

Trigger Warnings: Murder, Violence, Drugs, Abuse, Kidnapping, Captivity, Crimes against children.

COOPER

FEDERAL PROTECTION AGENCY

BOOK FOUR

BY EVIE RILEY

COOPER

The right path can save a life...

Growing up in foster care, the only true friends Cooper Jones had were the black hat hackers at the community center. At eighteen, after being caught by the government for hacking into Homeland Security, The Agent in Charge, impressed by Coop's skills, determined he needed to work for the government instead of hacking them. That Agent saved him from a life of crime, and almost certainly saved his life.

Now an analyst and hacker for Homeland Security, Coop prefers to be behind a computer to fight his battles. Recently scooped up by the Federal Protection Agency, he is a valuable asset to the team.

Detective Jonah West has dedicated his life to helping the people of Baton Rouge and he doesn't like it when criminals get to go free on a technicality. He spends countless hours every day being the best police officer he can to make sure that doesn't happen often. The downside to a cop's life is that his twelve-year-old son, Drew, spends much of his time alone with only his computer for entertainment. When his house is broken into and Drew comes up missing, Jonah contacts the FPA and asks them for help. Jonah is willing to pull out all the stops if it means getting his son back.

Can Coop and Jonah keep Drew safe while they track down the kidnappers, and will their growing closeness mean they have a future together?

CHAPTER ONE

Jonah

MY WHOLE BODY was sore. It had been a long night at work. Hell, it had been a long week.

I hated doing shift work, it was always hard getting used to going from days to nights without much notice in between. That was the life of a detective, though. Everyone had to take turns working overnights so we could all get the chance to enjoy sleeping in our own bed at night and being outside during daylight hours. The trick was, though, when I caught a case, it wasn't like I could just go home when my shift was over.

I worked in the homicide division, so when a case came in, we only had forty-eight hours to try and solve it before our chances of finding the killer went down drastically. Which meant it was quite often a lot of long hours, working all day and night just to try to get justice for the victim. Today, I had been going for thirty-six hours straight and I was in desperate need of some sleep.

It was eight in the morning when I pulled into my driveway. It was Wednesday, though, so I couldn't just head up to bed. I had to get my twelve year old son ready for school.

Andrew, or Drew, as he preferred, was the reason I worked so hard. I wanted to make sure these streets were safer for him, because I knew all too soon he would be off on his own and carving out his own path in this world. I wanted to try and make it at least a little bit safer for him to be out on the streets at night. My greatest fear was getting a call to go out to a crime scene only to discover the victim was my son. It was something I knew I would have to face when his mother got pregnant. I wasn't really sure I was ready to be a father at that point in my life, but I knew I couldn't walk away from him.

My whole life, I had tried to fit within the right box. The box that society said I was supposed to fit into. I had always been athletic. I played on the football team, and I was on the basketball team, too. I loved playing sports, I still do. I was a guy's guy. However, I was a guy's guy who liked to look at other guys naked.

I knew I was gay from the age of twelve. I knew it wasn't normal to enjoy watching the other guys change in the locker rooms or see them showering. I was well aware that I enjoyed it too much. However, I was also well aware that the other guys would never be cool with being around a gay man. I couldn't be gay, not back then, so I did what every other guy was doing. I dated girls. I had sex with girls, even though it wasn't really who I wanted to be with, and I told myself that was going to have to be good enough. I suppressed my gay self in favor of fitting in where society expected me to.

I was eighteen when I joined the police academy and once more, I was faced with an environment that wasn't open minded and welcoming of gay men. I continued to hide and I even got married to Melissa. When I was twenty-three, she gave birth to my son.

I was twenty-nine when I finally decided I couldn't do it anymore. I couldn't keep living the lie. I couldn't keep my desires at bay. I couldn't keep having sex with my wife and wishing it was a man underneath me. I just couldn't do it anymore.

So, one night when my son was six, I told Melissa that I was gay and wanted a divorce. She didn't handle it well. I knew she wouldn't. She tried telling me that I was just going through a phase. That I was confused. That I enjoyed having sex with her. After all, we had a son. She didn't appreciate it when I pointed out that I only got off on the friction of having sex with her and the vivid fantasies I would have while we had sex. Fantasies of a guy underneath me, whimpering and begging for more. She really didn't appreciate that part. Though, in her defense, I shouldn't have said it, but I was so sick of listening to her going on and on about how I was confused. I wasn't confused. I was just sick and tired of living in that small closet. After twenty-nine years, I had every right to live my life for myself. I wanted to explore my own sexuality, for the first time in my life.

I knew we would get divorced. It was going to be a very easy divorce, because there was no fixing us. I was into men and so was she. There was nothing either of us could do or say that would ever change that.

I had truly hoped that we would be able to co-parent and be friends. I knew it wouldn't be right away, but Melissa had always been open minded and okay with different sexual orientations. She had male and female friends who were gay. I figured once the dust settled and the hard feelings had passed, that she would be okay with me, too. I was very wrong. She was okay with other people. She was not okay with me. Not her husband. Nope. She had never been okay with me since the day I told her I was gay.

The divorce was simple. She signed it almost immediately and she wanted to avoid having to go to court. I thought it was great, that we were going to be able to get along and co-parent, that she had been taking this all so well. And then, it was time to work out the custody agreement and she ghosted us.

She had signed over full custody to me for Drew. According to the document she sent me along with the custody paperwork, she couldn't stand to look at either one of us. She felt that Drew would only remind her of the worst years of her life. Of the deception that I had put her through. She felt like I had somehow conned her into loving me and giving me a child. As if I was some sort of con man using her for her money and a kid. She wanted nothing to do with me and, even worse, she wanted nothing to do with Drew.

We hadn't seen or heard from her since that day. Six years, now. Not a single fucking word. Drew never received a phone call, no text message, no birthday card or Christmas card. Nothing. Having to explain to my son at the age of six where his mother was and why she wasn't coming back wasn't something I ever thought I would have to do.

At the age of six, he didn't understand why his own mother wasn't around. It wasn't like she hadn't been around for his whole life. When she was there, she had been a loving and doting mother. She was always helping with his playgroups and then with his school. She was on the PTA and spearheaded every fundraiser and bake sale. She was an active mom and I thought she loved being a mom.

I knew we were still young when we had him. She was twenty-two, but I figured we both had our jobs and we were responsible adults. I never missed going out to bars and clubs and partying all night. I didn't think she missed it, either. She never showed any signs of missing that life.

But at the first chance she had to leave and wipe the slate clean, she did.

For months afterward, Drew would sit in front of the windows in the living room, staring out at the driveway, waiting for her to come home. The first birthday and Christmas were hard. He was so confident that his mother would come by for them and when she didn't, there was no amount of comfort that I could give him that made him feel better.

That first Christmas was heartbreaking for me. He ran down the stairs Christmas morning and completely ignored the presents under the tree. He sat up on his knees on the couch and looked out the window and waited for Melissa to come over. When I tried to get him to open his presents from Santa, he refused and said he would do it when Mommy got there. All day, he sat there on his knees just watching the driveway, and every time a car drove by, he got his hopes up that it was Melissa. He went to bed that night crying his heart out and with not a single present opened.

I had to call my parents and they drove fourteen hours to come down to spend a few days with us. Only when his grandparents had arrived did he finally feel like opening presents.

My mom was amazing, because she had brought everything to cook for a full Christmas dinner. It had been a hard day, but we all got through it. Drew had gotten through it.

I had to hand it to my parents, they were older and they generally had traditional beliefs, but they supported me in being gay. It was a bit shaky at first, but when they discovered that Melissa had abandoned Drew, they were outraged. My father called her a closed minded bitch for not being able to accept me as gay and raise our son together. They were old fashioned, but to them abandoning your child was a far worse crime than being gay and raising one.

We didn't talk about my sexual orientation and I hadn't really brought a guy over to their house. We kind of had a bit of a Don't Ask, Don't Tell rule, but that was okay with me. It wasn't like I wanted to talk to them about my boyfriends, anyway.

As I walked inside the house, I was fully prepared to see Drew running around and grabbing the last of his things. I didn't have a babysitter for him when I worked nights. He was twelve and I knew he was responsible enough to handle being on his own. It wasn't like I went into work at five or six o'clock at night. I went to work at ten and he was in bed for ten-thirty. When he was younger, I'd had a babysitter, but now we both felt he was old enough to sleep alone in the house with all of the windows and doors locked.

I also had a security system with an alarm on every door and window so he was perfectly safe once he was in the house. And he wasn't old enough to go sneaking out at night. That would be something I knew I was going to have to deal with when he was around sixteen. Thankfully, I had at least four years before that would happen.

Drew was also very mature and responsible for his age. I never had to worry about him doing something incredibly stupid. He made it easy to trust him alone.

What I didn't expect to see when I walked into my home was the obvious signs of a struggle. The house was a mess and the further I walked in, the more worried I became. There were lamps shattered on the floor, the coffee table was broken, furniture was turned over, the picture frames on the walls were crooked and some were on the floor, the glass broken. What had my heart stopping, though, was seeing the directional blood drops leading from the living room to the front door.

"Drew!" I screamed as I ran from room to room, trying to find my son.

The detective in me knew I was being an idiot. I was running around an obvious crime scene, potentially destroying evidence, but I had to find my son. He could be hurt somewhere in my own home and I was not about to leave him injured on his own while I waited for the crime scene techs to get there.

I searched every room in the whole house, but Drew wasn't there. My son wasn't there. I could feel panic starting to claw at my throat, but I fought through it. Me panicking was not going to find my son any faster.

I had to focus.

I had to work the scene and follow the steps.

I had to think.

I had to follow proper procedures.

I sucked in a deep breath and let it out slowly. With a shaky hand, I pulled out my cell phone and called the kidnapping in. The fact that I had to actually call my own son's kidnapping in tore at my heart.

With the crime reported, though, I then turned to calling every single one of my son's friends to see if they had heard from him since last night. I needed to know if he had been missing only an hour or two, or if he had been missing all night. Just like with murders, the first forty-eight hours in a kidnapping were the most crucial. If we didn't find him within forty-eight hours of the time of his disappearance, we might never find him. Or worse, I might find him dead.

I had to work this case, but I knew there was no way in hell my boss would let me. It was too personal. I was too close to it. I understood that, I did, but I was not going to sit on my ass and let this son of a bitch have my son.

No one knew these streets better than I did.

I had informants and contacts in the Southside. They wouldn't talk to any cop but me, and if they knew my own son was missing they would help me. But in order to get them to help, I would need access to this case so I could point them in the right direction. And the only way I was going to get access to this case was if I was working it.

The second the patrol cars pulled in, I gave them my statement before I got into my car and headed off for the one place that I knew could help.

The Federal Protection Agency.

I had helped them with one case two months ago and they all seemed like stand up guys. They were all capable of stopping a serial killer. I knew they were making a rather impressive name for themselves within their area of expertise. They focused on crimes against children and my son's case was exactly within the realm of their specialty. I needed their help and I knew I would have a better chance at convincing them to let me work the case with them than I did with my own boss.

I also knew they didn't have to follow the letter of the law. They had immunity; they could break the law and do whatever they had to do to get their cases closed. To save children. I needed that right now. I needed to know that someone would kick in the door to save my son even without a warrant. I needed to know that we wouldn't have to wait around for evidence or for a judge to issue a warrant if we didn't have anything solid.

The FPA working the case increased the odds of my son being found and that was all that mattered.

The second I pulled up to the building, I ran inside and up to their office floor. I strolled right into their conference room without stopping. I saw some new faces as I walked by, but I ignored them. I needed to speak with Mason. He was the only person who mattered right now. I knocked on his office door before I walked in without waiting to be granted entry.

Mason was in charge of the Agency and his K9 partner, Koda, was never far from his side. I didn't have the pleasure of working with him on the serial killer case. He had been in the hospital with his boyfriend, Jarod. Their serial killer, Marcus Long, who was also a detective at the time, had been killing young teenage boys and torturing them before leaving them in a dumpster.

The Agency had been brought in by a FBI Profiler, Knox Hunter, to help after he'd had nothing on the killer for three months. At the last crime scene, Long had planted a bomb designed to hurt Ryzen, a man who worked for the Agency and was ordered to protect Knox. In that blast, Ryzen had ended up with some bruised ribs, but Jarod had taken a large shard of metal to his stomach. He had to have part of his liver removed and had been placed on medical leave, followed by desk duty for three months.

"Detective West, what brings you by unannounced?" Mason asked.

"My twelve year old son, Drew, has been kidnapped. I need your help."

I was hoping, I was praying, that he would say yes. That he would take this case over and then I could maybe take a breath, finally. I knew the guys in the Baton Rouge Kidnapping Division were good, don't get me wrong. The problem was, they had too many cases and not enough detectives. The Crime Lab was backed up, too, so any evidence that could help you find a missing child was delayed by weeks, sometimes months. They weren't fast at solving cases and that wasn't their fault, but I wasn't going to wait for months to find my son. I was going to find him before he was killed. There was simply no other option.

"Tell me everything," Mason said, and the tightness that had been wrapped around my throat started to loosen up, just a tiny bit.

CHAPTER TWO

Cooper

I HEADED INTO the conference room to see that Sebastian, Damien, and Max were the only ones there.

I had no idea what the case would be, but I knew we had a new one. It would be different for us, because for the most part, we had been working cases all together and one at a time. Within the past couple of weeks, though, the team had picked up some new guys and we were able to work more than one case at a time.

We currently had two cases going on. The first one was a drug trafficking ring that was using young kids as mules, dealers, and cooks. Ryzen, Roland, Rafe, and Hollingsworth were currently working that one. Jarod was also helping out on desk duty and I knew Mason was good to jump in should we need it. He had a shit load of paperwork he was stuck doing, because with everything one of his guys on the team did, he had to fill out paperwork for it.

The second case we had on the go was an underground brothel and strip club using underage girls as their workers. That was being handled by the new guys, Kruze, Gabe, and Deke. I didn't know much about them, but they had only started working with the team in the past two weeks. They seemed like good guys and Mason handpicked them himself, so I had to trust his judgment.

I was still the only computer guy, though, so I was working both cases and running whatever tracing they needed. Thankfully, they could run names themselves, but I was the one working any security cameras and doing a deeper dive into their victims and suspects. We needed another computer tech, another hacker, who could work the cases as well, because soon enough it would be too much for me to handle. Not that I minded being kept busy, but I had to sleep at some point, too.

"We got another case?" I asked as I slid into my chair.

"Mason didn't give logistics, just asked if we could come in and help with a local case," Damien answered.

"You know, with the amount of times you get brought in here, you really should consider moving here," I commented.

Damien, Sebastian, and Max were private detectives who worked for their own company in Gaithersburg, Maryland. We would often call them to come out and help us when we needed more guys. They came down for the last case a week ago to help with a major raid and had stuck around to help with the paperwork for it. Originally, they were set to be heading back out tomorrow, but it looked like they might just be sticking around for another case.

"It's something that we have been considering. We can move our private detective agency over here. We would get more work here," Sebastian commented.

"Plus, you would get to keep hanging

out with all of us," I said, flashing a grin.

The three of them didn't really do social very well. They liked to keep to themselves, but they were good guys and it was nice having them around. They were three more guys who could handle themselves out in the field and that meant I didn't have to go into the field as often.

I *could* work as a field agent, but I preferred to work behind a computer. I didn't like having to shoot people and I really didn't like being shot at. Bullets hurt. I knew that from personal experience and it wasn't an experience I wanted to repeat ever again in my life.

Before anymore could be said, Mason walked in with Detective West right on his heels. I wasn't expecting to see Detective West again. He had helped with our serial killer case and then we had all gone our separate ways. I figured this case must be one that he had been working on and now he needed some help.

"You all remember Detective West," Mason started. "His twelve year old son, Drew, has been kidnapped. Detective West was on the overnight shift at the station last night. When he arrived home this morning, just after eight, he discovered obvious signs of a struggle and his son was nowhere to be found. He has called his son's friends, but they hadn't heard from him since yesterday. Crime scene has already been called."

I instantly felt bad for the man. Working as a homicide detective was hard enough, but to be doing that *and* raising a twelve year old son... No way was that easy. I had to give him credit, he was doing everything he could to protect his city and the innocent people in it, while trying to be a father. Not many people could handle both lives.

"Have you called his mother?" Max asked.

"No. She walked out of his life six years ago. We haven't heard from her since. There's no boyfriend, either, it's just us," Detective West answered.

Now that was even more impressive. He was working full time as a homicide detective and raising his son *alone*. He was a single father and doing everything he could for his city. That definitely explained the dark bags under his eyes. He wasn't getting the sleep he needed while pulling double duty.

Still, a twelve year old boy getting grabbed from his home, that was risky. His kidnappers either didn't know that Drew was the son of a homicide detective or they did. My money was on them knowing. The kidnapping could have been connected to a case he was currently working.

"Was there a babysitter?" Damien asked.

"No. I didn't leave until ten last night. I made sure all of the windows and doors were locked and the alarm was set. I have an alarm on every window and door, so if someone tried to open them it would go off and I would immediately get an alert on my phone. The security company would be notified and they would notify the police. None of that happened and I *know* I set the alarm."

"If you set the alarm and it didn't go off, then that only leaves two options. Either your son turned the alarm off so he could let someone in, or you were hacked.," I stated.

"Except he couldn't have let anyone in. When the alarm is turned off for any reason, I get a notification on my phone. Nothing has come in."

"Does it still say it's armed?" I asked.

It was sounding more and more like he had been hacked. That would explain why no one had been notified of the break in. It also meant that whoever grabbed his son knew about the alarm system and knew how to hack into it to work around the notifications. This wasn't random. I'd bet my ass this was planned.

Detective West pulled out his phone and checked before he spoke. "It says it's armed."

"You were hacked. Can I see your phone?" I asked.

He handed the phone over to me and I started to go through it to see if there was any spyware or other backdoor access apps. His Internet usage was all normal and nothing stood out, though. I handed the phone back to him as I spoke.

"Does Drew have a cell phone?"

"He does, but it's still at the house. Along with his school bag."

"How easy is it to hack a security system?" Damien asked me.

"Very easy. Novice hackers can easily do it. I need to plug into the main security hub at the house and then I might be able to find the signature and backtrack it," I answered.

"All of you are going to Detective West's house. Do a full investigation. I have already informed local PD that we are taking over the case. Crime Scene is there on the scene and working it. Don't get in their way, but get what you need," Mason instructed.

We all gave a nod, almost in unison, and started to file out of the room. I quickly went to my office so I could grab the gear that I needed for the security system. With everything that I needed on me, I headed out and started to follow the others to Detective West's house.

I was surprised that Mason was going to allow Detective West to work the case with us, but I could understand why he made that choice. The victim was his son, there was no way, as a detective himself, he was going to let someone else handle the case. It would be better to have him working with us than for him to be out there drudging through the case on his own.

The second we arrived on the scene it was a madhouse of government vehicles. I parked in the first spot that I could find and followed the others inside. The first thing I noted was that the whole place was pretty much trashed and to me that made it pretty clear it was more than one kidnapper. All of that destruction didn't come from one twelve year old boy fighting off a single adult.

Usually, when a kid is kidnapped, there is hardly any destruction because they don't stand a chance against their kidnapper. This kidnapper either had some help, and Drew had a serious fight instinct, or they were looking for something. Maybe they had even added to the destruction to cover something up. I was completely confident the team would discover the answers soon enough.

I turned my attention to the main security hub by the front door. I plugged into it and started to run the diagnostics. I knew in my gut it had been hacked. That would be the only way for someone to get the alarm to not send off the notifications that it was programmed to do. It was also clearly not armed, but it was still registering that it was. There were multiple doors open, so if it was armed the whole house would be echoing with the alarm going off.

"Anything?" Detective West asked.

"I will have to run another, more in depth diagnostic on it with my computer back at my office. But, I can tell you right now, it was definitely hacked. It's still registering as armed and it's not even registering the doors being open. Once I'm back at the office, I'll be able to run some apps to find the hacker's signature and try and track it down, Detective."

"Jonah. You can call me *Jonah.*"

"Have you had any cases recently that someone could want payback for?" I asked as I unplugged my device from the main hub.

"No. I've been working homicides. They were all pretty straight forward, to be honest. There's nothing that stands out as unusual at all. I can't see this being connected to me, truthfully, but I can't see this being connected to Drew, either. He's just a twelve year old kid."

It *would* be odd for the motive to be connected to Drew. But at the same time, if it wasn't connected to Jonah, then it had to be connected to Drew or maybe his mother.

"What about his mother? I know you said you haven't spoken to her in six years. But could she be involved in something that could have gotten Drew kidnapped?"

"I don't know. I can't see her being involved in anything that would result in this. But it's been six years, I don't know what she's been doing since."

"We're gonna need to find her. This is too much destruction for it to be a simple kidnapping. You have to see that. I don't know how big Drew is, but he couldn't be muscular enough for a grown adult to not be able to grab him easily. To cause this level of destruction, it's overkill."

"I know. I didn't see it before, but now that my mind has started to process the events, I can see it. Drew spends all of his time on his computer playing video games. My son isn't athletic. He doesn't have any interest in playing sports or working out. He's a normal and average size twelve year old boy. He doesn't even know how to fight. I've taught him a few self-defense moves, but he doesn't have much interest in it. Whoever it was could have easily grabbed him without making a mess. This really is overkill."

I could see the wheels in his mind turning even as he spoke. He was trying to figure out who could have done this and why. Drew was just a kid, so it wasn't like this was directed toward him. He was just the weapon they were using to cause pain to either Jonah or Drew's mother. We had to figure out which one was the real target of this attack before we would be able to narrow down the potential suspects.

"Well, whoever they were, they didn't want anyone to ever get anything off of this," Max said, holding up a laptop that looked like a hammer was taken to it.

"That's Drew's," Jonah said.

Now that was interesting.

Why obliterate a kid's laptop?

The only reason I could think of was if something was on it that they didn't want anyone to get. I held my hand out and took it as Max spoke.

"Long shot, but can you fix it?"

"Depends on what is broken. If the motherboard is still in good standing, I could repair it long enough to download what I need off of it, but worst case I can just swap the hard drive into another system as long as its not damaged. I'm gonna head back to the office with this. I want to run the diagnostics on the security system and I'll see what I can do about the laptop."

"That thing looks impossible to fix, though," Jonah said.

"I've seen worse," I offered with what I hoped was a comforting smile.

With the laptop tucked under my arm, I headed out and hastily made my way back to the Agency. I needed to get into the system quickly to see what was so important for them to destroy it. People didn't smash a computer like that for the hell of it. They wanted it destroyed and that meant there was a reason for it. I just had to find it.

The second I got back to my office, I set up to start downloading the data from the security system and run the additional diagnostics. I then turned all of my attention to the laptop. I had to take it apart and then I would need to hook it up to my own special equipment that would let me get the data off of the drive even if it was encrypted or partially corrupted. There wasn't much that could stop me finding what I was looking for once I got started. This was the part that I loved about my job.

I had always loved working with computers. I started hacking when I was a young kid, and now, most would call me a hacking genius. There really wasn't anything I couldn't hack. Hell, when I was nineteen, I'd hacked Homeland Security just for the hell of it. I really wanted to know if I could do it, so I did. That success brought Homeland Security Agent Ronald Evans to my front door.

Evans, now that man was a good man. He had dragged my ass down to the Homeland Security Field Office, but instead of arresting me and sticking me in an interrogation room to face felony charges, he took me around their cyber security division. He showed me some of the cases they were working on; most of them were for counter terrorists. He showed me all of the white hat hackers who worked for Homeland Security. Up until that point, I'd had no idea someone could be a hacker and work for the government. The idea that someone could be a white hat hacker, someone that hacked for the good of the people and not just to commit crimes, blew my mind.

I had fallen in love the moment I stepped foot into that room. Evans had given me a job right then and there. I literally sat down and started working on a case. I instantly fell in love with the entire process. I was able to do a job where I could hack and gather intel, but I could also work on a puzzle that challenged my mind. Each new case was a new brainteaser and I loved every second of it. Evans had taken a lost and lonely boy, one likely headed for a life of crime and disaster, and not only had he given me a family, but a home and a true purpose. He saved my life and I would always be grateful for him.

***

"Yes!" I rejoiced as my program dinged to indicate I'd finally fixed the laptop drive enough to get into it.

It had been three hours since I arrived back at the Agency and I knew the others would still be at the scene going over everything, talking with the neighbors, and trying to find any security cameras that they could use. I was hoping by the time they came back that I would have something for them.

The diagnostics from the security system had come back, confirming that it had been hacked, but the code was very intricate, far too much for a simple code to hack into the system.

We weren't dealing with a novice, but rather a pro.

The thing was, this pro wasn't a normal pro. Most didn't go out of their way to make a hack harder than it needed to be. The code to get into the security system didn't need to be this intricate, but the hacker had chosen to make it that way.

Almost as if they wanted to show off their skills.

I pulled up the data from the laptop and started to look through the usual places. I hit the Internet web browser history first to see what Drew was into.

"Whoa," I said aloud as I started to see the places he had explored.

They weren't normal websites. Certainly nothing that a typical twelve year old boy would be looking at. These websites were places only a hacker could get into.

Drew had been spending time on the DarkNet.

He was exploring a world that was used by some of the world's most dangerous criminals and any one of them could have kidnapped him if he'd stumbled onto something he wasn't supposed to see. And based on how destroyed the laptop was, that was exactly what had happened. Whoever had kidnapped him wanted to destroy any trace evidence of themselves in Drew's life. It also meant that Drew might already be dead, and if he wasn't, he would be killed the second his kidnappers had what they needed from him.

"Shit."

CHAPTER THREE

Jonah

AFTER WE WRAPPED up at the crime scene at my house, I knew that I would never be able to live in again and feel safe. I knew I would need to sell it and move so both Drew and I would be able to move on from this whole nightmare.

Realistically, I should have probably moved already. This was the house that Melissa and I bought, the house that Drew had grown up in. It might have been better for him if I had moved us someplace new when he was six. Maybe then it would have been easier for him to accept that his mother wasn't coming back. At the time, though, I was scared it would traumatize him even more. I didn't want him thinking that Melissa couldn't find him when she came to visit. After this whole nightmare, though, we were moving. This house was cursed and it was time for someone else to deal with it.

Back at the Agency now, we immediately headed up to where Cooper's office was. I had never been in his office and I couldn't help but be surprised by how large it was. The first thing that grabbed my attention were the multiple flat screen computer monitors up on the one wall across from his desk, each one scrolling different information. There were computer parts and equipment scattered all over the place and I could tell he used everything in this room. It was clearly designed for him to be able to do anything with a computer and also repair any that were damaged.

I couldn't believe he had been able to repair the damage done to Drew's computer. The thing had looked like it had been run over and then backed up on it. Yet, he had called and said he had something major and we needed to come in right away.

I was hoping he had found something that would lead us to whoever took my son. At the same time, I was confused, because what could there possibly be on Drew's computer that would explain anything that had happened to him? He just used it to play video games and do his homework.

"What do you got, Coop?" Damien asked as he strolled into the room.

"First, the security system was definitely hacked, but it wasn't done by a novice. The code that was used was too sophisticated. It was actually more intricate than it needed to be, telling me this hacker wanted to show off and he wanted people to know he was experienced."

"Why, though? Why give us more than he needed to?" I couldn't help but ask.

"Because hackers can be assholes. Arrogant assholes. They like to show off. They like to hack into systems that they have no business being in just to prove that they can do it. That's not the bigger issue, though. I was able to reconstruct Drew's hard drive and I could see what he's been doing on the laptop. Drew's been hacking into different levels of the web. He's been playing around within the DarkNet."

"I'm sorry, what? No, Drew can't hack. He uses that computer to do his homework and play video games," I instantly retorted. There was no way that Drew could hack. Yes, he was good at math, but he wasn't some computer genius. I would have noticed if he was.

"What is the DarkNet, first of all?" Sebastian asked.

"Think of the Internet like an iceberg. You only see ten percent of it above the water and that ten percent is relatively safe, with the obvious exception of predators. The real stuff is the ninety percent that lives under the water, the parts you can't see. That's called the DarkNet or the DarkWeb. It's where the criminals live. Blackmarket selling, hitmen, child predators, you name it, it's there. But not all of the DarkNet is bad. A lot of novice hackers start out by hacking their way into the DarkNet and then they play around with other hackers. There are video games on there that companies create and get people to play to try and find the flaws within the system. They use hackers as beta testers to improve the games."

"Why hackers?" Max asked.

"Because in order to hack you have to understand computer code, how to write and read it. How it interacts with other codes to create video games. So, when up and coming programmers have a new game they want to test out before taking it to the market, they get hackers to play them and see what bugs there are. They look for ways to improve it. Hackers understand what can be done and they are able to pick up little details that are wrong within the code. The gamer gets to test out a new game for free and the programmer or company gets free feedback on a technical level they couldn't get from the average gamer. It's a win/win situation. Drew has been playing some of those games."

I couldn't believe it. I thought Drew was out of harm's way at home. I thought him having an interest in video games was safe. I didn't care what he did when he was an adult, but I figured if he was so interested in video games, then he would probably want to go to school to be a videogame designer. I'd figured it was best to encourage that and let him do whatever he wanted on the computer. I didn't need him to be a rocket scientist or a lawyer. I just wanted him to be happy with whatever career he chose. But I didn't know he was hacking to get into these games. I didn't know he even knew how to hack.

What kind of parent was I that I didn't know what my kid was doing on the computer?

I was a detective, for fuck's sake.

I should have known.

"How did he even learn?" I couldn't help but ask even as I ran my hand down my face, feeling entirely stupid at that point that I hadn't known what my kid was getting into.

"There's plenty of material out there to learn how to hack, including YouTube videos on it. If someone really wants to get onto the DarkNet, they'll figure it out," Coop explained.

"Okay, but even if he was playing those kind of video games, that can't be what got him kidnapped," Sebastian said.

"I don't know what got him kidnapped yet, but we can't count out the video games. Sometimes criminals will put in specific codes hidden in one of these type of video games. Hitmen have been known to do it to pass along messages. Black market traffickers as well. They hide their message within the game and the person who is looking for it plays and they see it. Most wouldn't think anything of it, but if Drew stumbled upon one of those messages and went somewhere online that he shouldn't have, it could have gotten him grabbed," I explained.

Great. This was just fucking great. My son was hacking and playing video games on the DarkNet with criminals and hitmen. Clearly, I had been failing miserably in the parenting department. I naively thought he was safe on his computer, but I was completely wrong. I didn't even monitor his online activity. I didn't see the need to invade his privacy like that. Apparently, I should have. Because then maybe, I would have seen what he was doing and I could have put an end to it.

I couldn't stop thinking about how scared he must be. I was also worried not only about his life, but his health, too. He'd had to have a pacemaker put in when he was an infant. We had to be careful with any stress on his heart. It was one of the reasons why he didn't like sports that much. He didn't need medication for it, thankfully, but if he was scared his heart rate would increase and there was no telling what it could do to him.

"Can you find out what he stumbled on or who could have taken him from this?" I asked, waving my hands at the multiple monitors covering the wall.

"It's gonna take time. These guys hide their tracks really well. It has to be hidden enough that not everyone stumbles upon it, but it's there so the person that they need to see it does. It's a fine line that they balance," Cooper answered.

"Is there anything we need to know about Drew. Anything you haven't told us that we could use to try and find who did this?" Damien asked.

"I don't know. I didn't even know he could hack. I thought it was just video games with his friends. He doesn't have a lot of friends, and the ones he does have all live online. He's not a sports kid and with his pacemaker, we have to be careful about strain on his heart."

"Whoa, he has a pacemaker?" Cooper

asked, sounding a bit too excited for my liking.

"Yeah, he had to get it when he was a baby to regulate his heart rate."

"You should have started with that," Cooper said as he immediately started to type away at his computer. I couldn't believe how fast he could type. I could barely get out fifty words per minute, but his fingers flew over the keys without him even looking at them.

"Why does that matter?" Max asked, before I could get the words out.

"Because pacemakers have microchips to make them work. And if it has a microchip, it can be hacked. I can trace his location from it."

There was no way.

Coop might be able to find Drew from the chip in his pacemaker?

I didn't even think that was possible. I didn't know I had a built in GPS in the kid. I watched as he hacked into my son's pacemaker and I held my breath as I waited to see if he was able to find him. I was praying that he could.

We needed to find my son and then we could figure the rest of this out once we got him back safely. We could figure out who took him and why, and I would sit down with him and discuss the dangers of hacking and the DarkNet. I had no idea how I was even going to have that conversation because I barely understood any of it, but I would figure it out. It was time to man up on my parenting skills.

"Got him," Cooper piped up as a map of the city appeared on one of the computer monitors with a red dot.

I assumed that red dot was my son. "Can you tell if he's okay?" I was terrified of what the answer would be, but I had to ask. I had to know what we were walking into. What *I* was about to walk into.

"The readings show that he's alive. Scared, if his slightly increased heart rate is any indication, but alive. I can't tell if he's hurt, but I don't think he is. The readings are pretty good."

And with those words, I could breathe again. He was alive. My son was alive and appeared to be doing well. And now that we knew where he was, we could go and get him.

"That a warehouse?" Damien asked.

"Yeah. Unfortunately, this just tells me that he's there. I have no way of knowing who else could be in there. I'm going to run any security cameras within the area and see if I can find anything we can use. You guys get geared up and I'll see what I can pull," Cooper said.

"Roger that. I'll let Mason know," Damien said, and spun on his heel, at a fast pace toward the door.

I followed Max and Sebastian out of the room to get my gear on as well. We knew where my son was and we were going to get him. I already knew I was not going to let Drew out of my sight ever again after this.

***

"Okay, so I'm not picking anything up," Cooper said, as we sat in the van outside of the warehouse.

"I find it hard to believe he's in there alone," Max commented.

It would be weird to kidnap a kid and then just leave him alone in a warehouse, but this whole situation was weird. At this point, I just wanted to get my son back and make sure he was okay. That was all I cared about.

"I don't know what to tell you. But I'm not picking up any other heat signatures but his. The pacemaker shows he's in there and it's not like they could have cut it out of him," Cooper pointed out.

"Maybe we're over thinking things. Maybe the kid stumbled upon something and his kidnappers just grabbed him to buy time. Maybe they were worried he would tell his dad. They could be just waiting until whatever they have planned is finished before letting him go," Sebastian stated.

That was possible. He *was* a kid and, unless these were hardened criminals, they might not be able to kill a kid. They could have something planned and they needed to wait it out. It's possible that Drew didn't even realize what he had seen and his kidnappers were just being cautious. It would explain why they had left him alone, why they destroyed my house. They needed to make it seem bigger than it was.

"Either way, we're going in," Damien said as he opened his door.

We all climbed out, but to my surprise Cooper stayed in the van. I figured he might not be a very active field agent with him working the computers. But still, he carried a gun and he was wearing a vest. I figured he would have been joining us.

Maybe he didn't go in unless the guys needed backup.

I followed Damien's lead. He seemed to be the one in charge out of the three of them. That was fine with me. I could lead, but I had no problem following either, especially if the person leading knew what they were doing.

Damien and I took the front while Max and Sebastian headed around to the back. With his go ahead, Damien pulled the door back and we stormed into the room. The whole room was empty. I had no idea what type of warehouse this had been, but it wasn't being used any longer.

There, sitting tied to a chair in the middle of the room, was Drew.

It all felt so weird.

His eyes weren't covered. He was just tied to a metal chair in the middle of the room. He had duct tape over his mouth to keep him from calling out for help.

"It's okay, hang on," I said to him as we worked on clearing the warehouse.

It was empty, though. None of this was making any sense and I suspected that there was more to this than we knew. I had a feeling we were in for one hell of a surprise by the end of it all, because even with Drew now safely back with me, I wasn't about to stop investigating. I was going to get down to the bottom of this whole thing and figure out who had kidnapped my son and why. I knew I couldn't rest until I had those answers.

I put my gun back in its holster as I went and started to get my son free. "Hang on Kiddo," I said as I pulled the duct tape off his mouth.

"Dad. I'm so sorry," he instantly said, tears welling in his eyes.

I could see that his lip was swollen and there was dried blood on it. I could also see there were a couple of cuts on his arm, from broken glass most likely. It was his blood that had made the blood drops out the door, but thankfully, it was from the cuts and nothing serious.

"It's okay. We're gonna figure this out. I promise, it's okay," I reassured him as I got the rest of the rope off of him.

The second he was free, he was throwing himself into my arms and I was instantly wrapping mine around him. My son was alive and he was safe, back in my arms. Nothing else mattered at that moment. I had my son and he was going to be okay. That was all that mattered. We would figure out the rest, but he was out of harm's way and I could finally breathe again.

CHAPTER FOUR

Cooper

I WAS RELIEVED that we had been able to find Drew, alive and well. I could see the love that Jonah had for him. I could see the deep relief that flooded his body when he was finally able to hold his son in his arms.

I had called for the paramedics to just check Drew over and, thankfully, he was mostly unharmed, minus a few cuts. He was going to be okay, though, and I knew with Jonah looking after him, he would recover from this trauma.

We made our way into the Agency

office and I knew we would need to talk to Drew to figure out what had happened and if he saw who had kidnapped him. I knew Jonah was going to want to do it, but I was hoping that he would allow me to speak with Drew first. I had a feeling he might open up more to me than his dad. I would also be able to connect with him and understand what he was talking about better.

Jonah brought Drew into the conference room, but I pulled him and the others away so we could chat for a moment.

"I know you want to talk to him and ask him about what happened, but I think it would go over better if I did it," I said as I looked Jonah in the eyes.

"That's my son. I'm not going to have someone interrogate him. He's been through enough," he said, instantly in defensive mode.

"I'm not going to interrogate him. We're just going to talk. I know he's your son, but there are things that kids don't tell their parents. He's going to be more open with me and I understand him," I countered gently.

"Coop is right. I'm going to have him

run the interview," Mason said, backing me up. When Jonah was about to protest, Mason spoke again, putting an end to it. "This is our investigation, West. You were not officially brought on. I have allowed you to be a part of this *because* he's your son and he was missing. He is now found, and if you would like to see this through, then you have to respect the chain of command. And you have to trust us. Your son is a young hacker and only Cooper knows what it feels like to be in his position. He can understand what Drew has to say. There will come a time for you to talk to Drew about what he's been doing, but that should be between father and son in a place where he feels comfortable. Not at a field office."

I could tell that Jonah wanted to argue, but he also knew better than to press his luck. It would be better for them to have this conversation outside of the field office. In a place where they could both feel comfortable and safe. The very last thing Drew needed right now, was to feel lectured or in trouble. That wasn't going to help us get anywhere. I needed him to be honest so I could try and figure out what he could have stumbled upon.

Jonah nodded, wordlessly backing off.

I headed into the conference room as I spoke. "Hey, Drew, can you come with me for a sec?"

I didn't want to have this conversation in an open conference room. I was going to take him to my office where he could maybe start to feel comfortable in and amongst all the computer equipment.

He simply got up and easily followed me. I suspected he thought he was in trouble, but that was natural. I still remembered how freaked out I was when I first went through Homeland Security. I thought for sure my ass was going to prison that day. That was another reason why I wanted Drew to see my office. I wanted to show him what a white hat hacker could do. That there was a whole other world out there for hackers and they could do what they loved and help people. As silly as it might sound with him only being twelve, he really was at a crossroads. He could either be a white hat hacker or he could be a black hat hacker and I didn't want him to be a criminal. Not if I could potentially stop it.

The second we walked into my office I saw his eyes light up. He was a computer nerd and my office might not be nerd heaven, but it was pretty close.

"Wow, is this your office?" he asked as he took it all in, his gaze flitting around the room rapidly.

"Yeah, it is. Pretty cool, huh? I get to spend all of my time hacking different systems and finding criminals to put away."

"You're a hacker?" he asked, surprise in his features.

I didn't blame him for being shocked. When I was his age, I'd had no idea that a hacker could work for the Government, either. I remembered my own amazement at the revelation when Agent Evans had brought me into the fold.

"I am. I'm called a white hat hacker. White hats are the hackers who use their skills to help people. We work for the government and different agencies, even the military, to help protect people and the country. Black hats are the hackers who look to hurt people and cause general mischief. They steal money, put people at risk, all different kinds of illegal activities. All they care about is the money and the reputation that goes with it."

"I didn't know there was a difference. I

thought all hackers were just hackers," Drew said, the awe in his voice evident.

"Yeah, I was like that, too, when I was your age. I grew up in the foster system. I didn't really have parents, but I had this huge hole inside of me that I couldn't seem to fill. One day, when I was nine, I went down to the community center to try and get some of my homework done. There were these three eighteen year olds there and they were hacking. I was really good at math and I was curious as to what they were doing. They started to teach me. It didn't take long before I was able to hack just as well as they could. I'm what is known as a hacking prodigy, apparently. If there's a microchip in it, I can hack it. It's how we found you. I was able to hack your pacemaker and I got your location from it."

"It's hackable? No way!" he squealed as he slid into one of my chairs.

"Yup. If there's a microchip or it's online, it can be hacked. Just like your security system was hacked. You know, hanging out with those hackers at the community center, it started to fill in that hole inside of me. I started to have real friends and I felt like I had something special. The better I got, the more impressed they got, the better I felt. I wanted to be their friend. I wanted them to like me. So, when they asked me to hack different databases, different banking systems, I didn't think twice. I jumped in with both hands." I chuckled at the variation of the typical expression.

"You were a *black hat hacker*?" Drew intoned.

It felt like such a long time ago. I was only twenty-nine, so it wasn't really all that long ago, but I had come such a long way since then.

"At one point in my life I was. I didn't know any better and I didn't want to lose the only people I thought were my friends. When I was nineteen, I decided to hack into Homeland Security. I wanted to see if I could do it. I was bored and decided it might be fun to try. I was able to do it, and then a Homeland Security Agent picked me up within an hour. Only, instead of arresting me, he showed me around their cyber division and I started working for them that same day. That was just over ten years ago now, and I haven't felt more complete in my life since making that decision to use my gift for good instead of bad."

"I want to feel complete," he softly admitted, his eyes downcast.

I suspected he was feeling like I used to. It wasn't Jonah's fault, but his mother was gone, had been for six years. And Jonah worked a lot of hours. As much as he loved his son, and I could see that he did, it didn't change that Drew would have a running tally of all the nights and days he'd spent alone. All of the holidays and birthdays that Jonah would have either missed or got called away from for a case. No matter how much Jonah loved his son, there was always going to be a dead body and another case that took precedence over Drew, unfortunately. It was part of the job and there was no getting away from that, sadly.

"I know your mom left when you were six. It can't be easy not seeing her. It can't be easy to know that your dad is out there chasing after criminals all day and night long. I don't know him all that well, but most cops have been hurt to some extent, which can be really scary for their kids."

"It is," he admitted truthfully. "I know he's a good cop and he always says he'll come home to me, that he's not going to let anyone take him out, but things happen all the time. I read about all of the cops who get killed all the time on the news. Most of the time they don't even see it coming. I just wanted to do something that made *me* feel good. That didn't make me feel so alone. I can't play sports with my pacemaker and I don't even like watching sports. I'm the math geek at school. I don't really have many friends. But online, I can be anyone I want to be."

"I get it. You are just about to start high school next year and I wish I could say it will get easier, but it won't. People like us don't find our place in the world until after high school. But when you graduate, you'll have this whole world at your fingertips. There is so much out there for you to learn. You will find your place and you will fill that hole, I promise you. Where did you learn how to hack?"

"I was playing a game online and some of the other players were talking about coding and hacking to play games on the DarkNet. I had no idea what that was and I started to talk to them. We started to communicate outside of the game on a hacking forum board. They started to teach me and they sent me some good videos for beginners. I got really good, I knew I was good, and then one day, I dived into the DarkNet and found all of these really cool games. I swear, I didn't do anything crazy. I just played the games. I even made a few bucks helping with the design of a few of them. It was just fun. That's all it was supposed to be. Something to pass the time and keep my mind engaged."

And for the most part, it would be fun. It would be safe for him to be on it and to explore, but he should be doing that with someone experienced who could make sure he didn't fall into any rabbit holes that could get him hurt or kidnapped, like what had just happened to him.

"The DarkNet is made up of a lot of different things. Some of those things are relatively safe, like playing those games. A lot of them are designed by novice game developers or start up companies and they are looking for honest feedback and help with the bugs. There's nothing wrong with that. But the DarkNet is also where dangerous criminals live. And not just hackers. There's black market organ trafficking, human traffickers, gun and drug traffickers, there are hitmen who get their contracts and payments through the DarkNet, and so much more. It's not safe to swim around in it, unless you know where you are going."

"I didn't know that. I thought it was just this hacker playground." Drew said and I could hear the honesty and surprise in his voice.

"And in a way it is, but you have to be careful you don't trip into someone else's sandbox. Which is what I think happened to you. Some of those criminals will hack into those games to leave a message for someone. I think you stumbled onto something, saw something you weren't supposed to, and they grabbed you."

"I didn't see their faces. They wore masks that covered them fully, even their necks, and they wore black, long-sleeved shirts. But there were three of them and the one guy said I shouldn't have gone *there*. I didn't get what he meant, but now maybe I do. Maybe I went somewhere in one of the games that I wasn't supposed to. But if I did, I don't know what it was or what I had supposedly seen. I play a lot of games, everyday. Nothing really stands out."

That's what I was afraid of. I could tell

from his browser history that he game-hopped a lot. It was going to take time to figure out what he'd seen and in what game. It wasn't going to be quick and I was going to have to dig into each of the games myself to see if I could find what he might have stumbled across. The trick was, he was still young. His mind wouldn't pick up everything that the games had to offer. So even if he saw something, he wouldn't have thought anything of it. These kidnappers either overreacted, or they were being extremely cautious. And if it was the latter, that meant whatever they were planning was going to be huge.

"That's okay. I'll go into the games and see what I can find. We'll find the guys who grabbed you. And now that we know you are on their radar, we can keep you safe. Come on, let's get you back to your dad and we can figure this all out."

I had no idea what was going to come from this, but I knew we would figure it out. I just hoped we would be able to figure it out before it was too late.

CHAPTER FIVE

Jonah

I HATED NOT being able to be in there with my son. He was *my son*. I should have been able to talk to him and figure out what was going on.

I still couldn't believe it. I couldn't fathom that I'd had no idea he was hacking or going into this DarkNet place. I still didn't understand it all. I wasn't against computers, but I only knew the basics of them. I was a homicide detective. I could check emails and run reports, but I couldn't hack into someone's computer if it was password protected.

I was never very good with math and science in school. I was more of an English person. Drew was the polar opposite of me. He could read, but he didn't love to read. He could do math, though, even from an early age when all of the other kids were learning their numbers, he had already figured out how to add and subtract them. He had always been gifted with numbers. Maybe that was how he learned how to hack. He would have had to learn how to code first, though.

It bothered me a great deal to know that my own son had this skill that I knew nothing about. I knew I was working a lot and I knew it left him alone often, but I was trying to be there for him. I thought we had good communication between us. I didn't think he was hiding anything from me. I wouldn't have understood most of what he said, but we could have talked about him learning how to code and wanting to explore that more. I certainly would have told him about the dangers of hacking, not to mention the fact that it was illegal. There was no telling what he could have stumbled upon. There was going to be a rather lengthy discussion about it when we got home tonight.

Finally, the door to Cooper's office opened and they both walked out.

"Why don't we grab Mason and meet in the conference room?" Cooper suggested.

"I'll go grab him," Sebastian said with a nod.

We all made our way to the conference room. I put my arm around Drew so he knew I was there for him. I was on his side. If he wanted to be a hacker, then there were other ways to go about doing it. I knew that law enforcement and different agencies employed hackers to help with evidence collection and to track suspects or victims down. I wasn't against that type of hacking. My issue was that in order to be good at hacking, he'd have to practice it and, as far as I knew, there were only illegal ways available to the general public to practice hacking. I wasn't going to tolerate any illegal activity, especially with him only being twelve. He was too young to be playing in that kind of volatile world and it needed to stop. We all sat down and a moment later Sebastian was back with Mason.

"It's good to see that you are okay, Drew," Mason started as he walked in the room, flashing a warm smile at Drew.

"Thank you, Sir," he said back, slightly awkward given the situation he was in.

"What do we know?" Mason asked, looking to get all of the information that he could.

"Drew has been playing some games on the DarkNet. I believe he stumbled upon something he wasn't supposed to see and that made some people nervous," Cooper started.

"We found him in a warehouse, completely untouched and not guarded. They'd just left him gagged and tied to a chair. We think the destruction at the house was done to throw us off. Whoever grabbed Drew, they didn't want to hurt him or kill him. Everything points to the idea that they have to be planning something that is time sensitive and they just needed to keep him quiet until it was played out," Damien added.

"But I didn't see anything," Drew lightly mumbled, his eyes downcast, but we were all able to hear him.

"And that is exactly what is going to be the problem. Whatever Drew stumbled upon in one of the games, he didn't pick it up. The only way to know what he saw is to play the games that he played and see if I can pick something up that will lead us to whoever kidnapped him and what they are planning," Cooper said.

"But could it still be there?" Mason asked.

"Depends on who they are. They could have pulled it out of the game code by now to protect themselves. It really depends on what the plan is," Cooper answered.

"We're also working against a clock. They didn't want to kill him. They wore masks, so they were going to let him go when this was all over and done with. Which means whatever they are planning, it likely has to be within the next seventy hours or so. A kid goes three days of no water and he's dead. Someone knew what they were doing. Knew he'd been found or escape in time," Max commented.

That was the thing. If they'd grabbed Drew to hold him off from reporting what he saw to anyone, then they had to be acting out their plan soon. If they waited too long they risked not only Drew dying, but him being found before they could put their plan into action. They had to have known I was a cop and if someone kidnaps a cop's son, the entire police force went looking for him on red alert. They had to know the streets would be flooded with cops just trying to find him. But maybe that was the point. Maybe it was more than Drew seeing something.

"What if we're missing something?" I said as I started to put the pieces together.

"We're missing a lot," Max stated.

"I mean about the kidnapping. They grabbed Drew to keep him quiet, I get that and I agree. He must have seen something for them to target him. But they knew where he lived, how to get through my security system. They had to have known I was a detective. And if they knew all of that and are criminals, then they had to have known that if you kidnap the son of a Baton Rouge Detective the entire police force would be out looking for him and running down leads. The streets are going to be flooded with cops working this case," I started to explain.

"Oh," Cooper said with complete understanding as he turned to his computer and started to type away.

"What?" Sebastian asked, confused.

"They have flooded the streets with police, but those police are too busy looking for kidnappers. Which means response times for other crimes are going to go down. They created the perfect window to commit a crime. My guess, a robbery," Mason said as he caught on to my train of thought.

"That's smart. Use a DarkNet game to communicate with your partners. No one within law enforcement would be looking for it; most wouldn't know how to get to the DarkNet. You set it all up and then you kidnap a kid and while everyone is busy looking for that kid, you hit your target," Sebastian said.

"But if this works that means they'll do it again. They could kidnap another kid of a detective to get the same result. They might have already been planning to do that the whole time and the fact that Drew saw something changed who they were going to pick," Max added.

"Drew, what time roughly were you grabbed?" Cooper asked.

"Um, I was asleep, but I think around four in the morning."

Goddammit.

He had been kidnapped and I was sitting at my desk at work trying to solve a case. I hated that I hadn't been home last night. If I had, this never would have happened. I would have been able to stop them from getting Drew and I might have been able to injure or kill one. We could have used that evidence to find the rest of the crew before they could kidnap any child. I was gonna have to talk to my boss. I couldn't do nights anymore, not until Drew was older. He was just going to have to accept that. It was too dangerous to leave him home alone. I knew that now.

"How many were there?" Cooper asked.

"Four," Drew answered.

"Okay, between four in the morning and now, there have been fifty-five robberies reported," Cooper started, but Max cut him off.

"It's been like seven hours, what the hell is wrong with this city?"

"It's not all major robberies. A few of them are business owners reporting a robbery for someone not paying their food bill and running out. That happens a few dozen times a day," I supplied. I didn't need to look at the list to know that would be on there.

"He's right. And we are looking for ones where the business owner or employees swear they turned the alarm on. They have an experienced hacker in their group, so they aren't going to be targeting Mom and Pop shops. They want high-end, but something they can slip into a bag easily enough. It could be diamonds or cash. They have connections within the DarkNet so they could easily sell the diamonds. Diamonds would be easier for them to move instead of cash that could have serial numbers reported and flagged," Cooper said as he continued to narrow down the possibilities.

"Diamonds have serial numbers, too," Mason pointed out.

"They do, but only the ones that came into the country legally. If they were conflict diamonds they wouldn't have come through the legal channels and then they wouldn't have the serial number. Just as valuable, though, on the black market," Cooper said.

"Wait, there was a shop in the one game," Drew said, speaking with more confidence now.

All eyes turned to him, but it was

Cooper that spoke. "What game?"

"Serial Subway. You're trapped in a subway tunnel and you have to run from a serial killer that is trying to kill you. While you are running, you have to avoid being hit by trains. The goal is to navigate through different subway tunnels and stores to try and find a way to escape and get up to the street level. I've played it a bunch of times to help the developer with the glitches. He was always having glitches because of the graphics. Two days ago, there was a new store, it had a diamond with a crown on it for the store logo. I ran into it thinking it was a new addition. I got to the back of the store and there was this tunnel, so I ran through it and it took me up to the street level."

That had to be it. They must have been able to see that Drew went through the store and they were worried he would tell someone about it. That tunnel must have been their real escape plan. It was pretty smart. They could code their own escape and run it like a drill without the fear of being caught. They must have been watching Drew somehow and were able to find him in real life. How, I had no idea and it bothered me a great deal that someone could easily find him.

"Do you know the street name?" Mason asked.

"No, it didn't show it."

"That's okay, that logo can't be that common in the city," Cooper said as he went back to typing.

"There could be other plans that were in that game or another game," Damien pointed out.

"I agree. Until we have these men in custody, I want Drew in protective custody," Mason ordered.

"We can go to a safe house that the department has," I easily agreed.

We were not about to go back to the house. Not when they had already proven that they could get into my house with ease. I wasn't going to be putting Drew at risk. We needed these men in jail and then, hopefully, I would be able to sleep better at night knowing that Drew was safe from them.

"Given their hacking capabilities, I would like for you both to stay with Cooper. His house is unhackable and if someone tries, he'll get an alert. Coop, you good with that?" Mason asked.

"Yeah, it's fine with me," he easily

agreed without looking away from his computer.

I wasn't too sure I wanted to be staying with Cooper. I could protect myself and my son. However, I was also not going to turn down the opportunity to be in a house where this hacker couldn't hack his way in. If it meant keeping Drew safer, then I was all for it.

"How long will it—" Damien started, but Cooper cut him off.

"Got it."

"Nevermind," Damien said under his breath.

"Jeweler King down on Fifth and Vine. I'll run the company and see if anything stands out. Right now, though, they haven't reported a robbery. But if they got their conflict diamonds stolen from them, they wouldn't be able to report it."

"So how do we know if they did or not?" I asked.

"We go in and look around. Immunity gets us through the door," Damien said simply.

Their immunity would come in handy for the cases that I worked. To be able to walk into anyone's house or business without a search warrant, and have it still it hold up in court, that was amazing. I would have a lot less killers walking the streets if I could have the same thing.

"Cooper, you take Drew and Detective West to your house. Start trying to see if you can find these kidnappers. And if you have to, play some games and see if they are planning something else. Damien, Sebastian, and Max, you hit the store," Mason ordered.

"Copy that," Max said as he stood.

We all started to get up and go our separate ways. I took Drew downstairs to the lobby while we waited for Cooper to grab whatever gear he needed.

"Look, Dad, I'm sorry about all of this," Drew started.

"I know you are and I'm not mad. But we do have to have a serious conversation about what you are doing on your laptop. I think what has happened here proves my point about hacking being dangerous, especially in places like the DarkNet."

"I know, but it was just fun. I was just playing some new games, making some new friends. That's all."

And I could understand that, but the problem was his fun was illegal and those new friends could be anyone. It wasn't like he was in a chat room with just teenage boys. He could be communicating with any criminal out there. It was very dangerous. Too dangerous for a twelve year old boy.

"First, the fun you were having was illegal. The DarkNet is filled with criminals and being a hacker is illegal. Only hackers within law enforcement are allowed to hack legally, and that's because they are trained and helping people. I don't know much about hacking, but I know that it's very easy to get caught up in the wrong crowd, regardless of what the crowd is doing. Second of all, the people you have been communicating with could be anyone. They can say they are fifteen, but in reality they are a fifty year old man who likes to play with little boys. You being in the DarkNet is pretty much the same as if you went to a Federal Maximum Prison and wandered around all of the dangerous criminals just for the fun of it. It being online doesn't change the danger factor. It's worse, because you can't *see* if the person on the other side of the screen is lying about who they are."

"So, what? I'm just never supposed to

hack again? I like doing it, Dad. I'm good at it, and Cooper is a hacker and look at what he's doing."

"Cooper works for a federal agency that allows him to hack to find victims and criminals. And I have no problem with you doing that type of hacking. If you want to hack to save people lives and put criminals behind bars, then I am all for it. I am against you hacking into a world filled with criminals."

"I have to practice hacking to get better at it. That's what the DarkNet is for."

"The DarkNet is for criminals to hang out without getting caught. I know this is way out of my league. I get that, I do, Son. But we don't know that the DarkNet is the only place you can practice your hacking. If this is something that you are truly interested in doing, if this is something that you could see yourself doing for the rest of your life, then I will support you, but we have to do it right. We can talk to Cooper. He probably knows how you can get the practice and training that you need without the danger of the DarkNet. I'm not saying don't be a hacker. I am just saying that there is a right and wrong way to learn. The DarkNet is the wrong way, so let's find you the right way."

I wasn't going to order him to never hack again. If that was his passion, if that was what he wanted to do for the rest of his life, if that was his calling, then, I was all for it. I would support him and be there for him, just like I would if he told me he wanted to be a doctor. But we had to do it safely. Just like if he told me he wanted to be a boxer, we had to make sure he was safe while he was learning.

"Okay, I'll ask him. I really do like doing it, Dad. I'm good at it and that makes me feel good about myself. I want to keep learning more about it and maybe work for a government agency one day. I didn't even know hackers could do the things that Cooper does. I didn't know there were black hat and white hat hackers out there. I want to know more."

"Then we can talk to Cooper and learn more about it. But from now on, no more DarkNet. We can't go through that again."

I couldn't go through it again. It was too hard and too much. The thought of losing him, the thought of not knowing where he was or if he was going to be alive when I found him. Nope. No way was I taking any of those chances again.

"I promise. I really didn't think anything like this would happen. It was just supposed to be fun."

I pulled him in for a hug as I spoke. "I love you."

"I love you too, Dad."

I let out a long breath. I had finally found Drew, but that didn't mean he was completely safe. He wouldn't be totally safe until we found his kidnappers. I was just glad that the Agency was still going to be helping me with this case and they were taking Drew's safety seriously. With any luck, we would be able to find these kidnappers and get them behind bars where they belonged. Then, Drew and I could finally start to put this whole mess behind us.

CHAPTER SIX

Cooper

I WAS SURPRISED that Mason wanted them to stay with me, but at the same time it made sense. If these kidnappers decided they needed to get rid of Drew, they wouldn't be able to hack into my house.

That was assuming they could figure out where he was being held. If they were able to follow basic police procedures they would know that he wouldn't be able to go back to his house with it still being a crime scene. Not to mention that the police force wouldn't allow Drew to be without police protection. The kidnappers only had two options, kill him or wait it out until the police moved on to another crime. That was why I thought they were going to kidnap another kid for their next heist.

And there would be another heist. It wouldn't make sense for them to only do this once, especially if it went perfectly. Yes, we found Drew, but chances were they had already done the robbery and were waiting for the right time to release Drew. They were operating in the DarkNet, meaning they would be targeting places that wouldn't want or be able to report the robberies. Places that used conflict diamonds would be perfect for this crew. They could steal them and sell them easily on the black market. Hell, they could sell them to a fence in town that would then unload them. It was a good way to make a quick hundred grand and the businesses wouldn't be able to report the robbery without putting themselves in jail. It was a victimless crime, if you ignored the kid they were kidnapping to make a clean getaway.

Everything within me was telling me this wasn't the first time they had done this, either. They had everything planned and executed without a mistake. They hadn't left any evidence behind that we could use to find them. They wore gloves, long sleeved shirts, and masks. They made sure to be covered up so they didn't leave any fingerprints or DNA. Plus, they covered their whole body so if they did have any scars or tattoos, the kids wouldn't be able to see them. They had thought this through and that could only come from experience. I had no doubt they had done this before and I needed to find their earlier crimes. Hopefully, that might lead us to them.

Pulling up to my house, I parked in my garage and then we all climbed out of my car. I used my phone to unlock my door and we trekked inside.

"You don't have a key?" Drew asked.

"Nope. Locks can be picked. Everything is electronic. It's my own system, so it's not on a circuit anywhere or on the market. There's no research that someone can use to hack into my system. And if anyone tries to hack into my system, I get an alarm and I can counter the attack."

It was a system I had created after I

started working for Homeland Security. I had discovered very quickly that my job was dangerous, even though I was behind the scenes. When you were as skilled at hacking as I was, there was always going to be someone looking for me to hack for them. And with killers and deadly criminals out there looking to hurt the person responsible for putting them in jail, it was better to have a proper secured system. It allowed me to be in my home and not have to worry about being hacked or someone breaking in.

"What if someone steals your phone?" Jonah asked.

I got asked that a lot. In theory, if someone stole my phone they would be able to use it to access my home. The trick was, my phone didn't have a normal security system in it like everyone else's phones. I'd made sure to upgrade it with my own software.

"Even if someone stole my phone, it can only be unlocked with my retina scan and my resting heart rate. If they try twice, it will automatically wipe itself and be useless to them."

"Seems like a lot of extra security just to avoid having a key," Jonah commented.

"Yeah, and how did that key work for you?" I countered with a smirk.

"Touche," he said under his breath.

"I have one spare bedroom. It's upstairs, third door on the right. Make yourselves at home," I said as I strode to the living room so I could get set up and started.

"You take the bedroom, Drew. I can crash on the couch."

"Okay."

I could hear Drew going up the stairs as Jonah came into the living room, tossing his bag down on the floor by the chair. I could feel the energy radiating off of him. He was anxious and antsy. He didn't like not being out in the field and chasing down leads, chasing down the bad guys. I had a feeling he was going to be antsy until we caught these guys. He finally sat down on the arm of the chair as I got my gear set up.

"I appreciate you letting us stay here."

"It's no problem. My place is the safest place for Drew to be."

I didn't normally have people over. I wasn't anti-social, but I did like my own space. I liked to live in the virtual world and I often spent my free time on the

DarkNet trying to find dangerous killers or pedophiles. There weren't many people who could hack as well as I could and, because of that, I tried to do everything I could to help eliminate criminals. I enjoyed the challenge of it and the reward of knowing that someone dangerous was put behind bars or in the ground, unable to hurt anyone ever again. I looked up as Drew came back down the stairs as he spoke.

"So, what do we do now?"

"*We* don't do anything. The Agency will find your kidnappers and arrest them. *You* need to focus on your school work so you don't fall behind while you are on house arrest."

I could tell that Drew wasn't happy that he was going to be sidelined, but Jonah was right. He was only twelve, this world was far too dangerous for him to be poking around in. Though, there was something he could do to feel like he was being involved.

"Actually, Drew, do you think you could write me a list of all the games you have played on the DarkNet in the past thirty days. And note any changes that you noticed in them within that time frame? That would help me to try and recreate what you have done and see if there are any new changes that weren't there before."

"Yeah, definitely. I can do that," he said, enthused.

"There was something that we wanted to talk to you about, Cooper," Jonah started.

"All right, what's up?" I asked, giving them my full attention.

As badly as I wanted to get started on tracking down these guys, I also didn't want to ignore any of their questions or concerns. This type of world was confusing and a lot of the time people got lost in it. I didn't want Drew to get lost in his interest for hacking and I didn't want Jonah to think it was all bad, either, because it wasn't.

"Drew is clearly interested in the hacking world. I told him that he wasn't allowed to be on the DarkNet anymore because of the obvious dangers. However, he is interested in learning more and growing his skills. Is there a way he could do that where it won't attract criminals?"

"Oh, for sure. Homeland Security offers a virtual course for hackers of all levels between twelve and eighteen years of age. They teach kids how to do white hat hacking with simulated cases. They also have camps in the summer for in person learning and to get to meet other hackers around your age. Then, once you are sixteen, and if you are skilled enough, they get you shadowing an analyst, which is what they call their hackers, and you get to help them with real case work. When you turn eighteen, you can go to the academy and you have a job with them right afterward. It's a great program. It allows kids to learn more about hacking without the dangers of them being manipulated by black hat hackers. Plus, Homeland Security gets to have new hackers every year with fresh energy."

It was a terrific program that I often volunteered for. I wished I had known about it when I was a kid because then I wouldn't have gotten into the wrong crowd like I did. At the same time, though, I might not have met Evans and I wouldn't have changed meeting him for the world. He had saved my life in so many ways.

"Really? That sounds awesome," Drew said, a big smile on his face.

"That sounds like a program that I would be happy to live with. Why don't you get the list that Cooper needs and then you can look into it, Drew," Jonah offered with a warm smile.

I could see that Drew was very pleased to hear that his dad would be willing to entertain the possibility of the Homeland Security analyst program. It truly was a great program and it allowed kids to explore their hacking skills without real life dangers. The DarkNet was not a place that any teenager should be playing in, especially one as young as Drew. He could easily be manipulated into doing something illegal and once that happened, it would be hard to get him out of that world.

Drew gave an excited nod as he headed off to get me that list created. I knew it was going to be a long list, but I would just work my way through it and see if I could spot anything that could lead us to their next target.

"It really is a great program. It's also a good way to keep kids that are interested in hacking away from the DarkNet and the criminals that flood it," I said once we were alone.

"I'm not against him learning how to hack, I just want him to be safe while he is learning. I also can't have him doing something illegal. If he were to be arrested, that would follow him for the rest of his life, juvenile or not."

"I volunteer with the program. I think he would really love it. And it lets him meet other people like him. That's the bigger danger when it comes to hacking. You want to connect with people who understand what you do and what you say. Only another hacker understands a hacker. Just like athletes are only understood by another athlete. The problem is hackers live online and underground. They don't hang out with the popular kids or go to school parties. The program can help him with connecting to other people like him. It will help him feel like he's not so alone in the world."

"It sounds like you are speaking from experience," Jonah said as he finally went and plopped down in the chair.

"I was around his age when I got in with the wrong crowd. Only, I grew up in foster care, so I didn't have any parents to make sure I wasn't doing something illegal. That I wasn't being manipulated and used for someone else's gain. Thankfully, the one time I did get caught as an adult, it was by a very understanding and open-minded Homeland Security Agent who offered me a job instead of sending me to prison. He changed my life and ever since I have been dedicated to helping other young hackers see that they don't have to commit crimes to feel like they belong somewhere."

It wasn't easy. There had been plenty of times even after I joined Homeland Security that I wanted to reach out to old friends. It took a couple of years before I was able to leave it all behind me, for me to understand that they weren't truly my friends and only using me for my skills, and no longer connect with them. Now, I was in a position to help kids grow their skills in a safe environment with other kids who they would be safe to connect with.

"I'm glad you were able to overcome your past and have been able to use your skills for good. And now, you are helping to put criminals behind bars and keep people safe. You doing that from a computer doesn't make you any less of an Agent or a good cop," Jonah said, flashing me a warm smile.

"Drew will find his place in the world, especially if he has you in his corner. And now he has me, too."

I wasn't about to leave Drew on his own. He needed someone who could teach him what he was capable of. Someone who would be able to show him the right way to hack. I was more than happy to do that. First though, we had to catch the people responsible for his kidnapping and then, he would be able to go back to living his life.

Hopefully, Damien, Sebastian, and Max were able to find something at the jewelry store that we could use to catch these bastards before another kid was kidnapped.

CHAPTER SEVEN

Jonah

IT WAS JUST after eleven at night and when I should have been able to relax and get some sleep, I couldn't get my body to do just that.

Drew had gone off to bed a couple of hours ago. He was exhausted from the trauma of being kidnapped and barely getting much sleep the night before. It was good that he was able to fall asleep, but I was fully prepared for him to have nightmares tonight.

Even though he hadn't been hurt, really, I knew being kidnapped was still a traumatic event. He was going to have nightmares about it, and I knew he wasn't going to feel safe in our home. We were going to have to move to give us a fresh start. I would have to find a place in the same area, though, so he could go to the same school. I didn't want to pull him out in the middle of a school year, not to mention he had friends at his school. He didn't have many friends and I was not about to take him away from the ones that he did have.

I had been worried about Drew at school. I had been worried about him not having that many friends and spending all of his time playing video games. As it turned out, I had a reason to be worried about the time he was spending on his computer playing video games. I didn't think he would be hacking and playing games on the DarkNet, though. Now that I knew about it, we could make sure he went about growing his skill and learning more the right way. I would be looking into this outreach program offered by Homeland Security. It sounded like a more than fair compromise where Drew would be able to learn more, but also be safe, and I wouldn't have to worry about him playing on the DarkNet.

I paced another round of Cooper's living room. I couldn't get myself to calm down. I couldn't get my body to relax. I was feeling antsy. I wanted to be out there looking for the ones responsible for kidnapping my son. I wanted to hunt them down and get justice for my son. Damien, Max, and Sebastian had gone to the jewelry store and were able to confirm that they had been robbed. They didn't report it because, as we expected, they were using conflict diamonds. They had two million in diamonds stolen from them. It was nowhere near the amount they could have gotten from a larger jeweler and we suspected this was just the dry run. They wanted to make sure their plan to kidnap a police officer's kid would work to keep the police response time down.

It didn't matter if the shop owner would report the robbery or not. If you were out on the street and saw four armed men going into a store wearing masks, you would report it to the police. They had to get in, get the diamonds, and get out before the police would have time to respond. On average, it would take less than five minutes for the police to arrive on scene of an active crime. However, with every cop being out there looking for a cop's kid, that response time could reach fifteen minutes, giving the robbers plenty of time to grab the diamonds and make a clean getaway.

Damien, Max, and Sebastian were working the crime scene. The owner said the thieves were fully covered head-to-toe in clothes, just like Drew had said, so we weren't going to be able to make an ID on them that way. Hopefully, though, there was a camera in the area that we could use to make an ID once they were in the getaway vehicle. They weren't going to be driving the whole way with their faces fully covered. They would have to take the masks off at some point and hopefully, we would be able to get them on camera and run facial recognition.

The shop owner was also not interested in reporting the robbery or filing an official complaint, but we didn't expect him to. Conflict diamonds were cheaper to buy, but they were still illegal. They were responsible for funding the war in Africa and as such, they were made illegal to mine and purchase.

"You are making me dizzy," Cooper said as he glanced up from his laptop.

I had been pacing back and forth all around his living room for close to three hours now. I couldn't help it. I had all of this anxious energy that I needed to work off.

More often than not, when this type of restless energy crept up on me, I would go for a run, but I wasn't about to leave Drew here alone with someone he hardly knew, even if I was sure deep down that I could trust Cooper. If I didn't feel like going for a run, I would sometimes call one of my fuck buddies up and work it off sexually. That was not a possibility right now, either, because again, I needed to be here with Drew to ensure he was safe.

"Sorry. It feels like my skin is crawling."

"I get it. You don't come across as the type of man who likes to wait around for something to happen. You're more proactive," Cooper said with complete understanding to his voice.

"I can sit for days on a stake out, but it's this part that I hate. Having no leads and waiting around for the criminals to commit another crime. And that is before you factor in that they could be going after another kid of a fellow cop. We're stuck in this waiting period and there isn't anything I can do because I don't play video games."

Our best chance of catching these guys was through the games that they hacked into and set up the code that would lead us to their next target. But I didn't play video games. That was never something that I held much interest in. Not to mention, I didn't understand how it all worked. Cooper understood how the games worked, how the coding worked, etc. To me, it might as well be written in Chinese and unless it was on a Chinese menu, I had no clue what the hell it would say.

"I get it. This isn't exactly a case that would be right up your alley and there isn't anything you can do right now. I have to play the same games that Drew did to try and see if there are any patterns or anything that could lead us to the crew or their next target. Damien, Max, and Sebastian are running any camera footage in the area, but so far they have nothing. The jewelry store wasn't in a very populated area and the city doesn't have many cameras up within the area. Our best bet of catching these guys is through the DarkNet games."

I knew that, I did, but that didn't mean I was happy about it. I wanted to be more proactive. I wanted to be able to hit the street and make these arrests. I wanted to be able to send my son to school and not have to worry about him being kidnapped. I wanted this over and done with so we could both move on from this traumatizing experience and, hopefully, be able to get back into a normal routine again.

"I know. I'm just not used to not being able to chase down a lead or hit the streets to try and find my perp. They are all online and I can't do anything to help catch them right now."

"I get it. So what do you usually do when you are feeling like this?"

"Usually, I call up one of my fuck buddies and have sex with him, but that isn't an option, obviously," I said with a smirk.

I wasn't sure if Cooper knew I was gay. I was working under the impression that he didn't with me having Drew. Most people assumed I was straight when they found out I had a son. As if that never happens with gay men.

Some of the guys I had been with didn't care. They were good with me having a child. Others, though, they got very weird about it. As if me not being out and open when I was younger was some type of insult to them and the gay community. It never made any sense to me, because plenty of men were in the closet and had children. Plenty of men got a little too drunk one night and made a baby. Me having a child didn't change that I preferred to be with men and was finally out of the closet and very proud of it. If Cooper had an issue with me being gay, then that was his issue and he could get over it.

Cooper closed his laptop as he spoke. "Works for me."

"What works for you?" I asked, confused.

"Sex. I'm game if you are."

"Wait, what?"

He couldn't be serious. We didn't even know each other. He couldn't be offering to have sex with me just to get me to stop pacing. It wasn't that I was a prude. I'd had one-night stands before, especially in the beginning after I came out of the closet. And Cooper was cute. He had that sexy nerd look going for him. Still, he *couldn't* be serious.

"Sex relaxes you. I enjoy sex and I haven't had it in a year. So, if it gets you to stop pacing and I get an orgasm, I'm all for it." He grinned cheekily.

Okay, he was serious. Still, I wasn't saying no, but I wasn't sure it was a good idea with Drew right upstairs. The very last thing I wanted was for my son to hear me having sex, especially when we were supposed to be looking for the men who kidnapped him.

"Drew—" I started, but Cooper cut me off, already knowing what I was going to say.

"My bedroom is soundproofed. He won't hear us."

"Why is your bedroom soundproofed?" I couldn't help but ask.

"I get loud and I don't believe in denying myself sex if someone is over," Cooper said with a simple shrug.

"I like it a bit rough," I warned.

Cooper stood up as he spoke. "Perfect, I like being tossed around."

This was a terrible idea, but I was not

about to look a gift horse in the mouth. If Cooper was in need of sex—and after not having any for a year, he had to be in desperate need—I was not about to pass up on an opportunity to have sex.

I followed him up the stairs to his bedroom and the second the door closed, Cooper was starting to remove his clothes. He had his back to me and I saw the telltale scar on his lower back. I reached out and placed my hand on his back, letting my fingers trace the edges of the scar.

"Bullet and a surgery scar. How does an analyst get shot?"

I would have figured that Cooper would have been safe working in a computer lab. I didn't think he would be in a position to get shot. Instantly, that made me concerned for Drew if he did decide to follow in Cooper's footsteps and work for a Government agency.

"I am trained to be a field agent as well. I took a bullet protecting an agent who saved my life previously. Evans, he was the one that got me into Homeland Security when he could have just arrested me for hacking and tossed me into a cell. The bullet would have killed him. Instead, we are both alive, and I am missing a kidney, but I would do it all over again. I know scars can be a turn off."

I couldn't help the small huff of a laugh. Maybe scars could be a turn off to some, but I didn't have that issue. It was crazy, though, that he had lost a kidney. I knew people could live a normal life with just one, but if something went wrong with that one kidney, your life could be in serious danger. It made sense now, why he didn't get out of the van when we found Drew. He had to be extra careful to ensure he didn't injure the only kidney he had.

I could have told Cooper that scars didn't bother me, but I figured I could also show him. I pulled my shirt off and I could see the shock and understanding in Cooper's eyes.

"I don't have a problem with scars," I said.

I had plenty of my own. Being an active cop in Baton Rouge led to injuries. I had been shot a couple of times, I'd been stabbed and beaten, broken bones, all of it.

Cooper ran his hand over my scars as he spoke. "Bullet and stab wounds. Either you have been very reckless, or you have the worst luck." He chuckled.

"Maybe a bit of both. I'm an active cop and that can result in injuries," I answered as I moved my hands down to his jeans and started to remove his belt.

He followed suit and I pressed my lips against his as we worked on divesting the other of the rest of their clothes. I didn't care too much for kissing, but I did enjoy a bit of it. Cooper easily allowed me to have control of the kiss and the second our tongues touched, he let out a soft moan. I kept the kiss short, though. I was far more interested in other activities with him. I pulled back and spoke.

"On your knees."

He gave me a playful smirk before he easily got down onto his knees. I could see the shock in his eyes and I knew exactly what he was thinking. I wouldn't call my dick *big*; it was *massive.* That really was the only word to describe it. I had been very blessed in that department. Oral sex with me was an Olympian sport. My nickname in high school and it had followed me on the force, was Hammer. The guys used to joke about how I could probably kill someone with it.

Cooper ran his tongue along my tip and moaned at the taste of my pre cum hitting his taste buds. I threaded my hand into his hair and started to guide his mouth onto my dick. I knew he wasn't going to be able to take it all, no one had ever been able to take me all. But I was curious to see how far he could go. I would let him set the depth and then I would set the pace.

Bit by bit, I watched as Cooper took more of me into his mouth, but when most people couldn't help but gag, he relaxed his throat and continued until he took me all the way down to my base. I couldn't help but moan at the sight. Not once had anyone been able to deep throat my whole length and it was only turning me on even more.

"Fuck, your throat feels amazing," I moaned as Cooper started to work his way back up my shaft.

Cooper moaned around my dick, sending vibrations all the way down it. I could see that he was hard and his own dick was dripping with precum. It would appear that Cooper really liked to give blowjobs. He most likely had an oral fixation and that was more than fine with me.

I started to lightly thrust my hips, picking up the pace, and Cooper only moaned his appreciation even more. I couldn't get over how glorious his mouth felt. How incredible it felt to be all the way into someone's throat and know that they were getting just as turned on by it. My balls pulled up tight and I felt electricity race up my spine. At this rate, I knew it wouldn't be long before I was coming. I would usually stop, but I wanted to feel his throat swallowing around my dick.

"I'm gonna come right down your throat," I moaned out, giving a slight tug on his hair in a light warning just in case he wasn't on board with that.

Cooper let out a deep groan as he started to suck even harder around my dick and I knew that meant he was good with it.

I snapped my hips forward and gave a deep groan as I came hard down his throat. It had been a few months since I had been with anyone, so I had a lot of cum to offer him and Cooper eagerly swallowed every last drop. I couldn't help but moan and pulse more as I felt his throat working my shaft, milking even more out of me.

I continued to thrust my hips, pressing my cock in and out of his lips, ignoring how sensitive my dick was. I wanted to be fully hard so I could fuck the hell of out him. Cooper hadn't had sex in a year and I was going to make sure tonight was a night he would never forget. Once I was fully hard again, I pulled Cooper's head back as I spoke.

"On the bed with your ass up in the air."

"Yes, Sir." Cooper whimpered. He went to get onto the bed in the position that I wanted, while I went over to the bedside drawer to grab some lube. I had a condom in my wallet that would fit me, but I didn't carry lube around. I opened the drawer and immediately saw the lube, but also a couple of sex toys. I grabbed the lube before quickly grabbing the condom as I spoke.

"Sex toys, huh? Naughty boy."

"I get lonely."

I gave Cooper's ass a slap as I got onto the bed and spoke. "I bet you do. If it's been a year since you've had sex, you must be in desperate need of a real dick by now."

I added some lube to three of my fingers as Cooper spoke. "You have no idea."

I could imagine. I couldn't go a year without sex, that was for sure. I would have gone insane by now. I had a high sex drive and when I wasn't working, I was often trying to hook up with someone. It was a great way to relieve stress, but also to make up for all of the years that I had denied myself what my body was craving.

I inserted two of my fingers at once into his tight hole and right away Cooper began moaning and moving his hips back to get more of my fingers inside of him. I placed my free hand on the back of his neck and put my leg against the left side of his ass to keep him in that position. It would stop him from moving his hips and give me total control over him.

"I'm in control of your pleasure, not you," I said as I started to finger fuck him.

Cooper whimpered at either my words or the roughness, perhaps both. Either way, he was clearly loving this. I quickly stretched him enough so I could add a third finger and then, without delay, I started to search for his sweet spot. I knew I hit it when Cooper let go a loud moan and curled his hands into the comforter. If I had allowed it, he would have been bouncing on my fingers.

I turned my hand and started to rub my middle finger over his prostate at a fast pace. I wanted to make him come without even touching his cock. I wanted to show him just how high the pleasure could be. It didn't take long before Cooper was a moaning and whimpering mess on the bed.

"Please, fuck me," he begged as his legs shook.

I knew I had brought him to the edge and I was keeping him from falling off of it. I was also getting closer to the edge just by listening to his moans. It was time we both got what we wanted.

I quickly pulled my fingers out and slipped on my condom before I lined myself up with his hole and pushed my massive dick inside his hot ass. I had to close my eyes as the pleasure shot all down my spine. Even though I had stretched him, he was still tight and his hole was wonderfully hot. Cooper was panting underneath me as I pushed every last inch of my dick inside of him.

"So big," Cooper panted out, the hitch

in his breath telling me he was straining with the intrusion, but his body was craving more and he ground his ass around my dick.

I bent forward, pressing my chest to his back, and whispered into his ear, pushing even deeper inside of him. "I'm going to ruin you for other men. You ready to be craving my dick for the rest of your life?"

"Oh, yes, please," he begged.

I moved back and started to pull out just slightly before I was pushing back in. I went slow at first. I knew he needed time to loosen up and adjust to my size. The second I felt Cooper's ass loosening up, though, I was pounding into him. I made sure to aim for his sweet spot and I knew I hit it when he let out a small scream of pleasure and arched his head back.

"That's it, baby, scream for me," I growled as I picked up my pace.

I looked forward to feeling his ass tightening around me when he came. I anticipated milking him and taking him to heights of greater pleasure than he'd ever experienced before. I was going to make sure Cooper never forgot about this night. I had this odd desire to make sure he would be ruined for other men. That other men's dicks would never bring him the pleasure that mine could. Maybe it was cruel of me, considering we were only doing this for one night, but I couldn't help it. I wanted to make sure that Cooper never forgot about me or about this night for the rest of his life.

I kept my pace fast and hard, making sure to hit his sweet spot dead on with each thrust. I could feel him getting closer, his muscles tightening around my cock now. But I didn't just want to feel it. I wanted to *see* it as he dropped over that edge.

I quickly pulled out and flipped Cooper around so he was on his back. I grabbed him by the knees and lifted his legs up toward his chest, opening him up for me.

Cooper easily held onto his knees and made sure his ass was up in the air.

I hissed as I saw his needy hole spread open and ready for my dick once again. I moved so I could slam right down into his hole and the second I did, Cooper was screaming from the dead on hit to his prostate.

I could feel his legs trembling and I knew he was going to come soon. My own orgasm was building at a rapid pace. After a few more thrusts, Cooper's walls were tightening around me again and then, he let out a scream as his dick started to pulse.

I growled as I watched his beautiful dick pulse with cum, rope after rope shot out of him as I continued my assault on his sweet spot, milking him for all he had.

With a final thrust, I pushed myself as deep as I could go inside of him, hissing at the white-hot electricity that raced up my spine, and came inside the condom with a long, drawn out groan.

Cooper moaned at the feeling of me pulsing inside of him and it made him come just a bit more. My whole body was tingling and I had a feeling Cooper's was as well. He wore a complete look of bliss on his face and I knew my mission had been accomplished tonight. Once I finished pulsing, I grabbed the edge of the condom and slowly pulled out. By the time I had pulled the condom off, tied it and tossed it into the garbage can beside the nightstand, Cooper was asleep.

CHAPTER EIGHT

Cooper

THE SECOND I began to wake up, I remembered what happened before I fell asleep. I couldn't help but moan slightly at the memory. Not to mention the ache in certain parts of my body.

Jonah had said he was going to ruin me for other men and he did not disappoint. That had been the best sex of my life and I knew there would never be another man who would ever bring me that level of pleasure. I swear my body was still tingling from last night. I didn't even remember falling asleep. The sex was just *that* good.

I pushed myself up into a sitting position. I made sure to go slow, because I already knew I was sore and I anticipated feeling more of it as I moved. He was the largest man I had ever been with and I was fully prepared to be sore and feeling him inside of me for days to come. I wasn't upset about that part. I did enjoy the feeling, after all.

There was a slight stab of pain that made me cringe a little, but it quickly passed, settling once more in to the pleasurable ache. I climbed out of bed and shuffled my way over to my en suite bathroom. I needed to take a quick shower before I could get dressed and go downstairs and face the music.

I wasn't sure how well this morning would go over. I was no stranger to one-night stands. I'd had my fair share of them. I didn't go out of my way to have them, though. I did prefer to have more of a friends with benefits relationship. Someone who I could enjoy and have fun with, but could also share a coffee in the morning without it being awkward.

This morning with Jonah could either be awkward or comfortable. I wasn't certain which one it would be, and it would all depend on how Jonah reacted to our one-night stand.

I was perfectly comfortable being around him after last night. Sex wasn't something that I shied away from. However, I knew some guys would find the next morning to be awkward. I was hoping that we could avoid any awkwardness between us this time around. I needed him to be okay with it all, especially if he and Drew were staying at my place for the foreseeable future.

I allowed the hot water to sluice over my body as thoughts of the case flitted through my brain interspersed with memories of last night.

Damn.

I gave my head a shake as I leaned back under the spray and washed my hair. I needed to try and get my head back in the game. Being distracted by thoughts of my time with Jonah wasn't an option right now.

We had four kidnappers out there who could already have their next target within their sights. We needed to grab them up before they tried to snatch another kid to increase their odds of getting away. The part that I didn't understand, though, was how many times they truly believed they could do that and get away with it. Sure, the first heist they might be able to grab a detective's kid and be able to get in and out from their target without much trouble. But that was only the first time. Every time after that, it was going to get harder. Eventually, the kidnappers had to either stop all together or find a new plan. They had to know the police would eventually catch on. Not to mention, even if the officer's kid was found unharmed, that didn't change the fact that the cops would be hunting the city for the kidnappers. They had to have an endgame plan, but I just couldn't see it yet. I couldn't help but feel like it was a player in one of the games. The question was, which one.

I was going to have to play the games again today and see if I could pick anything up. I had been doing that most of the day yesterday and I hadn't seen anything that stood out to me. That was the issue, because whatever message or signal these guys were using to communicate, it was something specific enough for them to notice, but vague enough that others wouldn't. This was also the first time I was playing the games so I didn't know what was different. It would have been helpful if I had played the games before, because then I would have been able to pick up on anything that was different, even if they were subtle differences.

The one person who would be able to tell me what was different was Drew, but I had a feeling Jonah was not going to allow him to play any of the DarkNet games anymore, even if it was to help me track down what I needed to catch the fuckers. I could understand that of course, but it also meant it could take me longer to find anything actionable.

It wasn't a position I wanted to be in, but I knew I might have to talk Jonah into letting Drew help me. I would supervise him and make sure he didn't do anything crazy, but I needed another hacker who could assist me with the games. Drew was here and he had the added bonus of having already played the games. The trick was going to be getting Jonah to give his permission.

I got out of the shower and made quick work of drying off, brushing my teeth, and pulling on some clothes. A quick look at my clock told me it was just after eight.

I headed downstairs and heard noise coming from my kitchen. I walked in and saw that Jonah was busy cooking up some bacon and eggs.

Could this man be anymore perfect?

I didn't see Drew anywhere, though, and I couldn't help but wonder if he was still sleeping.

"Morning," I said as I made my way over to Jonah where he stood in front of the stove.

"Morning. How did you sleep?" he asked, flashing me a playful smirk.

Good, we weren't going to be doing the awkward dance with each other. I was relieved, because I didn't want things to be awkward between us. We were going to have to work this case and considering we'd already crossed paths on a previous case, Detective West was likely going to be a frequent flier within our cases. It would be easier if we could handle being around each other without feeling like twelve year old boys getting caught making out in a church.

"Amazing. I had a very good workout before I fell asleep," I said, flashing him a grin as I leaned against the countertop.

"Just *very good*? That sounds like an understatement to me."

"Okay, the workout might have been the best workout of my entire life. It might have been so amazing that any other workout is going to pale in comparison." I chuckled.

He gave me a lusty smile as he moved closer to me and softly spoke so we wouldn't be overheard. "I did warn you that I would ruin you for other men." He winked and nudged my hip with his.

"You did warn me. And you definitely made my future sex life very disappointing. But I think you like that part. I think you get pleasure out of knowing that you get these poor guys addicted to your dick, only to leave them completely unsatisfied for the rest of their lives."

Jonah gave me a dark smirk as he went and placed his hands on either side of me, trapping me against the counter top. He closed the distance between our bodies and he spoke into my ear. I could feel his crotch right against mine and just feeling how big he was, even soft, was enough to make me moan slightly.

"Is that what you are? A poor man who is now addicted to my dick? I'd say you certainly seemed like you enjoyed having it down your throat last night. I could become addicted to you, too. To your mouth and needy hole." He ground his hips against mine as he playfully bit the bottom of my ear, causing a soft moan to escape my lips. "Maybe we could be each other's fixes. You give me what I want and I'll give you what you want."

"Like, um..." I had to get my mind to work. It was not very easy right now, though, because all I could think about was how close his body was to mine. How close his dick was to mine and how all I wanted was to feel it against me once again. "Friends with benefits?"

"Exactly. You down?" he asked as he moved so his mouth was just a breath away from mine.

"Yes," I said, softly.

"Good."

He moved even closer to my mouth, his warm breath tracing across my lips and sending chills over my skin before he was pulling back and moving over to the stove once again.

Asshole.

Apparently Jonah enjoyed teasing, which meant it was going to be a very long day for me.

A long and frustrating day.

The sound of my phone ringing thankfully snapped my mind back to the situation at hand. I pulled my phone out of my pocket and saw that it was Mason. I finger punched the green phone icon.

"Hey, Boss," I said as I answered the phone.

"We have another kidnapping. Officer Danny Montanna. His fourteen year old daughter was grabbed last night. He works the night shift and he allows her to stay home alone while he is working. Mother is dead. Security system was hacked and the place was destroyed. It's the same MO. Damien is on scene with Sebastian and Max."

Crap, if they had already kidnapped someone else, that meant they were going on a heist today. These guys were moving fast and not allowing for much of a cooling off period. It made sense, though. The longer they waited in between, the greater the chance of them being caught.

"I'll play the games today and see if there is anything different in them that wasn't there last night. I'll try to figure out how they are doing this and see if I can find their next target."

That was only part of what we needed to do, though. We also needed to come at this from a different angle. We couldn't wait around for them to do another heist. We knew they would be going after conflict diamonds. We needed to get out there, be more proactive. It was time the guys hit the streets and started looking into potential targets.

"I'll text you the address. Keep me posted."

"Will do." I ended the call and turned my attention to Jonah. I had to tell him what we had, but now, I was also going to have to have that conversation about Drew. I had hoped to maybe feel him out a bit more and discuss it with him today, but that all changed. We needed Drew to help me with the computer end of things now more than ever.

"What's going on? Jonah asked.

"Officer Danny Montanna's fourteen year old daughter was kidnapped last night. He works the night shift and she is home alone. He came home this morning to the house being destroyed and his alarm hacked. Damien, Sebastian, and Max are on scene. Mason is going to text me the address."

"Fuck, we gotta do something about this. We can't just have them out there kidnapping kids so they can rob someone. If word about this gets out on the street, criminals everywhere will be using their blueprint for their own robberies."

"I know. That's why we need to hit this from all angles. I will keep working the games and DarkNet, you and the guys should be working it from the streets. Run it like any other investigation. I will try and find the hacker and, hopefully, that will lead us to the rest of the crew."

"So, we focus on the rest of the crew and hope it will lead us to the hacker. Makes sense. We both come at this from opposite ends and, hopefully, we'll meet in the middle with some definitive answers. All right, I'll go and start working my sources on the street," he said as he moved the cooked bacon onto a plate before he turned off the stove.

"There is one more thing I want to talk to you about real quick. It's about Drew."

"What about him?" he asked instantly and I could see him getting defensive before I'd even pushed the idea. I was going to have to choose my words carefully.

"Playing these games, trying to see what is different from when he played and now. It's a lot. I know it might not seem like it, but it's a lot of work and it would help if I could have someone else helping me going through them," I started, but Jonah cut me off.

"Absolutely not. Him playing those games is what got him kidnapped."

"I know, but he would be doing it right beside me. He's safe in this house, Jonah. I promise. My system is flawless. He would just be playing the games and he's already spent hours on them. He knows what is the same and what would be different. It will be easier for him to spot any differences, and it might allow me track down the hacker faster."

"I don't want him on the DarkNet. That's not a place for him to be."

"And I understand that completely, I do. And I agree, he shouldn't be on it. But these are extenuating circumstances and he will be with me the whole time. I will make sure he doesn't go anywhere he's not supposed to go. And after this case is wrapped up, he won't ever be on it again, I promise. Jo, we have a crew kidnapping teenagers just so they can steal conflict diamonds. It's only a matter of time before they slip up and accidentally kill one of their captives. We gotta catch them before that happens."

I hoped he would be willing to allow Drew to do this with me. I completely understood why he didn't want Drew on the DarkNet, even if that was just playing a game. It was dangerous, especially if you were smart like Drew was. There was no telling what he could have come across, but that was the point. We needed him to play the games so we could see what he could find. If he found their plan once, then he could find it again.

Jonah let out a sigh before he spoke. "All right, but he doesn't go anywhere but the games. I don't want him talking with anyone or doing anything that could put him in danger."

"I promise. I'll be there the whole time and I will make sure he is safe."

"Okay. I'll go wake him up and then, I'll head out and see what intel I can gather. I don't suppose you happen to have a list of the places that sell conflict diamonds?" He chuckled, dispelling some of his tension in that one breath.

"Not really something people advertise. And I am only assuming they are going after conflict diamonds again. I could be wrong, but they would be easier for them to sell."

They could be going after anything, but conflict diamonds was what they had already gone after and most thieves will steal what they know, especially once they become more comfortable with the burglaries.

"Untraceable, fit in their pockets, and can be sold for a pricey amount. I agree, it makes the most sense to go with. I'll see if there is anyone on the streets who might have an idea of any places that could be the next target. Maybe we'll get lucky."

"I hope so."

The life of a fourteen year old girl depended on us finding her. I hoped that they would leave her alone like they had done with Drew. So far, they weren't killers, and I was really hoping that they would keep to being thieves and not cross that line. The issue was, though, I wasn't entirely confident that they wouldn't become murders if they were pushed into a corner. If one of their captives fought back or escaped, they could be forced to kill them. We had to find them and stop them before they escalated and did something that they couldn't walk back.

CHAPTER NINE

Jonah

I MADE MY way into the bar down on the Southside.

I hoped that I would be able to get some type of intel out of the guys there today. I knew most of the people, almost everyone, who lived on the Southside didn't talk to the police, but I wasn't just another cop.

I worked hard to make sure everyone knew that I would be there if they needed help. That I wouldn't let their dead loved ones go without justice. I always did everything I could to keep my promise to them and, so far, I hadn't let them down. It took time to build that trust, on both ends. I had to be able to trust them with the intel that they had given to me.

It wasn't often when someone would reach out to me, but it had happened. Usually, it happened when Fentanyl hit the streets and they needed my help to get it shut down. Fentanyl was one of those drugs that even the gang leaders didn't want on their streets. It killed their customers and brought a great deal of police presence, reducing the money they could make. Going to talk to a gang leader was not how I had expected to spend my morning, but it was what it was and I knew the chances that the leader or his members could give me some insight was strong.

When I woke up this morning, I'd decided that I wanted to have more than a one-night stand with Cooper. Our time together had invaded my dreams. I dreamed of him all night long, and when I woke up this morning, I was harder than I had ever been. It was like being a teenager again. It took everything in me not to go up those stairs and slide into his ass. I felt like he was invading my entire body. I wanted to touch him. I wanted to hear his moans. I wanted to watch as I milked him again. I thought maybe it was just an after effect of great sex last night, but when I woke up this morning with that need stronger than ever, I knew it had to be more than a single night.

I had originally planned to tease him all day before we would be having sex tonight. I was a fan of teasing. I loved being able to wind my lover up and then watch as he exploded. I wouldn't get to tease him today, unfortunately, but tonight, he was going to be all mine.

I didn't get to taste him last night, either, but I would tonight. I was going to take my time this evening and make him come multiple times. If he thought I ruined him last night, he had no idea what he was in for.

I made my way inside the bar and nodded to the bartender who was cleaning up behind the bar. The place wasn't open to the public, but it was a command center of sorts for the Southside Hustlers. I had been here before, so most of the crew knew me.

I made my way into the back and knocked on the door to the office before I opened it and walked in. Drego was sitting at the table with a couple of his guys. They were busy counting the money that they would need to move into another stash house. They didn't bother with covering it up or trying to give me some bullshit excuse. They knew I didn't care that they were slinging drugs. They knew as long as they didn't get any minors involved or sell to kids, I was good. Drug addicts were going to use if they wanted to. Taking every last gram of drugs off of the street wouldn't stop them from finding something else to use to get their fix. If they kept kids out of it, I had no problem with their business.

Especially the Southside Hustlers.

They did give back to their community. The community center and some youth sport teams were only in existence because they gave money back into the community. They cared about their community. They were gangsters and drug dealers, but they did it because that was the environment that they grew up in. It was all they knew, and even if someone came into power and decided to offer decent paying jobs to low income areas, the gangs would still be there. It would take decades before they were able to eliminate the gangs in the Southside. It was part of the environment and all I could do was try and make it safer for the kids and the people outside of the gangs who had no choice but to live in the area.

"Detective West, kinda early for a visit, don't ya think?" Drego said with a friendly smile.

"Trust me, I would much rather be in bed right now. I got a problem," I said as I grabbed one of the chairs and turned it around, straddling it.

"Don't remember hearing anyone got popped," Drego said.

"It's not a homicide, thankfully. Two days ago, I got home from the night shift and my house had been broken into and my twelve year old son was kidnapped."

"Shit, Drew got grabbed. You need ransom money?" Drego asked, and I could hear the concern in his voice.

I had mentioned Drew a few times to him. He knew about my ex-wife taking off and it disgusted him that a woman could turn their back on their own child. The fact that he would willingly offer up the ransom money, fully prepared for me to never pay it back, only showed the level of respect that we had for each other.

"I appreciate that, but we got him back the same day. It turns out that Drew has been hacking and playing video games on the DarkNet," I started to explain and Beta cut me off.

Beta was one of the worst street names I had ever heard. It all made sense, though, when I saw the inside of his house. He had twenty beta fish all over his house. The man was obsessed with them.

"DarkNet is no place for a kid. He's lucky he didn't get popped between the eyes."

"Oh, he got a long lecture about it. He was playing one of the games when he stumbled upon a robbery crew's heist plan. It was a jewelry store that had conflict diamonds. It's a four man crew, one of which is a hacker. This hacker was able to get into my security system and compromise it. They grabbed him and left him in an old warehouse, unharmed and alone. They then used the distraction of the force looking for Drew to hit the jewelry store. They made off with two million in conflict diamonds."

"Smart plan. While everyone is busy

looking for your boy, they can get in and take their sweet ass time. I haven't heard about no robbery, though," Drego said.

"Probably won't. Most people won't file a complaint when their illegal diamonds get stolen. Last night the same crew kidnapped a fourteen year old daughter of another officer. If they follow the same pattern, they will hit another spot with conflict diamonds. I am hoping you might be able to point me in a direction."

They were drug dealers, but I knew lots of different criminals had plenty of different connections. When someone went to jail, there was no telling who their cellmate would be or who would be on their cell block. The guys all talked and connections were made. They could have easily come across a thief or someone in there who could be connected to illegal diamonds. Or even someone with connections to the black market. If we could find out who these guys were selling the diamonds to, we might be able to catch them.

"I ain't got any ties to no illegal diamonds or the black market. I'm strictly drugs. But I do know a guy. He's a stripper," Drego started.

"Not where I thought you would be going with this. Do we need to have a chat?" I asked, flashing him a friendly smirk.

Drego gave a rich laugh before he spoke. "Naw, man, he's not an exotic stripper. He's a diamond stripper. The man is very good with the delicate process of removing serial numbers off of gems. A lot of major jewelry thieves go to him to get the serial numbers erased before they sell their goods. Now, he might know who has conflict diamonds. If nothing else, he'd know the places that have no problem buying diamonds unmarked. Name's Laser. He's down at one-eighteen Cosway Ave. Tell him I sent you."

"Thanks, man, I appreciate it," I said as I stood up and held my hand out.

He easily took it as he spoke. "No problem. And you tell that boy of yours that the DarkNet ain't no place for a good kid. And if you need someone to scare him straight, you just send him down here and we'll take care of it."

"I appreciate that. I think getting kidnapped has been a very eye opening lesson for him."

"No doubt. Be safe, Detective West," he

said with a warm smile.

"You, too. I don't want the next homicide scene I get called on to be yours."

And I meant that. Drego was a good man, despite him being a drug dealer.

I had to give it to him, though, the guy running the Southside Hustlers before him, it was a bloodbath. The man had no problem killing anyone who dared to step foot in their area unless granted permission. There had been constant gang wars happening on these streets. That was until five years ago when Drego had enough of innocent people dying on all sides. He killed his leader and took over.

Ever since, gang on gang violence in the Southside Hustlers had gone down. The other gangs still feud, but the Southside Hustlers were known as more Switzerland than anything else. As long as you stayed away from their people and didn't hurt them, you didn't have to worry about them.

Drego had even helped to mediate feuds between two gangs to get the killing to stop when a war reached its peak. All Drego wanted was for kids to be able to play out in the streets, no matter the time of day or night it was, without the risk of getting shot in the crossfire.

I climbed back into my car and headed off to speak with Laser. Hopefully, he would have something that we could use to find these guys.

***

Just as I pulled up out front of Laser's house my phone went off. I looked at it and saw that it was a number I didn't have saved into my phone.

"Detective West," I said as I answered.

"It's Damien. Cooper said you were out working the streets. Did you get a lead?"

"Sort of. I'm just about to go speak with a guy who removes the serial numbers off diamonds. I'm hoping he might know which shops use conflict diamonds. What about you? Any news on the girl?"

I was hoping we would be able to find her quickly like we did with Drew. The problem was, we only found Drew that fast because he had a pacemaker. He had something in him that could be hacked so we could get his location. If this girl didn't have anything like that, or some type of smart watch or something, we wouldn't be able to track her.

"Hopefully, your guy can give you something. We have nothing over here. The crime scene was the same as yours. It was a mess; the laptop was destroyed. We have a uniform bringing it to Coop as we speak. Hopefully, he will be able to put it back together and maybe get some intel off of it. The officer's security system was hacked, so no alarms went off. According to her father, she doesn't have any medical conditions and her cell phone was left at the house. She doesn't have a watch or anything that we could use to find her location. We've already searched the warehouse that Drew was left in."

They were being smart. They probably had a whole list of warehouses that were abandoned that they could leave the kid in. And without her wearing anything with a microchip, Cooper couldn't find her. What bothered me was the smashed laptop. Maybe they did it to make it seem like they were after something, but my gut was telling me otherwise. They smashed Drew's laptop so we couldn't get to his browser history and discover he had been playing video games on the DarkNet. So why smash hers?

"What do we know about this girl?" I asked.

"Jessica Montanna, fourteen, goes to Seaway High as a freshman. We've sent uniforms over to speak with her friends at the school. So far, though, nothing has come up. She's a good student, according to the report cards that were up on the fridge. No Juvi record. Her mom is deceased as of three years ago. Officer Montanna has been raising her on his own ever since. He hasn't even dated yet. Said he didn't want to bring another woman into her life until she felt ready."

"What were her grades in Math and English?"

"Seriously?" Damien asked, and I could tell he didn't understand why that would be relevant. It might not be, but I was running on a hunch.

"Humor me."

I could hear him walking before he spoke. "Math she gets all high nineties and in English she's in the upper seventies, low eighties range. Why?"

"From what I have recently discovered, hackers excel in Math, but can be pretty average in English. It's how their mind processes the numbers versus words. Maybe she wasn't targeted just because her dad was working the night shift as a patrol officer. Maybe her laptop was smashed because she saw something that she wasn't supposed to, just like Drew."

It was a long shot, I was fully aware of that fact. However, both Jessica and Drew had this one thing in common. It can't be a coincidence that the second time a law enforcement official's child was abducted and they were both good at math and computers. We would need Coop's diagnostics on her laptop, and hopefully, he could get it to confirm my theory. But at least we had a theory, now.

"You think they were both targeted for their hacking skills. It's possible, but I mean, how many young hackers could there be with parents in the police force?"

That was the question, because if they were targeted, then how were our kidnappers finding them?

My gut was telling me this was connected, that they were targeted, but I had no idea why.

Sure, maybe they could have stumbled upon something, but what would the odds be that two young hackers in the same city would stumble upon a heist?

Plus, they just happened to be the only child of single law enforcement officials. The odds were too high to make this coincidental. It had to be connected and maybe if we could discover that connection, we could find out who their next captive would be.

"I don't know, but I'm not buying that they only learned how to hack using YouTube. I'm sure there are plenty of videos on how to hack on YouTube, but it has to be pretty basic. If it was that easy that anyone could get onto the DarkNet, then criminals wouldn't be using it. I mean, we're not talking about how to hack into a phone or your school's database. The DarkNet is used for hitmen and human traffickers, there's got to be more to it than these kids are learning from YouTube."

"You make a valid point. Seems like you are going to need to talk to your kid and see what else he knows."

"Yeah. I'll let you know if I get something."

"Copy."

I ended the call, but I didn't get out of my car right away. Damien was right, it was starting to seem like Drew had been keeping something from me. He was only twelve, he shouldn't be caught up in anything dangerous. I just couldn't see it. At the same time, though, he had to know more than what he had told us. There was no way these two just happened to get grabbed out of all of the children in the city.

I let out a sigh and rubbed my hand over my face. I was going to have to talk to Drew when I got back. I just prayed that I wasn't going to hate his answers.

I climbed out of the car and made my way toward Laser's place. Hopefully, he would be able to point us in the right direction. We needed something that we could use to pick these guys up. I knocked on the door and a moment later it opened part way.

"What?" a guy said, and I had a feeling this was Laser.

"I'm here to see Laser. Drego sent me." It would be best to skip the part about me being a detective. At least, until I got inside.

The guy stepped back and allowed me to walk inside. The house looked normal, but I knew there was a basement and that would be where he did his work. I didn't need to see it. I wasn't about to arrest this man. I wanted the kidnappers. I didn't care about whatever he was doing with the gems to clean them.

"You got something you need scrubbed?" Laser asked as he moved into the living room. He was a sketchy and skittish type of guy. But I guess in his world it was better to be paranoid than trusting.

"No. I'm Detective West with B.R.P.D. Don't start freaking out, I'm not here for you," I said quickly. I could see him starting to panic the second that I said I was a detective. "I'm looking for a four man robbery crew. They are kidnapping teenagers to keep the cops busy while they go in and rob a jewelry store. They target the ones with conflict diamonds. Drego said you might have an idea of what stores are using conflict diamonds or ones that are open to illegal diamonds."

"I might, but I ain't no snitch."

"Look, I don't care about what setup you have in your basement. I don't care about the unknown amount of money you have in stolen gems in said basement. I don't care about your clients or you, for that matter. However, I could start caring about it all and that's not going to bode well for you. I promise you, a few nights in the county jail and you will snitch on everyone, including your momma. You are not the type of guy who does well in prison. So, tell me what I want to know and I'll leave and you can go right back to your illegal activities."

Some cops would care. In fact, most would. A bust like that could be career making. Myself, though, I cared about preventing kids from being kidnapped. I wanted the kidnappers. What Laser was doing wasn't my department and I didn't care. If he wanted to wash stolen jewelry that was his business, and most of it would be covered under insurance so the victims would be able to get compensated for it. Was it justice, no, but they were still living and that was what mattered.

I could see him thinking about it. He was going to tell me, we both knew it. He was not the type of guy who was hard enough for jail and he knew it.

He got up and strolled off somewhere for a moment before he came back with a list. "That's all I know," he said.

I took the list and saw that there were

twenty-three jewelry stores on it. This was going to take a long time. We were going to have to run the owners and investigate to see if they could be the target of this crew. It was, unfortunately, not going to be a quick lead.

"Appreciate it," I said with a nod before I headed out.

I heard the lock being thrown the second the door clicked closed. Laser was going to be looking over his shoulders for weeks after this. Every time someone knocked on the door, he was going to be expecting the police. He would calm down eventually, though, and he might be a nice resource of information for a later case. I got a lot of homicides from home invasions. There was always a chance he might come across some high-end jewelry from one of them.

I climbed back into my car and started to make some calls. We were going to need to run these names and do a surveillance check on these stores. My hope for getting back at a decent hour to speak with Drew was going right out the window. At this rate, I wouldn't be getting back to Cooper's until late. That talk was going to have to wait until tomorrow.

CHAPTER TEN

Cooper

IT WAS NEARING ten o'clock when Jonah finally came back home.

Whoa, not his home, *my* home.

That was weird. I shouldn't think of this as Jonah's home. We'd only known each other for less than five days. I shouldn't be thinking how good he looked walking through my front door. I shouldn't be noticing how easy it was for me to spend the day with Drew. I shouldn't be thinking about how nice it would have been for us all to eat breakfast together. I shouldn't be wondering how it would feel to fall asleep in his arms, to wake up in his arms.

Or better yet, to wake up with his erection pressing against my ass.

I couldn't allow myself to have feelings for him. He didn't come across as someone who was interested in feelings. He had already been married, to a woman. He most likely wouldn't want another serious relationship like that.

Not that I was looking for a serious relationship, either. I had never really been in one and I wasn't sure it was the best idea to get into a relationship with someone in law enforcement. Yes, he would understand why I worked long hours and could be called away at a moment's notice. However, he would also work long hours and be called away at a moment's notice. He was also an active field detective and had the scars to prove it. He was more likely to be killed in the line of duty and I wasn't sure that was something I would be able to handle. He wasn't going to change his job or how he did it. And I would never ask him to do that. Even if we were in love, I could never ask him to change his career. Just like he would never ask me that. What we did for a living, it was special, and it was work that needed to be done. It wasn't something either of us were looking to walk away from. It would be better to leave any emotions out of this and just enjoy the amazing sex.

"Hey, you're back," I said, flashing him a warm smile.

"Yeah, sorry for being so late. I didn't mean to dump Drew on you," he said as he removed his coat and boots.

"You didn't dump him on me. He's not an infant; he's twelve. It's not like he requires a lot of work. We just hung out on the couch working away. We haven't found anything yet. They might not be using those games again and it's not like there is a shortage of games on the DarkNet. What about you?"

Jonah spoke as he leaned against the doorframe that led into my living room. "Well, we have twenty-three possible locations that the crew could hit. And those are just the ones we know about. No one has found Jessica yet, so there's a chance they haven't hit their target yet. We spoke with the owners of the jewelry stores, but they are all playing stupid and denying any type of illegal activities. We don't have warrants to search them, so all we can do is monitor them. We have unmarked cars at each location. Can't really say we got anywhere today. What about the laptop? Is it a goner?"

That laptop was a lot of work to try and repair. I wasn't certain I would even be able to do it, but I was able to half fix it. They had destroyed it more than Drew's and I didn't think that was an accident. I think the hacker somehow discovered that we were able to grab Drew and he wanted to make sure we couldn't get into it this time around. That told me there was something on the laptop that could lead us to something.

"Sort of. I couldn't fully fix it, not like Drew's. I do believe that you're right. I think both Jessica and Drew were targeted and it has to do with whatever is on their laptops. Jessica's was destroyed twice as badly as Drew's. They made sure nothing could be recovered. I was able to get into it, but I couldn't get to the browser history. It was most likely double scrubbed so it couldn't even be rebuilt. What I did find, though, was a pretty sophisticated firewall and a large amount of hidden files."

"Hidden files?" he asked, confused.

"Every computer has the option to hide a file. So when you look at your documents or desktop, no one will see that you have it. You have to go through the computer to search for hidden files. I couldn't get into them, but the file was very large. I'm talking just over three gigabytes with something in it."

"She's hiding something, but what?"

"No idea. It could be a shitload of documents or it could be videos. For all I know, it could be a video game that she is creating. It doesn't have to be a bad thing, but it is there and with the damage done to the computer, I can't access it."

I wasn't certain what would be in the hidden files. It could have easily been a draft for a video game. That would explain why it was rather large. It also would explain why she was hiding it. She could have been worried about someone looking to steal her idea. It could also explain why she was on the DarkNet, assuming she was. She could easily be an up and coming video games designer. It didn't have to mean something illegal.

"And there is nothing you can do to Frankenstein it back to life?"

"No. This thing is dead, we were lucky I was able to even get it to turn on once."

"Okay. Were there hidden files on Drew's laptop?"

I could tell he was afraid to ask the question, not that I could blame him. He was clearly thinking that Drew and Jessica were involved in something illegal, something shady, and it got them targeted by this crew. I wasn't getting that from Drew, though. I genuinely didn't think he knew who they were or what was going on.

"I didn't search for any. I can tomorrow. My eyes are too burnt out to keep staring at a screen. For what it's worth, though, I don't think he's involved in anything illegal. I spent all day with him and he genuinely just loves playing the games. When I mentioned Jessica, there was no recognition in his eyes. He doesn't know her. That doesn't mean he doesn't know her online handle, but we don't even know what that is so we can't ask him. He's a good kid. I can't speak for Jessica, but he's a good kid."

Jonah let out a sigh as he tiredly rubbed his hands over his face. I could tell he was stressed and worried. That he had been worried about this all day, not that I could blame him. It couldn't have been a good feeling to wonder if your own son was doing something illegal and could be setting a target on his back. With that said, though, I did think they knew each other, but only online. And that was what we needed to get out of Drew tomorrow. We had to know the full story, because I believed he was holding something back. Like every teenager, he was only giving us what he thought would answer our questions and get him in less trouble. We needed the whole truth if we were going to solve this case.

"I just don't know what to do about that. As stupid as this is going to sound, I almost would have preferred the whole issue to be about drugs. At least that I would be able to understand and fix. I could end that. But all of this computer stuff, the coding, the hacking, the DarkNet, I can't fix that and I don't understand that world. It's like being dropped in a foreign country where English isn't even their second language and told to figure it out."

"If you asked me a question about football, or any sport for that matter, I couldn't answer it even if my life depended on it. You can't be expected to know everything about every topic out there. You are going to have topics that Drew will be interested in that you won't know about. Just like there are topics he doesn't know that you do. It's not about you being able to talk computers with him, Jonah. It's about you *listening* to him when he does talk. Showing him that you are interested and willing to be there for him."

It meant everything to a kid. I wished I had that growing up. I wished I had someone who would listen to me and allow me to share with them what I thought or felt. I had to keep it all to myself and that led me to the wrong crowd and almost landed me a federal prison. I was all on my own, but Drew wasn't.

"I know you said you grew up in the foster care system, but did you ever have contact with your parents? Or one of your foster parents who listened to you?"

"No. I don't really know who my parents are. I have no memory of them. My foster parents were mostly abusive and neglectful. I bounced around a lot and was ignored. It wasn't until I met Evans did I finally have a home and someone who understood the real me. The hackers that I met at the community center, they understood what we were doing, but they didn't know who I truly was. Evans was the only person who took the time to listen to me. Even when I would go on these long technical rants. He just sat there, smiled, and gave the occasional nod. Drew doesn't need you to understand the words, he just needs to know that you care enough to listen to them."

He gave me a warm smile and I knew I had managed to make him feel better. I was happy that I could help him. I wanted to make him feel better and not feel like he was failing his son, because he wasn't. He had stuck around when his wife left him with a son. He didn't have to be a single father, but he *chose* to be and it was honorable. He shouldn't feel guilty or bad about not understanding everything there was about coding or hacking.

"Well, I can tell you right now that today has not gone how I thought it would."

"And how did you expect for it to go?" I

asked with a smirk.

"How about I show you?" he said, flashing me the sexiest smile I had ever seen in my life.

I was instantly getting up and following him upstairs to my bedroom. I had no idea what was going to happen or what his plan was, but I so didn't care. I doubted there was anything that he could do to me that I wouldn't love.

We quickly made our way into my bedroom and the second the door closed his hands were on me, stripping me of my clothes. I turned around so I could remove his clothing as his lips finally touched mine. My whole body felt like it was on fire with just a single touch. No man had ever made me feel this way and I didn't understand what it was about Jonah that could do this to me.

The second we were both naked, he was guiding me back toward the bed. I was all too eager to get onto the bed with him. He pulled back from the kiss as he spoke.

"Lay down, but put your head toward the end of the bed."

Well, that was new, but I was more than willing to do whatever he wanted me to. I quickly scrambled into the position that he wanted.

He grabbed me under my shoulders and moved me so my head was hanging off of the end of the bed and I couldn't help but wonder what he planned to do.

"Open up, I'm gonna fuck your throat."

A moan escaped me the second his words registered in my brain. I had never given a blowjob like that before and I was already hard just thinking about it.

I willingly opened my mouth and he started to slide his massive dick inside of my mouth. He went slow, but unlike before, I felt every glorious inch of him as his dick worked its way across my tongue and down my throat.

The second he was all the way inside of me, he was moving back to lightly fuck my mouth.

"You feel so good, Baby, but how do you taste?" he said, and that was the only warning I had before he bent all the way forward and licked at the tip of my hard and weeping dick. He moaned as he spoke. "Nice and sweet, just how I like it."

A second later, I felt his hot mouth engulfing my dick and it was heaven. He continued to thrust into my mouth, making sure he got all of his cock inside of it, his balls butting up against my nose.

I had never experienced this level of pleasure before from mutual oral. This was better than some of the sex I'd had with other guys. I had no idea where Jonah had learned all of these things, but I couldn't wait to find out what else he would be teaching me.

It didn't take long before I was a moaning mess underneath him. He worked my dick with his mouth like he was an Olympic champion in blow jobs. I was gripping the sheets with both hands just to try and keep my body still. I didn't want to lose the heat of Jonah's mouth or the amazing feeling of him being down my throat. I would have easily done this all night long if it had been possible.

I was getting closer and closer to falling over that cliff, and right before I was about to come, Jonah was pulling his mouth off. I let out a whimper at the loss of his mouth and at the denial of my orgasm. I was seconds away from pure bliss and then it was gone.

"Don't worry, Baby, I'll make you come, but not until I'm buried inside of your tight little ass. I got a drink for you, though," he said as his thrusting picked up to a whole new level.

I vaguely wondered if my throat was going to be sore tomorrow, but that thought quickly vanished. Even if it was sore, I didn't care, because this felt far too good to get him to stop.

I wanted to taste him again. I wanted to feel him inside of my ass and to feel the highest level of pleasure that he would be able to give to me. I knew he would deliver, too, because last night he definitely did not disappoint.

It was a moment later when he snapped his hips forward one last time and came hard down my throat with a groan. I eagerly swallowed everything he had for me, not wasting a single drop. He moaned each time he felt my throat constricting around him, and when he finished pulsing, he went back to lightly thrusting to get fully hard again.

Tonight was going to be the best night of my life.

CHAPTER ELEVEN

Jonah

IT HAD BEEN a long time, years, since I woke up with someone in my arms. I hadn't been planning on falling asleep with Cooper, but after finally coming for the last time, we were both exhausted and had fallen asleep almost instantly.

And I do mean *instantly*.

I was still buried inside of his ass with him curled up in front of me. The sex last night had been even better than the previous night. Part of that was due to the fact that I didn't have another condom, but with us both being tested regularly and both negative, Cooper was perfectly fine with me not wearing a condom. It had made the sex even better and after I came twice inside of him, and him three times, our bodies had given out on us.

I should be bothered by the fact that he was curled up against me. That I had slept with him. Even with my friends with benefits we never fell asleep afterward. I had always made the point and effort to leave once we were finished. It was a boundary that I enjoyed keeping. At the same time, though, I didn't tend to kiss them, and for whatever reason, I couldn't seem to stop kissing Cooper.

I don't know what it was about him, but he made me want to break all of my rules. He made me want to kiss him and feel his body against mine all night long.

I didn't date. I hadn't dated since I'd built up the courage to leave my wife. I never thought I would ever want to be in a relationship again. I had been tied down to a female for a good majority of my life. And with being gay, it felt like a prison sentence that I was never going to escape. I wasn't ready to date, then. I wanted to play the field and just have fun. I wanted to explore everything I had been missing in my life.

And I did.

Oh how I had explored and enjoyed.

I had been with a lot of guys and each one taught me something new. None of them, though, had ever felt as good as Cooper did. None had ever made me want to feel them in my arms or kiss them.

Cooper was special.

I wasn't stupid enough to not notice it. Maybe it was time that I finally allowed myself to be open to the idea of dating someone again.

Cooper let out a soft moan and I knew he was waking up. I started to kiss along the back of his neck as he spoke in a gravelly voice.

"Good morning."

"Oh, it's a very good morning," I said with a slight thrust of my hips.

He moaned as he wiggled back against me. "What time is it?"

"It's just after nine."

"Drew is gonna be up, isn't he?"

I gave a light snort to that. "Not likely. He's a twelve year old boy. He'd sleep until noon if we let him."

My son was becoming a teenager. He was just starting to sleep in all day and getting weird about his personal space. I knew soon enough I was going to have to have the sex talk with him, but thankfully, that was not going to be right that moment.

I pressed kisses along Cooper's neck as I spoke. "We have two options. We could get up and get some breakfast. Or, you could play cowboy and ride my dick and then we get breakfast. Which would you prefer?"

I already knew which one he was going to choose and I was very much looking forward to it. So far, I had been doing all of the work and this morning, I was feeling a little lazy. I wanted to lie there and watch, just enjoy the view and the pleasure as he rode me.

"I'll take the second one," he said, and wiggled his hips, grinding his ass back on my hardness.

I pulled out of him so we could move into the right position. I reached over the bed and grabbed my belt from my pants.

Cooper moved so he was straddling my hips, but before he could slide my hard cock back inside of him, I grabbed both of his wrists and tied them behind his back with my belt.

"No touching," I said, flashing him a smirk as I ran my finger along his hard shaft, causing him to hiss and let out a shaky breath.

I lay back and watched as Cooper lifted his hips and started to take my dick into his ass. I knew he was already stretched, I had just pulled out of him, so he didn't have to go slow.

I moaned as I watched as my dick disappeared inside of his hungry hole. The second he had me buried inside of him he didn't even wait before he was moving almost all of the way off before slamming right back down.

Cooper let out a whimper as the position made my cockhead hit his prostate dead on, just like I knew it would. He was instantly doing it again, and again. Rapidly thrusting his ass over my cock, moaning and whimpering, more and more precum leaking from his slit to dribble down his hardness each time he pressed downward.

I moaned at the sight of him using my body to pleasure himself. "That's it, Baby, use my dick. I want to watch as you make yourself come."

I ran my hand over Cooper's dick,

causing him to moan deeply. I collected some of his precum that was dripping off of his tip with my finger and then brought it up to my lips, flicking out my tongue and tasting his essence.

I moaned my appreciation as his flavor burst across my taste buds and Cooper returned the moan at the sight of my digit disappearing into my mouth.

"You taste so sweet, perfect for breakfast." I gathered more precum from his tip, but this time I brought it up to his lips.

Without saying anything, Cooper parted his lips and, with his gaze locked on mine, he easily sucked my finger into his hot mouth.

I moaned deeply, panting heavily as I watched as he licked his own precum right off of my finger.

He was so sexy, so perfect.

Cooper started to move faster and I knew he was chasing his own orgasm. It wasn't easy for him, though, because he didn't have any friction on his dick. I had tied his hands back so he couldn't touch himself. I knew the desire to touch his dick would be too great for him and that wasn't what I wanted. I moved my hand to his cock once more, gripping him tightly in my fist, and slowly started to jerk him off.

"Do you want to come?" I teased.

"Yes, fuck, feels so good," he moaned as he picked up his pace once again.

"So then come. I'm not stopping you. Come for me while you fuck yourself on my dick. You better come soon, though, because if I come first, then you'll have to wait until next time we're together," I said as I stopped jerking him off, causing Cooper to let out a whine at the loss of friction.

I loved teasing and I loved knowing that I could make this man go insane with the need to come. I was torn between hoping he would come and not. I would have loved to have been able to keep teasing him all day.

Cooper started to bounce even harder and faster. I knew he would be close to coming soon. I could see the precum running out of him. He was going to milk himself on my dick and it was going to be magnificent to watch as he spilled over that cliff.

It was a few moments later when Cooper gave a soft scream as he came hard, his cum pouring out of his slit in long, white ropes, splashing on his belly and over my chest.

I grasped his hips and started to brutally thrust up into him. He let out another scream as the angle made my cock constantly rub over his sweet spot, milking out even more cum from him. The tightening of his muscles around my dick became too great and forced me over the edge. I snapped my hips up hard once more and emptied everything I had inside of him with a deep, throaty groan.

We were both breathing heavily and I could feel his legs trembling slightly from the workout. Now, I really needed to feed him breakfast. That had been amazing, though.

Once again, *he* was amazing.

I had said I wanted him to become addicted to me, but I knew I was already addicted to him. I didn't think I would ever get tired of being around him, of being inside of him. It was like he was heroin and I could never get enough of it.

"You made a mess. Now, you have to clean it up," I said as I lifted him off of my dick.

Cooper instantly knew what I was

talking about, and without any hesitation, he bent forward and ran his tongue up my stomach, collecting his cum. He continued to lick it all up and the sight of it almost had me fully hard again.

Once every drop of the cum was cleaned from my belly and chest, I grasped his hips again and flipped him around so he was up on his knees, bent over, face down, ass in the air.

I spread his ass cheeks and ran the flat of my tongue over his engorged, leaking hole. He gave a shaky moan at the contact of my tongue across his highly sensitive entrance. I didn't care, though. I loved this part.

I knew most guys might be bothered by it, but there was just something about the taste of my own cum from my lover's sweet hole that I enjoyed. I also loved how sensitive the guy was after sex and I wanted to build Cooper back up, only to leave him when he needed more.

"Fuck, Jo," Cooper hissed, moaning his appreciation of my efforts as he pushed back to get my tongue to go further inside of him.

I was all too happy to push my tongue into his needy, soaked hole. I continued to eat him out until I knew he was rock hard and on the edge once more. When his balls pulled up tight, and I knew he was getting too close, I pulled back and gave his ass a light slap before reaching over to untie his wrists.

"We need to get to work. We can't spend all day in bed."

He gave a whimper and I couldn't help but chuckle lightly. I knew at this point he was in desperate need for more, but he would have to wait until tonight. For now, we had to get ready for work and get some real food into us. But after we finally did find these kidnappers, we would be spending an entire day, or weekend for that matter, in bed.

CHAPTER TWELVE

Cooper

"I TAKE IT you're a breakfast guy," I remarked as I sat down at my ridiculously small kitchen table, watching as Jonah stirred together the ingredients for pancakes.

"Most important meal of the day. Plus with Drew, I have a habit of cooking him something. Often, especially since he's been older, I have been working nights so I make sure I cook him a real breakfast to make up for me not being there at night. I know he's just sleeping, but still, if he had a nightmare or was sick, I wouldn't be there for him. I know it's not much, but I feel better knowing that I am at least sending him to school with something real in his stomach."

"It's nice that you make him breakfast. Most of the foster homes I was in, it was either cereal or no food in the morning. Those moments that you can spend with him and get to talk and catch up, they're important, even if they are only for a few minutes at a time."

He was a good dad and I hated that he always seemed to be second guessing himself. I could understand it. He was a single dad working a full-time job and, as a police detective, his job wasn't exactly nine to five. He could be called away anytime outside of his shift. He could have to work past his shift and on holidays and birthdays. There were no guarantees in his line of work, but he had taken that on when he signed up to be a police officer.

The problem was, Drew didn't sign up. The kid was enlisted to the life and it could be very hard on a child, especially as he got older. Drew was twelve now, he understood that his dad could be hurt. He would have seen him hurt over the years with those scars. It would be natural for Drew to be scared and pull away as he got older. It was something that Jonah would need to keep a very close eye on to ensure that Drew didn't go down the wrong path.

I would also be keeping an eye on him. Even once this case was over, I would be making a point of regularly seeing Drew and helping him with his skills. I would be making sure he knew that he had someone in his corner, even when his dad couldn't be there.

"I try. I thought as he got older it would be easier, but now I'm starting to think it's going to be harder."

"Have you talked to him about the dangers of your job and what will happen to him if you die in the line of duty?" I knew it wasn't an easy conversation to have with anyone, but I couldn't help but wonder if Drew was worried about where he would go should the worst ever happen.

Jonah let out a sigh before he spoke. "No, and I know I should have that conversation with him. He's old enough to understand that my job is dangerous. He's seen me hurt, shot, and we've worked through it and I have always downplayed it a bit. The problem is, I don't really know where he would go. His mother wants nothing to do with him, hasn't had any contact with him for five years. I have no siblings, and my parents are older and on a fixed income. They wouldn't be able to afford to raise him if should I die tomorrow. I don't know."

I could hear the deep feeling of conflict and pain in his voice at not being able to have that answer. I could understand fully that he was apprehensive about sending Drew to his parents. I'd had a couple of older foster parents and it wasn't a good situation. They barely had enough money for food and they were sick a lot. Taking on a child, it wasn't easy. And it sounded like Drew's own mother wasn't even a possible option. Even if she could be found, she had abandoned Drew five years ago. The woman had made the incomprehensible choice to no longer be a mother. Without a relative, Drew would be placed in the foster care system and that was the last thing that either of us wanted.

I figured it had to be taking a toll on both of them. Every time Jonah went out for work, the "what ifs" had to weigh on his mind and that could make him distracted in the field. It wasn't a good position to be in.

"He can stay with me." The words were tumbling out of my mouth before I even registered that I was saying them.

Jonah instantly turned around and gave me a confused and shocked look, not that I could blame him. I was fairly certain I had the same look on my face.

Was I a kid person?

Not so much. I was a teenager person, sure, but younger children, I didn't tend to be around them. Not since I had aged out of the foster system. I never wanted to have children of my own or someone else's. It was a direct result of having to care for so many different children in my life.

Once I was thirteen, I started to become one of the oldest foster kids in all of the homes I had been placed in. The older kids, their job was to help take care of the younger children. When I was fourteen, for six months I had to share a room with a newborn who was addicted to heroin. I spent six months out of school and stuck twenty-four hours a day, seven days a week with this crying baby. I never wanted to have children, not after that.

Drew wasn't an infant, though. He was a twelve year old boy and he might never have to be placed with anyone if Jonah didn't die. However, just the thought of Drew having to go into the foster system, it made my stomach turn into knots. There was no telling what could happen to him and I didn't want him to experience any trauma or abuse. I didn't want him to get caught up in the wrong crowd and become a black hat hacker, either. He didn't deserve it.

"What?" Jonah finally managed to ask.

"Yeah, I didn't expect that either." I took a moment to collect my thoughts before I spoke again. "Look, I am not a child person. I had to raise a shit load of them during the last five years I was in the system. I'm a cat person. But, I also know what happens to kids in the system and I don't want that for Drew. He's too good of a kid. He's too talented to end up being abused and used by criminals. So, if you don't have anyone else, you can leave him with me should the worst happen. I know you don't know me all that well, but he would be safe with me. You wouldn't have to worry about him being abused or neglected. I suck at cooking, so I can't promise anything in that department, but he would be safe."

He gave me a warm smile and I could see he appreciated the offer. I was hoping we would never have to enact it, that he wouldn't die before Drew was an adult, but I also knew there was no telling what could happen in the line of duty.

"Thank you. I can't tell you how much I appreciate that. I don't plan on kicking the bucket anytime soon, though, so you shouldn't have to worry," he said, flashing me another warm smile.

"It would be great if you didn't die anytime soon. Not just for Drew, but for my sex life," I said, smirking.

He let out a rich laugh as he turned back around to get the pancakes off of the stove. We both heard the bedroom door opening upstairs and I knew Drew was awake.

Aa few minutes later, when we were all sitting around the table eating, Drew asked, "Did you find Jessica?".

"Not yet. We're still looking for her. I have to go back out shortly and help with the search. There is something I need to talk to you about, though," Jonah answered with a quick glance in my direction.

"What is it?"

"I know Coop showed you a photo of her yesterday and you didn't recognize her. However, the odds of you both not knowing each other are pretty slim. Coop, wasn't able to repair her laptop enough to get into the browser history, but we are operating on the assumption she was a hacker as well. That you both were targeted for a specific reason."

"But I've never seen her. I have no idea who she is. And what could we have done to be targeted?" Drew asked instantly, and I could hear that he was getting defensive.

"No one is saying you are lying about knowing her. But maybe you do know her by her hacker name. When you play the games, have you ever talked to anyone?" I piped up, trying to calm Drew down.

"Not in the games, no."

"But you have somewhere else?" Jonah asked.

"On comments for YouTube videos, sure."

"Nope, try again. I know you said you learned from YouTube videos, but I don't believe that is how you discovered how to get onto the DarkNet. If it was that easy, criminals wouldn't be using it. Someone had to teach you," Jonah said.

"You're not in trouble, Drew. But your dad is right. YouTube didn't show you how to get into the DarkNet. And it didn't show you how to hack like you have managed to do. Hackers talk to each other, they offer tips and help beginners get onto the map. I had it in person, but now everything is done online. We need the truth. Jessica needs the truth."

"Full immunity, right here, right now. It doesn't matter what you tell us, you won't be in trouble. This is very serious, Drew. I need the truth before someone loses their life," Jonah added.

Drew let out a soft sigh before he started to explain. "I was watching a YouTube video about basic hacking, pretty simple code work. And it was just for me to learn more about coding and how to design an app. I thought it might be cool to try and create a new app for a game. At the end of the video, there was a link to a free coding workshop. I was curious, so I clicked it, and it was completely free, so I enrolled. I learned all about coding, but halfway through, it turned into hacking. I did the exam at the end and got perfect. The next morning, I got an email from them with another offer for a free hacking workshop. I took it and it connected me with a hidden chat room where the students could all talk with each other. No real names were given. It was one of the rules. You had to always go by your code name and never reveal anything personal about yourself. We were told the owner of the workshop would monitor the chat room and if we broke the privacy rule, we could be kicked out. That part of being a hacker was anonymity."

That was what we had been missing. I needed that link and I needed to get into that workshop. I was willing to bet every dollar I had that our hacker was running that group. Jessica would have been a student and there was no telling who else could be.

"Do you still have access to the chat room?" I asked before Jonah even had the chance.

"I don't know. I can try, though."

"Do you know if that video is still up for the first workshop you went to?" I asked next.

"I think so, yeah. I can show it to you."

"What are you thinking?" Jonah asked me.

"I think our hacker is running it. Black hat hackers, they like to do things alone, but they also like to work in groups. Hackers can be very creative, and when they work together in a group, they can accomplish more. They can build something pretty amazing. Unfortunately, sometimes those things are not a new video game or a security system. It sounds like our hacker is looking to recruit the next generation of hackers. People he can easily manipulate."

"Kids who don't fit into normal school society. The kids who aren't popular. Maybe the nerds who get bullied. The ones who are ignored. They are vulnerable to being manipulated with the promise of fitting in and having a place where they belong," Jonah said, clearly understanding.

"I'm sorry, Dad."

"You don't have anything to be sorry for. High school is hard for everyone who doesn't fit in with the athletes or the popular kids. You're a smart guy who just happens to have an interest and skill when it comes to computers. I know you don't fit in perfectly right now, but after high school you will. And with this outreach program, you will find kids like you, who enjoy the same things you do, who you can connect with. Guys like this hacker, they know what they are doing and they know how to prey on someone. It's not your fault that you didn't see that. You're not old enough to see it."

"He's right, Drew. You didn't do anything wrong. You discovered something you were interested in and had a natural talent for. It's only logical that you would want to explore that more. I do need to know, though, if there are any hidden files on your computer," I asked.

"No, why would I?" he asked, confused.

"You know what hidden files are?" I asked first.

"Yeah, it's where you make a file or document hidden on your computer so it can't be found on a surface scrub. I mean, everyone knows that," he quipped with a small smirk and an eyeroll.

I couldn't help, but look over at Jonah with a big smile on my face. He simply rolled his eyes at us before I turned back to Drew.

"Jessica had a massive, three gigabyte hidden file on her laptop. The hard drive is too damaged for me to open it. But it's a massive file and clearly not documents. Do you have any idea what it could be?"

"Maybe. At the end of the workshop, the runner connected six of us for a private conversation. He said he was so impressed with all of our skills, he wanted us to work on a different project. That if we did really well, we could be hired in his company to work for cyber security and major corporations, backtracking hacks and preventing a cyber attack on their system. We were all for it. I mean, it was a huge opportunity. Completing this project had to be done together. If one of us didn't do our part, the whole project would fall apart."

"And what was it that he wanted you to do?" Jonah asked.

"My part of the project was to create an algorithm that could mutate within different databases. He wanted us to create a skeleton key, but he swore it would never be used. That it was only for a simulation to prove that our key would actually work. It was never supposed to be used in real life. It was just supposed to be some virtual thing that couldn't actually work in real practice."

"Shit," I immediately said.

"Hold up, what's a skeleton key?" Jonah asked me.

"It's like a key to the city, only that city is the world. It's a virtual key that, when created properly, can be used to unlock anything and everything. And I do mean *everything*. You download it onto a USB drive and you can take it with you to access anything that has a USB port. It's a series of complex codes and algorithms that, when they work properly, can unlock anything with a microchip. I'm talking about online banks, the stock market, power, water, gas, cell phones, anything connected to the Internet. Military bases, nuclear missiles, hospital equipment, everything nowadays is connected to the internet, and anything that is still controlled from an offline circuit, you can use the USB to get in. All you have to do is plug it into a hub at that facility. And it works anywhere in the world. Some guy could be sitting in his mother's basement and start World War Three with a few keystrokes."

This was a nightmare, a complete clusterfuck nightmare.

If this hacker was able to create a skeleton key, there was no telling the damage that he could do to the country; to the world. We had to find him and make sure any traces of a skeleton key were wiped out.

"And you made one?" Jonah asked Drew, now feeling the urgency and the panic.

"No, I swear I didn't. I don't know, it just felt off. I knew it was only supposed to be in a virtual simulation, but it still didn't feel right to make something like that. To help create something that should never be made. I left the group. I left the workshop and went back to playing video games. That was about two months ago. But if Jessica has a large hidden file, it's possible she was one of the other five hackers and that she did do her part."

"It seems like the most likely scenario. He would have easily been able to hack into your IP to see where you were located. The other four might be local or they could be close by. If Jessica did her part, which I think it's safe to assume she did, it's possible the other four did theirs as well. But without your algorithm, the skeleton key is useless," I said.

"But if he has five out of six parts, why can't he just finish it himself? If he's this powerful hacker, why does he even need kids to do it?" Jonah asked.

"There's different skill levels for hackers, but also specialties. Not every hacker can create a complex mathematical algorithm that has the ability to mutate. It's a serious skill and it is something that you are born able to do or not. You have to be a math genius. Our hacker probably can't do it and has probably tried to finish it, but if the algorithm is even one number off, it all falls apart," I explained.

"And you can do this?" Jonah asked Drew, clearly impressed.

"Yeah. I don't know why or how, but I get numbers and the puzzle of it all. I like the challenge."

"Me, too. It's my specialty as well. And there are not many of us out there who can do it. Which is going to be a problem, because this hacker wants the skeleton key, and if he can't find someone else who can finish it, they could come for Drew. I suspect that is why you were grabbed first. They were probably going to come back for you and try to get you to finish the skeleton key."

"Why leave him alone in a warehouse if they need him to finish it, then?"

"Because I don't think the kidnappers know what is going on. We've been operating under the assumption that the hacker is one of the kidnappers, but I don't think he is. I don't even think he's even in the city. He could be in another country, for all we know. I think he's using the kidnappers as a distraction."

"They were probably told to bring Drew somewhere after the heist, but we got to him first. The hacker probably didn't know he had a pacemaker and we could track him. The kidnappers get to be paid in conflict diamonds and he gets to finish the skeleton key," Jonah said, nodding. I could practically see the wheels turning in his mind as everything clicked into place.

"But why take Jessica? If she did her part, why grab her?" Drew asked, confused.

"Maybe they didn't. She did finish her part, that's the only logical explanation for the hidden files. Maybe she left willingly and is going to meet up with the hacker or the others. If the hacker still promises them all work, for doing their part, he could be building an army that could break through any cyber wall. He's not just going to stop with a skeleton key. Even having it, he would need more hackers to help him go through all of the layers of security. And to keep modifying the key on the fly as the Government works to redesign their cyber systems to prevent the key from getting in."

"So it's something that he would need ongoing help with. If he's planning on keeping the young hackers, it makes sense that he has them being kidnapped. If they run away, they would still be looked for, but it opens them up to questioning about why they ran away. If they are kidnapped, it explains why they have been gone and they have an honest reason as to what happened to them without divulging the hacking ring," Jonah said.

"But why would she agree to any of this?" Drew asked.

"We might not know that answer until we can talk to Jessica. But I have a feeling our hacker has been seducing her.

I would be willing to bet that she is the only female hacker who moved on. Her mom died a few years ago. She's an only child, dad is working as a cop. He's probably working extra hours to start saving for her college tuition. She's probably not popular in school, feels like she doesn't belong anywhere, has no one to talk to. Then, this man starts paying attention to her, telling her all the things she needs to hear to feel good about herself. He has probably given her private one-on-one lessons, bought her stuff. She probably figures they are going to be together and right the wrongs of the world. She has no idea that he's just using her, that he's a predator and she's just his latest prey."

"We gotta find this hacker and shut him down before he keeps doing this," Jonah said with a great deal of determination in his voice.

"Assuming we can. I'll work with Drew today to find the other four within the group. I'll also see what I can dig up on Jessica. You gotta find Jessica. She could be the one to give us the kidnappers and the hacker."

"Do we need to warn someone about

this skeleton key?" Jonah asked.

"They don't have the algorithm. If they did, we would be reading about it. I'll inform Mason and he can run with it through the proper channels."

"Is Drew going to be in trouble for any of this?" Jonah asked, worried about how this could turn out for his son.

"No, he'll be fine. He's just a kid doing a workshop. He didn't do anything illegal and he didn't make the algorithm. He had a bad feeling and he got out. He's not going to be in trouble for it."

I would make sure that Drew was protected if anyone wanted to give him crap over his involvement. He had no idea that the hacker was running the workshop for ways to recruit new hackers for his evil plan. Most of the young hackers probably didn't even know the true reason behind this hacker's motive.

"I'm sorry about all of this, Dad," Drew said, his eyes downcast, and we both could tell he was feeling guilty, but he didn't have any reason to be. He had no idea that this would happen.

"You don't have to apologize for what is happening. You didn't know that this hacker would try something like this. And if you hadn't said *no* to your part, we might never have known about this skeleton key until it was too late. Now, we have a chance to stop him. You did the right thing and I am proud of you," Jonah said, flashing his son a warm smile.

Thankfully, Drew had walked away from the online threat from this hacker. Because if he hadn't, if he had gone along with the narrative and belief that the skeleton key was just part of a virtual simulation, things could have been really bad. There was no telling the level of damage that this hacker could have done before he was found and stopped. Now, we had to find him and Jessica, more than ever. Hopefully, Jonah could find Jessica and I would be able to find the other hackers and make sure they hadn't been grabbed either.

It looked like it was going to be another long day. Hopefully, at the end of it, though, I would get to have my reward with Jonah in my bedroom.

CHAPTER THIRTEEN

Jonah

THIS CASE WAS never going to end.

We had spent all day trying to find Jessica, but so far we hadn't been able to locate her. I knew her father was losing his mind. Everyone in the department knew that Drew had been found within hours of our search. They had all expected to find Jessica within the same amount of time.

Only, Jessica didn't want to be found.

It was not going to go over well when we did find her and I had to interrogate her. Everyone who knows her father, hell, who knows she's an officer's kid, would know that I was interrogating her. It wasn't going to be a good time and I was going to get some shit about it even after the truth came out. I was fully prepared for it, though, and it didn't matter what other cops thought. This was about keeping people safe and making sure a skeleton key that could wipe out our country was prevented.

My phone rang and I pulled it out to see that it was Sebastian calling me. "Hey, tell me you have something good," I pleaded into the phone the second I picked up.

"Two things. The first, we were able to find the crew's latest heist. It was another jewelry store that was not on our list. Turns out they are completely legit, but when you go into their basement it is filled with conflict diamonds and stolen pieces. The crew made off with ten million this time."

"Jesus fuck."

This crew's plan was working and as long as it was working, they were not going to be changing it. My gut said they would already be scooping out another kid to grab and I had no idea who it could be.

"Second, we found Jessica, or technically, she found us. She walked into a police station about an hour ago crying and putting on a huge show. Her father is with her now, and they are going to be brought into the Agency to be interviewed."

Son of a bitch.

She knew she couldn't be kidnapped the whole time. She would have to be found at some point.

Why not control when she was discovered by her showing up claiming to have escaped?

She was clearly going to keep up with her show and I was going to have to break her. I just hoped that her father would allow me to do it. I would have to interview her with him out of the room. She would feel comfortable and protected with her father there with her. I needed her to feel the pressure of the reality she was facing. Though, it would help if we had something that I could use as proof to get her to open up.

"I'm on my way," I said, before I ended the call. I then quickly dialed Cooper's number to see if he had anything.

"Hey," he said, and I could already hear the exhaustion in his voice. I might have kept him up too late last night.

Oops.

"Jessica just walked into a police station an hour ago. Apparently, she put on a big show about being kidnapped. She is being taken to the Agency with her father for an interview. I am heading there now. Tell me you have something that I can use against her."

"Okay, so I was able to get all of the other five hacker's names from Drew. I ran the names and was able to get a match on each one. The other four hackers are spread out across the country. I've sent their names off to Agents so they can be picked up and questioned. They won't be in trouble, all are minors, but they need to be made aware of the situation. Now, all of the conversations in the chat room are gone, they delete automatically after a few hours. However, with the help of Drew, I was able to narrow down each part that was assigned to each hacker for the skeleton key. Now, Jessica doesn't know that I wasn't able to open her hidden files, so you could bluff her."

"She's only fourteen, she should be easy to bluff. What was her part?"

If I could get her alone, then I would be able to bluff her. She was young, she wouldn't know how to control her emotions or be able to keep her lies straight. If I could get the truth out of her, it wouldn't matter what anyone said.

"She is an information hacker. Their specialty is to curate information."

"How is that a hacker?" I asked, confused.

"Information hackers aren't building lists of cigarette brands. They go into a company's system to generate information that could be used against them. Take a bank, for example. The hacker will get every single name of everyone who is hired by the bank, their physical characteristics, age, marital status, social security number, their parents, mother's maiden name, any pets, literally everything about their life. They will then sell that information to someone looking to do a heist, or they steal their identity and steal tens of thousands of dollars from them. Information hackers can be very dangerous. I once arrested one who stole three cents a day out of a million bank accounts. Made thirty grand a day and they did it for a year before anyone caught on."

"Wow, okay. Well, that explains why our hacker liked her so much. She could have made millions of dollars for him. What would she have been collecting for the skeleton key?"

"Like I said, most of everything is done online, but there are main hubs for power that have to be done in person. Unless you want to make a big explosion by sending in a team with guns, you would want someone to take over someone's identity. If she could gather the proper intel, they could put one of their own guys into the hub and turn the power off for a third of the country. Based on the large size of the hidden files, she was putting the intel into a video game that would then be released into the DarkNet for the hacker."

"Got it. All right, I'm going to speak with her and see if we can get the crew or the hacker from her. Keep me posted if you find something else."

"Will do."

I ended the call and started to make my way toward the Agency. I now had something that I would be able to use against Jessica and I was hoping it would work. The last thing I needed was Officer Montanna trying to shut down the interrogation or demand that she had a lawyer.

***

The second I walked into the Agency's interrogation area I could tell that Officer Montanna was annoyed. He didn't appreciate that he was down here with his daughter as opposed to in an office upstairs. I knew this wasn't going to be easy for him to hear, but there were no other options right now. We needed to get Jessica talking and, hopefully, identify this robbery crew or the hacker.

"Officer Montanna, I appreciate you coming down here with your daughter. I know it's been a trying couple of days for the both of you," I said as I held my hand out to him. I didn't need to introduce myself, he was well aware of who I was.

"Thank you Detective West. I am glad to hear that your son was okay."

"Thank you. He's doing really well. I know you want to get Jessica home, but given the targets this kidnapping and robbery crew are after, we need to catch them before another kid is grabbed. If I could just speak with Jessica for a few minutes, I would truly appreciate it."

"Of course, we're happy to help."

I guided them over to an empty interrogation room and led them both in. I didn't sit down, though, or close the door as I spoke. "This is Damien. He works with the Agency. He is going to speak with you, Officer Montanna."

He looked over my shoulder and saw Damien behind me. Instantly, I could see the objection in his body language. He was not going to go quietly on this one.

"I am staying with my daughter. He can speak with me later."

"I understand your reluctance to leave your daughter, but I'm not actually asking. It's an order," I said with complete authority to my voice.

He could take Jessica and leave, but that would not go well for him. The Agency didn't need a warrant to question or hold her. If he wanted this to go smoothly, he would have no choice but to cooperate.

"Follow me, Officer," Damien said with a deadly edge to his voice.

Officer Montanna looked at us both before he turned to look at Jessica. He then gave a nod and headed out behind Damien. I knew he wasn't going to be going far, just on the other side of the two-way mirror. I wanted to make sure he heard what was going on so if Jessica tried to stonewall me, he would be able to help me get it out of her. I just needed him to hear the evidence first, before jumping to his daughter's defense. I also needed Jessica to speak freely, something she would be more open to doing with her father out of the room.

I closed the door and just leaned against it. I was in charge, not her. She looked scared, but I couldn't tell if it was all an act or not. I suspected a bit of both.

"Why don't you drop the act. We both know you weren't kidnapped," I started, and instantly she was upset and putting on another show.

"What are you talking about? I was kidnapped. I got grabbed by these men right out of my bed and then tied to a chair. I was there for over a day. I was screaming for help, but no one could hear me."

"You were screaming? How did you get

the duct tape off of your mouth?"

"They didn't put any on me. They tied my wrists and ankles down to the chair with rope and then they put a gag around my mouth. I was able to spit it out and scream for help. But no one came."

"How did you get out of the chair if you were tied down?" I countered.

"I fought against the ropes and was able to finally get it loose enough on my wrists. It took forever."

"You're lying," I said as I started to move around the room.

"No, I'm not. Why do you keep saying that?" she asked, with tears rolling down her cheeks. No doubt she suspected that she was being watched and wanted to put on a good show for the camera.

"Because I was there when Drew was found. I was the one who cut the ropes off of his wrists. I know how tight they were. And even though he didn't fight against them, his wrists and ankles were red and burned from the rope. If you did, in fact, fight free of the rope, your wrists would not only be red, but also bloody from cutting into your skin. You have no marks on them. You were never gagged and you were never tied up. You were never kidnapped. You faked the whole thing."

"No I didn't. What is wrong with you? I am a victim. I was kidnapped, I could have been killed. Why are you doing this to me?"

"You are putting on a good show, but that's all that it is. Do you really think I would bring you down here without any proof? You're done, Jessica."

"I don't know what you are talking about. I'm a victim and you can't keep me here. I know my rights."

"Your rights went out the door the second your father brought you in here. This Agency has full immunity from the Governor. I can throw you in jail right now, if I want to. I don't need a warrant or probable cause to arrest you and charge you. And I know you were the one who destroyed your home. That you were the one who destroyed your laptop, or I should say *tried* to destroy it. But you see, the thing with laptops, unless you have obliterated it, someone smart can always rebuild it and recover the data. You might think you're good at hacking, but you are nothing compared to the hacker who works here. He rebuilt your laptop. He found your browser history. He found you playing on the DarkNet. He found your chat room for that hacking workshop you signed up for. He found your hidden files with the video game that you designed to upload onto the DarkNet filled with information that will help to build a skeleton key and start Armageddon. We have it all. You're done. So, drop the helpless victim act, you're not fooling anyone, and Daddy isn't here to save you."

I could see her processing the words and it didn't take long before the tears dried up and she was no longer a scared little teenage girl there in front of me, but rather someone with cold eyes. She was still thinking because she was a teenager that she would be able to get away with it all. That no one would charge her with anything. Unfortunately for her, that would only be true if she cooperated.

"My father wouldn't save me no matter what. He stopped caring about me a long time ago. When Mom was alive, he was working day shifts so he could be home with us at night. He would leave for work after breakfast and be there just after I got home from school. We got to have two meals every day together. I actually got to see him. But two days after Mom dies, he goes back to work and starts working night shifts. I almost never saw him. I was left with a babysitter all night and now that I'm old enough, I don't see anyone at home. Even on his days off he's working. He's doing everything he can to not be around me. He doesn't love me. If he did, he would be there."

"I saw your Dad's timesheets. He's working a lot of overtime, close to sixty hour weeks. But he's not doing it because he doesn't love you. He's doing it because when you work the night shift you get a two dollar premium an hour for working at night because it's more dangerous and the hours suck. That two bucks might not seem like a lot, but that's an extra eighty a week, before the overtime kicks in. Eighty a week might not seem like much to you, but it's three hundred and twenty dollars a month, just shy of four grand a year, and in four years it'll be over fifteen grand that he would have saved up. That's almost a full year of College tuition. *Your* College tuition. Your father loves you. He's working himself to the bone to be able to give you a future."

If she cared about the new

information, she didn't show it. I doubted that she cared about the reasoning behind her father's working hours. To her, it wouldn't be a good enough excuse. She would turn it around to make it seem like her father didn't love her. That she was a poor little girl being abandoned by her own father. She was going to work it in her favor. She was going to twist everything that her father did to make it seem like she was neglected.

"I don't need him to pay for my College. I could get student loans, not that I actually want to go. I have a real skill that is very valuable. Companies all over the world are going to want me to work for them. I'll be making millions of dollars a year. I don't need College," she said, a cocky smirk plastered on her lips.

"You are aware that hacking is illegal. Unless you are a Government Agent or work in the military, you are committing a crime. And that's not even including you working with four other hackers to create a skeleton key. Something that can be considered an act of terrorism and have you placed in a maximum federal prison for the rest of your life. The only way to avoid that, is by telling me everything you know about the kidnapping crew and the hacker behind it all.”

“But, Detective, I’m just a little girl,” she said, flashing me that cocky smile again.

Before I could even respond to her, the door to the room was opening and Officer Montanna was walking in. I could see the hurt and shock in his eyes. This was why I wanted him to hear what she had to say when she thought he wasn’t around. I needed him to hear the truth right out of her mouth. For him to see that she was behind her own kidnapping and that there were serious charges laid in front of her.

“Dad?”

“Jessica, what have you done? I just heard everything. You faked your own kidnapping. You have been hacking and exploring the DarkNet. Did you really help make this skeleton key thing?”

“I haven’t done anything wrong. I was doing an online workshop to learn how to hack. I didn’t do anything wrong.”

“Except you knew that the skeleton key wasn’t actually going to be used in a virtual simulation. You knew the mastermind behind all of this was going to use it in real practice," I argued.

"What— what is it?" Officer Montanna asked.

"It's a complex code that requires multiple parts to be put together in order for it to be created. However, once you have it created, you can hack into anything that is connected to the Internet. You can also copy it onto a USB drive to plug it into any hub and hack into it. It can be used for the Stock Market, all the way to the Nuclear Launch Codes. The person could use the skeleton key to send us all back into the Dark Ages, or use it to drop nukes on any country in the world and start World War Three," I explained.

"Oh my god," Officer Montanna said as he started to pace around the small room.

"Your daughter is the one who provided our mastermind with the intel he needed to ensure he would be able to have access to any location that was not connected to the Internet. She was an active member of the group and has helped to create it. Her part was already handed over. The only reason it was not finished, is because Drew's part wasn't finished. He didn't do it. He felt like something was wrong and he wasn't about to do something that created a world danger," I started as I went and turned the chair around and sat down in it. "But see, that's where it gets interesting. Because Drew is one of a few in a small circle of hackers who can create, from scratch, an algorithm that can adapt and change depending on the system the skeleton key is being used for. It's very mathematical and complicated and the mastermind can't do it. That's why he was kidnapped and left alone. He was going to be moved and then convinced to do his part. As for you, you played kidnapped so the crew could steal ten million in illegal diamonds."

"Drew betrayed our hive. He knew that going into the final project that his part was vital to completion. He betrayed us. He betrayed our family that Danthor has created for us," Jessica said.

Bingo.

We now had a name for our hacker and I knew that Cooper would be able to track him with it now.

"What are you doing? Jessica, that crew kidnapped someone, they have stolen twelve million dollars worth of diamonds. They are facing multiple felony charges that could get them twenty-five plus years in prison. You can be charged as an accomplice to it all. In addition to being an accomplice for helping to create a skeleton key. Detective West is right, you could be charged with crimes against the country. It doesn't matter that you're fourteen, you can be charged as an adult at your age. You wouldn't be the first fourteen year old to be charged as an adult."

Officer Montanna was beyond pissed, not that I could blame him. However, I could also hear the fear and worry in his voice and concern over what future was laid out in front of his daughter. He understood how serious the situation was. How dangerous the situation was for his daughter. He let out a sigh, then he went and sat in the other chair right next to his daughter, before he continued.

"The robbery crew and the mastermind have not been arrested. That means that you can tell Detective West everything you know and you can get a deal. You can avoid going to jail or juvie. We could make a deal for probation and we can put all of this behind us. We can fix this together. You just have to tell us what you know."

"What I know is that Danthor loves me. I'm not going to turn on him. He hasn't done anything wrong. He would never use the skeleton key to hurt anybody. We're going to use it to catch criminals that the justice system has failed to put away. He's not a bad guy," Jessica said, still not willing to give any of them up.

"Jessica, he doesn't love you. He's just a predator using you. It's not a coincidence that you were the only female who got to move on. He is a predator and he is using you for your skills. Everything he told you was a lie, even down to whatever age he said he was. He doesn't love you. You're just someone he can manipulate and leave to take the fall for this whole mess," I said.

I had a feeling, though, that no matter what either of us said, Jessica wasn't going to give them up. She was completely at Danthor's mercy. He had her wrapped around his finger and she was going to keep believing in his cause. She was going to keep believing that the court wouldn't put her in prison for any of these crimes. The thing was, though, they would. This wasn't what I wanted, but this was the path she wanted to walk. Hopefully, she would change her mind soon. Maybe after she spent the night in jail, she would think twice about her decision to stay quiet.

"I'm sorry," I said to Officer Montanna and I could see he understood what would happen. "Jessica Montanna, you are under arrest for two counts of grand larceny, one count of kidnapping, and an accessory to crimes against the country. You have the right to remain silent. You have the right to an attorney. If you cannot afford one, one will be provided to you. Do you understand your rights?"

"Sure," she said as she rolled her eyes.

"Where... where will she go?" Officer Montanna asked with a shaky voice as I went and put the cuffs on Jessica.

"She will be taken to the county juvenile hall, where she will be held until her court date. Due to the charges, though, she won't be eligible for bail. Unless she decides to plead out, it could take a year before her trial date."

"Chill out, Dad, I won't be there for a year. Danthor won't let me be in jail for more than a day or two. He'll hack the system and make sure someone comes to get me," Jessica said with that snarky attitude still dripping from her voice.

"No, he won't. But maybe a couple of days rooming with criminals will teach you that," I said as I started to walk her to the door. It opened and I passed her off to Damien who would take her the rest of the way.

"I'm so sorry," Officer Montanna instantly said when we were alone.

"You have nothing to apologize for. Her actions are not your responsibility. I'm sorry that things turned out this way. Hopefully, the night in jail will make her realize the seriousness of her situation and she will sing."

"I should have seen this coming. I shouldn't have changed my shift. I would have been there more."

"Don't do that. You can't second-guess yourself. This isn't your fault. She was manipulated by a predator who has done this before. We will find him and make sure he pays for all of this. Get her a good lawyer and maybe a therapist in the jail. Maybe, they will be able to get her to see what is really going on."

Whether I liked what Jessica had done didn't matter. She was still a fourteen year old girl who had been taken advantage of by an adult male. She had no idea just how serious this situation was because she wasn't old enough to understand the true implications of it. Hopefully, with time and some professional help, she would, and then she would be more open to talking. For now, we had to focus all of our efforts on finding the kidnapping crew and Danthor before they all disappeared.

CHAPTER FOURTEEN

Cooper

IT WAS NEARING eight o'clock when Jonah walked through the door. He looked exhausted and I had a feeling that meant his interrogation with Jessica had not been an easy one.

He had texted me Danthor's name, but that was all he had said. He told me he would tell me once he got back. I had been spending the day with Drew, trying to find the other hackers from the workshop, and trying to find the mastermind based off of the YouTube video.

What concerned me, was the number of views the video had. It had over two million views, and even if people didn't watch it all the way through, it was still a huge pool of potential hackers that this man had been cultivating from his workshop. Even if only twenty percent of the people who viewed the video took the workshop, it was a large number of hackers that he could have at his beck and call.

Thankfully, what was needed to finish the skeleton key was not something your garden variety hacker could pull off. We were most likely still in the clear with him not having it completed.

"You okay, Dad?" Drew asked, with a great deal of concern lacing his voice.

"Yeah, I'm okay. It was just a long conversation and it didn't go the way I was expecting or hoped it would."

"She didn't know anything?" I asked.

"Oh, she knows something, but she's not talking. She believes that Danthor loves her and that they were going to use the skeleton key to get justice for those that the justice system has failed. He has her completely snowed. Even after Officer Montanna came into the room, she wouldn't give anything up. She is on her way to juvie and hopefully, after spending the night there, she will realize that Danthor isn't coming for her."

"She really won't give anything up?" Drew asked, surprised.

"Not even after we told her the charges. Because of what the skeleton key can do, she could be charged for acts of terrorism. She's facing life, but she believes she will be saved by the love of her life. She's a young and dumb fourteen year old girl who got played by a predator. It happens, unfortunately, and by the time she realizes what happened to her, it most likely will be too late for her to make a deal. I just feel bad for Officer Montanna. He went through the trauma and horror of having his only child kidnapped, only to discover it was all fake and now, she will be spending her life in prison."

"It's not something any parent should have to go through. Maybe her lawyer will be able to talk some sense into her," I said.

It wasn't that surprising, though, that she didn't give anyone up. Like Jonah said, she was young and dumb, and had been manipulated by an older man.

Danthor knew exactly what he was doing when he recruited her. It was going to take a long time before she would finally give it up, and I had no idea if it was ever going to happen in time for her to save herself.

"Hopefully. What do you got?"

"We found the other four hackers and they were all picked up by Homeland Security Agents and brought back to the field offices for questioning. I heard back from all four agents, all four hackers did their part of the skeleton key and submitted it onto the DarkNet in a video game format already. Now, all four said they had no idea it was going to be turned into a real functioning key. They all believed that a security company or a recruitment office for Government Agencies was running the workshop. The Agents weren't sure if they believed them, so they were all hooked up to a polygraph test and they all passed. They were all under eighteen, most were fifteen or sixteen, and they will be placed on a watch list. They were all offered the opportunity to use their skills for good when they turn eighteen, should they be interested. Who knows if they will be, though," I stated.

It was good that Homeland was offering them a position in their academy, but I also knew that not every hacker wanted to be buff and attend boot camp to get a job as a hacker. It would depend on their personality and if they truly wanted to do some good in the world. If not, they could keep being a hacker for a company, a black hat hacker, or they could stop all together and go work for a tech firm. Really, their futures were completely up in the air, but we might have saved four young hackers from going down a bad path.

"At least that's something. Did they know anything we could use?"

"No, they just knew the name Danthor. They had no idea that there was a kidnapping/robbery crew out there. They did say that Danthor paid more attention to Jessica in the chat room. He was always praising her and sending her bitcoins as a reward for her learning efforts."

"Which supports our theory that he had been courting her to manipulate her into being his puppet. Where are we on finding him?"

"*Nowhere.* We are nowhere. It's great that we have his hacker name, but just like in real life, having just a name and no photo to put it with makes it very difficult to track the guy down. He could be anywhere, and with just a hacker name, I can't even run it in a system to see what pops. I have to work the DarkNet to try and track down his movements and see if anyone has been able to see him, and try to get his real name to then use to track down in the real world. It's not something that is going to be a quick resolution. It could take years to find him."

That was the issue. When we had a suspect, we had their name that we could then run. Then, we find their photo online, either from social media or a driver's license. With just a hacker name, I couldn't run it through our databases. It was going to take a long time and a lot of work to track down someone who could give me his real name and then, I could try and get a photo of him to run in the system. It wasn't something that was magically going to get done within hours or even weeks.

"That's not good. He could have a skeleton key finished by then," Jonah said, clearly worried.

"I informed Mason about all of this and he told Ryzen. Ryzen used to work for the CIA and he got into contact with some of his connections there. They then reached out to me. The other Agents sent in the video games that were uploaded from the four other hackers, plus one of the hackers knew what video game Jessica had uploaded to the DarkNet. I created an algorithm-coded virus that would completely destroy the video games and any information within. The CIA hacker was able to adapt their own code to my virus so it would destroy any information gathered from the video games that was uploaded onto any computer. So even though we don't know who Danthor is, all of his work for the skeleton key is completely destroyed."

It was very complex and I could tell that Jonah had no idea what I was talking about, but all that mattered was that the skeleton key was destroyed and if Danthor wanted to create one, he would have to start all over again and with new hackers. At least it was buying us time.

We would also, hopefully, be able to get into the chat room for the last workshop and shut it down with the help of the other four hackers. Drew no longer had access to it because he left, but the other four hadn't left yet. From what I had been told, they were all willing to cooperate with Homeland to get it all shut down.

"I understood that last part of that. That's good, though. That means he will have to start from square one and that buys us the time we need to, hopefully, track him down. He's not going to give up, not when he was so close to having it made."

A loud beeping interrupted our conversation and I instantly knew what it was. My fingers flew over my keyboard as Drew spoke.

"What is that?"

"I'm being hacked," I answered.

I knew it had to be Danthor trying to get into my system. Only, my system wasn't like the ones that he was used to. Mine was far more complex and sophisticated than a typical security system. He wasn't going to be able to hack in, but I might be able to pinpoint his location while he was busy trying to get into my system.

"If he's trying to hack in, that means the kidnappers are coming here. They might be trying to get Drew to make the skeleton key," Jonah said. He was up and already looking out my front window.

"They won't be able to get in if they are. The doors can't be hacked and there's no lock to pick. Even if they tried to shoot their way in, the windows are all bulletproof," I said.

"Why do you have bulletproof windows?" Drew asked, completely confused and scared.

"Because I've put a lot of dangerous criminals away and they would love to have me killed."

"We got company. There's four masked guys right outside and they have automatic weapons. It seems like Danthor told them we were on to them and now they want us dead," Jonah said as he pulled out his phone.

"Okay, but if they can't get in, then don't we just wait for the cops to show up?" Drew said.

"That's what we're doing," Jonah said as he moved back before speaking into the phone. "This is Detective West, I'm at 1223 Southshore Lane, the kidnapping crew is at my location. I'm secured in the house with my son. Four men are armed with automatic weapons. Have everyone available to roll out to my location."

"Dammit," I said.

"What?" Jonah asked as he put his phone away.

"He disappeared. He must have figured out that he couldn't hack in and he left before I could trace him."

I wasn't expecting for him to give up that easily. Once he saw my system, he had to know that they wouldn't be able to just waltz right in. I would have figured he would have tried harder, but he just gave up.

"Um, what is that?" Drew asked and we both looked to see what he was looking at out the window.

The one man had opened the trunk and pulled out an RPG. "Shit, yup that's a flaw," I said with urgency.

We both jumped into action and started to move away from the window. We were only going to have a few seconds before that thing was flying into my house. We both pulled out guns and flipped the dining room table over before the three of us got behind it. Then, there was an explosion and the sound of glass shattering throughout the front of my house. My ears were instantly ringing and I knew it wouldn't be long before the bullets would be flying. Thankfully, there were only four of them, but they had automatic weapons, making it feel more like twenty guys. I could hear the dull sound of the bullets flying toward us and Jonah covered Drew's body with his own. The wooden table was not going to do anything to protect us. We had to move.

"Get behind the island," I yelled at them.

Jonah was instantly pushing Drew to move and I poked my head up enough to be able to provide cover fire. We also only had one clip each, so we had to make each shot count. The second they were behind the island, I was moving. I managed to take out one of the kidnappers in the process and I was relieved that we were down to three. All we had to do was hold them off long enough for backup to arrive.

"Dad!" Drew cried, and I turned my head to see a large blood pool forming underneath Jonah.

He had been hit.

Most likely when he was protecting Drew behind the table.

Shit.

I moved my hand over and checked for a pulse. It was there, but it was weak. I grabbed one of the towels that were hanging on the bottom cupboards as I spoke. "Drew, listen to me. I need you to push this against the bullet wound. Push as hard as you can to try and slow the bleeding down. Backup will be here soon."

Drew took the towel with trembling hands and pushed it against the lower part of Jonah's back. I was worried that the bullet could have hit his spine. I knew he had moved over to behind the island, but that could have pushed the bullet around more into his spine. There was no telling what damage could be done and we wouldn't know until a doctor was able to run scans.

None of that could happen while we were trapped here.

I didn't have my phone, but Jonah had placed his in his pocket. I quickly pulled it out and keyed the radio option for his phone.

"This is Agent Jones, I need immediate assistance 1223 Southshore Lane. I have an officer down. I repeat, an officer has been shot. We are taking on heavy fire. I need a bus on a rush to my location and every available unit in the area. Start an officer down protocol, and notify Med."

I dropped the phone and started to fire back as the calls came in. Every available unit was responding that they were on their way. I knew within moments the street was going to be flooded with cops, whether they were needed or not. Every cop within a decent distance of our location would be coming here to see if there was anything they could do to help. When it was one of their own down and needing help, they all came.

I could already hear the sirens and I knew we would be getting out of here. I just had to hold them off a bit longer.

"Talk to me, Drew, how is he?" I said as I returned fire again. I needed to keep them back so they wouldn't be able to approach. If they got too close, they could easily kill me and take Drew.

"I don't know," Drew said, his voice warbly and panicked, and I didn't need to look at him to know that he was crying.

This was not what I wanted him to see or go through, but there was nothing I could do about it right now. Right now, we just had to get through this, and then, Jonah would be able to be in the hospital where the doctors could, hopefully, save his life.

"I know this is hard, but help is coming. I can hear the sirens, can you?"

"Yeah," he said with a shaky voice and a sniffle.

I could hear more gunshots, but this time they weren't from an automatic weapon. Help had arrived and I knew it wouldn't take anytime at all before the last few guys were down.

A long series of single gunshots echoed all throughout my house and I knew there were at least ten cops all firing at once. With the last gunshot, the whole house went quiet and I knew we were safe.

"Back here!" I called out as I turned my attention to Jonah.

I took over for Drew as the officers made their way around to my island. I could tell they were shocked by the sight in front of them, but they snapped out of it quickly. The one officer went over to Drew and moved him away, getting him out of the house where he wouldn't have to see the carnage. Another two officers joined me in keeping Jonah stabilized as we waited for the ambulance to arrive.

I could feel my own body shaking. I couldn't believe this had happened. I never thought I would have to go through something like this. It had been a long time since I had been involved in a shootout and never one quite like this. I was terrified about what would happen with Jonah. I knew the gunshot wound was bad and I was very afraid that he wouldn't be able to pull through on this one.

He had just come into my life.

I couldn't lose him.

Not now.

Once the paramedics arrived, I was pushed out of the way and I had no choice but to watch as they fought to save Jonah's life.

***

My back was killing me, the same as my ass. I had been sitting in an uncomfortable plastic hospital chair for twelve hours now. The whole waiting room was filled with cops and the guys from the Agency. We were all waiting on news about Jonah.

He had been rushed into surgery the second the paramedics got him off of the ambulance and so far, we hadn't heard anything yet. I knew no news was good news, but at this point I would have really appreciated something. Even if that was just a nurse coming out to say he was still alive and they were still working on him. At least that would have been something.

As for the case, all four kidnappers were dead. All dead at my house that was now not only a crime scene, but looked like it had been in a war zone. I was going to be moving. There was no way I was going to ever be able to live in that house again. Even if I repaired it, I would always be able to see Jonah's blood all over my kitchen floor. It was better to sell it and let someone else deal with it all. I would make sure it was professionally cleaned and I would have a new wall put up, but I wouldn't be living in it.

Damien, Sebastian, and Max were able to identify the kidnappers and found the stolen diamonds at the stash house they had all been staying in. We had been hoping to get something out of the kidnappers that would lead us to Danthor, but that intel died with them. I suspected Danthor knew that would be the case. And even if they were able to succeed in killing Jonah and I to get to Drew, he would have still won.

As for Drew, he was a mess, but I couldn't blame the kid. He was only twelve and he just went through a shootout that resulted in his father being seriously shot. He would be thinking worst case scenario and terrified for what the future could hold. I hadn't told him it would be okay, because I didn't know and I didn't want to lie to him. I needed to know what Jonah's situation was first before I tried to comfort the poor boy.

The second a doctor walked out to us, we were all on our feet. He came over to me as Drew was standing next to us and without a next of kin, he would have to tell Drew.

"I am Dr. Charles. I was the surgeon for your father. I want to let you know that he is alive and I do expect for him to make a full recovery."

The second the words were out of his mouth there was a palpable great relief that flooded through the entire room. Officers started to hug each other and clap at the good news. I was beyond relieved, but I also knew that depending on where the bullet hit, that recovery could be a very long and painful one.

"Where did the bullet hit?" I asked.

"It hit the bottom of his spine and ended up moving just slightly. From what I was told, he moved for better cover and that is probably when the extra damage was done. I was able to remove the bullet and repair the damage to his spine and the nerves. He will be able to return to active duty in time. However, it's going to be closer to six months before that happens. Due to the damage and the repair, he will need extensive physical therapy to relearn how to walk again."

"He's paralyzed?" Drew asked, horrified.

"He's not paralyzed. He can feel his legs and he can move them. However, his nerves and muscles need to relearn the movement of walking. He's going to be in the hospital for six weeks before he will be able to be released. He will be in a wheelchair until he progresses in his physical therapy and relearns how to walk. I know it sounds scary, but your father is otherwise healthy and he is still young. He will blow through the physical therapy faster than you think. Within six months, he'll be back to running and be active," Dr. Charles said, flashing us all a warm, comforting smile.

I wrapped my arm around Drew's shoulders as I spoke. "All that matters is that he is alive and will make a full recovery. We'll get him through the rest."

"Can I see him?" Drew asked Dr. Charles.

"Of course. I'll take you to him. He's not awake yet, but he will be within a few hours."

We followed the Doctor down the hallways until we reached the recovery room for Jonah.

He looked pale as a ghost, but I knew that was from the blood loss. He had a blood bag as well as an IV to help get some blood back into him. It was going to be a long road ahead of him, but I was determined to make sure he got there.

"What's gonna happen to me?" Drew asked as we went and plopped down into a chair at his father's bedside.

"You're gonna be okay. While your dad is healing, you are gonna be living with me. For now, we'll be in a hotel until I find a new house. Then, when your dad can leave, he'll live with us and we can get him through this. In a few days, when you feel ready, you can go back to school and start getting back to a normal life."

I knew it wasn't going to be easy for him to do that. He had been through a lot in the past couple of days, but eventually, he would get there. We all would get there. I was not about to let either of the West men go through this alone. We were family now and we would get through this as a family.

EPILOGUE

Six Months Later...

Jonah

THE HOUSE WAS filled with people from the Agency.

Today, we were celebrating my return to active duty. The past six months had been life changing, to say the least. Waking up in the hospital to discover that I had not only been shot, *again*, but had to relearn how to walk, well, it was a lot.

I'd had a great deal of some not so proud moments when I snapped at Coop or one of the nurses during my stay at the hospital and even afterward. I wasn't used to not being able to do things on my own. I wasn't used to not being able to move around how I wanted, having to use a wheelchair and then a walker.

Fuck yeah, it was hard.

It was the hardest thing I had ever had to do and it was not something I wanted to ever have to do again.

Over the past six months, though, I had discovered just how much I had fallen in love with Cooper. I didn't even know it, but I was. Seeing him every day at the hospital, seeing him interacting with Drew, it only warmed my heart.

Knowing that Drew was living with Cooper and going back to school, that he was starting to heal from it all, it only confirmed that Cooper was the perfect man. He loved my son, he cared for him, and he would be an amazing dad to him.

I didn't want to die, I didn't want to leave Drew, but if it did happen, then I could do so knowing he would be loved and well cared for. That Cooper would make sure he had a bright future and would recover from the loss one day. And that was all I wanted for him.

Cooper and I had decided to try our

hand at dating after I got out of the hospital. I wasn't sure if it would be a good idea. I mean, I wasn't exactly a catch with being stuck in a wheelchair, but he wouldn't hear any of it.

We had taken things slow. With me not being able to have sex, we were able to learn a great deal about each other. We grew something real that would only make the sex better. And when we finally could have sex last month, it was earth shattering. I thought the previous times were good, but they were nothing compared to the build up and wait over the past five months.

The man was perfect.

Absolutely perfect.

Even when I was able to be living on my own again, neither I nor Drew wanted to leave. This had become our home, a home for all three of us. Thankfully, Cooper was in agreement with us. Drew had even decided to change schools to one within the area. He was ready for a change and he didn't want to be the kid who got kidnapped at his old school. I could understand that. He wanted a fresh start and I was more than happy to give it to him.

Drew was set to attend hackers camp in a couple of weeks for the summer. He was already packed and excited for it. He was like a little kid on Christmas Eve all over again and it was such a relief to see. He had found something that he was not only good at, but passionate about.

There had been many nights that Drew and Cooper would practice hacking into things and Cooper would let him help on the cases he was working on. I had discovered that Cooper would actually pose as an underage kid in different chat rooms to help catch predators. He would then pass off the information to the local police for them to catch the guy when he went to meet up with who he thought was an underage minor. It was just further proof of what a good man he was.

He was a tremendous role model for Drew and I was so happy that he could have Cooper in his life. That he could have an adult in his life who understood what he was talking about and could show him different tricks and skills with a computer. Drew was learning a lot and his attitude was so different. He was back to being a happy and fun kid, and it was all thanks to Cooper.

"Have you thought more about my offer?" Mason asked as he strolled over to me.

Mason had offered me a position within the Agency a couple of months ago. I hadn't given him an answer yet, because I wasn't sure how I felt about it. I still needed time to get my head wrapped around everything that had happened and what I was feeling. Now, though, I did have an answer for him.

"I have and I am going to accept it," I said, flashing him a warm smile.

I would miss being a detective, but I would still be doing what I loved for the Agency. The only difference was, I would have more freedom to do it. I would also be going after criminals who were out to hurt children and that was something I was passionate about. It was time for a change and I liked knowing I would be getting to spend more time with Cooper. We made a good team and I was looking forward to my future within the Agency.

"Perfect. You start tomorrow. Be prepared to be busy. We have cases coming at us from all directions," Mason warned before he headed off.

I knew they were getting busy. Mason

had been trying to find more people to work for him. From what I had heard, Sebastian, Damien, and Max were looking to move down here to help out as well. It should be interesting and I did like working with the guys. I was looking forward to seeing what life had in store for me.

There was one thing that I needed to do today, though, and with some luck it would be another reason to celebrate. I had already spoken to Drew about it and he was over the moon excited. We were both hoping this would turn out well and go the way we wanted it to.

"Excuse me, can I have everyone's attention, please?" I called out into the backyard.

Everyone with the Agency was here and they all turned to look my way. I let out a small sigh, trying to get my nerves to calm down. I had only ever done this once, but I didn't mean it that time. This time, I was going to mean it and I had no idea what I would do if he said no.

"Thank you so much for coming out today and celebrating my return to work. And it looks like I am going to be seeing a lot of you, because I have accepted

Mason's offer to work for the Agency." I paused as everyone clapped or cheered. Once they quieted down I spoke again.

"There are a lot of reasons to celebrate today, but I am hoping to add one more." I turned to Cooper and took his hand in mine, my eyes finding his.

"Cooper Jones, I was not expecting you. After my last failed marriage, I never thought I would want to date someone ever again. But then you came into my life when I least expected it. You came into my son's life when he needed you the most. You saved him and you saved me in ways I cannot begin to explain. I can't imagine my life without you being in it. I want to wake up every morning with you in my arms. I want to fall asleep every night holding you against me. I want you to be my last kiss, my last love." I got down onto my knee and pulled out a ring box, opening it as I continued.

"Cooper Jones, will you do me the honor of being my husband?"

I could see the tears building in his eyes. He wasn't expecting this. I couldn't blame him, I never thought I would get married again, either, but I couldn't imagine not having him in my life. I wanted to call him my husband. I wanted everyone to know that he was mine and I was his. I wanted to get married for love this time. I wanted it to last and there was no one I wanted to do that with more than him.

"Yes," he said with a huge smile, happy tears slipping down his cheeks.

Everyone started to clap and cheer as I slipped the ring onto his finger.

I stood and pulled him in for a heated kiss. I didn't care who was watching, he had said *yes* and I was too damn excited to keep it as a simple kiss.

Tonight, though, we would be celebrating this alone and we would be putting our soundproof bedroom to great use. For now, though, we were going to celebrate our new engagement with our family. The future was ours and I couldn't wait.

Thank you for reading!

If you enjoyed Cooper, do me a solid and go leave a review?
Even a few words can make my day and give me the motivation to keep on plugging away at the stories you love.

Thank you!

Next up is Noah!

That's right, we are going to get to know Ryzen's brother a little bit more.

This story is definitely going to be the one that turns up the heat to the super steamy level, so be forewarned.

Turn the page now for Noah's story!
Can we just say YUMMY? lol

NOAH

FEDERAL PROTECTION AGENCY

BOOK FIVE

BY EVIE RILEY

NOAH

Letting go is truly the most powerful control of all.

Federal Prosecutor, Noah Riley has had enough of what he feels is a failing justice system. He's watched one too many times as young victims are let down and the men who have caused them harm go free. It's time for a change in his life, but he has no idea where to start.

Fire Captain William Clarke doesn't get close to the men who work under him at the firehouse. He keeps his distance and his personal life entirely separate to avoid his secret coming out. His men could never respect him if they knew his preferences, so it's simply better to stay in the closet. No man could ever make him come out—until he meets Noah and what he believes is all shot to hell in a single heartbeat.

Can these two men find the love that will change both their lives forever?

Dear Reader

If you read the preview for Noah, then you already know it hits the mark on delicious MM steam, and I hope I've done it justice in getting a bit more involved in the character relationships vs some of the previous books that were more about the action and adventure in the story, without losing plot and becoming straight smut, of course.

See, I do read your reviews and I have noted many readers wishing for more depth/intimacy with the MCs earlier on in the book, so hopefully this one floats that boat and then some. Please let me know!

Yours Always,

Evie Riley

CHAPTER ONE

Noah

I WALKED INTO the club tonight on a mission. Tonight, I needed sex, but not just any old vanilla sex. I needed to be dominated, manhandled. I needed to find myself a Master.

I didn't care for taking orders outside of the bedroom, but when I was in it, I did enjoy it. Working as a Federal Prosecutor, I saw some of the worst that humanity had to offer this world. I saw a lot of cases that were forever burned into my brain and I would never be able to stop the nightmares from them.

EVIE RILEY

I always had to be in charge. Always forced to make literal life or death calls. I had to make sure the person I was prosecuting was, in fact, guilty, and then, I had to get the jury to see it. It took everything out of me and left me feeling more exhausted than I could possibly put into words.

So, when it all became too much, when I felt like I couldn't breathe, I would go to a club like the one I'd just walked into and seek out sex with a Dominant. Someone who would dominate and control me. Someone who would make the decisions, so all I had to do was what I was told. There was no thinking involved. There were no lives on the line, no victims in desperate need of justice. It was just him and I and nothing but pleasure. It made my brain turn off and made me feel something other than stressed and sick. After the last few months that I'd had, I needed it now more than ever.

For the past three months, I had been working on a huge case to prosecute a brothel owner who filled his smarmy business with underage girls as prostitutes. It should have been a slam-dunk, but the defendant was claiming he was innocent. That he had no idea those girls weren't eighteen, even though they were clearly fourteen to fifteen. He refused a plea deal, and wanted to take it to trial. And I knew why, too, because at trial the only way we could prove that he had knowledge of their ages would be to have each girl testify.

Out of the dozen girls that he had working for him, young teens that he had raped, abused, and trafficked out to the highest paying customer, only five agreed to testify.

I had to listen to them talk about how he had raped and abused them. How the customers had forced and used them in all sorts of disgusting, sexually deviant ways.

I had them on the stand and testifying, telling their stories, only for his defense attorney to try and make it seem like they were using him. That the girls had lied. The defense kept trying to make it seem like the defendant was the victim in all of this.

He brought up all of their past history, how they ran away, how they were addicted to drugs. The only reason they were addicted in the first place was because he had forced the heroin into them. He was a monster who had done this before. He had done this in different cities with different girls. He had never been caught. He always shut his brothels down when the heat was starting to get too hot.

We had finally caught him in New York.

We were finally going to be able to put his ass in jail.

We were finally going to be able to stop him.

The jury deliberated for three hours before they came back with a not guilty verdict. They actually believed that he was a victim in this and not the girls.

Not guilty.

After three months of having to listen to their stories, their horrors, only for them to be treated like lying drug addicts who tried to take advantage of a businessman.

Unfuckingbelieveable.

He had a legal license for a brothel, so we couldn't even get him for that. He was off to another State for a whole new set of victims and there was nothing I could do about it.

I was done.

I had put in time for three weeks off, packed a bag, and I was out of there. I didn't even wait for a plane. I just got into my car and drove. It took two days for me to get to Baton Rouge and I was planning on staying at a hotel. I knew I could stay with my brother, Ryzen, but he was busy living with his new boyfriend, Knox. I did not want to hear them having sex.

Plus, this was going to be my vacation. My time to unwind and have as much sex as I wanted. I wanted to be able to do whatever I wanted; if that meant drinking at nine in the morning, if that was what I chose to do, then that's what I was going to do.

I made my way over to the bar and ordered a whiskey from a cute bartender who eyed me up and down with a nod. This was a gay club, but it was one that catered to those that were into the kink lifestyle, doms and subs, mostly. It was a place where you could go and meet a new partner for a single night or even for a new relationship.

I wasn't looking for a relationship, because I would only be here for three weeks. I just wanted some fun. I wanted to feel good and I wanted to not have to think and plan and strategize. I just wanted to escape feeling all of this pain.

I grabbed my drink and turned around to look at the club patrons. I needed to find someone who was clearly a Dom, but was also attractive. I didn't just sleep with anyone. I had a standard and I liked what I liked. I never settled for anything less. If I was going to trust my body with someone, then they were going to have to meet my standards. With that said, I was really hoping someone here tonight would match my standards.

A lot of people were already paired off, so I ignored them and kept scanning the crowd. My gaze landed on a man roughly my age. He was muscular and rugged looking. I liked my Doms to be rough around the edges. I didn't need them pretty, I was man pretty enough for the both of us.

I knew I wasn't a typical submissive. I was a bit bigger than most and I had muscles. I didn't spend all day at the gym, but I did enjoy working out. I kept my gaze on him and his eyes locked onto mine, one brow arching above a chocolate brown eye. He appeared to be interested in me, so I decided to make the first move.

I finished my drink before I strolled out onto the dance floor. I kept my gaze on him as I started to sway my hips, making it clear I was up for some fun. He didn't look away. He kept his eyes on me and I could tell he was enjoying what he saw.

I slowly turned around and started to move more to the music. As I danced, I could already feel my stress starting to melt away. I relaxed more when I was able to be around people who understood me. Men who didn't care what I liked in the bedroom because they enjoyed it as well. It was a few minutes later when I felt strong hands being placed on my hips and his hardness pressed against my ass. I didn't even have to turn around to know it was the man I had been watching. The man I wanted.

I pressed my ass back against him, reveling in the feeling of his already hard dick against my ass. It was big, very big, and that made me extremely excited. He ran his hand down my chest, over stomach, and he didn't stop until his hand skimmed my dick. I couldn't help but moan at the simple touch. It had been close to six months since I'd had sex and I was in desperate need.

"You're already hard, my sweet boy. Tell Daddy what you want," his husky voice growled into my ear.

Daddy, huh?

Hmmm.

That was a new one for me, but it wasn't a turn off. I was used to the typical Master or Sir, I had never had a Daddy. I knew that it was one of the names some Doms liked to be called, though. It wasn't a fetish that involved treating your partner as a child, despite what many people thought. It was more about taking care of their partner, making sure the submissive knew they were safe with the Dominant and felt good. I didn't care what he liked to be called just as long as he made the noise in my head quiet down.

"You feel so big, Daddy. I'd love to feel your dick against my tongue, deep in my ass," I answered as I ground back against him some more, his body heat surrounding me.

"Follow," he ordered, and the command sent shivers up my spine.

"Yes, Daddy."

He took my hand and guided me through the crowd toward the backrooms.

This club had ten backrooms that could be used for hookups. It was why I chose this club over the other ones. I was not about to bring anyone back to my hotel room.

The second we walked into the room, Daddy slammed me against the door. He wrapped his hand around my neck and captured my mouth with his own.

I moaned at the roughness and easily kissed him back. I allowed him to have all of the control. I loved it when the man I was with took complete control in the bedroom and Daddy didn't seem to have a single issue with taking what he wanted.

His tongue slipped into my mouth as he deepened the kiss. I couldn't believe how amazing it felt to be kissed after the past six months. He knew exactly how to take control of it and make me feel weak in my knees.

After a moment, when we both needed air, he pulled back, but kept his hand on my neck, his hips pressed to mine as he panted.

"Tell me what you want me to do, Daddy," I said, flashing him a playful smile.

"I want you on your knees with my

dick in your mouth, my sweet boy," he ordered.

"Yes, Daddy," I whimpered, before I got down onto my knees. I was all too happy to take this man in my mouth. I could feel how hard he was against his jeans and I couldn't wait to see his dick uncovered. I knew he was going to be big and I was really hoping he knew how to use it.

I made quick work of popping the button and unzipping his jeans. The second I pulled his hard dick out, I was moaning, my mouth watering at the sight. He was as big as I thought he'd be. He certainly didn't disappoint. Now, I was just hoping that he would be talented with it.

"I love a huge dick, Daddy," I moaned. I ran my tongue along his shaft from his base up to his tip, getting my first taste of him. I took his tip in my mouth and sucked, humming my appreciation as the taste of his precum hit my tongue.

I needed more. I needed to know what Daddy's cum tasted like, what it felt like as it pumped down my throat. I started to work my way down his large shaft.

I was a slutty submissive, and I was proud of it. I had made peace with my desires a long time ago. I also knew that my sexual interests were most likely connected to the lack of a father figure in my life. I didn't care, though, because it felt good and that was all that mattered to me.

I felt Daddy thread his hand into my hair, getting a good grip. I moaned at the slight pull as I worked my way down to Daddy's base.

"You like that?" Daddy asked in a husky voice as he pulled my hair a bit harder this time.

I whimpered as I looked up at Daddy through heavy-lidded eyes as I pressed my lips around his base, his hardness stretching my throat. I could see the heat in his eyes and I was willing to bet that not many guys would be able to take him all the way into their mouth. But for me, I loved the feeling of a dick in my throat.

"Holy fuck," he moaned as he started to lightly thrust his hips.

I returned the moan as I felt him start to fuck my mouth. I could feel my dick pulse with need as he thrust his hips and his balls slapped my chin. This was exactly what I'd wanted. I'd needed someone to use me for their own pleasure. Someone who could make everything disappear all around me.

Daddy started to move his hips even faster and I felt his dick getting harder, his cockhead swelling. He was getting close to coming and I wanted it desperately. I wanted to drink every last drop he had for me.

Daddy was moaning deeply now, as his pace picked up even more. I knew my throat was going to be sore tomorrow from the abuse, but I didn't care. I would buy lozenges by the dozen just to make this go longer.

After a few more thrusts, Daddy snapped his hips forward and let out a deep growl as he shot line after line of scorching hot cum down my throat. I whimpered like a bitch in heat as I greedily swallowed everything he had for me.

Fuck, he tasted so sweet.

I couldn't remember the last time I had tasted anyone that sweet before. I moved back, pulling him from my throat, and sucked at his tip, getting the last few drops out of him before he pulled out. I instantly mourned the loss of the feeling of his dick against my tongue.

"You taste so good," I moaned out as I licked my lips.

"You're a bit of a cock slut, huh?" Daddy groaned.

"More than a bit," I replied, flashing him a grin before I wrapped my lips around him once more and sucked on his tip again, getting a couple of stray drops of his precious essence. "I could suck your dick all day," I said as I looked up at him.

He pulled me up by my hair with a growl and smashed his lips against mine. He shoved his tongue into my mouth and I moaned as he licked and sucked at my tongue, getting a taste of himself. I could feel the passion and desire within him. He needed more and I was all too happy to oblige. After a moment, he pulled back and spoke.

"Get naked, up on the bed on your hands and knees. I want your ass in the air."

"Yes, Daddy," I moaned.

I quickly began to remove my clothing as Daddy did with his own. I scrambled over to the bed and got into his ordered position while he went around and grabbed the lube from the bedside drawer.

I leaned onto my elbows and spread my legs nice and wide for him, making sure he had the perfect view of my ass. I heard him groan and I knew exactly what he had seen.

He ran his hand down my ass and pushed on the end of the plug that I had inserted before I left the hotel.

"And what do we have here, my sweet boy?"

"I stretched myself before coming here, Daddy. That way I wouldn't have to be stretched. Plus, I like the feel of it." I moaned, jutting my hips backward as he pushed it in even further.

I found something comforting about having a plug in. I knew it was weird. No, not at the top of the weird scale, but it wasn't normal, either. I had always enjoyed the feeling of having a dick inside of me. I didn't know why and I couldn't explain it, but the fullness, the stretch, always brought me comfort. I felt connected to someone and I had missed that growing up. It was safe to say I had a healthy sex toy collection, some of which I'd brought with me.

"I like that you enjoy having something

inside of you, my sweet boy. So many others deny themselves what they find joy in. It's good for you to embrace it," Daddy said as he ran his hand over my ass.

I felt a light slap to my ass and it caused me to let out a light moan. I did enjoy being spanked, by either a hand or a belt. I enjoyed a bit of pain with my pleasure. Anything to make me feel something other than empty and sad.

"You like it rough, my sweet boy?" he asked as he slapped my ass even harder this time.

"Fuck yes. You can be as rough as you want, Daddy," I said and moaned as I thrust my ass up hoping to encourage him to continue. I wanted more. I *needed* more. I wasn't a masochist by any stretch of the imagination, but I did enjoy the rough and painful sex if there was pleasure with it.

"Good to know," he breathed and chuckled. He slapped me as hard as he could, the sound echoing out in the room and red-hot fire blooming over my skin.

I gave a deep moan and again pushed my ass in the air. "Again, please, Daddy."

He did it again, but this time he also made sure to hit the end of the plug to drive it even further inside of me. The end rubbed my sweet spot and I squealed.

I couldn't help but push my ass out even more. I needed more and Daddy did not disappoint. He continued to slap my ass as hard as he could. White-hot fire burned over my cheeks and thighs and I was already looking forward to seeing the red marks and light bruising there tomorrow. My ass throbbed and I loved every moment of it.

"I'm negative. I've got the proof in my pocket. I got tested last week and I haven't been with anyone since. Tell Daddy it's okay for him to fuck you without a condom." I could hear him panting behind me as he said the words and I knew he was as on edge as I was at that moment.

Usually, my immediate answer to that question would be a solid no. I'd learned not to blindly trust what people said in the heat of the moment, but somehow I knew he wasn't giving me some line.

Call it gut instinct.

He most likely did have those test results in his jeans and I was confident he was negative like he said. I was negative as well.

I'd always had a condom policy, but this vacation was about being reckless, letting go, even adding some danger to my life, whatever it took to quiet the voices in my head. It was about escaping and not feeling the last three months. I was throwing caution completely out the window for the next three weeks and I didn't care that I might regret that decision later.

"I'm negative, too, Daddy. I want to feel you come inside of me."

"That's my good boy. Daddy is going to come in your sweet, tight ass and then watch as it drips out of you," he said as he started to pull the plug out of me.

I whined at the loss of the plug, but I knew it would soon be replaced by something so much better. I heard him open the lube and slick up before I felt his tip against my already stretched hole. The plug wasn't as thick as he was, but I didn't care. I didn't want him to stretch me any further. I wanted to feel the sting of him entering my hole. Of his dick stretching me out further. I couldn't stop moaning as his tip breached my hole and pushed inside of me. He felt so good. He was huge and this was exactly what I needed.

"So fucking big. Don't stop. I love the feel of the burn at first, Daddy." I groaned, hissing at the pain even as I pushed my hips back to get him to go even deeper inside of me.

He growled as he slammed his hips forward, pushing himself inside my ass all the way down to the base. I let out a small scream as the pain and pleasure mixed within my body. This man knew exactly what I needed and he wasn't afraid to give it to me.

And I loved it.

He was the perfect Daddy. He didn't give me any time to adjust before he pulled all the way back out to his tip, and then slammed right back inside of me, hitting my sweet spot dead on and making me scream out once again.

"Oh, Daddy, yes. Fuck me harder," I whimpered as he snapped his hips and drilled into me.

This man certainly didn't need to be told twice. He put his hands on my hips, his grip bruising, and started to pound into my hole like his life depended on it. I had no idea how long he was going to be able to last at this brutal pace, but I was hoping the fact that he already came once meant that he would be able to go long enough for me to come.

With each thrust, he hit my prostate and I saw stars. I couldn't stop moaning and whimpering at each thrust, each solid pass over my sweet spot. I was so hard I felt like I was going to explode soon.

"Oh yes, Daddy, don't stop. You're gonna make me come soon," I breathed out, panting deeply.

Daddy snaked his hand around my hip, wrapping his fist around my hard dick with a firm grip and it made me whimper at the sensation of his rough touch over my velvet skin.

"You're so hard, do you want Daddy to make you come?" he asked as he slowed his thrusts down to barely even moving.

"Yes please, Daddy, I need to come. Please make me come, Daddy. I'll do whatever you want," I easily begged. I knew that was what he wanted and I was all too happy to give it to him.

"Come for me. I want to feel your ass tighten around my cock," he ordered as he started to jerk me off, pulling roughly at my cock yet still keeping his thrusts deep and slow.

He shifted his hips once more and I moaned at the contact of his dick hitting my sweet spot once again. It didn't take long before I let out a long, deep groan and came long and hard into his hand.

I heard Daddy moan as the walls of my ass tightened around him. I knew I was tight as I clamped down around his hardness. He had to stop moving so he wouldn't come yet. I was thankful for that, though, because I wanted to feel him inside of me longer.

When I stopped pulsing, he threaded his free hand into my hair, fisting a chunk of it. He then pulled me up and back so I was on my knees with my back against his chest. He kept a tight grip on my hair and tilted my head back.

"Whatever I want, my sweet boy?" he asked, his voice a husky growl in my ear, sending shivers snaking down my spine.

"Yes, Daddy, anything."

Daddy held his cum covered hand up to me as he spoke. "Good boys always clean up their messes. Lick it clean."

"Yes, Daddy," I moaned, licking my lips. I took his hand in mine and brought it to my mouth. I started to lick up my own cum. I loved the taste of cum, even my own. I truly was a cock slut, but I was proud of it. At least in the bedroom.

"How does it taste, my boy?"

"Good, Daddy. I love the taste of cum," I whispered, pressing my ass back against his still hard dick, hoping he would take the hint that I was more than ready for more.

"Such a naughty, dirty slut you are. Daddy loves it," he said before he sucked hard on my neck, causing an appreciative moan to slip from my lips.

I loved being given hickies. I always felt like I was being marked and I loved that feeling. I loved feeling like I belonged to someone, that I had someone who wanted me enough to mark me as his.

Once Daddy's hand was clean, he pushed me back down onto the bed. He removed his hand from my hair and placed it on the back of my neck. Holding me down, he let go of all control and started to pound deep into my ass.

We were both a moaning mess and my legs were trembling from the overwhelming pleasure my body was experiencing. Neither of us ever wanted this to end, that much was clear, but I could feel him getting closer, getting harder, swelling once more.

After a few more rapid thrusts, Daddy snapped his hips forward until he was balls deep inside of my ass and was coming with a loud groan. The second I felt his hot cum scorching the inside of my walls, I was whimpering and writhing underneath him. I had never felt someone coming inside of me before and I instantly felt like I was being marked. That as long as his cum was inside of me, I belonged to him. That feeling alone had washed away the past three months. It removed that empty hole that I'd had inside of me. I knew it wouldn't last, but for right now, I felt complete bliss.

We were both breathing heavily and I already knew I could easily become addicted to him. I was hoping he was a local and we would be able to meet up again before I had to go back to New York. I needed this to be more than just a one-off.

I felt Daddy pulling out and I was disappointed that he wanted to watch the come drip out of me. I wanted to keep it there a bit longer. To my surprise, though, I felt the plug being pushed back inside of me as he spoke.

"I like the idea of you walking around with my cum inside of you."

"Me too, Daddy," I instantly said, and it was the complete truth. I didn't want the feeling of belonging to him to disappear just yet. I wanted to embrace it just a bit longer. I *needed* to.

He removed his hand from the back of my neck and I felt him climbing off of the bed. I knew we were finished for the night, but I was really hoping we could meet up again. I was hoping he would want that, too.

"You a local?" he asked.

"No, just visiting for three weeks, Daddy," I said as I moved and started to get dressed.

"Care to meet up again, my sweet boy?" He pulled his jeans up over his thick hips and buttoned them closed as he gazed at me, a cat that ate the cream look on his face.

"Definitely," I easily agreed, flashing him a smile.

He pulled out his phone and handed it to me as he spoke. "Give Daddy your number."

"Yes, Daddy."

I took the offered phone and typed in

my number before I handed it back to him. I'd let him decide on what he was going to put the number under.

Once he had my number saved, he tucked the phone away into his pocket as he spoke in that husky voice of his. I couldn't help but wonder if maybe he smoked for it to get that way.

"When Daddy texts you, you will answer and you will meet me when I tell you. Do I make myself clear?"

"Yes, Daddy. I'll be a good boy," I promised. For now, at least. I was extremely interested in seeing what a punishment by this man would feel like.

"You better or Daddy will punish you. You go straight back to your hotel room. You won't let anyone touch you while you are in town. You belong to me until you go back home. Do I make myself clear?" he ordered and damn, didn't that almost have me fully hard again.

"Yes, Daddy. I only belong to you."

He didn't say anything else. He simply turned and strolled out the door.

I let out a shaky breath as I tried to get my emotions back under control. That man had a way of making me feel pleasure on a whole new level. He knew exactly what I needed and he gave me more than what I could ever have hoped for. I had no idea who he was or when he would text me, but I was hoping I would be seeing him again tomorrow. I only had three weeks down here and I wanted to spend every chance I could with that man.

CHAPTER TWO

William

I MADE MY way into work just after eight in the morning.

As a fire Captain in Baton Rouge, I had a grand number of responsibilities that rested on my shoulders. The lives of my men depended on me to be able to make the right call. To be able to read the fire and know what path it was going to take. If I failed, my men could be seriously hurt or killed. It was a great deal of stress, but it was a stress that I took on each and every day.

I had joined the fire department when I

was eighteen, fresh out of high school. It had been twenty-two years since then. I have had my moments where I felt pure joy and felt the brotherhood, and then there were times when I had wanted to quit and I wasn't sure I was going to make it through. I knew I had changed since I was a probie.

How could I not?

Back when I first started, I was filled with so much excitement and hope. I was naive and thought I could handle anything that came my way. Even when the fires were bad and the victims were innocent and destroyed, I still thought I would be able to handle it for the rest of my life. And then, the years started to add up. The victim count started to add up. And now, twenty-two years later, I had been chewed up and spat out so many times I had lost count. I was no longer happy-go-lucky. I didn't socialize with the other firefighters in the station. I kept to myself.

It wasn't just because I was their Captain and I had things I needed to do while they were hanging around waiting for a call. It was also because I couldn't get attached.

I had discovered that it hurt a lot more, that the guilt was worse, if I allowed myself to get close to my men and they died. I refuse to allow myself to get close to anyone, ever again. It was why I didn't interact with my men outside of work. I kept things completely professional, including the conversations that we had. It wasn't often we had any type of conversation, even a professional one, unless it was warranted. My men were good and they knew what they needed to do.

As for any personal life, I kept that simple as well. I didn't date. I had no interest in it. Dating meant feelings and I was not interested in feeling anything toward someone. I wanted to just be able to feel pleasure without any drama associated with it.

I also had a different style of sex. I needed to be in control. I needed to be dominant and control my partners in the bedroom, even a bit out of it. I didn't need a slave, but I needed someone that would do as they were told, and there would be no surprises.

I relied on a routine. I relied on knowing that I had complete control over my life. My mental health depended on it. I didn't like surprises, good or bad. I didn't like the unknown and uncertainty. I found comfort and mental stability in knowing I could control the environment around me, including the people in it. That was why I did so well as a Captain. Everyone in my firehouse had to follow my rules and listen to me.

That didn't always work out well in a relationship. Most men wouldn't tolerate being dominated and controlled. I would never take it too far, of course. I didn't need a mindless slave or someone who couldn't make a single decision for themselves. I just needed a person who was able to play by my rules. Someone who had no problem giving up complete control to me during sex.

I would never take advantage of someone, either. I always made sure to read how my sex partners were responding to me so I could act accordingly. I usually had to compromise here and there to make sure it was pleasurable for the both of us.

That was, until last night.

I had gone to the club to find someone to play with for the night. I'd tried to have a fuck buddy, someone who I could go to for my type of need, but my most recent one had found someone they wanted to date. I was happy for them, don't get me wrong, but when it's difficult enough to find a play partner you mesh with, well, let's just say I ended up rather frustrated when it ended. That was six months ago and I hadn't found a replacement for him yet.

Just my luck.

I'd been going to the club to get my needs filled and, hopefully, find a new submissive who would be interested in me being their dominant. So far, I had been striking out. Yes, some were interesting and good in bed, but they weren't what I was looking for. They didn't take me to the height that I needed to hit in order to get the stress to wash off of my body. To bring a calm and peace to my mind.

That was, until last night.

I had no idea who he was, I didn't even know his name, but he was amazing. He was perfect for me. I had never been with someone that much in love with being a bottom. That much in love with dick. He even wore a plug to the club. I loved sex toys.

I loved to play with them. I even had a sex room in my house that I kept locked. The guys that I took in there, they only cared for some of it. They were never truly willing to let me play full out. I got the feeling, though, that the submissive from last night would die to be in that room.

He didn't even blink twice when I referred to myself as Daddy. It wasn't because I wanted a child, it was because I didn't like the term Master and I heard Sir all day long at work. I wanted something that was more personal, something that I wouldn't hear coming out of one of my men's mouths. Daddy did the job perfectly and the guys I had been with tended to be okay with it.

The man from last night, though, that was pure bliss.

It was freeing, because he loved everything I did to him and I knew he would love everything else that I would plan for him.

I had to see him again.

I had to get him into my sex room.

He was only going to be down here for three weeks, but I was planning on taking complete advantage of that time. I planned to text him tonight and get him over to my house. If I was only going to be able to get three short weeks out of him, I was going to make every second count.

I pulled into my parking spot at work and got out. I worked at Station Twenty-One on A shift and had two trucks. One was a normal firefighter truck, a fire engine, and the other was a rescue truck, or Squad, that was equipped to do specialized rescues such as natural disasters, people who were injured at work, people that needed to be removed from a vehicle after an accident. I also had an ambulance with two full time paramedics. I had twenty guys, including the paramedics, under my roof, and it was my job to make sure they all got to go home at the end of the day. I hadn't lost anyone in the past five years and I hoped to keep it that way, but I knew fires could turn deadly without any notice and there would be nothing I could do about it.

"Morning, Boss," Hawke said, and gave me a mock salute.

Hawke was my lieutenant for my fire truck. I gave him a nod just as the alarm sounded followed by the dispatcher's voice.

"Truck forty-three, Squad eighty-nine,

Ambulance nineteen, structure fire at 3245 Main Street. Reports of multiple people trapped inside."

"Let's go!" I called out as I ran over to my service truck.

This was going to be a long day. It was barely eight in the morning and we were already getting sent to a fire that could have deadly consequences. I headed off first, pulling out of the driveway with sirens blaring, knowing that my guys would be right behind me.

I sped down the streets, weaving in and out around the morning traffic. We were roughly ten minutes away and I was hoping by the time we got there the people who were in the house had been able to get out. The second we arrived on scene, though, I knew that wasn't the case. The whole house was engulfed in flames.

The street was thick with smoke due to the lack of wind that morning. People from the nearby houses had already left their homes and were standing on the opposite side of the road, spread out on the sidewalk.

"Get the hoses going. Probie, go to the neighbor's and make sure no one is there," I ordered as I made my way toward the house.

It was completely on fire and I knew there was no way we were going to be able to save any of it. Now, it was about containment and making sure that the other house close by didn't catch fire. I glanced over and saw police were pulling in and I knew they would make sure the crowd stayed back. Good. Less for me to worry about right now.

My guys quickly got the hose hooked up to the fire hydrant and started to blast the line of water onto the fire. We had to control it from the outside, because the fire would make the building unstable, too unstable to send them in. I was not going to risk them being inside when the roof collapsed.

"Call said people were inside. Do we know if they got out?" I asked an officer who approached me.

"We got a witness who said he tried to get the door open when they saw the flames, but it was bolted shut from the inside. He couldn't get it open and the windows are all safety glass. Another ran around to the back and the door there was bolted as well. Someone wanted to make sure whoever was inside didn't get out.”

Fuck, this was arson and the people inside that they wanted dead, were definitely deceased now. There was no surviving the heat or the smoke from this blaze. We had a new arsonist and, hopefully, they were only interested in this house.

“Why the safety glass?” I asked.

That was different for a typical house. There wouldn’t be a need to have safety glass up. This house had to be used for something and I was willing to bet whatever that something was, had been the reason this house was targeted.

“System has it as a foster home for children who are at risk of retribution. Some are testifying against dangerous criminals. Others have been taken away from abusive parents. This was created as a safe haven.”

Double fuck.

That meant that the bodies we were going to recover would be children. This day was going to be a disaster and I was already not looking forward to it. It also meant there would be a lot of possible suspects. Someone in the home had clearly been targeted, and this was a final way of making sure that target never spoke their truth.

"We'll have the fire out soon and then you can have the crime scene start," I said.

"Crime scene will be here shortly, but my Boss is already calling in the Federal Protection Agency. They'll handle this and make sure whoever is responsible pays for it."

That was a good thing. I knew the Federal Protection Agency. Hell, everyone in a first responder position knew about them. They were making serious waves and had one hell of a reputation for getting justice for children. That was the only positive aspect out of this crime. The FPA would make sure the arsonist was caught, and they would make him pay. These people, however many there were inside, would get to have justice.

Once we got the fire out, it would be their turn to take over. My job was to get the fire out and make sure they would be able to get inside safely so they could recover the bodies and start their investigation. I just prayed that this arsonist wasn't a fire bug and only just getting started.

CHAPTER THREE

Noah

WAKING UP, I instantly could still feel last night in my body. My throat was a bit sore, but I could easily fix that. I had taken the plug out last night, but I hadn't taken a shower so I could feel a stickiness on the back of my thighs.

I still couldn't believe how amazing last night was. It was everything I could have dreamed and more. I was really hoping that Daddy, whoever he was, would call me again tonight so we could have more fun. I wanted to know what else he could do to me with more time. Hell, I would even consider having him come over to my hotel room.

Said hotel room was a penthouse suite that I had all to myself. I spent extra just to have the luxury of this place. I wanted a vacation. I wanted the chance to get away from every demon that had been plaguing my mind. The penthouse had its own bedroom with a king size bed. The living area had a full kitchen and the one wall was completely floor to ceiling windows. The bathroom had a full glass shower big enough to fit five people in, as well as a full size hot tub. The place was perfect and worth every penny.

As much as I would have liked to spend all day in bed, I had planned to surprise my kid brother today at his work. Growing up, I had always wanted a brother but my mother was not interested in having more children. I grew up with just her and her parade of boyfriends. My mother was not very good at being alone so she always had a boyfriend. Whenever one relationship ended, she had someone new that same day. One thing they all had in common was that they didn't care for me.

Growing up, I had made excuses for

her. She was young when she had me, just eighteen, so it would make sense that she wanted to party and enjoy life after having to be a single mother at a young age. Now, though, I knew what it was. She didn't want to be a parent, but she didn't want to be the mother that gave her kid up, either. It didn't make for a loving home. Still, I had never been abused and I never went without food or clothing. She made sure to keep me alive and in a decent home.

When I was in my late twenties was when I discovered that I did actually have a younger brother. Ryzen was nineteen when we first met. It was a complete coincidence that we had run into each other. Our father had died and we were the only ones who showed up for the funeral. The man was not well loved or even liked.

The only reason I was there was because I had hoped it would provide some type of closure. I knew from my mother that he wasn't a good man and that when she discovered she was pregnant she had ran away to protect the both of us. Ryzen's mother didn't have the same belief. Ryzen's mother had stayed with our father and it ended up getting her killed.

Meeting my brother for the first time was surreal. I had always wanted a brother. I always wanted someone that could be there with me and help me not feel so alone. I don't know what was wrong with me, but I always felt alone. I always felt like there was a hole inside of me and nothing I did helped me find that missing piece to complete me.

Having Ryzen has helped, but he has his own demons he is still trying to work through. It had taken a few years before I'd discovered that he had been a child soldier. That at a very young age, he had been living in a warzone and killing people, only to be picked up and employed at eighteen by the CIA. Obviously, he was good at what he did and I guess working for the government was better than the alternative, at least.

It had taken a long time for Ryzen to start to come to life and I couldn't be more proud of him. He'd come a long way from that eighteen year old man. He was still a sniper, but now he worked for the Federal Protection Agency helping to keep children safe and prevent them from having to go through any of the horrors he'd had to experience when he was a child. He was also able to find love. Knox Hunter was a FBI profiler who had actually been behind my brother being fired by the CIA. They had worked through it, though, and they were both madly in love with the other. I couldn't have been happier for him. He was finally working through his demons and building a life for himself.

Me on the other hand, I was sinking and just trying to keep my head above the water. I wasn't too certain I was succeeding in that regard. I kept telling myself it was just this case, that I needed a break from criminals. From crimes against innocent people. I just needed this vacation and then I would be able to go back to New York and take on the next case. The problem was, I wasn't certain that was my issue, or that a vacation would fix it. I was getting burnt out and I wasn't certain I would be able to keep going. The problem was, though, I was Federal Prosecutor. That was literally my job, my career. And at thirty-eight, I was too old for a career change. Even if I could entertain changing my career, I had no idea what it would be. All I had ever wanted was to be a lawyer, to help people and put dangerous criminals in jail where they belonged. If I wasn't doing that, I had no idea what I would do or who I would even be.

That was literally my life, how could I just walk away from it?

Letting out a sigh, I climbed out of bed and strolled into the gorgeous bathroom. I needed to start getting ready if I wanted to be able to catch Ryzen at work. I wasn't certain if he was working a case or not, but I hoped he would be there.

I knew the Agency was getting very busy and they were taking on more agents to help with the large flow of cases that were coming their way. Ryzen often had to travel all over the country to work different cases. He was madly in love with his job and I was both proud and jealous of him for it. I was no longer in love with mine. In fact, it felt more like I was married to someone I couldn't afford to divorce. We were just trapped being tied to each other until one of us died. It was clearly an unhealthy relationship.

I don't know, maybe spending some time with Ryzen would help me to figure out what I wanted to do. Or maybe it was going to make me feel even more confused and depressed.

In the meantime, though, I truly hoped that Daddy texted me. I knew that would put a big smile on my face.

At just the thought of the man my whole body tingled. I didn't know what it was about him, but he was so attuned to my body already. It was like we had already done this dance with each other before and we were reconnecting. All I wanted was to see him again, to feel the peace he brought me.

I didn't even have his number, so I couldn't text him. I had to wait for him and that both annoyed me and excited me. He was a man who enjoyed being in complete control and I was fine with that. But I couldn't help but wonder what he did for a living.

He was muscular, so he clearly spent time working out or he did a great deal of manual labor. His hands were rough, like he used them often, so I was leaning toward manual labor. Maybe he was a builder, but I wasn't too sure. He had some scars on him that I could have sworn looked like old burns. I wasn't an expert on that, though, so I couldn't say for sure. That also didn't mean he was a firefighter; he could have been burned as a kid. Hell, he could be ex-military and was injured by an IED. Ex-military would fit and explain a lot. They tended to like to be in control, especially if they ran a unit. Plus, he would be used to working out and having to stay in shape. They also worked with their hands, so he could be a mechanic or a builder who was just out of the forces.

What the man did, though, it didn't really matter to me. I didn't care if he was rich or poor. All I cared about was his ability to help me not feel so empty. His ability to make me feel something that wasn't complete exhaustion and sadness.

I knew there was something wrong with me. I knew I was depressed and I was using sex as a way to avoid that feeling. I also knew I shouldn't be doing it, but it was the one thing that worked. I had tried therapy, but there wasn't really a good enough reason for me to be there.

I had never been abused. I didn't have some horrible trauma that had left me scarred. I was a prosecutor who got to hear the stories of victims, yes, but that shouldn't make me depressed, because they weren't *my* stories.

I had tried antidepressants, but they made me feel even more miserable and made my brain foggy. I stopped taking them pretty quick. The only thing that worked was this type of sex, so I'd stuck with it.

The last therapist told me I needed a lifestyle change. That I needed to change careers or find something else that I could do that wouldn't make me so depressed all the time. But again, it wasn't that simple.

Letting out yet another sigh, I stepped under the hot water from the shower, letting it sluice over my skin. I needed to stop thinking about that stuff right now. I was supposed to be here on vacation and that meant leaving all of my problems in New York. Here in Baton Rouge, I was just Ryzen's older brother down for a fun three week visit. I told myself enough was enough. There was going to be zero shop talk, from now on, and I was going to focus on having a good time.

I made quick work of getting cleaned up before I got out of the shower, drying off with a huge fluffy white towel. I headed back into the bedroom and grabbed some blue jeans and a black t-shirt. I also grabbed one of my favorite plugs, slicked it up, and slipped it inside of myself. I had a feeling I was going to need the comfort today.

I made quick work of getting dressed before I slipped on my converse shoes and black leather jacket. I headed out and made my way to my car. I would pick up something to eat along the way, plus coffee. I typed in the address for the Agency and then I was off.

***

It was roughly thirty minutes later when I made my way up in the elevator to the main area of the Agency where my brother would most likely be. This was going to be the first time I had actually seen a place where my brother worked and I had to admit I was a bit excited for it. I would get to see his office and meet his friends.

It was very simple and domestic, but we never got to do this before. I never got the chance to meet his friends growing up or to take him to work. We never got the opportunity to be normal brothers growing up.

I strolled off of the elevator and made my way down the hallway. I could hear his voice coming from one of the rooms. The second I walked in, his gaze landed on me and he flashed me a warm smile.

"Noah, what are you doing here?"

"Surprise," I said as he made his way over to me and I instantly pulled him in for a hug.

It felt so good to be able to hug him. To know that he was here with me. Whenever we were around each other, Ryzen had a way of making me not feel so alone, even if we weren't in the same room. Just knowing that he was around, it made me feel better. It always had from the very day we first met.

"It's good to see you," I said as he pulled back, wrapping his arm around the waist of a dark-haired man who'd slid up to his side with a grin.

"This is Knox. Knox, this is my brother, Noah."

"So you're Knox. It's nice to finally meet you," I said as I held my hand out to the man who had stolen my brother's heart.

"It's nice to meet you. Ry has told me

so much about you," he said as he took my hand in his.

"How long are you in town for?" Ryzen asked.

"Three weeks. I just finished a long and brutal trial and I decided to cash in some of my vacation days. I got in late last night."

"Where are you staying?" Ryzen asked, confused.

"In a hotel, and before you jump on me, I *like* the hotel. I want to be in a hotel. I know I could have crashed with you, but it's not a real vacation unless you have room service and tiny liquor bottles to work your way through," I said with a cheeky grin.

Knox gave a chuckle at that before he spoke. "He's right, babe. Part of a vacation is getting waited on hand and foot."

"It's good that you are here. You've sounded stressed the last few times we've talked. You look like you could use a break. And who knows, maybe I'll be able to convince you to move down here."

"Oh yeah, and do what? Kick down doors with you?" I asked with a playful smirk.

Though, the idea of moving down here

didn't sound terrible, but again, what would I do?

There was no point in moving down here just to keep being a prosecutor and having the same issue. I might as well stay in my condo and keep going through the motions.

"I'd pay to see you kick down a door. And you could be a lawyer down here or teach at the University. That job is making you look old," he teased, and I couldn't help but roll my eyes.

I was thirty-eight. I was far from old. Still, he was right, the job was starting to age me. And I had never considered that I could be a teacher. I was easily qualified to teach law. Maybe that would be something for me to look into. Again, I didn't have to figure it out right now.

"Well, with you in town, we will need to try and all meet up a few times for dinner," Knox said.

"Definitely. Assuming this one doesn't get sent away," I said with a nod at Ryzen.

"I just got back, so it's someone else's turn to do an away case. I'm next on deck for a local issue."

"Are you guys getting a lot that are local?" I asked.

"We seem to be getting a shit load of cases that the local PD can't solve. Anything that has to do with children, we handle it. None of us mind, though. If it gets someone dangerous off of the streets, it's worth it."

I did know from my own research that Baton Rouge was pretty bad for human trafficking and the foster care here wasn't that great. I knew from my conversations with Ryzen that they were working really hard on repairing the foster system and trying to set up safer options for the children. It was a long process, though, and often he asked me for advice on different legal paperwork that they needed to sort through. I was happy to help, because that was something that I could do to help children. I didn't have to deal with a jury or a defense attorney trying to make it seem like the victim was actually in the wrong. What Ryzen needed help with was paperwork that you just had to know how to fill out and what channels to send it through to get it approved. It was simple and pure.

"How has the foster system been?" I asked.

"It's a work in progress. Knox has been

helping with doing interviews with potential foster parents to make sure they aren't trying to fool anyone. All we can do is take it one house at a time," Ryzen said with a shrug.

"Unsolved cases against children, though, have started to go down and that is a huge accomplishment," Knox added.

"Absolutely, it's a huge accomplishment and you all should be proud of the work you have done," I said.

"Sorry to interrupt," a man said from behind me.

I turned around to see who it was just as Ryzen spoke. "Mason, this is my brother, Noah."

"It's a pleasure to meet you," Mason said as he held his hand out.

I easily took it as I spoke. "It's a pleasure to meet you. Thank you for giving my brother his passion back."

"I was very fortunate that he said yes to working for us."

I could tell he meant that, too. And I knew that Ryzen had saved a few of their lives with his sharp shooting skills.

"We have a case?" Ryzen asked.

"A call just came in, a foster home was set on fire. The FD are already on the scene and the fire has been put out. Fire Captain William Clark has stated it was arson. He didn't give details over the phone, but we have ten dead bodies, one adult and nine children. Everyone who was in the home didn't make it."

"Shit," I softly said.

I was supposed to be here to get a vacation and now Ryzen would be working a mass homicide that involved nine children. This was not what I had been expecting when I came down here to get away from death and pain.

"It gets worse. The foster home that was targeted, it was a safe haven. All of the children in the home were there because they needed protection. Either from abusive parents that the system failed to put away, or dangerous criminals that they were set to testify against," Mason added.

"Someone in that house had to be targeted and the rest were collateral. I don't have any active cases right now, why don't I go down with Ry and see what I can pick up," Knox suggested.

"I would appreciate that. We are running thin. Everyone else is working a case, I myself am about to head out for

Utah. We have a suspected cult that is recruiting homeless teenagers to commit crimes. I'm heading there with Hollingsworth. Gabe and Kruze are working on wrapping up their case and then they will be all yours, but it could be a few days before that happens. I have also been informed that Captain Clark is more than happy to lend out anyone you need from his department to run threat assessments on any of the other foster homes."

"We're gonna need to do that. We can't afford to assume this is a one off. I'll get to the scene," Ryzen said.

"I'll text you the address. It was nice meeting you, Noah."

"You as well," I said with a warm smile before he turned and headed off.

"Sorry, but I gotta run," Ryzen said.

I shook my head. He didn't need to apologize for it. I understood why he had to leave.

"No need. Why don't I come with you? You're shorthanded. I can speak with witnesses and people in the area. They might be more willing to talk to me than someone in law enforcement," I offered.

Did I want to go somewhere with nine

dead children, no. But I also knew it was going to be a long and difficult case for him and I didn't want him to feel like I wasn't willing to help. Plus, these children could have been targeted because of a case they were connected to. They might need a lawyer to help them get the proper warrants and court documents to try and track down the arsonist. As much as it went against what my vacation down here was all about, I also couldn't ignore the severity of the case.

"You sure?" Ryzen asked, and I could tell he was picking up on my need for this vacation. He didn't want to push me if I wasn't in a mentally sound state of mind. I loved him for that, but I was also the older brother and it wasn't his job to worry about me.

"I'm good. You drive," I said with a warm smile. He simply gave me a nod, but I knew the conversation was not over.

We all headed out and climbed into Ryzen's truck. I truly hoped that this was going to be an isolated incident and it wouldn't take him long to wrap up. I really didn't want to spend the next three weeks helping with cases.

I checked my phone, but there were no

new messages. Now would have been a perfect time for Daddy to reach out to me. I really hoped he still wanted to meet up before I had to head back to New York. I could really use it.

CHAPTER FOUR

William

IT WAS JUST after nine when I was alerted that the Agency had arrived on the scene. We had spent an hour making sure the fire was fully out and the house was structurally sound so they could walk around in it.

I had gone inside and counted ten bodies, one adult and nine kids. I had no idea what their genders were; they were burnt right down to the bone. They were going to have a hard time making any identifications. We would help where we could, but we didn't do investigations. We were the ones who handled the fire and it was on the police to handle any investigations. Still, these people, these children, deserved to have all of the help they could possibly have. So, I would be keeping a close eye on this case and make sure someone paid for their deaths.

That was not how I wanted to start my day, or spend it, that was for sure. Those children belonged to someone. They had parents, or a family who would be mourning them. The story was going to hit the papers and shock the whole city. It was good that the local police weren't going to play around with it. That they weren't going to try and work the case and then bring on the Agency when they had nothing. The Agency would be able to find who was responsible for those children's deaths and they would make sure they paid.

A man in a suit climbed out of the passenger side and I recognized him. Knox Hunter. He was a profiler with the FBI. They were clearly taking this very seriously and that made me feel better. A profiler would be able to have a deeper understanding of this arsonist and, hopefully, they would be able to catch him before another home was hit.

I didn't recognize the man who got out of the driver's seat, but I didn't expect to. I had never worked with any of them. There had never been a reason for me to before. I wasn't sure how they were going to react to me being involved with their case. This was one fire I was not going to just forget about. I was going to be involved and make sure this arsonist never set another fire ever again.

When the back door opened and a third man got out, my stomach instantly dropped.

There was no way.

Why was he here?

It was the man from last night. The man who had shown me a whole world of decadent pleasure. The man that I was craving with every ounce of my libido.

Why would he be here?

He said he was on vacation, so why would he be showing up to a crime scene?

That was not something I was prepared for. My sex life was not something I could risk getting out. No one knew I was gay and I was not about to let that come out. I was not going to be the gay firefighter, the gay captain. I couldn't afford to have my men questioning if I was looking at them while they were coming out of the shower or half dressed. I couldn't have my men questioning my motives or my capabilities. Not to mention, I was not going to have my personal life floating all around and being the house gossip. If my men knew how I enjoyed my sex, that I had a sex room in my home, I would lose their respect. I was not going to be someone that every firefighter in the city talked about. It was one thing for them to be impressed by my accomplishments. Hell, for them to bitch about how much of a hard ass I was. All of that was acceptable. But I was not going to have my personal preferences being the talk of the town.

"Captain Clark?" The man who had exited the driver's side of the car said.

"Yes, you must be from the Agency."

"Ryzen. This is FBI Profiler Agent Hunter," Ryzen said as he gave a nod to Knox.

"I know the name. And who is that?" I asked with a nod to the man I had slept with last night.

I made sure to keep my voice hard. I didn't want anyone to know that I knew him and I wanted to make sure he understood that there would be no recognition on my part. That him trying to say something wouldn't be tolerated. I could see the surprise in his eyes as he fought to hide it. He wasn't expecting me to be there any more than I was expecting to see him.

"Noah Riley. He's a Federal Prosecutor down on vacation. He was with me when the call came in," Ryzen said.

So that was his name. *Noah.* It fit him. I was surprised he was a Federal Prosecutor, though. He didn't come across as the lawyer type. At least none I had ever met. At the same time, though, it could make sense why he enjoyed being submissive. He probably spent all day long in court having to be demanding and in power. I knew from some of my previous submissives that they enjoyed the break in power. They enjoyed spending some time in a position where someone else made all of the decisions for them. The break from having to have all of that pressure on their shoulders is what they needed to be able to keep going. Being a Federal Prosecutor had to be extremely grueling at times.

And now that we weren't in the club, now that I was getting to see him in daylight without the haze of sexual need clouding my eyes, I could see the pain in his eyes. I could see the exhaustion. This vacation wasn't for fun, it was a necessity. He was drowning and he was hoping that this three week vacation would be what he needed to come up to the surface.

I doubted it would be.

That level of pain and darkness in his eyes would have already seeped into his soul. I'd seen that look on plenty of men who stayed in their career far too long. Police officers and firefighters who continued to do the job long past the time they should. If you see too much darkness in your career, it eats away at your very soul. Lose too much of your soul, and you become a shell of the man you were. Noah looked like he was right on the border of losing himself completely.

That thought shouldn't bother me. I didn't know him. We had only slept together once. It was amazing, the best I had ever had, but that didn't mean I had feelings for him. I had lust, a deep lust that I would be acting on again very soon. Still, that shouldn't be enough to make me wish I could remove the pain inside him, that I could tell him it would be okay, that he could figure something else out with his life. The one single night we'd shared together didn't change that we were strangers. That we were only a hook up in a dark club's backroom. I couldn't let his eyes distract me. We were all here for a case and I was not about to let some random submissive get me twisted up inside.

"The bodies are this way," I said, purposely ignoring Noah.

I guided them to the house and through the front door. The bodies were mostly all in the same area. They all had clearly been trying to escape the house before the flames and smoke got them.

"Jesus," Noah said as he closed his eyes for a moment.

There was a pang of guilt that shot through me. I knew he was struggling in his life, I could clearly see it on him. I should have warned them about the bodies. I should have advised that he be kept outside. He wasn't my submissive, but that didn't change that I had been with him, and was planning on being with him again. As a dominant, it was my job to know what my sub needed. Even if it was for one night. That was the last thing he needed to see.

"They would have died from the smoke before the fire got to them," I said, trying to offer what little comfort I could. I knew it wouldn't be much, but sometimes knowing that the smoke killed them before they would have felt the flames was enough to bring peace.

"And you are certain it's arson?" Knox asked as Ryzen started to look around.

"The windows are all safety glass, so no one would be able to break them and climb out. The front and back door both had a metal plate that was screwed into them to ensure no one could get out. We haven't found the starting point yet, but we know accelerants were used. This house was already overrun with flames by the time we got here. Within ten minutes, this house was a goner and everyone inside along with it."

There was a lot of debris we had to go through before we would be able to find what started the fire. Maybe once we found where it started, we might be able to discover who in the house had been targeted.

"Noah, why don't you go and see if any of the neighbors know anything or saw someone?" Ryzen suggested and I could tell that Noah was all too happy to leave.

"What's a prosecutor going on vacation down here for?" I couldn't help but ask once he left.

"He's my brother," Ryzen simply said as he bent down to get a better look at the only adult victim.

That made sense as to why Noah would come down to Baton Rouge and show up at a crime scene. He must have been at the Agency seeing Ryzen when the call came in and offered to help. Or maybe Ryzen asked for Noah to come along.

I wasn't certain if Ryzen had noticed the darkness threatening to swallow his brother whole. If he was struggling with his job, this was not the crime scene he should be walking around.

"This was obviously done by someone who knew what they were doing. It wasn't an amateur who had done some online research. They knew what metal to use on the doors to keep everyone in, even as the heat and flames overtook the doors. They knew the safety glass would keep them inside. This arsonist wanted someone in this home dead and they didn't care for collateral. This suggests that it was a professional who had been hired for the kill," Knox said as he moved around.

"This place was being used as a safe haven. There's no shortage of possibilities here for targets. Was there only supposed to be nine kids here?" I asked.

"Social Services confirmed that it was one female adult with nine children living here, all under sixteen," Knox answered.

"That doesn't seem smart. Why have one female be the protector of these kids? They were here because their lives were in danger. Shouldn't there have been more protection?" I asked.

I had never heard of a safe haven foster home, but to me it seems pretty stupid to leave nine potential targets in a home with just a single female.

What was she supposed to do if a crew stormed in here?

Bake them cookies?

I knew there were some badass females in the world, but still, they weren't Wonder Woman. There should have been at least two males living here to help protect the children.

"The system isn't perfect. Safe havens

are pretty new. Normally, if a child needed to be protected so they could give testimony, they would be placed within a federal safe house with agents. However, it was hard on the children. Some were as young as six and needed their parents. The system figured a foster home might be easier for the children to adjust and adapt to. But then, there's not enough people who want to take on the added risk. Plus some of the kids are there because their parents are abusive and the system can't get them in jail. It's a pilot program that isn't working, clearly," Knox explained and I could tell he was annoyed by how the system was handling these cases.

I could understand that there was this grey area. If the person who needed to testify was under eighteen, it became very tricky to protect them, especially if they didn't have any family you could trust them with. But there had to be a better way than a foster home and just praying they stayed alive.

"We need to know how it got started. If it happened internally or externally," Ryzen said.

"I'll get my guys on it," I said with a

nod before I headed out.

"Hawke," I called over as I walked out the door.

He half-jogged over to me before he spoke. "Yeah, Cap?"

"Get the guys and start to do a preliminary investigation. The Agency guys need to know if the fire started internally or externally. Let's find out how our arsonist got the house ablaze."

"Copy, Boss," he said with a nod, before he made his way off.

I scanned the crowd to see if I could find the one person I wanted to speak with. I knew I shouldn't be talking with Noah right now, not with people all around, but everything in me was telling me to find him. I saw him walking in between two of the homes and I suspected he was trying to get a minute alone to get his own thoughts and emotions under control.

I made my way over, making sure no one was following me or that I had eyes on me. I walked the short distance to Noah, who was leaning with his back against the brick wall trying to get his breathing to even out.

"This is not exactly how I planned on

seeing you again," I said as I stood right in front of him.

His eyes snapped open at the sudden sound of my voice. I could tell he was surprised to see me here with him, but he was also pleased about it and that sent heat rushing throughout me. I refused to analyze why I felt that warmth from something so simple.

"I was hoping I would see you again," Noah admitted.

"I took your phone number. I didn't do that for practice," I pointed out.

"I know, but lots of people take someone's number and then never reach out. I wasn't confident if you would want another round or not. I know I'm not what a typical submissive looks like," he said with a slight shrug and I could hear the insecurity in his voice.

I hated that he was feeling insecure. That he felt like I wasn't going to reach out to him, that I had just taken his number to be polite. He had no idea how amazing he had been last night. Sure, he had muscles and he wasn't your typical submissive spinner, but I didn't care about that. I cared about how well we clicked in the bedroom and we certainly did that. I cared that he made the storm within my body and mind go quiet, something that no man had ever been able to do before. That's what mattered to me.

"You're beautiful, every inch of you is perfect. If someone else can't see that, then why would you want to waste your time on someone who is clearly a moron? I was planning on texting you after my shift. But seeing as how you are here, now I don't have to. You will be out front of my home for eight o'clock tonight. I will text you my address and I expect you to be there on time. Daddy doesn't let late little boys into his home. Do I make myself clear?" I ordered.

I could see the heat starting to flood his eyes. He wanted me just as desperately as I wanted him. He needed me as desperately as I needed him. If I was only going to be getting him for three weeks, I was going to make sure I spent every moment I could with him.

"Yes, Daddy," he said softly.

"Good boy. Now, tell Daddy, are you wearing a plug?"

I was confident he wasn't, but I was asking to see if I could get any sort of reaction out of him. I wanted to try and offer a bit of a distraction from the horror he had just seen in the house. The slight blush that tinted his cheeks was delicious and I wanted to see more of it.

"Yes, Daddy."

At hearing his answer, I was instantly having to fight off an erection. I was *not* expecting that answer. I thought for sure he was going to say *no*. As it turned out, he apparently liked wearing them even when he wasn't about to have sex. I didn't think he could get anymore perfect.

"Naughty boy. You better not be wearing it because you were planning on having someone else touching you," I said with a false edge to my voice.

We weren't exclusive. He had every right to see who he wanted, just like I did. But the thought of another man touching him made my blood boil. I didn't want anyone touching him. He was *mine*, even if that was only for three weeks. He was *mine* to touch, to pleasure, to fuck, and I couldn't stomach the idea of another man touching him, being inside of him.

"No, Daddy, only you."

"Then why wear it, my sweet boy?"

"It's comforting. It makes me feel like

I'm not alone," he softly admitted as he looked down.

I could tell it had been an issue in the past with guys he had been with. Though, I didn't get why. The thought of him walking around all day with something inside of him, knowing that he enjoyed it and all of the other toys I could have inside him, it was only turning me on. It was just further proof that he had only been with morons in the past if they had an issue with it. The fact that he found comfort in it wasn't foreign to me. I knew other submissives who enjoyed wearing a toy during the day or at night. They liked the feel of it and that was all that mattered. He shouldn't have to feel like he needed to hide that from his partner.

"I understand that, my sweet boy. Keep it in for me, okay? The thought of you walking around all day with a plug deep inside of you is driving me crazy. We are going to play all night in my sex room. Daddy is going to show you a whole new world of pleasure," I promised.

The heat was once again back in his eyes and I could tell he wanted to go right now. We couldn't, we had work to do, but tonight it was going to be just him and me and a lot of sex. He needed the break from the pain he was feeling and I was all too happy to be that break for him.

"I can't wait, Daddy."

I turned on my heel without another word and headed back over to where the crime scene was. I needed some time to cool my own body down. I was looking forward to tonight, though, and every other night for the next three weeks.

CHAPTER FIVE

Noah

I STAYED THERE in the alley for a few more minutes to try and get my emotions back under lockdown. I was not expecting to see Daddy, *William*, here today. I had been hoping he would text me, but I really hadn't been one hundred percent confident that he would.

I knew things could be said in the heat of the moment and not mean anything real. Plenty of guys had taken my number and said they would call, only for them to completely ghost me. I hated it, because they got my hopes up only to destroy them. It would have been nicer for them to tell me they were only interested in one time with me. I would have understood, because maybe *I* was only interested in a one time thing. I also understood that sometimes you could have zero emotional chemistry with someone that you felt physically attracted toward. Or you could have chemistry, but you just didn't click. It happens and it wasn't something to be ashamed of. I always preferred honesty over false hope.

Letting out a sigh, I made my way back out toward the main street. I was here to help and I wouldn't be any help to anyone if I was hiding in an alley like some drug dealer. I stood there for a moment scanning the crowd. I wasn't in law enforcement. I didn't run investigations. However, I had been around enough investigators in my career to know certain things. Like how arsonists liked to come back to the scene of the crime to take in the aftermath. They liked to watch their art and that was either done in person or with a camera. I doubted a camera would have lasted in the house, which meant there was either a hidden camera somewhere across from the house or he had been here.

Possibly, he was still here, watching.

The bodies hadn't been brought out yet. The crime scene techs needed to take photos and be very careful with moving the bodies. I knew from past cases that burnt bodies could fall apart and turn to ash if you grab them the wrong way. There was a specific way you needed to handle their remains, making it a slow process.

I didn't see anyone appearing more interested than others. There were approximately twenty bystanders looking around, talking amongst themselves. It was perfectly natural for people to be here. For them to be gathering around in little groups to talk about the tragedy that had taken place. They had probably known the woman who lived in the house before it became a safe haven. They had probably all seen the children coming and going, maybe even getting on the bus with their own children.

This wasn't an area of town where you would expect an arsonist to attack. It was a shock to their community and it was going to live within them for the rest of their lives. Every day they got up, every time they walked out their front door, they would see the burned out house. It wouldn't surprise me if the owner of the home tore it down and sold the land to be built on. It would take a long time before this community would be able to heal and that couldn't start until they all felt safe in their homes.

Until the person responsible for this attack was caught.

I made my way over to the first group that contained two rather upset women and one man. He appeared to be trying to comfort them the best that he could, but it wasn't going well for him. They were very upset about the loss of life across the street and their grief appeared genuine. If I had to guess, they were close friends with the victim. The man, I wasn't certain. He appeared to be upset, but he wasn't crying or showing any pain. That didn't mean he didn't care about the situation, he just might be better at keeping his emotions in check.

"Excuse, I'm sorry to have to do this right now, but I was hoping I could speak to you about what has happened," I started.

"No, of course," the man said, his voice

shaky with emotions. Maybe he wasn't holding up as well as he appeared.

"I'm Noah Riley, I'm a Federal Prosecutor. I'm going to be helping on this case. Did any of you know the victim?"

"Yeah, we knew her. She was such a sweet soul. Mel has been living in that house for six years now. She used to have a husband, but it didn't work out. He couldn't keep it in his pants. She was only thirty-eight, but she felt like maybe her time for her own children was up," the blonde female started.

"She approached us with the idea of her becoming a foster parent about six months ago. She was really excited about it and Sandy and I live across the street, so we told her we would help, should she need it. We just wanted her to be happy," the brunette added.

"Kate and I are dating, she called me at work this morning to tell me about the fire. I came right back here. We had all been hoping that everyone had made it out," the man said.

"And your name is?" I asked.

"Alex Nesbitt. I tend to be here at night with Kate and Sandy. Normally, one of the kids is over looking for some help with their science homework," he said with a warm smile at the memory.

"Mel had no idea she would be up to nine kids, but I swear she loved each and every one of them. Whenever one needed a home, she never said no. She told us once it didn't matter how many of them there were. She felt like if she said no to them, she was telling a child they weren't wanted. She grew up with pretty crappy parents. She never wanted to make a child feel unwanted. She never wanted to make a child feel like they weren't good enough for a home," Sandy said with tears building in her eyes.

"And the kids were amazing. Some of them we could tell had a rough life already. They were shy and took a bit to open up and get used to being around people. Mel was telling us about one little boy who was six, Austin. It took her weeks to get him to sleep in his bed instead of hidden underneath it. We knew they all came from a dangerous background. Mel knew that going in, but she just said they were the ones who needed the most love and attention. We never thought something like this could happen to any of them," Kate said as the tears started to roll down her cheeks.

"Who would do this? Mel would have been bad enough, but the others... They were just children. What could they have possibly done to deserve something like this?" Alex asked, with anger starting to show.

None of them were faking their emotions. They were genuinely confused and upset by the fire. Alex also had an alibi that could easily be checked. He wasn't our arsonist. As most arsonists were white, middle-aged males, so that ruled out the women. Not to mention women didn't tend to kill children. They were caring and nurturing, generally. They wouldn't kill a child in this type of fashion. Poison tended to be more their go-to for killing methods. It was simple, easy, and the child just went to sleep. There was minimum pain or mess involved, so it was as close to humane as you could get where murder was concerned.

"Did Mel have any problems? Was there anyone hanging around, maybe?" I asked.

"She's never told us of anything. And if there had been a problem, she would have. She knew that the kids with her needed added protection. If there was even a whiff of an issue, she would have reported it," Kate answered.

"This area is mostly families. We're all close. We have block parties with all of the kids. We take turns on Halloween with taking the kids out so the rest of us can stay home and give out candy. We're always helping each other with projects or school fundraisers. We're a tight knit community. Even our delivery drivers are all the same," Sandy added.

"Someone would have stood out if they were snooping around someone's home," Alex confirmed.

Hmmm, that's interesting. I'd have to see what the other bystanders said, but if that was true, then the arsonist was able to get to our victim's house without anyone noticing him. Or he lived in the community. He could have easily assimilated himself within the community. Either by being a delivery driver, or dating someone in the community. This arsonist had clearly done his homework. He knew how close the community was. Which meant, he had watched this community. We might be able to catch him scooping out our victim's home weeks before the fire.

"Thank you. I'm truly sorry for all of your loss. I know this isn't going to be easy to recover from and the last thing you want to do is have to answer any questions. I really appreciate you taking the time to talk with me about this," I said, flashing the group a kind smile.

"We just want to help. We want justice for Mel and all of the children. None of them deserved this. If any of us can help, we're going to," Sandy said with determination flooding her voice.

I got the feeling that she was speaking for everyone in the community and not just her and her two friends.

"I appreciate that. If you think of anything, please don't hesitate to call the Federal Protection Agency and ask for myself."

"That's that new agency that has been helping to solve crimes against children. I've seen them on the news a few times after a big arrest. They're working this case?" Alex said, and it was clear he was surprised that it had been handed over to the Agency so quickly.

"Your friend's house was only targeted

because one of the children was the target of this arsonist. We don't know which one yet. However, your friend didn't just take in any children. Every child she had in her care was there because they needed the added protection. Some were being kept away from violent parents and others were set to testify against dangerous criminals, but had no family to live with while they waited for their court date. Your friend took in the children who needed the most help, the most love. She was an honorable woman and I wish more people in the world were like her," I explained with a small smile.

"Oh my god. I had no idea. She never said anything. When she got the safety glass put in, she said it was just to make the kids feel safer. Some of them were really terrified to be in the house or around anyone. It made sense that she would want them to feel safe in the house," Kate said, clearly upset by the new piece of information.

I wasn't surprised that Mel had kept that aspect away from her friends. She most likely didn't want them to worry about her or about the children. It also would have been easier to protect them as well. If her friends didn't know the full story, then anyone who came around asking about the children, they wouldn't have to play dumb. They would truly be in the dark and not worth assaulting for the information. Still, that didn't make the blow of the information any easier to accept. They most likely felt like their friend didn't trust them with that information.

"We could have helped her. We could have kept a better eye on the house. Had cameras installed. We would have helped her," Alex said.

"I'm sure she knew that. She was probably trying to protect you from any blowback. Your friend did an amazing thing by taking in those kids. She was just trying to keep you all safe as well," I offered.

The girls started to cry again and Alex was instantly wrapping his arms around them. I turned away and allowed them to mourn the loss of their friend and her children in peace. I had a feeling the rest of the people I spoke with were going to have the same things to say, but I was going to talk to each and everyone of them. I was going to get all of the information that I could out of them and maybe, just maybe, we might get lucky and someone saw something that could lead us to the piece of shit who did this.

CHAPTER SIX

William

IT WAS A few minutes before eight that night and I was a ball of anxious energy. I had been waiting for this all day, craving it, and now, Noah was going to be here soon and we would get to play.

I already had my sex room ready and set up for him. I had a lot planned for him and it was going to be amazing for the both of us. I knew today had been hard on him. I could see him struggling all day and I wanted to take him away from it all. To take him away from the crime scene and all of the pain that was connected to it.

There was a very dark and black cloud that was hanging over his head and it was getting bigger and bigger by the day. Part of me wanted to talk with him and find out what was going on with him. Why he was filled with so much hurt. It wasn't any of my business and I knew I had no place in even considering asking him, but I couldn't help it. He just looked so hurt, on the edge of that cliff and I wasn't certain he wouldn't jump off.

The sound of my doorbell snapped me out of my thoughts and I was instantly smiling. Now, it was time to have fun. I pushed all thoughts away about the pain that was haunting Noah. Time to focus on the good things.

I went to the door and opened it. Noah was standing there in the same clothes that he had been wearing earlier in the day. I was happy to see that he hadn't changed, because that meant he likely still had the plug in as I'd asked.

"Come on in, my sweet boy," I said as I moved back.

"Thanks, Daddy," he said as he edged past me and headed inside.

I wasn't certain how he felt about the

Daddy part yet. If he was bothered by it, I would be fine with dropping it. It wasn't a need that I had. It was more that I didn't want to be called something that the guys at work would call me. He hadn't cringed when I first said it, and he continued to use it, so I was hoping he was okay with it.

I could tell my house impressed him as he strolled through and looked around. It was an older home that had been abandoned and set on fire several years ago. I had actually been one of the firefighters who had been on call to put it out. Where everyone else saw a piece of garbage, I saw potential. Thankfully, the bones of the place hadn't been affected by the fire.

The owner had been more than happy to sell it to me at a steep discount just so he could get out from under it. I had done most of the work myself, gutting the inside completely and rebuilding it from start to finish, and I was very proud of it. I had worked hard on it. I even had a hot tub on my back patio with a big outdoor kitchen. I spent most of my time outside, enjoying the stars and listening to the peaceful night. That was my thing, what I did to relax, and this house was perfect for that.

Once he'd taken a few moments to familiarize himself with the layout of my home, impatience flooded through me and I pushed him up against the wall in the living room, pushing my hips against his groin with a growl.

His eyes reflected back the heat and excitement I was already feeling, and without waiting another second, I claimed his lips with my own. He let me control the pace of the kiss, melting into it as if he'd finally been given a reward he'd been waiting for all day. I took everything he was offering, running my hand down the front of his shirt, over his hips, and around to grab his firm ass. I pulled my mouth from his, my breathing already heavy.

"You still wearing the plug in here? You left it there for Daddy as requested, right?" I confirmed, even though I knew he probably was. I needed to hear him say it.

He licked his lips, the action sending a jolt rushing to my already hard cock. "Yes, Daddy," he breathed out, pushing his ass back into my hand, a little grin turning up the corners of his lips.

"Good boy," I praised, nipping once more at his mouth before pulling away reluctantly.

"Come," I ordered as I turned away from him and strolled off down the hallway.

I heard the sound of his footsteps as he followed me without questioning where we were even going. He obviously needed this just as badly as I did.

I guided him down the hallway until we reached my playroom. I had already unlocked it, so I simply opened the door and walked in. I turned around so I could see his reaction and he did not disappoint.

His eyes flooded with a mixture of surprise, anticipation, and arousal. I could tell he knew that he was going to have one of the best, if not *the* best, night of his life in my playroom.

In the room, I had a wooden Saint Andrews cross along the one wall, a sex swing hanging from my ceiling, and in the middle of the room, there was a wooden sawhorse type spanking bench bolted to the floor that had restraints attached to it. In the back of the room, behind red draperies, a king size, four poster bed covered with crimson satin sheets lay in wait, but he'd see that later.

Along every wall, there were different types of restraints, paddles, floggers, and whips. I even had leashes and collars, for those who accepted that type of play. I had a dresser along the right wall that was filled with even more sex toys including vibrators, dildos of all sizes from small to enormous, cock cages, and an assortment of butt plugs. The top drawer also contained several boxes of condoms and packets of lube. I had put in a lot of money toward building this playroom and outfitting it with everything I liked, but it was all worth it.

"Strip," I ordered as I faced him.

"Yes, Daddy."

He urgently began to remove his clothing as I watched him, my cock starting to thicken with each piece of clothing he discarded. The second he was naked, I could clearly see he was rock hard and ready to play.

"Safe words?"

Red, yellow, green, Daddy."

"Thank you. Good boy."

I walked over to him slowly, stalking

him in a sense, before I stood behind him. I grasped the back of his neck and guided him over to the spanking bench. I pushed on the back of his neck so he bent forward over it.

I went around and attached the restraints to both his wrists and his ankles, making sure they were snug but not too tight. It would keep him bent over the spanking bench and with his legs fully spread, putting his ass on perfect display for me. It also kept him completely at my mercy. I could do whatever I wanted to him and he wouldn't be able to stop me.

I left him there and went over to my dresser and pulled out a vibrating cock ring before I went over and grabbed one of the collars and a leash off the hooks on the wall. I strode confidently back over to my boy and attached the collar around his neck before adding the leash to the back of the collar where the metal ring was. I dropped the leash over the top of the spanking bench for later. I then went and slipped on the vibrating ring as I spoke.

"Have you ever worn one of these before my boy?"

"No, Daddy." I could hear his breathing had gone up a notch.

"You are in for a very special treat tonight, my boy," I said as I turned the vibrating cock ring onto the highest setting.

He instantly let out a deep moan, his cock already leaking pre-cum from the slit as the strong vibrations sent a wave of pleasure up his body. I had known he would enjoy it. He loved playing with toys, so it made logical sense that a vibrating ring was going to be something he was going to love. I wouldn't be surprised if he went out and purchased one after this. He might be interested in purchasing a few other toys by the end of the night, too.

I went back over to the dresser and pulled open the bottom drawer. I dug out one of the silver aluminum dog bowls before I went back over to Noah. I placed it down on the floor right where I knew his cum would go as I bent toward him and spoke gruffly in his ear.

"You can come as much as you want, but you'll have to clean it all up afterward."

"Yes, Daddy," he said in a breathy voice, his breath hitching as he began to breathe faster.

I moved and stood behind him, still fully dressed. I ran my hand down his back and over his ass. I then proceed to slap his ass as hard as I could, causing Noah to let out a deep moan as the sting brought him a great deal of pleasure.

"You like that, my little slut?" I asked as I slapped him once again, enjoying the bloom of crimson that spread across his ass cheek.

"Yes, Daddy," he moaned out, panting heavily now.

"You're going to count each one until you come," I said as I slapped him, this time making sure to hit the end of the plug, enjoying the little jerk of his body as I connected.

"Yes, Daddy," he whimpered, and I knew it wouldn't be too long before he was coming.

With each slap on his ass, Noah counted like a good boy. I loved spanking my submissive and it was even better if they got pleasure out of it as well. Noah clearly loved to be spanked so I didn't have to hold back. I spanked him until his ass was nice and red.

After twenty, open-handed slaps, ten

on each pale ass cheek, I slid my belt from my pants and folded it in half before I spanked him with it. The added sting caused Noah to give a whimper of mixed pain and pleasure on each stroke, his cock leaking copious amounts of fluid now.

I knew his pleasure had spiked, that he teetered on that edge, and it wouldn't be long now before he was coming. I was also going to have the pleasure of seeing the red welts on his ass for the next few days.

After another ten lashes across his ass, Noah bucked, his balls pulled up tight, and he let out a long, low moan as he came. I watched as his cum hit the bowl like it was supposed to.

"That's my good slutty boy. I want that bowl full of your cum," I ordered as I hit him once more with my belt, laying one final welt across his crimson, swollen skin.

"Yes, Daddy," he cried out with a shaky voice as he continued to jet rope after rope of milky fluid into the bowl below him.

I tossed my belt down to the floor before I got down on my knees behind him. I spread his cheeks and pulled out the plug, tossing it down on the ground as well. His hole was stretched and perfect, it was just waiting for a dick to fill it up. He wasn't stretched enough for me, but that was good. I liked it when he was all tight and I knew he enjoyed the sting of pain of me entering him.

It was just another way he was perfect.

Licking my lips, I leaned in and ran the flat of my tongue over his hole. The second I made contact, Noah hissed and let out another long and deep moan. Eating ass was one of my favorite things to do. He tasted sweet and I knew it would drive him crazy. He was sensitive and I knew he would enjoy it even more post-coital.

He tried to push his hips back, begging me for more, but the restraints kept him in place. Squeezing his ass cheeks in my grip, I spread him as far as I could and then I pushed the tip of my tongue inside of him. The sensation seemed to break Noah for a second time and he let out a wail.

"Fuck, Daddy," he moaned, whimpering as he came again from the pleasure coursing through him.

"Coming so much already. Such a good boy you are. You taste so sweet, I could do this all night."

I went back to licking and sucking his tight hole and he couldn't stop moaning and bucking at each invasion of my tongue. I continued to lick him until he came twice more and his legs were trembling. The sounds of his moans each time he came were almost enough to make me come in my pants without being touched. I needed to be inside of him, though, and I needed it now.

I stood up and made my way around to the front of him. I grabbed a chunk of his hair and pulled his head up. I rubbed his face into my still-covered cock as I spoke.

"Is this what my sweet boy wants?"

"Yes, Daddy. I want it so badly. Please, fuck me, Daddy," he begged, panting.

I used my free hand and undid my pants and pulled my hard dick out. I brought it over to his mouth and he easily opened up wide for me. I pushed myself in all the way until my balls hit his full lips. I didn't go slow or easy with him. I knew he wanted it rough and I knew from the last time that he could handle my size. He was, after all, quite the cock slut.

I started to thrust my hips and I fucked his mouth hard and fast. Noah didn't stop moaning his appreciation as my dick slid all over his tongue. He was a true bottom, he loved having a dick inside him, no matter which hole was filled, and I knew he was going to love everything I did to him.

I knew I wasn't going to last long. I was too worked up after listening to him moaning and coming for close to an hour now. It was only a few minutes later when I snapped my hips forward and buried myself completely within his mouth. Fire burned through my spine and my balls pulled up tight as I let out a deep groan, and then I came hard and deep down his throat.

Noah was instantly swallowing everything that I had to offer him. He didn't miss a drop, and that made me so proud. I stroked his hair, murmuring over and over how good a boy he was as I continued to pulse, emptying myself in his hot mouth.

I was still half hard, so despite the sensitivity, I continued to thrust a few more times to get fully hard again before I pulled out. Noah whined at the loss of my dick inside of him, but I knew soon enough he was going to be whimpering and begging for more.

I moved away from Noah and began to remove my clothes rapidly. Once I was naked, I went back over and grabbed the chain leash that I had left over the spanking bench. I pulled it so tight it lifted Noah's head up. The tightness from the collar and the pull of the chain increased the tightness around his throat. It was enough to push Noah over the edge again.

"Fuck, that's it, fill up that bowl," I said as I slapped Noah's still scarlet ass, causing him to whimper even more. "I'm going to fuck you now, my sweet boy."

"Yes, please, Daddy. I can't wait to feel you fill up my hungry ass," he pleaded, wiggling his ass as much as he could on the bench despite the restraints.

I lined the broad head of my cock up with his partly stretched hole and then slowly pushed inside of him. We both moaned at how glorious his ass felt as it stretched around my girth. I continued to push myself all the way down to my base without stopping. I knew he loved the sting so I didn't even bother with letting him adjust to the intrusion.

I instantly pulled out and then slammed back into him. I kept my pace fast and brutal, something I knew we were both craving. We were both moaning as our bodies took pleasure from the other. It was rough and aggressive, but it was exactly what we both needed in order to feel that much-needed stress relief. This was only just the beginning, though, because I wouldn't be stopping for a long while. I was going to get everything I could out of Noah before I allowed him to have a break.

***

It was a good two hours later when I finally ran out of steam. My legs needed a break and I was confident Noah did as well. We were both breathing heavily and there was cum running down Noah's legs from his ass.

It was beautiful.

He was so beautiful.

I turned off the vibrating ring before I pulled it off his cock and then went and removed the restraints. I kept a hold of the leash and dragged Noah down by it so he was kneeling on the ground as I spoke.

"Lick it all up, my naughty boy."

"Yes, Daddy," he said with a heavy breath and a lick of his lips.

He bent forward and started to slurp up his own cum from the bowl. Seeing him doing that almost made me hard all over again.

He could not get any more perfect.

The peace that he brought, it was intoxicating, and I was starting to doubt that I would ever feel it again with anyone else.

"That's my good little slut," I praised as I watched Noah lick up every last drop like a good boy.

Once Noah finished, his tongue tracing his lips for any stray drops of his cum, I pulled him to his feet, but I had to catch him as he swayed slightly.

"Hey, you okay?" I asked, worried as I leaned Noah against the spanking bench.

"Yeah, sorry, my legs are a little numb," he said, flashing me a small warm smile.

I spoke as I removed the collar and leash. "Sorry, I probably should have changed up positions on you a couple of hours ago."

"I'm not sorry," he said with a big

smile, and I knew he was very pleased with himself.

"Come on, I know just the thing we both need to relax for a bit," I said as I took his hand.

I shouldn't be doing this. I should be telling him to get dressed and leave, but I wasn't ready for him to be gone yet. I wasn't ready for the calm and peace that came with him to be gone. And I suspected he wasn't ready for it to be gone either.

CHAPTER SEVEN

Noah

MY WHOLE BODY was tingling, I almost felt high, and I was loving the sensation. Nothing beat the feeling of headspace to chill out the voices in my head. My legs were starting to come back to me. I hated when they fell asleep, that pins and needles sensation, but it was worth the insane amount of pleasure that William had given to me.

This round of sex had been even better than last time. And just like last time, he had brought this calm feeling over me. Everything disappeared when I was with him and I knew I was going to become addicted to him. To that quiet and peace. I didn't know what he felt around me, but I was hoping he was enjoying the time he got to spend with me as well, in more than just a sexual way.

I wasn't sure where we were going, but I easily followed him as he guided me outside. It was dark, so I couldn't see too well, but I did make out a pretty fabulous outdoor kitchen and seating area. He guided me over to an extra large hot tub and I instantly knew what the plan was.

"It's already hot. You hop in and I'll grab us something to drink," he said, flashing me a warm smile.

I didn't need to be told twice. I climbed into the hot, steaming water and the second it hit my sore legs I was in heaven all over again. It was a nice hot tub and it was deep with wide seats. Whoever designed this had clearly been thinking about someone being in it for a long time and planned it to be comfortable. The hot water felt amazing on my muscles and I was in no hurry to get out. I thought tonight I would have had to spend a couple of hours in the tub at the hotel to ease the aches, but this was more than doing the trick.

William strolled back out with two water bottles and two bottles of beer. He handed me one of each after opening them before he climbed into the hot tub himself, and slid onto the seat across from me.

"Thanks," I said before I took a long drink from the water bottle. The cold water felt good on my throat. I was very thirsty and my throat was dry from all the moaning and oral sex.

William moved so he was lying back on the bench seat facing me. He then reached out to grab my free hand and pulled me over to him. He turned me to lie with my back against his thick chest before he draped his right arm over me and rested his hand against my chest. I easily leaned back against him taking in all of the comfort he was giving to me with the simple cuddling.

I hadn't tended to cuddle with any partner I had been with, not even my long term ones. Though I usually just preferred to have sex and then go our separate ways, it wasn't always like that. When I had first started dating and having sex, the guys used to hang around. We would fall asleep and go out on dates, like most of the other couples I saw around us. That quickly changed, though, as I got older. It was like I was suddenly not good enough to take on a date. To be more than just some submissive they could use in the bedroom.

I knew part of that was my fault. I had gotten used to being treated that way. It had gotten to the point that I accepted it and expected that things would go that way. I had accepted that I would be treated like I was some cheap whore they'd picked up for the night. I knew I should've been demanding more, but I also didn't know how well that would have gone over so I didn't. I didn't want to lose the stress relief that they were providing me with the sex so I kept my mouth shut and dealt with it.

That had become my life and something as simple as a cuddle was now so foreign to me. It was pathetic and sad, but it was my life and once I got back to New York it would be my life once again.

"It's beautiful out here," I said as I gazed up at the stars. I didn't need to be thinking about my past or what awaited me back home. I needed to soak in every moment with William that I could. It was going to be what got me through the darker days when I got home.

"It is and so are you," he whispered into my ear.

I knew it could have easily been some cheesy line, but I chose to believe he meant it. That he did see me that way and wasn't just telling me some line that he thought I wanted to hear.

"Can I ask you something?" he asked, and that surprised me.

Most of the dominants I had been with never asked permission before they said or did anything. They always did what they wanted regardless of what I said.

"You're the Dom, you can do anything. That's how it works, right?" I said with a small smirk.

"That's not how I operate. Yes, I like to be in control in the bedroom and there are things outside of the bedroom that I like to control. I like having a routine and I like picking where I eat. However, I don't have to control every conversation or every little decision. I have no interest in having a slave in my life. If there is something you don't want to talk about, then just say so.”

I was surprised by that. I would have figured he would want someone to do what he says all the time and to stay quiet. He didn't come across as someone who would want to hit pause on the control outside of the bedroom. Him wanting to control certain aspects of his life, I was good with. I didn't really care where I ate and it made sense that he would want a routine with his job.

It was refreshing, though, to be with a Dom, even for a little while, who didn't want to have control twenty four seven. I was pretty easy going and I could adapt to just about anything. I liked it when the guy I was with picked where we ate or what we did. Not that I'd really had much of that in the past decade. Still, when I was younger, I had enjoyed it.

“Does that mean I don't have to call you *Daddy* outside of the bedroom?” I asked.

“No, you don't. I know the Daddy thing can be weird. Honestly, I just didn't want to be called *Sir*, because the guys at work call me that. I didn't like *Master* because that felt like I was a slave owner. Someone suggested *Daddy* a long time ago and I stuck with it."

Now that made sense. I would imagine it would be weird to be called *Sir* all day long and then have someone you are having sex with call you that, too. A lot of the guys I had been with preferred *Master*, but they loved their guys to be slaves. One I had slept with had even wanted to control when I could eat and when I could take a piss. I turned him down right quick. I was not looking to have someone control every second of my life.

"It's not weird. I've never called anyone that before. But I never really liked *Master* and you not wanting to be called *Sir* makes sense. I'm good with it. What did you want to ask me?"

"You can tell me it's none of my business if you want. I was just wondering what it was that made you take a three week vacation. When I saw you this morning at the crime scene, I could see a lot of pain in your eyes. You have a look that is all too familiar to me. I've seen it plenty of times with other first responders," he started, gently.

"What look is that?" I asked, trying to postpone the obvious question.

I had been worried Ryzen would notice that something more was going on with me, but he hadn't. At least, not yet. That might have had something to do with getting called away to the crime scene so soon after I had arrived at the Agency. I knew it was going to be a conversation that came up in the near future with him, though. The problem was, I wasn't sure what I was going to tell him when he asked. He knew I didn't take vacation days really, and never had I ever taken three weeks off before. Not even when I was sick and ended up in the hospital with a bad case of pneumonia. I was back to work within a week of getting out of the hospital. I was always working, so it was against my behavior to take three weeks off.

It shouldn't have been surprising that William had seen the pain within me, but it was. It would make sense that he would be able to see it. He was a fire captain. He would have seen plenty of people struggling with the darkness in his job. Still, I didn't think he would be paying much attention to me. I didn't think I would be worth the effort of him paying attention to me.

"The look of someone who is drowning and has lost the energy to swim up to the surface. There's a lot of pain in you and I have to wonder if you took a vacation with the hope that it would give you the energy to keep swimming up for air. Or if you took it knowing that when you got home you would let the water take you."

He didn't say it outright, but basically he was concerned that I would kill myself when I got home. It wasn't that surprising with the statistics of suicide for first responders. I would never take my own life, that wasn't something he had to worry about. He shouldn't even be worried about me. We didn't know each other outside of the bedroom. I didn't understand why he seemed to care about me.

"I'm not going to drown. I don't take vacation time. I barely take sick time. The last few months, I had been working a case that fell through and the asshole walked free. It was kinda the last straw for me. I packed up that night and drove down from New York City. I didn't even tell Ry that I was coming. I arrived last night and headed to the club after checking in at my hotel. I guess I just figured that maybe this vacation would turn the clock back or something. I don't know."

And I didn't know. I didn't know what to do. I felt like I was having this mid-life crisis, only I wasn't buying a sports car or a motorcycle. I had no reason to be feeling this way. There were prosecutors ten years older than me and they were still able to show up for work every day. They didn't feel the way that I did.

So why did I?

Why couldn't I do it like they were?

I didn't understand, and I didn't know how to stop it. I didn't want to be this weak. I was supposed to be strong. I was supposed to be brave and unstoppable and yet, the only peace I found is when a man was controlling me and using my body as their own personal sex toy. It was screwed up.

I was screwed up.

"There's nothing wrong with wanting to get away from it all. With needing a break from the stress of your job."

"Says the firefighter. You literally run into burning buildings. You see dead bodies all the time and you aren't running away. I have no real excuse for not being able to do my job."

"What was the last case that you worked? Care to talk about it?" he asked, gently.

I let out a soft sigh before I spoke. I really didn't want to have to talk about it, but he also had a right to know why I was down here. What had brought me out here. Who knew, maybe talking would help.

"Gil Ramirez, he was a human trafficker that federal agencies had been chasing for years all across the country. He'd always been able to get out of town just before the raid happened. He used under age girls, some as young as eleven, to run a string of brothels. The brothel itself was always legal, but he filled it with girls who are runaways or in the foster system. Girls who don't get reported missing. He finally came to New York City and the Feds grabbed him. It was my job to make sure he went away for life. I interviewed every one of the girls and had to listen to their stories and the horrors he put them through. Not all of them agreed to testify, but the ones who did had to do it in open court. Ramirez' attorney made it appear like they had lied about their ages. That he couldn't possibly have known they weren't eighteen. The jury believed him. That was our one chance to shut him down and put him in jail where he belonged and the jury listened to those girls' stories and they believed him. For three months, I had been working with them to build the case and the system just tossed them away like they weren't important." I sighed and sucked in a breath.

"Seeing the look on those girls' faces when the verdict came in, fuck, I could see it destroy each and every one of them. They had been told that their case would be easy to prove. That it was going to be hard on them to testify, but all the jury would need to convict was to hear their stories. And they had heard their stories and only heard lies. They didn't hear the deep pain within their voices. They didn't see the trauma that those girls were now going to have to live with. All they saw were young girls who had tried to ruin a good businessman." I shook my head.

"I knew that trial outcome was going to be a tipping point for some of them and there would be nothing I could do to keep them from falling off the cliff. I had seen it so many times. Victims of sex crimes who are told it was their fault or they must have wanted it but now regret it. Too many times I'd seen victims of rape and human trafficking turn to drugs and prostituting because was all they knew. It was what they thought they were only worth. It was just too much that time." I was aware that my voice hitched, my emotions raw again as I finished telling William about the case.

"I'm sorry that happened to them. The system isn't perfect, but it's allowed to be imperfect when you are dealing with a minor crime. Crimes where lives have been destroyed, they should never be taken lightly. Victims should never have to feel ashamed or unheard. It shouldn't have happened to them. I don't blame you for wanting to get away after all of that. You might not run into burning buildings, Sweetness, but you still hear and see trauma every day. You have to listen to the victims and their stories. You have to relive the worst days of their lives with them over and over again. You have to fight for them. It's not a fire, but your job is extremely stressful and that isn't something you should take lightly."

"I'm just hearing it, though. I didn't go through it. There are prosecutors far older than me who have been able to handle it. I should be able to, too."

"That's not how trauma works. I know guys younger than me who quit being a firefighter because it was too hard. Not the physical aspects, but having to see people's lives being destroyed. I know people older than me who have killed themselves because of all the loss they had experienced in the job. Everyone reacts differently to trauma. You can't compare yourself to the others, because you don't know how they are handling it. What people see on the outside isn't always what is going on internally. Those other prosecutors could be drunks for all you know. There's nothing wrong with taking a breather. With considering a career change. You're entitled to be happy and healthy, Sweetness."

"I don't know what to do. I know I'm supposed to go back, but everything in me is screaming for me to stay here, find something new. But I'm a prosecutor, damn it, what the hell would I do otherwise?"

William kissed the side of my head as

he ran fingers through my hair over and over in a soothing motion. He was trying to comfort me and I appreciated it. The only thing keeping me together right now was feeling his skin against mine. To know that he was there with me. Even being next to him was helping the chaos within me to calm down. I don't know what it was about him, but the world was more bearable when I was around him. Which was not helping me in making a decision on if I should stay in Baton Rouge or go back to New York. I had to remember this was just a temporary thing between us. I couldn't let myself foolishly hope that it would be something more if I lived here.

"No one said you couldn't be a lawyer still. You could teach at the University. You could switch to business law. Hell, you could probably work for the Agency. You have options, Sweetness. You just have to decide if you would like to go back to New York or not. If it is hurting you, and I can see that it is, why go back to a life that will only cause you more pain? If there is one thing I know, it's that life is short and no one is guaranteed tomorrow. Live your life with as much joy that you can because you might not get the chance tomorrow to do it. You have three weeks off. Take the time to get your own thoughts and emotions back in control. Once you are able to think more clearly, you'll be able to make a proper decision."

He was right, no one was guaranteed a tomorrow. I had been trying to live my life with that philosophy, but I had been more focused on trying to help as many people as I could before my time was up. I realized I hadn't been focused on *my own* happiness and health. I needed to take some time to get my thoughts back in proper order and then I would think and plan what I wanted to do. I had three weeks, so I could look into the option of staying here and what that would look like. See how I felt about any of it.

"Sorry for dumping all of this on you."

"I asked. And you have to talk about it with someone. Though, I have to imagine your brother would understand. He seems like a dark and tormented man."

I couldn't help the small snort at that. He had no idea how screwed up Ryzen could be. "He had a hard life, including being a child soldier in Africa. He would understand, but he would also worry and tell me to stay. If I stay, I want it to be because I want to stay. I want it to be because I feel like it's the right decision to make and not what other people want me to do. This isn't a decision I can allow someone else to make for me, unfortunately. I have to be the one to make it."

There had been plenty of times in my life where I had allowed someone else to make the decisions. However, this was my life, my career, the decision was only mine to make, even if it would be easier for me to let someone else do it. I had to be the one to live with it.

"You're absolutely right. This is a decision only you can make. However," he started, before he turned me around and I was instantly straddling his lap. He slipped inside of me and I was instantly moaning at the feel of him. "I could think of a few perks if you stayed longer than three weeks, my sweet boy."

"And what would they be, Daddy?" I said, flashing him a smirk as he grasped my hips and started to lightly move me up and down on his hardness.

"A very healthy sex life, for starters. I don't know how you feel, but when I'm with you the storm that consumes my mind goes quiet. I've never had someone make me feel so at peace before, and I'm not in any hurry to lose that."

That surprised me, because I didn't think he felt the same. He brought calmness to my own storm. He was the first man to ever make it all go quiet and peaceful. It warmed my heart to hear that I was bringing the same peace to him.

"You make me feel the same. I don't know why, but you make me feel better than anyone ever has. Getting to keep seeing you would be a very big perk to me staying here."

I let out a loud moan as he hit my sweet spot. I was beyond sensitive right now and I wasn't certain I was going to last very long, even at this speed. His lips captured mine as he started to move me even faster on top of him. He lightly thrust up to match my downward motions, pushing himself even deeper inside of me.

My whole body was tingling already and I knew it wasn't going to be long before either of us came. We were both so sensitive and worked up. You would think after all the sex we'd just had that we would be too tired to even be able to get an erection, but our bodies sang for one another. Our need was too great and I loved how he could make me feel so needy. It was weird, because I figured by now I shouldn't still be craving his touch. Logically, I should want to go back to my hotel room and rest, but I felt like I could go for weeks with him without stopping.

He devoured me with his kiss, allowing me to feel everything that he himself was feeling. He showed me all of his passion and desire for me through his lips, his touch, and I gave it right back to him.

I let out a whimper as I felt his calloused hand wrap around my dick, gripping me tightly as his thumb spread a pearl of pre-cum over my slit. I was never going to get tired of the way his strong hands felt on my body.

"That's it, my sweet boy. Come for Daddy. I'm right behind you," he said with a heavy breath as he picked up his pace.

My whole body felt like it was on fire as my balls pulled up tight and I cried out as each thrust battered my prostate.

How was it possible to crave someone this badly?

I didn't know what was happening

between us, but I never wanted it to end. It didn't take long at all before I was tumbling off the cliff once again.

"Daddy..." I moaned as I pulsed in his hand, my ass muscles clamping down around his cock.

The tightening of my walls pushed him over the edge and he snapped me down onto his dick as he came hard and long inside of me. I had no idea how he even still had cum left in him with the amount of times he'd come already this evening. But once again, I felt his heat flood my insides and it brought me a feeling of completeness. I never wanted this to end. He could have locked me up in his bedroom right then and I would have happily spent the rest of my life there.

I placed my forehead against his as I fought to catch my breath. The heat from the hot tub was not helping my head any at all. I was starting to get all floaty from the heat and the pleasure. William pulled back and placed a kiss on my forehead before he spoke.

"I think it's time to head into the bedroom."

I just gave a nod and he lifted me up and off of him. We both climbed out of the water and dried off with fluffy warmed towels.

I followed William into his bedroom and saw that he had a king size, four poster bed, so there was plenty of room to roll around in it. It was a nice bedroom and he had clearly taken his time working on it. There was a flat screen television mounted on the wall across from the bed. There was an electric fireplace underneath the tv and a bathroom just off to the right of it. It was a very nice bedroom and I could picture someone spending a lot of time in here.

"As much as I would love to play again, we both need sleep," William said as he pulled the covers back on the bed.

I was prepared to have sex again, but hearing that he wanted me in here so we could sleep sent a whole different type of pleasure rushing through me. He actually wanted to *sleep* with me, to cuddle and wake up next to each other. I couldn't even remember the last time that had happened in my life.

I climbed into the cool sheets as William turned the lights off and went around to the other side. The second he got under the covers, he wrapped his arm around my waist and pulled me over to him. I turned so my back was against his chest like he wanted me. He curled up behind me and I could feel his dick against my ass. He kissed the back of my neck as he spoke.

"Perfect, you can have that when you wake up in the morning. Good night, my sweet boy."

"Good night, Daddy," I said back as I enjoyed the feeling of his dick pressed against my ass. I closed my eyes and it didn't take long before I was able to fall asleep curled up in his arms.

CHAPTER EIGHT

William

I HAD NEVER been one for cuddling, but for some reason with Noah I couldn't help myself. I wanted to be able to hold him. I wanted to try and give him some strength to keep fighting, to keep moving forward. At the same time, I wanted to feel him pressed against me. I wanted to continue feeling the peace that he brought into my life.

I didn't understand why he made me feel that way, but I didn't care to dissect it, either. The fact was, he made me feel more at peace. He made the storm within me go quiet and I loved that feeling. It had been so long since I had been able to feel that way and I'd honestly never expected to ever again. Getting to spend this time with Noah had been a dream come true and I wasn't ready to let him go.

I knew there was a high chance that he would go back to New York. I had seen the same thing plenty of times with first responders. They went back to work when they shouldn't and it continued to eat away at their soul. I didn't want that for Noah, though. I didn't want him to become a shell of a man, because from what I had seen so far, he was one hell of a man. He didn't deserve to lose anymore of himself, especially to his job.

I knew what he did was important and I would never say it wasn't. He helped to put dangerous criminals behind bars. He was doing this world a great service, but I also knew how draining it was on him. How draining it would be on anyone. It was one thing to get there when someone's house was on fire, and quite another to have to listen to the victims retelling their story over and over again and then having to have someone argue that it was their own fault. It was soul wrenching and after so many years, it simply took a toll on a person.

I could see that toll all throughout Noah's eyes and I hated it. I wanted to see his eyes full of life, excitement, joy. I wanted to know what he looked like when he wasn't haunted by his job. When he was free from the trauma of it all. There were other avenues that he could take where he was still a lawyer and still helping people without it destroying him. I had every intention of trying to get Noah to see the benefits of staying here, and not just in the bedroom, but for his own life.

I glanced over at my clock and saw that it was just after eight in the morning. I had to get ready for my shift that started at ten, but I still had a bit of time this morning, so I had every intention of making the best of it.

Noah was still sleeping with his back against my chest, putting us in the perfect position for some morning fun. I knew he would still be lubed up from all the sex we'd had not that many hours ago. I was already hard and I knew soon enough, he would be as well.

I moved very carefully as I lined myself

up with his hole. I didn't want to wake him up just yet. I slowly pushed in as I knew he wouldn't be fully stretched anymore and I didn't want to hurt him. I let out a groan the second my tip breached his hole.

How was it possible for one person to feel this good?

As I continued to push inside of him, Noah let out a soft moan as he started to wake up. I kissed the back of his neck as I spoke.

"Good morning, my sweet boy."

"Morning, Daddy," he breathed out as he pushed his hips back a bit to try and get me to go in even deeper.

"Someone's needy," I teased.

"Yes, Daddy, you feel so good." He wiggled his ass and I slipped in all the way to the hilt.

Once I was all the way inside of him, I didn't stop for a second. He felt so good, so fucking good. I was never going to be able to get enough of him. Based on his reaction to my touch, Noah was feeling the same. I was already addicted to him and the thought of him not being in town made me go crazy. I didn't care what I had to do, I was not going to allow him to go back to New York. Even if that meant I had to restrain him in my bed. He was *mine* and he was always going to be mine.

He let out a loud moan, whimpering as I hit his sweet spot dead on. His body was responsive and I loved it. I hated it when the guys I was with were so quiet. I wanted to hear their pleasure. I wanted to hear their moans and pleas for more.

"You feel so good, my sweet boy. So tight and hot around Daddy's dick." I gently bit the side of his neck, causing him to whimper from the pleasure.

His phone rang, breaking the beautiful song of our moans in the room. We both looked over at it and saw that it was his brother calling him. When he made no move to answer it I spoke.

"Answer it. Could be important."

I stopped moving and he gave a whine at the loss of pleasure. He reached over and grabbed his phone and answered it.

"Hey."

I didn't hear the other end of the conversation, but I didn't need to. I immediately pulled out before I slammed back in. Noah bit down on his lip to keep himself from making any noise.

"I never said I was going to stop," I

whispered into his other ear.

"Yeah, I can do that for you," Noah said into the phone as he fought to not make a sound.

I picked up my pace, making sure to hit his sweet spot each time. A couple of times he had to turn his head into the pillow to muffle the sound of his moans.

"Yeah, I'll get started on the paperwork and submit it," Noah said.

I rolled us so he was on his knees with his upper body against the bed. The new position put even more pressure on his prostate as I brutally pounded into him. I snaked my hand around to his dick and started to stroke him in time with my thrusts. I could feel how hard he was and his tip was already wet with pre-cum dripping out of it.

I bent forward and whispered into his ear once again. "Keep him talking. I want to hear you come with your brother on the phone."

He let out a deep groan as I picked up my pace even more. I didn't care if Ryzen could hear the sound of our skin slapping against each other. I loved that I could make Noah do this. That I was going to make him come while his brother was on the phone. Every time he saw his brother from now on, he would be reminded of this and hopefully, get turned on. I was going to make him crave me all day long.

"What? No, I just hit my foot on the corner of the bed," Noah said, trying to explain the sound he'd made. "You'll be at the Agency later?"

I felt Noah's dick getting even harder and after a moment, he pushed his face into the pillow and held the phone as far away as he could as he gave a loud and deep moan as he shot line after line of cum into my hand.

"Yeah, sorry I was just trying to think of what I needed for the documents," Noah said back into the phone once he was able to form words again.

I smirked as I grabbed a chunk of his hair and pulled him up so he was up on his knees and had his back against my chest. He bit his lip once again to keep from making a sound. I held my cum-covered hand out in front of him and without even having to say anything, he started to lick it up despite the fact that his brother was on the phone.

"Okay." He paused in his cleaning. "I'll get the documents ready and file them with the court and then, I can be in with the records. We should have them by lunch time." Noah continued to lick my hand clean.

I sat back on my heels and placed my hands on his hips, pulling him tightly to my groin. I started to move him up and down on my dick, thrusting my hips upward each time I bottomed out in his ass. I kept my pace fast and brutal, making sure each time he slammed down on my dick, I was hitting his sweet spot dead on.

"Okay, I'll see you soon," Noah said, before he ended the call. He tossed his phone down onto the bed and let out a loud moan that echoed in the room.

"Such a naughty boy, coming with your brother on the phone. I think my sweet boy likes the danger of someone potentially discovering what you are doing."

"Oh yes, Daddy. I like being watched," he moaned.

Just knowing that he enjoyed a bit of exhibitionism filled my head with plenty of possibilities. All of those possibilities had me seeing stars and it didn't take long before I was coming hard and deep inside of him with a loud groan.

Noah moaned as my cum hit his walls and I knew he loved the feeling of the heat bursting inside him.

I kissed the back of his neck as my body rocked with each throb and pulse. This was never going to get old. I was never going to tire of his body.

His perfect body.

It was like he was made for me.

Like we were made for each other.

"You shower and I'll cook us some breakfast. You are to not wear a plug today, nothing inside of you. Daddy wants you nice and tight for what I have planned for you tonight, my sweet boy."

"Yes, Daddy," he said with a shaky breath, goose bumps spreading over his skin.

I slowly moved him up and off of me. I didn't let him stand, though. I pushed him down so he was lying back on the bed with his ass up in the air. I spread his cheeks so I could watch as my cum started to drip out of him. This was one of my favorite parts. Being able to see my cum dripping out of the person I was with, the physical evidence of how I owned their body, it always excited me.

"Such a perfect hole you have, my sweet boy. Such a good boy you are. Daddy is going to reward you tonight," I moaned, as I watched the spunk slowly dripping out of him.

"Thank you, Daddy."

I gave his ass a light slap as I moved back and got off of the bed. "Go get showered, I'll make breakfast. You need more than just cum in your belly."

"But it tastes so good, Daddy," he said, flashing me a playful smile that almost had me climbing back into the bed with him. I couldn't, though, we both had work to do and there would be plenty of time to play later.

I strolled out of the room without a backward glance, knowing that he would take a shower like I had instructed. I made my way into the kitchen and started to get some bacon going. I was already planning on what I was going to do with him tonight. I wanted to take him out. I didn't normally do the dating thing, but Noah was different.

He was special.

I wanted to show him that he was special to me. That he wasn't just another submissive I would use until I was bored and moved on to a new one. He was different and he deserved to be taken out and shown off. He deserved to be treated properly and I was not about to let anything stand in our way.

I knew he could be going back to New York, but I was hoping I would be able to prevent that. I hadn't been planning to try and prevent it, at first, but after last night, after waking up with him in my arms, screw it. I didn't want him to leave and I was going to do everything in my power to ensure he would stay here. Him leaving would be a mistake, I truly believed that. And it would be a mistake for the both of us.

What we had, even though it was new, it was special and not something that most people got to experience. I was not about to let Noah throw that away and I was not about to let him slip through my fingers. Not if there was something I could do about it. This was one relationship I would be fighting for.

It was ten minutes later when Noah came out of the bathroom all freshly showered and dressed for the day. I had to give it to him, he looked good in a suit.

"Is there anything I can do to help?" he

asked.

"You can keep standing there and looking sexy," I said with a smirk curling the corners of my lips.

"I think I can do that. You said you had something planned for tonight?" he asked.

"I do. I'm taking you out on a date. I'll text you later with the details when I have them."

"Okay." His eyes lit up in surprise and excitement for a split second before the emotion disappeared and he glossed over my announcement. "Do you work today?"

I knew from our short conversation that he wasn't used to someone taking him out on dates. My guess was that he was excited, but also nervous, and probably too afraid to get his hopes up for fear of being let down. That was what he was used to, after all. Which was just too bad for him, because he was going to have to get used to being treated better than he ever had before, and that included wining and dining him, because I planned on taking him out on a good number of dates. I planned on showing him he was worth so much more than he'd ever had before.

"I do. I get off at six. What did your brother want?"

"Oh, he needs access to the victims' foster care records. Even though they are dead, they are still protected under the law and the social worker for the victims is not willing to give up their files without a court order. I'll have to file the paperwork and then get the files, but like I said, we should have them by lunchtime."

"Is that normal for someone to not want to give them up?"

It didn't seem normal to me. I mean, the children were dead, had been brutally killed, I would think the social worker would want to do anything in her power to make sure they got justice.

"Yes and no. It depends on the social worker. Some of them are more than happy to hand files over. And others are more picky about it. It mostly comes down to if the social worker feels the need to hide something. If they feel like they missed something or didn't do something right, they are more inclined to hide the files unless given no other choice. That might not be the case here, but I find it weird that she won't just hand them over.

From what Ryzen has told me, there has been a serious problem with the foster care system in town. It's part of why the Agency was relocated here. They are supposed to be cleaning house and making sure every foster parent and social worker are good people and not criminals. It's a process that they are still going through."

It was a procedure that would take a long time in a town this size. However, it sounded like a course of action that they needed to do badly, so it would be worth the time and effort involved.

I shook my head. "Glad I'm not stuck on that job. Good for them, though. Sounds like it was long past due. I'm going to head for a quick shower. Keep an eye on that bacon, will you." I gave Noah a quick peck on the mouth and then made my way into the bathroom. I had to be at work in a little bit and I wanted to get my showering over and done with. It would allow me more time to spend with Noah before we would both need to head out.

The hot water felt amazing sluicing over my sore muscles. Yesterday had been a work out for myself as well as for Noah. The hot tub had felt marvelous, but we weren't in it nearly long enough to be able to really relax our stiff and sore muscles.

I gave my body a good wash so I could attempt to get Noah's cologne off of me so no one at work would be able to smell him on me. As much as I liked his scent, I couldn't risk the guys at work questioning me on why I smelled like another man. I wasn't anywhere near ready for that yet.

Once I was all cleaned, I climbed out and dried off with a fresh fluffy towel. I didn't bother with putting on clothes just yet, though. I enjoyed being naked in my own home, though I would have preferred for Noah to still be naked as well, but that might've been for the best. I was afraid we would both get too caught up in the other and it would make us both late for work.

I made my way back out to the kitchen and I smirked as I saw the heat rise in Noah's eyes as his gaze landed on my naked form. He was standing by the stove, making sure the bacon didn't burn. I had to remind myself to keep my hands to myself or we were going to be right back in my bedroom where we'd started this morning.

Once the food was ready, we went and sat down at the table to eat. I enjoyed the comfortable silence and the small talk we made about our work. It was very relaxing and felt completely normal for us. As if we had been doing it for years already.

I wasn't bothered by the fact that I was still naked and he was fully clothed. Normally, it was the other way around, the submissive would be the one who was naked, but the difference didn't bother me. It probably should, but it'd only worked out that way because he came out of the shower and got dressed. I hadn't told him not to dress after his shower, which was a mistake on my part. It would have been much more enjoyable to watch him eat naked.

"See something you like?" I asked, once we had finished eating. Noah kept looking down at my hard dick and licking his lips. I knew he wanted it. He had told me he loved giving oral and that he could do it all day if he was allowed.

"Very much so, Daddy," he answered as he glanced down once more, his tongue flicking out to trace over his pink lips.

I sat back and picked up the newspaper as I spoke. "You can play for a little while, my sweet boy, but then I have to go to work."

"Yes, Daddy."

He eagerly got down on the ground and crawled the short distance over to me. I watched as he took me into his mouth with an appreciative moan as he started to work my dick with his mouth.

I turned my attention to my newspaper. This was going to be a very good day.

CHAPTER NINE

Noah

WALKING INTO THE Agency, I couldn't help but feel terribly annoyed. I was in such a good mood this morning with William and that went downhill pretty quick when I had to deal with Ronald Johnson, the social worker for all of the victims in the house fire.

I thought that after forcing us to go and get a court order just to have the case files for our victims, he would be more than willing to hand them over. Especially considering he was the one who denied Ryzen the files when he asked, citing *policy and rules*. Mr. Johnson was the one who demanded we get a court order before he would release them. So we mistakenly thought walking into his office with said court order would make it easy for him to hand them over. I mean, he had to know we were coming with the necessary documentation.

Nope.

It took him close to an hour to slowly find them all and collect them for me. He had me waiting in his office while he dicked around for over an hour. It was bullshit and I knew he was doing it on purpose. He either had something to hide, or he didn't like that the Agency was now going to be involved with the case. I wasn't certain if he had something to hide, but I knew there were a good number of social workers who had already been terminated since the Agency came down here to clean up the system because of their handling of some cases.

I was in such a good mood this morning, too. I'd had an amazing night. I'd had the best sleep that I'd had in close to a decade. I couldn't believe that I'd slept that deeply. More often than not, it would take me forever to fall asleep, and even when I did finally get there, I slept light. I always woke up at any little sound and I could never get more than five hours of sleep on any given night. Some nights, I wouldn't even sleep. Yet being in William's arms, it brought so much comfort and security to me that I had fallen asleep almost instantly and I didn't wake up until he woke me up in the best way possible.

We were going to go on a date tonight. I couldn't believe it. I hadn't thought he would want to do anything with me outside of the bedroom, but once again he was surprising me. I had no idea where we would be going, and I didn't care. I would go anywhere with him. I would do anything with him. As annoyed as I was about Ronald, I was not going to allow him to ruin my good mood. I was looking forward to my date with William and I was going to hold onto that.

I made my way up to Ryzen's office with the box of files. Hopefully, we would be able to find something in them that would lead us to who this arsonist was, or at least who he was targeting. Once we knew who the true target was, we could look up who the defendant was that they would be testifying against.

I strolled into Ryzen's office and saw that he was there alone, tucked up behind his desk and scrolling through something on the computer. I placed the box down on the table as he spoke.

"Afternoon. That took longer than I was expecting."

"No shit. The social worker still didn't want to hand over the files. He slow-walked his ass around trying to collect everything," I complained as I sat down and removed the box lid.

"You think he's hiding something?" Ryzen asked as he joined me at the table, sliding into the seat across from me.

"I think he's old as dirt and is just trying to make it until he can retire. I got the feeling that he didn't really care that these kids were dead. He was just relieved he wouldn't have these nine cases in his roster any longer."

"Nice," he said, his voice dripping with sarcasm as he shook his head. "All right, we can go through them. There's something we have to talk about first, though."

"What's that?" I asked, hoping that he wasn't going to be asking me about the phone call we just had and doing my best to appear nonchalant. I was trying very hard not to blush at him knowing that he had listened to me not only having sex, but coming as well. Though with any luck, he wouldn't have known that was what had been going on.

"The reason you came down here. We didn't get to talk about it before this case popped off. Why didn't you tell me you were coming down?" he asked, calmly.

"It was a spur of the moment decision. It's not a big deal," I said, trying to downplay it, but I could tell by the look Ryzen was giving me he didn't believe me.

"You never take vacation days. Now all of a sudden, out of the blue, you take three weeks worth. Come on, Noah, I'm not blind. I can see that you are exhausted and struggling. What's going on?"

I knew I could tell him anything, I did. At the same time, though, it was hard, because I didn't want him to think of me as weak.

To tell me to suck it up.

He had been through so much in his life, all before he was even an adult. He had survived so much and he was incredibly strong. Stronger than I ever could be and the last thing I wanted was for him to see me as weak. I was supposed to be the big brother. I was supposed to be the one he could come to when he needed advice or help. I wasn't supposed to be the one unloading onto him. And really, compared to the things he'd been through and seen in both his childhood and his time with the CIA, I didn't really have any right to complain to him about the things I'd seen or the issues I had with it now.

"It's nothing, I'm fine," I said, trying to blow him off. I was hoping he would take the hint and let it go, but of course he didn't.

"Don't give me that shit, Noah. What's going on?" he said, with a hard edge to his voice. I knew that meant he wasn't going to let this go and he was not going to tolerate me lying to him, either.

Letting out a sigh, I sat back and told him everything. "I was working on a bad case for the last three months. A case involving underage girls being forced into sex work at a legal brothel. The few I was able to get to agree to testify were torn apart by the defendant's attorney. He claimed the same bullcrap I have heard a hundred times, that it was their fault. They lied to him about their age. They were never raped, they were willing participants and that his client was the true victim in all of this. Blah, blah, blah. It was total bullshit. Federal Agencies had been after this guy for years and we finally caught him red handed and had the chance to put him in bars. The jury deliberated for three hours before coming back with a not guilty verdict."

"Son of a bitch. So he gets to get away with it all and to start all over again in a new place. Unbelievable. So you packed up and came here?"

"I didn't even think it through. I got home and I knew I just couldn't do it. I packed my bags, loaded my car, and just started driving. All I could think about was just getting away from it all. I'm tired, Ry. And I don't know what to do. I should be going back. I should be sucking it up and going back to work. But honestly, thinking about going back, about being in another courtroom having to listen to the victim's story, it makes me feel like I can't breathe. I don't know what to do," I said, sounding completely lost and hating it.

"Then you don't go back. No job is worth your health, mentally, emotionally or physically. You look like shit, Brother. I can see the toll this job is taking on you. Even a three week vacation isn't going to hit the reset button. Stay here."

"And do what? That's what I can't figure out. What am I supposed to do? I'm a Federal Prosecutor and if I can't handle the cases, then what do I do?"

I knew I could switch legal areas. I was trained all across the board, but I was a criminal prosecutor. I had never practiced any other type of law. It wasn't like I could start my own family law or business law firm. I knew enough, but not enough to handle a serious caseload.

"You could teach. The University down here might be looking to hire a new professor. You could work with our social workers to help them with the system. I know there is a lot of legal work that needs to be done to get through all of the red tape. We can find you work, that's easy, Noah. We can find you a place to live. All of that is easy. The hard part, is you admitting that your health is more important than any case you work on. I don't mean any disrespect, but there's always another prosecutor who can take on your cases. But there's not another *you* in the world. Keeping you in the world is far more important than any job."

He was right. I wasn't irreplaceable at work. It wasn't that I wasn't good, I was excellent at my job, but so were a lot of other prosecutors. I wasn't in the middle of any cases and any future cases that would have gone to me could easily go to someone else. I could argue that right now was the perfect time for me to make the move, because I didn't have any active cases. My clients wouldn't have to deal with someone else taking on their case and having to build a rapport with them. It really might be the best time for me to make the switch, assuming I could find work down here.

"Maybe. I'll think about it, okay?"

"That's all I ask," he said, flashing me one of those rare smiles of his.

We got to work on going through the files and it was about three hours later when my phone vibrated. I pulled it out of my pocket to see a text from William.

Be at my place tonight for 6:30pm sharp. Wear your tightest jeans and a short t-shirt.

A shiver of pleasure raced down my spine. I had no idea what we were going to be doing tonight, but I was already looking forward to it. I didn't even care what we did, because we would be together and that was all that mattered to me.

Yes, Daddy.

I sent him my text back before I tucked my phone back into my pocket. I had to get through these files and then tonight, I could let it all go. I would be getting to spend the evening with Daddy all over again and I couldn't wait.

CHAPTER TEN

William

IT WAS NEARING six-thirty when my doorbell chimed through the house.

I had showered before I left work so I wouldn't smell of smoke and would have time to get home to change before Noah came over for our date. I had plans to take him out to a restaurant that was well out of my station's district. I was planning on making this a very memorable first date and I couldn't wait to get started.

I went and opened the front door and saw that Noah had indeed listened to my instructions. I had told him to wear the tightest pants he owned and to pair them with a t-shirt that didn't hang down so low. He was wearing tight, dark blue jeans that were skinny and looked almost painted on. Delicious. He had clearly brought them to wear at the club for his vacation. He was also wearing a black t-shirt that hit him right where his belt was and he'd paired it with his black leather jacket. He looked amazing and he was dressed perfectly for what I had in store for him.

"Come on in, my sweet boy," I said, licking my lips as I moved back to allow him to enter.

"Thank you, Daddy. I hope this is okay to wear."

"It will do, but there is something that you are missing before you look perfect for tonight. Come," I ordered, turning on my heel to head down to my bedroom.

Noah easily followed behind me and once in my room, I spoke again. "Pull your pants down."

"Yes, Daddy," Noah said, flashing me a big smile.

He easily pulled his pants down and I saw that he was wearing boxers. That wouldn't do. "Remove your boxers. You will never wear any underwear again, even if I am not with you. I want to always be able to take you whenever I want."

"Yes, Daddy. Sorry," he easily said as he went through the process of toeing his shoes off so he could remove his boxers.

Once he was naked from the waist down, I strolled over to him and lightly gripped the back of his neck. Using minimal force, I guided him over to my bed and pushed him to bend down so he was standing with his hands flat on my bed, ass exposed.

"Don't move," I ordered.

"Yes, Daddy."

I turned to the bedside table and opened the top drawer. I pulled out a new toy that I had picked up just for him. I spoke as I turned back to him, admiring his ass as he displayed himself for me.

"I got this today just for you," I said, running a hand over his pale globes. I gave the left one a hard smack.

"Thank you, Daddy," he said on a moan as I rubbed over the pink handprint that had risen on his flesh.

I picked up the cock ring and easily slipped it on him. I then grabbed the vibrating bullet and pushed it inside of his tight hole. I pushed my index finger in along with it so I could place it right against his sweet spot and ensure it would stay there for the rest of the night until I decided it could come out. With that done, I slapped the right ass cheek as I spoke.

"Get dressed, my sweet boy."

"Yes, Daddy."

I moved back and watched as he slipped his pants and shoes back on. When he was fully dressed, I placed my hand on the small of his back and guided him out of my house and into my truck. I opened the door for him before I made my way over to the driver's side. Cranking the ignition, I flashed him a wicked grin before I pulled out of the driveway and headed off for the restaurant.

The drive was silent for a few moments between us. After a few moments of simply enjoying the silence and concentrating on the road, I reached into my pocket and hit the button on the device that was connected to the ring and bullet. Noah was instantly jumping as the ring and bullet started to vibrate simultaneously. I knew the devices were causing instant pleasure to shoot up his spine, and grinned mischievously at his reaction.

"Holy fuck," he moaned as he looked over at me.

I gave him a big smile as I spoke. "Oh, did I forget to mention what that new toy does? As you can feel, they vibrate and the ring will keep you from coming. I am going to enjoy watching you sitting there at dinner, knowing that you are being driven to the brink again and again right in front of all of those people."

I was really looking forward to seeing it. I couldn't wait to see Noah across from me in the restaurant as he wiggled around as his dick grew hard enough to pound nails. I was going to enjoy knowing that everyone would be able to see that he was hard and he wouldn't be able to do a damn thing about it.

I reached over and ran my hand along his shaft through his jeans. He was already hard and I could see the clear outline of his cock pressed against the tight material across his hips. He moaned and wiggled his hips at my touch.

"That is only the first setting, my sweet boy. Daddy is going to love seeing the look on everyone's faces as they see your hard dick through your pants. As they see all of the pain and pleasure you experience while we eat. If you are a good boy, then after dinner I'll let you have *my* cum for dessert."

He moaned as he wiggled his hips again, pressing his cloth-covered cock upward against my hand. "I'll be good, Daddy."

"That's my sweet boy," I said, removing my hand from his lap. He let out a delicious whimper at the loss of contact and I grinned, feeling rather pleased with the thoughts of what he'd have to go through this evening as everyone watched.

We drove the rest of the way to the restaurant in silence. I was loving how much he wiggled around as his body was flooding with pleasure. The second we pulled into the parking lot, I turned my truck off and gave Noah my full attention. I hit the button on the remote and turned it up another couple of levels. He let out a deep moan and I could see the strain start to show in his face.

"Come on, my sweet boy, we have dinner reservations," I said with a smirk as I climbed out of the truck.

I moved around to his side as he tumbled out of the passenger side, barely able to stand already. I placed my hand on the small of his back and guided him over to the entrance as I spoke.

"No covering up that hard dick. Keep your hands by your sides and keep your eyes up."

"Yes, Daddy."

I guided him inside and I instantly noticed that the place was packed. I felt my own arousal pick up at the idea of how many people would witness Noah's situation this evening.

The hostess gave us a warm smile and I could easily see her gaze traveling down to see the shape of Noah's hard dick through his jeans. I chuckled and she quickly snapped her eyes up to meet mine and I could tell she was shocked and didn't know what to do.

"Reservations for Clark," I said, snapping her out of it with a lustful grin in Noah's direction.

"Um, right," she said as she now stared down at the restaurant seating map, a blush staining her cheeks. She grabbed two menus as she spoke again. "Follow me, please."

I placed my hand on the small of Noah's back once again and we followed the hostess over to our table. I was very pleased to see that it was in the middle of the room. I guided Noah through the room, making sure to go slow so everyone would be able to see him.

Once we arrived at our table, I pulled the chair out for him before I went and slid into my own. Usually, I wouldn't be touching him or pulling his chair out. I would never want anyone to know that I was there with a man, especially on a date, but there was something about Noah. I wanted people to know that he was mine. That he belonged to me. I wanted people to know that he was spoken for and they couldn't have him. For some reason, Noah brought out my possessive side and it was overpowering my need to keep myself in the closet.

"This place is nice. I've never been here before," Noah said, his voice a little warbly and slightly higher pitched than usual as he peered down at the menu.

"It is a nice place. I've never been here before, either. Do you have a favorite pasta dish?"

"Not really. I'm pretty easy when it

comes to food," Noah said with a small shrug as he closed the menu and set it aside, shifting his hips on the chair.

He was perfectly content for me to choose what he ate and that only turned me on even more. Some guys liked to give me a hard time about wanting this type of control, but Noah had no problem with it at all.

The waiter came over and I ordered us both a drink before telling him we needed more time with the menu. We didn't really, I just wanted to delay this for as long as I could.

I reached into my pocket and turned the device up a bit higher. I looked over at Noah with a smirk on my face. His breathing hitched as the vibrations picked up. He wiggled and I saw him bite down on his lip and he gave a soft groan.

"You okay?" I asked, playfully.

"Don't suppose we could just skip to dessert, huh?" Noah asked, flashing me a small smile.

"Now where would the fun be in that, Sweetness?" I asked right back with my own smile and a wink.

The waiter came back over with our drinks and I placed our order for our food.

Once he was gone, I turned back to Noah.

"How was work today?"

"Um, considering I am supposed to be on vacation, it was frustrating, actually."

"What made it frustrating?"

The fact that he was supposed to be on vacation and he was working an arson case would make it frustrating, but I had a feeling it was more than that.

"I got the paperwork in and the judge approved it. I went to collect the case files from the social worker, but he still gave me shit about handing the files over. Then he slow-walked collecting everything. I have a feeling he knows something more, but he's not giving anything up yet. Ryzen is going to look into him and see what he is hiding. If it's not connected to this case, then he'll pass it off to the Agency's agents that they have assigned to investigate all of the social workers."

I could see how that would be frustrating. They wanted to get this arsonist and the only way they could start to track down who the target was is through the records. If they had to fight to get the records, then it would slow down their investigation.

"Did you find anything in the records

yet?"

"Not yet. Everything looks pretty normal and typical. The children were all placed in that home because they didn't have anywhere else that would be safe to go. None of them had any family. Most of them had the same story: their parents were either dead, in jail, or on drugs. All of them had been in foster homes previously, before they witnessed a crime and they were placed in Mel's home. What the crime was, though, that isn't in the files," he said, and I could tell he was annoyed to just be talking about it.

"Shouldn't it have been?" I asked.

"Typically, yes. Usually, everything possible is in the file so if the file were to be transferred over to another social worker, they would be made aware of the full situation. Because the information wasn't in their files, we spent the day having to search the police database for it. It was a long and frustrating day, but hopefully tomorrow, we will start to get some answers."

"Hopefully. I know it's gotta be frustrating on your end. We did discover how the fire was started, at least. Were there any open cases or previous ones with the same MO?"

I had called and spoken with Ryzen this afternoon once my team and I were able to determine how the fire started. It was started from two fronts. The first was internally. The arsonist had been able to get in the home. My assumption was they did it at night when everyone was sleeping. They had poured gasoline all over the floor. Then from the outside, more gasoline was poured, the doors were locked, and then it was started at some point in the morning. It explained why no one saw anything. They wouldn't have noticed someone in the middle of the night getting their fire ready. And then first thing in the morning, he could have been walking a dog by the house and dropped a lit match in the grass. The house would have gone up quickly and it would have burned hot. The arsonist was smart and I suspected he had done the same thing previously.

"As it turns out, arsonists really like gasoline."

"Shocking," I said, sarcastically.

"I know, right? There's over a thousand open suspected arsonist cases all involving gasoline as the accelerant of choice. And even more that are closed. We might not catch who the arsonist is through the MO, but rather who would have hired him to kill one of the children," Noah continued as he wiggled and moved around in his seat.

I couldn't help but smirk as I watched him try and get comfortable with the pleasure that was scorching through him. By now, he had to have become more sensitive to the vibrations from the toys. Being solid as a rock for that long had to be a challenge. He wasn't complaining, though, and I was enjoying every minute of it.

He closed his eyes and started to pant. I couldn't help but smile. I could only imagine how much he would *need* to cum by the time we left. I turned the remote on the device as high as it could go, causing him to let out a decent sized moan that caused people to look our way. I could see the faint blush that tinted his cheeks as he looked around the room.

"That's the highest setting. You seem to attract quite the attention, Sweetness. Tell me, though, how much do you love it?" I asked with a knowing grin.

"This is the best date I've ever been on,

Daddy," he said with a heavy breath, and I knew he meant every word.

Some guys liked being watched, but most people didn't enjoy it. I loved that Noah was so open and comfortable with his own sexuality and his interests in the sex department. This was a man that wore a plug out in public because he enjoyed it. He was not shy and I loved that he was so comfortable letting me have some fun with the toys tonight. It was going to be the first of many interesting dates, I could promise that.

"Just think, if you lived down here, this could be a weekly thing. We could go out for dinner, go to a bar or a club. We could go out grocery shopping with this toy in you. We could have so much fun together, in and out of the bedroom, Sweetness."

"Are you trying to convince me to move?" he asked, flashing me a small smirk as he shifted his hips once more.

"I'm simply stating a fact. If you lived here, we could have a lot of fun. Exclusive fun," I emphasized.

"We could, but don't think I didn't notice how we are on the opposite side of the city, from your station house. If I were to entertain the idea of living here, I won't entertain the idea of being a dirty secret. I won't commit to a man who can't openly commit to me."

I knew what he was saying. He was out and proud and I was hiding in my closet. If I were to be with him, I would have to come out, something I wasn't certain I was ready for. It wouldn't be fair for me to ask him to move here to be with me and force him to hide our relationship. Sure, it would be fun at first, but it wouldn't take long before that got old and he would become resentful and unhappy.

Two things I never wanted him to feel.

I wasn't certain I would ever be able to give him what he wanted, though. I had no idea if I would ever come out. I'd never wanted to. But I would definitely need to think about it. I'd never done anything like this with my past submissives before and I never would, even if they were here now. Noah was special and maybe, he would make me want to come out of the closet with the people that I worked with.

"I understand that. And that would be something I would consider changing if it meant being with you. It looks like we both have some things to consider. For now, let's enjoy the time we get together, Sweetness."

"Yes, Daddy," he said with a warm smile.

I couldn't wait until dinner was over and then we would be able to go back to my place and I would be filling him up with my cum. I was going to make sure that when he went into work tomorrow, he did so with his ass filled with my cum and a plug in him to keep it there. He belonged to me and I was going to make sure he knew it all day and night long. If I was only going to get him for three weeks, I was going to enjoy every waking minute with him that I could.

CHAPTER ELEVEN

Noah

PULLING INTO THE parking lot at the University had me feeling an assortment of emotions. I was nervous, anxious, but there was also a small amount of excitement.

I was there just to see about an open position in the law department. They were in need of a professor for criminal law. It would be full-time and would have the potential for tenure later on, should I wish for it. From what I had read on their website, the job came with a very good pay. I would actually be making more than I did now.

There were a lot of great benefits of switching to a teaching position. I wouldn't have to work on cases. I wouldn't have to listen to the stories of victims. I wouldn't have to deal with scumbag defense attorneys trying to make it seem like the victim was lying. I wouldn't have to deal with any triggers and I could just go into work, teach, go home, and prepare lessons for the next day. It would be simple. Easy. I wouldn't have any added stress, no more nightmares. I could just be a normal person. There was a lot of appeal to that.

As I made my way through the University parking lot, I couldn't stop thinking about last night. The date had been perfect. Beyond perfect. I had never experienced something like that before. I never expected that I would enjoy going out into public and being teased the entire time, never being allowed to come the whole time we were out. That I would enjoy people knowing that I was rock hard and was leaking cum continuously but never achieving release.

On the way home William had allowed me to suck him off during the drive for my dessert and then we had sex all night until the early morning hours. I was tired and relieved by the time he finally allowed me to climax, but it was well worth it. Every second of the torture to that long-awaited orgasm was well worth it. I very much looked forward to other date nights with the same or similar types of edging and the frenetic coupling with William afterward.

I needed to head into the Agency to continue to go through the files after my interview. Ryzen was working with Knox to try and find any evidence or leads they could use that would point them in the right direction of the arsonist. We now had the MO, but it wasn't very specific, and certainly not enough to narrow it down to a workable suspect pool.

Walking inside the University, I made my way to the law department. I was meeting with the University Hiring Director to see about the position. I easily followed the signs and once I arrived at his office, I knocked as per the instructions. After a moment, I was granted permission to enter. I walked in and gave the man a warm smile as he spoke.

"Noah Riley, it's a pleasure to meet you," he said as he stood up and offered me his hand.

"It's nice to meet you as well, Director Samson," I said as I took his hand.

"I'm curious, what makes you want to make the change from being a Federal Prosecutor to working as a Professor?"

I answered as we both sat down. "I have been thinking about relocating down here. My younger brother is here and it would be nice to be around family. I've also recently realized that the cases are getting harder for me to handle. I deal with some of the most violent criminals and their victims are often killed or left severely damaged. It's a hard life and it's getting worse. I think it might be past time for a change."

"I would imagine after some of what you've seen in your career that it would take a toll on you. Why the interest in teaching?"

"I can't work the cases anymore, but I am very good at my job, at my success rate. I would like to pass on what I have learned to the next generation of lawyers so they can continue to put criminals behind bars. Each generation should pass on what they know so we can continue to have competent lawyers."

I meant what I was saying, too. I did think it was important for lawyers to pass on their knowledge and experience to the next generation. It was the best way for new lawyers to learn and adapt to the changes in laws and evidence collection. As science evolved, lawyers had to as well. If I could help the future generation of lawyers learn something that could work to put a dangerous criminal behind bars, then it would be worth it. I would still be helping to make the world a safer place. I just wouldn't be going through the trauma of it.

"I can't speak from personal experience, I'm not a lawyer, my job is to find the right candidate for the right profession, but I will say that I agree. Sometimes, it's better to step away from an occupation that is impacting your life in a negative light than to keep going and continue to hurt yourself. I think it's noble that you would like to help with growing and shaping the minds of the next generation of lawyers. Our current position is in the criminal law class. It is a program that offers four levels, from basic to working real life cases. The first level is an introduction to criminal law and by the end of it, the students can decide if they wish to move on to level two or focus on another area of law. Level four is mostly the students achieving placements and working small time, simple criminal cases. It's designed to get their feet wet while they have supervision so they can avoid beginner mistakes. You would be teaching five days a week and the class time varies. You would meet with everyone in the legal department to come up with a schedule that works for everyone. Do you have any questions on that?"

"No, that sounds all very straight forward."

It sounded good. I liked that I would potentially be teaching students at different grade levels. I would have colleagues who wouldn't need to ask me about a case. I could have a more normal life.

"Perfect, we are just finishing up our last semester before summer starts. So, you wouldn't need to be here for two months. Summer break is four months. In two months, all of the professors come back and they start with their lesson planning and work out a schedule. It's pretty light work for the first while before all of the students come back. That would also give you time to get everything you needed wrapped up in New York before making the move down here. I would like to offer you the position. Your track record is very impressive and you would be a huge asset to the students and the University. That is, if you are indeed interested in making the change," he said, flashing me a warm smile.

I had been on the fence the whole time on whether I should make the move or not. I wasn't expecting him to offer me the position today. I thought he would tell me he had other candidates that he was interviewing and he would let me know. I thought I would have more time to consider and weigh my options. However, I had to admit listening to him telling me more about the job, I was getting excited. There were a lot of possibilities in the position, a lot of good. It had been a long time since I had felt excited over new employment. It had been a long time since I had felt excited about *anything* outside of a sexual nature, actually. I knew it was the right decision.

"I'm very interested and I would be honored to be a member of your staff," I answered with a warm smile.

I meant it, too. This was the change I needed and as an added bonus, I would also get to spend time with William still. Maybe we could build something real between us and that was something I was more than looking forward to.

"Perfect, that is great to hear. I have some paperwork for you to fill out and we can make it official," he said as he pulled out a file.

We spent the next thirty minutes going over all of the paperwork and I felt elated about the choice I'd made by the end of the interview.

I was going to be the new criminal law professor.

I was going to have to reach out to my current employer and give them my notice. I would also have to pack up my condo and sell it. Plus find somewhere down here to live. It would be a lot of work, but I was hoping it would all be worth it. I was getting a fresh start and that was something I think I truly needed.

Now all I had to do was help my

brother catch an arsonist and I could start a life away from crime.

CHAPTER TWELVE

William

I WAS SUPPOSED to be focused on the paperwork that was sitting in front of me, but all I could think about was Noah.

Our date last night was beyond epic.

It was one of the best times I'd ever had out in public. It was made even better knowing that Noah was enjoying it just as much as I was. The man was perfect.

Absolutely perfect.

I was already trying to think of something else we could do that would be a lot of fun. That maybe neither one of us had done before. I was happy that Noah was also going to speak with a hiring director at the university. There was a criminal law professor position and I was truly hoping the interview went well and Noah would be offered a job.

It would be great for him to be working at the university so we could continue to see each other. Not to mention, he desperately needed the change. His mental health wasn't going to survive working in New York City for much longer. It would be best if he got a fresh start somewhere else with a whole new job.

Why not start fresh here in Baton Rouge where he had his brother and, hopefully, a new boyfriend to enjoy it with?

I was pulled away from my paperwork as the loud talking coming from the lounge area began increasing. I had no idea what my guys were doing, but they were making a lot of noise while they were doing it.

Letting out a sigh, I pushed up from my desk and strode out. The station house was divided up into different areas. There were bathrooms, both guys and girls, with showers. There was a large, coed locker room. Then there was the bunk room where there were enough beds for everyone who worked there. We all had our own little area. The beds were in their own little cubicles to offer a bit of privacy and each had a small shelf to have a photo on them or a place to put their book when they had to go out on a call.

I had my own quarters that were set up as an actual bedroom with a desk; it was almost like a dorm room. The rest of the house was the kitchen, living room, and dining area that we referred to as the lounge. It was all in one area and open concept so I could see where all of my guys were. We also had a gym, and multiple storage rooms for all of our food and gear.

I walked into the lounge to see three of my guys sitting on the couches in the living room area. I could tell that Hawke was upset about something. I tried to think of a recent call we had gotten that could make him upset, but nothing came to my mind. At least, not since the arson call a few days ago. He was sitting with Jase and Zander and both of them seemed to be upset as well, but for a whole different reason. Where Hawke looked sad, they looked angry. Something had obviously happened.

"What's going on?" I asked the three of them.

"Oh hey, Cap. It's nothing," Hawke instantly said, and I could tell the response was a bold face lie.

"He's an asshole," Jase said, not even bothering with hiding his anger.

"Who's an asshole?" I asked. I was trying to keep the order from my tone, because if this wasn't connected to a call, then I had no business being there.

I kept my guys at a distance and I was not about to change that now. It was easier to keep a wall between us. It made it easier to send them into a dangerous situation if I wasn't emotionally connected to them.

"Chris," Zander answered.

"Is that another firefighter?" I asked, still not sure what was going on.

"No, he's a cop. Which should have been my first clue that things weren't going to end well," Hawke said, with a small shake of his head.

"What didn't end well? Is there a beef that I need to be made aware of?"

We relied on the police to have our

backs in the field. There had been plenty of times where we had arrived on a scene and there was an active shooter or someone attacked one of us. We need the police to have our backs, just like the police need us to have theirs. A beef could be a serious problem and could make our calls even more dangerous.

"No, Cap, no beef. We just broke up," Hawke said, with a sad shrug.

"You're gay?" I couldn't help but be surprised.

I had no idea anyone in my Station House was gay. I thought I was the only one. Hawke had never given any indication that he was seeing a man. And both Jase and Zander seemed perfectly okay with it.

"Since I was a kid," Hawke replied with a nod and a slight grin.

I went and sat down in the chair as I spoke. "What happened?"

It was none of my business, but I couldn't help it. I had no idea that Hawke was gay and I felt like I should have known. I should have noticed that one of my guys was gay.

And yet, I'd had no idea.

The way Jase and Zander were

reacting to him, there was no hatred or disgust. They treated him like he was one of the guys. I never expected for them to be so open and accepting of someone who was gay. That didn't mean I thought they were bad guys, but I also knew it wasn't easy for most men to accept a homosexual, especially in our line of work.

"Chris and me had been dating for three years. He's in the closet and that was fine, at first. But after three years of him still giving me empty promises, I couldn't do it anymore. I was tired of having to play *friend* around the guys at his work or when we went out. I was tired of having to go to another town just so we could go out on a date. That's not the life I want. So, I told him last night either he was coming out or we were done. He said he was never coming out, that he won't be the *gay cop.*"

"I'm sorry," I said.

It all sounded familiar, though. Being in that closet, it was very easy to be in it, and it was incredibly hard to walk out of it. There was security and comfort in the closet. Nothing changed as long as you were in it and sometimes, it was easier to keep everything the same than risk it all changing.

The thing that hit me was eventually Noah and I would be in the exact same position. He was out and proud and he was not going to tolerate me living in the closet forever. He didn't want to be kept as a dirty secret for the rest of his life and I could completely understand that. I wouldn't want that either, if I was in his position.

"It's okay. I'm upset and annoyed, but I'll get over it. If he wants to be in the closet for the rest of his life, that's his decision. Though, the next guy I date will be one that is out and proud."

"I told you he wasn't a good idea," Jase said.

"Yeah, I know. I should have ended it years ago. All I can do is live and learn from it." Hawke sighed, lifting his shoulder in a small shrug.

"It's his loss, man," Zander said. "When you are ready, we can go and hit the gay clubs and find you a rebound man," he added with a big smile.

That caused Hawke to chuckle lightly. "Let me lick my wounds first, and then totally."

I couldn't believe how easy the conversation was between the three of them. They didn't seem to care that Hawke was gay. They were acting like he was one of the guys.

It was blowing my mind. I thought I would have to hide who I was from everyone, because they wouldn't be able to handle it. But these three didn't even bat an eye about any of it.

"Does everyone know you're gay?" I asked.

"Oh yeah. It's not something I've kept hidden. I told everyone from the jump," Hawke answered.

"Everyone is good with it, Cap. We're all an accepting bunch," Jase added.

"Good, that's good," I said as I stood, my mind reeling. "I'm sorry about your boyfriend, but it sounds like you're better off without him. You deserve to have someone who will be happy to show you off."

"Thanks, Cap," Hawke said, flashing me a warm smile.

I headed back to my quarters. I needed some time to think and get my thoughts in order. I never expected that the guys at the house would be so open minded and accepting. I never thought I would ever be able to come out to any of them. The revelation had my mind spinning and I needed to try and get myself back under control before we got a call.

One thought did keep repeating itself over and over again in my head. And that was maybe I wouldn't have to live in the closet forever. That maybe I *could* come out and still have the respect of my guys. I never expected for that to be a possibility, but maybe it truly was.

It was something that I needed to think about. I needed more time to process the information before making any major decisions. But I liked knowing that I at least had the option now, which was more than I thought I would ever get to have. Something about the new knowledge added a pep to my step as hope blossomed in my chest.

Today was going to be a good day. I just knew it.

CHAPTER THIRTEEN

Noah

I LET OUT a sigh as I rubbed my eyes for what felt like the hundredth time.

I had been holed up in Ryzen's office going through all of the case files from the social worker and the corresponding cases from the police for the victim's cases. It was a shit load of paperwork and so far, nothing really stood out.

I was trying to narrow down who might have been the intended target so Ryzen and Knox could focus on trying to track down anyone who would have gained something from their death. The problem was, so far, all of them could have easily been the intended target, including Mel. She was keeping these kids safe, giving them a chance at a good life, and that could be resented by the kids' parents, or even a gang that was trying to keep their hold on them. Anyone of them could easily have been this arsonist's target. So far, no one else had been attacked. That was a good thing, but I also knew that if there was another victim we would have more to go on. It wasn't a positive thought and not what any of us wanted.

I had been over these files multiple times and I hadn't found anything. Yet, my gut was telling me there was something in them. There was something that I was missing and I was going to keep going over it until I finally found that something.

I kept coming back to this name, Blane Titsex. I didn't know why, but I couldn't help but keep going back to it. I knew it was perfectly logical that it was a real name, but it just felt fake to me.

I grabbed a piece of paper and wrote it down. I then went back over every other social services report on the victims. Every single file had a name that just felt off about it. A quick look at the names and I could see that every single one of them had the same letters, but they were in different orders.

I started to work my way through all of the possible combinations that the letters could make that would give me a real sounding name. It was a lot, but I knew that was my answer. I just had to find it first. My phone vibrated in my pocket and I pulled it out to see a text from William.

Call me, my sweet boy.

I was instantly smiling and I dialed his number as I closed Ryzen's office door. It only took him a moment before he answered.

"Hello, my sweet boy."

"Hi Daddy," I said as I went and sat back down.

"I know you are working, and I won't keep you long. I just wanted to call and see how your interview went."

A warmth spread through my chest at knowing he was calling to check in on me. That he cared enough to call and ask how my day had gone so far. It was sweet and not something that I was used to.

"Well, you are talking with the newest criminal law professor at the university," I said with a proud smile tilting the corners of my mouth.

"Oh, am I now? That is amazing, Sweetness. How are you feeling about it?"

"Surprisingly, really good. I wasn't expecting for him to offer me the job on the spot, but he was very interested in me coming on. I thought I would have more time to think about it, but when he offered it to me then and there, I didn't even hesitate to say yes."

"That's good, though, Sweetness. It means you are ready for the change and you want the change. When do you start?"

"The students are about to start their four month summer break. So, I don't start for two months, which is good. I have to put my notice in with my current employer. Plus pack everything up, sell my condo and find a place to live down here. The two months will allow me to get it all worked out."

"It's good that you get some time in between to work everything out. It will make the transition easier on you. Will you stay for the next two and a half weeks or are you planning on going back early?"

"I haven't thought that far ahead yet.

I'm just trying to help Ryzen with this arsonist case and then I can plan the future. I might go back early to get a head start on everything, but I don't know yet."

I really had no idea what I was going to be doing yet. I hadn't thought that far ahead. I could figure it all out later, though. There wasn't anything major that I needed to have an answer for right that moment.

"I'm happy for you, my sweet boy," he said warmly.

"Thank you, Daddy.".

"How is the case coming?"

"I think I've finally found something. I've been going through the social worker cases and the police reports for each of the victims' cases. I came across a name in each file that was fake, but they all contained the same letters, just in a different combination. I'm trying to go through the names and see if I can figure out a real one and then run it. It might be nothing, but it might lead us to someone that could give us the arsonist."

I knew it was a long shot, not to mention there could be any number of combinations for the names. It was most likely going to come back as a complete waste of time, but it was still something that needed to be run down.

"It sounds like a viable option. If someone went out of their way to make a fake name in repeated files, there has to be a reason for it. I'm on shift until eight tonight, but afterward, I'd like to see you again."

"Definitely. Text me when you want me over, Daddy," I easily agreed.

"Be safe, my boy."

"Promise, Daddy. You too."

He was the one who had the dangerous job. I was sitting here in an office going through paperwork. The biggest threat to my life would be a paper cut. He was running into burning buildings.

"Always, Sweetness. I'll see you tonight."

He ended the call and I couldn't help the warmth that flooded through me knowing that I was going to be seeing him again tonight. Now I had even more motivation to figure out the real name that this person was using. I didn't even know why they would be using different names.

What did this person have to gain?

They were in every file, but not in any of the witness reports, and there was no real reason for them to be in the victims' files with Social Services. This person had gone out of their way to make sure their presence was known and they were placed in these files. The reason wasn't filled out on any of the forms, either.

Which was odd in and of itself.

Typically, when someone was involved with a child for Social Services they had to fill out a form and it specifically stated their relationship to the child. But that part was left blank and it never should have been. The caseworker should have made sure it was filled out. Apparently, the kids' lovely Social Worker was so lazy he didn't even care to make sure the paperwork was filled out properly.

"Finally," I said aloud as I was able to get the letters to form a proper name. It only took a hundred tries.

Alex Stibent.

I went over to Ryzen's computer and logged in to run the name. I was hoping he would be listed somewhere and then I could go and have a chat with Mr. Stibent and find out why he was listed on all nine victim's files.

Well, the information that returned was not what I was expecting. As it turned out, Alex Stibent was a foster parent.

A Safe Haven foster parent.

Well, that was a curveball. That could easily explain why his name was scrambled in the folders. I'd seen it before with foster parents using false names in a Social Service's file. They do it to protect their identity in case someone is trying to track down a child. Mr. Stibent must be the foster parent that the children would go to if something were to happen to Mel.

I wrote his address down and headed out. I needed to speak with him. He might know more than what was in any of the files. I sent a quick text to Ryzen letting him know where I was going and that I would keep him updated on what I discovered.

***

After knocking on the door it opened to reveal Mr. Stibent. Only, Mr. Stibent was actually Alex Nesbitt, Kate's boyfriend, who I had interviewed just the other day at the crime scene.

"Mr. Riley, what brings you by?" Alex

asked with a warm smile

"I just had some follow up questions. Do you have a minute?" I asked.

That was not what I was expecting to discover. I needed to let Ryzen know, because there was a very real possibility that Alex Nesbitt was our arsonist. The trick was, I couldn't walk away, because then he would know we were on to him. I just had to play this off as a follow up interview and get the hell out of there.

"Yeah, of course, come on in," Alex said, gesturing with his hand and maintaining the warm smile.

I stepped over the threshold as I spoke. "I'm sorry, when we spoke last I wasn't aware that you were also a foster parent."

"I am. I'm sorry I didn't say anything. Kate doesn't know. I didn't want to put her in danger so I've been keeping the two worlds apart. It's not always easy, but Kate is very understanding."

"I would imagine it has been very difficult for you at times. Do you have any children now?" I needed to make sure he was alone so no one got hurt when Ryzen stormed in here with backup.

"No, not right now. I only take in children who have nowhere else to go. If any had survived the fire at Mel's, they would have been placed with me. There are two levels of security, the first place is Mel's and then they come to me if they need more than what she can give them."

"Okay, I was wondering why the system placed the kids with Mel. I'm not being sexist here, but I would have figured the children would have gone to a home with multiple men to protect them."

"Part of how the Safe Haven homes work is that it's one adult. You can fly under the radar easier. You don't want to stand out. And Mel was one hell of a fighter. She took self-defense classes and made sure all of the kids did as well. She also knew how to shoot. She was pretty amazing," he gushed.

There was a bad feeling growing in the pit of my stomach. We had been operating on the premise that the children were the targets, but maybe it wasn't about them. Maybe this was about love, or rather unrequited love. The way he spoke of Mel, there was a warmth to it, but I could also see the love he had for her in his eyes. It was more than that of a friend.

"You loved her," I simply stated.

"What? Of course, she was my friend,"

he said, clearly trying to backtrack and cover the emotions he'd displayed.

"But she was also more than that. You cared for her, but I'm assuming she didn't want to be with you in that sense," I pressed.

He sat there for a moment just staring at me and I could tell he was trying to figure out how he should be handling this. He didn't want to confirm, but he also knew there would be no point in denying it, either.

"She didn't want to risk our friendship," he said, his voice tight.

I suspected it was more than that. I suspected that Mel didn't want anything to do with him in a sexual manner. She might have not wanted to hurt Kate or maybe she held zero attraction to him. It was upsetting to him, though.

"That must have been frustrating for you. There she was, working all of those hours with the kids. She had been active on dating websites. She was trying to build a life for herself, build a family, and she didn't want you."

I had no idea if she had been on dating websites. I was trying to see what type of reaction I could get out of him. The instant anger that flashed through his eyes told me he suspected that Mel had been seeing other men. I was willing to bet that Alex had seen her with another man and that was the stressor for him. That was what made him snap. It wasn't about the children, they were just casualties. He wanted Mel dead. He wanted her to pay for not loving him.

It all made sense.

Of course no one saw someone outside of the community that morning. Because Alex was a member of that community. Him being around Mel's house wasn't anything out of the ordinary. He could have easily started the fire. His alibi could have been fabricated; it wouldn't have taken much work to do. My phone ringing broke the silence. I reached into my pocket and saw that it was Ryzen.

"Excuse me," I said as I stood.

I moved away slightly as I went to answer my phone, but I never even got to hit the answer button when pain exploded in the back of my head. I was instantly on the floor as the world around me blurred. I was just able to see Alex picking up a gas can before it all went black.

CHAPTER FOURTEEN

William

IT WAS NEARING four in the afternoon when we pulled up to a house on fire.

When the call came in, I had been hoping it would be a quick one. Our shift was almost over and there was nothing I wanted more than to head home to see Noah. God, I wanted to see him so badly. It was crazy how much I could care for someone that I barely knew. It was crazy how much my body could crave the touch of another. There was nothing I wanted more than to go home and see Noah there waiting for me. To see Noah naked and ready for sex. And what made it better, there was a very real chance of that happening one day.

He had gotten the job. He was going to be moving here and I couldn't have been happier. I wasn't going to be losing him in less than three weeks. He was going to have to return back to New York City so he could pack up his condo and sell it, but that would only be temporary. I would still get to have him once he returned and depending on when he was going to go up, maybe I could take some time off and go with him. It would be nice to see where he was living and I had never been to New York. It could be a little vacation for the both of us. I could bring it up tonight once I saw him.

The second we pulled up, we noted that the house was engulfed in flames. There were people already on the street looking at the tragedy that was playing out before them. I scanned the area and I saw a couple of patrol cars that had arrived before us. I had no doubt that the police had helped to get the neighbors out of the houses surrounding the one that was on fire. I went over to one of the patrol officers to see what they knew.

"Captain Clark. What do we know?" I said, once I was close enough as my guys got the lines set up.

"House came back to Alex Nesbitt. That's his car in the driveway. Neighbors said he is normally home all day and they saw him not that long ago letting another man into his home. We ran a black car parked on the street and it came back as a rental. The rental agreement has Noah Riley as the renter. We suspect both are still in the home. We tried to get in, but the smoke was so thick we couldn't see anything."

The second he said Noah's name my blood ran cold. If he was, in fact, still inside, he could easily be dead. The fire was burning hot. There had clearly been an accelerant used and there was no telling what condition the victims could be in.

"They're in there?" I asked with urgency to my voice.

"From what we can gather, we suspect that two people are in the home."

That was all I needed to be told before I took off at a run. I went to my rig and tossed on my jacket and grabbed my tank. I could hear my guys calling out to me; it wasn't normal for me to gear up. I stayed outside. I didn't go into fires anymore, not unless I had to go in to help my guys. For me to be gearing up, it instantly put them on edge, but I didn't have time to try and calm them down or explain.

I had to get to Noah.

With my tank on, I ran to the house and was instantly going inside.

"Noah!" I yelled.

The thick, black smoke was everywhere along with the hot flames. If anyone was in here, they were going to be burned and unconscious. There was no way for them to be awake with that level of smoke.

I suspected that gasoline had been used once again to set the house ablaze. I had no idea if Alex was the target or if he was the arsonist. I knew that Noah had been trying to track down a name from the files and I was assuming that man turned out to be Alex Nesbitt. However, I had no idea if he was a witness or the arsonist. I did know that some arsonists would set themselves on fire if they were at risk of being caught.

I kept myself low, knowing that Noah

would be on the floor. I worked my way through the main areas on the first floor. I went slow, making sure to check everywhere so I wouldn't miss him. If he came here to speak with Alex, then he wouldn't have gone upstairs. He was most likely on this level. I saw a leg poking out behind a chair and I was instantly running over to it. I bent down and my heart sank at the sight of Noah. He was unconscious, but there wasn't any part of him on fire, so I was hoping that meant he hadn't been laying here for long.

"Hang on, Sweetness." I said as I picked him up bridal style and made my way out of the house, just as my guys were going in.

"Medics!" I yelled out for my two paramedics. They were instantly running toward me with a stretcher just as another voice called out.

"Noah!"

I looked over and saw Ryzen and Knox running toward me. I placed Noah down onto the stretcher and my guys were instantly on him, administering oxygen and setting up an emergency central line.

Now that we were outside, I could see the redness of his skin. It wasn't a first degree burn, through. I was leaning more toward a second degree, and they would hurt. I knew that for a fact. The heat had been so hot, that even though the flames hadn't touched him, the heat still got him.

"We need to intubate," Calvin said.

Those were words I never wanted to hear in regard to Noah. I never wanted to hear that he needed to have a tube down his throat. I knew the smoke inhalation was going to be bad, but I had been praying that he would be able to bounce back without a whole lot of intervention. He was young and healthy. He should be able to come back from this if they could keep him breathing.

I had to trust the process, I knew that.

I knew Calvin was experienced. He had been a paramedic for over a decade now. He knew what he was doing. That still didn't make it any easier to watch as he pushed a plastic tube down Noah's throat.

It wasn't until that moment did I realize that Noah wasn't just any man. I was in love with him. I didn't even know how it happened or when. It was too soon, way too soon, but I was in love with him. Knowing that he was in need of help to breathe, knowing that there was a chance that he might not make it through this, all of my emotions hit me head on with full force.

I was in love with him and now I might lose him.

I could feel my body starting to tremble from the realization of how bad the situation was. At the realization that I could lose the man that I loved before I even got the chance to truly be with him. Before we got the chance to be in a real relationship. Before I got the chance to come out and tell the world about him. I was going to lose him before I even got to make him truly happy. Before I got to see him free from all of the mental pain that his job had put him through. We were about to get our fresh start and we could lose it all right now.

We could lose it all to a fire, of all things.

"We gotta go," Calvin said as they started to push the stretcher onto the ambulance.

Ryzen was instantly following them and getting inside the rig. As badly as I wanted to be the one to go with them, I couldn't. I wasn't family, and no one knew we had been seeing each other. I also had my guys here and I was the only Captain on scene. I couldn't leave. Not until the fire was out.

"I'll meet you at the hospital. I'll stay here and work the scene," Knox said to Ryzen before he closed the ambulance doors.

Knox banged on the back door of the ambulance to let them know they were good to take off before he immediately went over to the patrol officer I had spoken with earlier.

I on the other hand, couldn't seem to move. I stood there with my gaze on the ambulance as it drove down the street, my heart breaking as they drove away with the man I loved.

I desperately wanted to be going with him. I wanted to be in that ambulance holding his hand and making sure his heart didn't stop. The next time I saw Noah, he could be dead and I would never get to tell him that I loved him. I would never get to have a proper goodbye with him. He could just be gone and there was nothing I could do about that.

"You okay, Cap?" Hawke asked.

I hadn't even realized he had come

over to me. The ambulance was long gone, I couldn't even see it now, but I still hadn't moved. I felt like I was frozen. As if my legs were cemented into the ground. I had never felt like that before and I never wanted to feel like that ever again. Assuming Noah survived his injuries, I'd decided then and there that he was going to be restrained to my bed where he would be safe. It wasn't until Hawke placed his hand on my shoulder did I finally snap out of it enough to be able to turn to look at him.

"He'll be okay. Come on, let's get this fire out and then get you to the hospital, Cap."

I should have been bothered that Hawke had figured out Noah meant something to me. I should have been telling him it was nothing and blowing it all off.

The thing was, though, I didn't want to.

I was so tired of having to carry around the huge secret. The weight of it was so heavy, too heavy for me to carry right now. Hawke was gay. He wasn't going to care that I was as well. He was right, though, I had a fire that needed to be put out. There was another person that we needed to find, too. Once the scene was contained, then I could go and see Noah and, hopefully, by the time I got there he would be okay.

***

Four hours.

How could a couple of tests take four hours?

Once we got the fire out, we'd discovered Alex Nesbitt's charred body in the kitchen. With the fire out, we had left the scene to Knox to work and figure out what the hell had happened.

I had arrived at the hospital four hours ago to Ryzen telling me they took Noah for tests. All of my guys had stuck around, even though we were now off shift. I wasn't going to admit it out loud, but it meant a lot to me that they had stuck around. They didn't know Noah and they didn't owe it to me, but they stayed so I would have their silent support and it meant a lot.

I saw Ryzen sit up straighter in his chair and I was instantly lifting my head. I was expecting to see a doctor, but instead it was Knox walking toward us.

"Hey, Babe, anything?" Knox asked first.

"They are running some tests. What do you got?"

"Nesbitt was the one that set fire to our victim's house and he set this fire. As it turns out, Nesbitt was an active writer on his computer. Cooper was able to get the data off of his laptop and it was filled with journal entries. Nesbitt went on and on about Mel and how he was in love with her but she was cheating on him. The entries go from loving to violent over the course of a year. From what I could piece together, Nesbitt was stalking Mel. She probably didn't even know he was obsessed with her until it was too late. In an entry from the morning after the fire, he talks about how she was with him forever, that they would see each other again and they could be together properly." Knox shook his head in disgust.

"Noah probably figured out something wasn't right with him when he arrived at the house. Before he could get out of there, Nesbitt knocked him out and started the fire," Ryzen added.

"But he killed nine kids," I said.

It was one thing to be obsessed with someone and want to keep them all to yourself, to be a stalker, that I understood.

But to kill nine children in the process, what the hell was the point in that?

Those children had already been through hell as it was. They didn't deserve that pain. They didn't deserve to have their lives taken from them.

"He was jealous of them. He wrote about how he didn't like all of the attention Mel was giving to the children. That they ruined what was so special between them. At first, when Mel had started talking about being a foster parent, Nesbitt thought it was a great idea. He joined himself, but he never received any children. I was able to pull his file with Social Services and he was placed as an emergency foster parent only. He was literally who they would place a child with if they had no other option. I think in his mind, he thought he would get to foster a child, have that in common with Mel, and they would get to spend even more time together. But once again, something was blocking his path to Mel," Knox explained.

This whole situation was fucked up.

A woman decided to do something good with her life, she decided to give back to children who were in need, and then that asshole comes along and decides to kill them all.

And for what?

Because she didn't want to date him?

It was bullshit and completely pointless. The whole situation was pointless.

"Wow," I simply said. That was all there was to say at that point.

"At least he's dead and they all have justice now. It doesn't count for much, but at least their extended families and the people who cared about them, if there were any, will know the truth. They will get the closure they need," Ryzen said.

It wouldn't count for much, not in the long run, but at least one less monster was out of this world. He couldn't hurt anyone again and that was really all that we could ask for.

It was a moment later when a doctor started to walk toward us. Instantly, I was on my feet along with Ryzen. Everyone moved closer to see what the doctor had to say.

"He's going to be okay. He has Superficial second degree burns to his arms, his neck, and his face, but they will heal and they won't scar. He got lucky there. The smoke took a toll on his lungs, but we are confident they will recover. We have him hooked up to a ventilator to give them a break and help them heal faster. He is sedated right now, to help him get over the bulk of the pain from his burns, but also so he won't fight with the tube. In a few days, we can lighten the sedation and start to allow him to wake up. At that point, if his oxygen levels are good, we can start to wean him off of the ventilator and switch him to a normal oxygen nasal line," the doctor said.

Just being able to hear those words, that Noah would be all right, I felt like I could breathe again. I had no idea how badly I needed to hear those words until they left his mouth. My whole body was no longer tight. I felt like I could get a deep breath in again.

Noah was going to live.

The man that I loved was going to be okay.

He was going to have a bit of a road ahead of him with his lungs healing, but I was going to be there every step of the way. I was going to make sure he was fully healed and ready to take on his new job in two months.

"That is great news, Doc," Knox said with a warm smile.

"When can we see him?" Ryzen asked.

"He has been moved to a private room on the fifth floor. Room five-fifteen. You may see him two at a time, and only for a few moments, but that is it. Even though he is sedated, he still needs rest."

"We'll be quiet," Knox promised.

"Thank you," I said, sincerely.

The doctor nodded at each one of us, shook Ryzen's hand with a tired smile that reflected in his eyes, and then, without anything further, he turned on his heel and headed off.

I looked over at Ryzen to see what would happen, who would be going in to see Noah first. I suspected that he'd figured out that his brother and I had been seeing each other. We hadn't spoken about it, but I could tell by the way he looked at me. He knew, but he was respecting my privacy. I knew, though, that he and Knox would want to see Noah and I was worried that meant I would have to wait until one of them left before I could get my eyes on the man that I loved.

"You two go. I will grab some coffee," Knox said, flashing a warm smile at the both of us.

"You sure?" I asked. The last thing I wanted to do was overstep.

"Yeah, it's fine. Go," Knox said with a nod.

"What are you waiting for, Cap? Go see your man," Zander said.

I was instantly turning to look at my guys and to my surprise, none of them looked upset or disgusted. They all shared the same look of understanding and acceptance. I couldn't help but look over at Hawke, who put his hands up in a mock surrender as he spoke.

"Hey, don't look at me. They figured it out. Not that it was really hard to figure out."

"Yeah, Cap, for the past week you've been happier. You've even come out to eat with us and you sat down and talked with Hawke, Zander, and myself today, and you never do that. We could all tell you were seeing someone. We just didn't figure out who until you ran into that fire like your life depended on it," Jase added.

"We're happy for you, Cap," Calvin said, a smile turning up the corners of his mouth.

And I could see that they were. It was written clearly on all of their faces. They were genuinely happy for me. It warmed my heart to know that they weren't going to think less of me for being gay. I was no longer going to have to hide who I was from them.

A huge weight had been lifted off of my shoulders and for the first time in years, I felt true joy, true belonging. Maybe it was time I reevaluated my stance on not getting close to them. Maybe it was time I reevaluated a lot of things in my life. That internal reflection could wait, though.

The man that I loved needed me and that was exactly where I was going to be.

EPILOGUE

Two Months Later…

Noah

TODAY WAS THE day. Today I was going to be starting my new job at the University.

I never thought I would be making such a drastic change in my life at this point. Becoming a teacher, much less a Criminal Law Professor, and in love with the most amazing man in the world.

Although I had agreed to take the position, I wasn't completely sure I was doing the right thing, though it certainly had made me feel better to accept the job and with it, the hope for a less stressful future. I wasn't positive that a change in job was going to make enough of a difference in my life for me to be truly happy. I had simply been going through the motions for so long and I wasn't sure what it was that I'd been missing in my life, what would need to change to be truly happy and content.

At least, not until I woke up in the hospital and realized that I was madly in love with William. It was insane, because I shouldn't have been.

Not yet.

We barely knew each other. We had spent less than a week together and yet, I was deeply in love with him. When I thought I was dying in that house, I figured I would have thought about Ryzen. He was my brother, the only family that I had. It *should* have been him that I was thinking about, that I was sad about leaving, about not getting to say goodbye.

And yet, all I could think about was William.

All I could think about was never getting to see him again. Never getting to feel his hands on my skin. Never getting to feel the peace that he brought to me when we were together. Never getting to bring that same peace to him. It was at that moment, that I realized I was in love with him. That our casual, three week fling had grown so rapidly into something serious.

And it happened so fast I hadn't even seen it coming until it was too late.

Waking up in the hospital and seeing his face, I knew that my decision to take the new job had been the right one after all. I couldn't leave. New York was no longer my home. Baton Rouge had become my home and it was all thanks to William.

I was truly happy here.

Waking up in the hospital with a tube down my throat had been terrifying, but William had been there to get me through it. He had explained that I had inhaled a good amount of smoke and the tube was needed to help heal my lungs. I had also sustained some superficial second degree burns all over both of my arms, my neck, and face.

Thankfully, they hadn't left scars, but they had hurt like hell and my skin had been sensitive to the touch for weeks afterward as they healed.

My lungs had sustained some serious damage and I still had to carry an inhaler around just in case something aggravated my lungs. The doctor had assured me that with time, my lungs would fully heal and I would be able to live my life normally again.

Currently, I was taking things very carefully and not doing anything too strenuous where my lungs would have to work overtime.

Our sex life certainly took a hit, though. Instead of going multiple rounds without a break, I could only handle one or two a night. Anything more than that and I'd end up wheezing and that just wasn't sexy. Not to mention the unusual fatigue after any sort of workout or sexual activity.

All of which the doctor assured me was completely normal with the injuries I had sustained. He told me to be patient and not to worry. I would be right as rain and back at all my old activities soon enough.

I had a difficult time being patient, though.

William had been amazing with me over the past two months. He had spent every day in the hospital with me, not even caring that his firehouse now knew that he was gay and in a relationship with me.

I was relieved to hear from Ryzen that none of the guys seemed to care all that much that their fire Captain was gay. In fact, a couple of the guys at the house had admitted they were gay as well. It was an enormous relief for me to hear that William's men were accepting of him and some even understood where he was coming from.

It was also a huge relief that William had been taking things so well. I hadn't been certain if he would want to go back into the closet or pretend like it never happened, but thankfully, he was out and proud now. He didn't think twice about holding my hand or kissing me in public.

It was really nice to not feel like a dirty secret any longer.

Not that it wasn't fun while it lasted, but I simply couldn't be in a long term relationship with someone who couldn't be proud to be seen with me. I wasn't going to be kept hidden or denied basic public displays of affection from someone who claimed to care about me.

When I got out of the hospital after a week, it had been decided for me that I would be staying with William and not Ryzen. I was all too happy to be spending my days with William, resting in his bed.

To my surprise, though, William had taken two weeks off of work so he could be at the house with me and make sure I was healing up okay. I could tell he was worried about my lungs. They were pretty crappy those first few weeks, but they did get better as they healed from the smoke damage.

Those next two weeks, though, were amazing on a whole different level. We spent the days curled up in his bed watching movies and eating take out. He took very good care of me. He helped me in the shower and we even spent some time in the hot tub. We didn't have sex or even touch sexually for two weeks, which was extremely hard for the both of us, but we got through it.

The second the doctor said I would be fine to resume more physical activities, William had spent the day spoiling me. I had never come so much in my life and the best part was I just had to lie there while he did all of the work. We took breaks, we had to, but by the end of the day I had come close to twenty times. The next day I was broken, I could hardly move and we knew we'd overdone it. We took things a bit easier for a little while after that.

Day after day, William continued to take care of me and he continued to steal a piece of my heart.

As he came up behind me and wrapped his thick arms around my waist, I turned and gave William a warm smile. I had been in the bathroom just finishing getting ready for work. He was on the night shift this week so we would be like two ships passing in the night, but I knew it would go by quickly. Soon enough, he would be back on days and we would have our evenings together.

"You look beautiful," he said as he brushed his lips over my freshly shaven cheek.

"You mean now that I am not all red and wheezy," I teased.

"You were beautiful then, too, but I am glad that you are back to being healthy, or close to it. How are your lungs today, Sweetness?"

"They're good. I have my inhaler with

me just in case. I'll be fine, William."

That was one thing that I had noticed that picked up. Ever since the fire, William had been incredibly protective of me. He was always worried about what I was doing and making sure I didn't overdo myself. I didn't take offense to it, though. I knew what happened had terrified him.

Shit, it terrified me and I hadn't found myself half dead.

From what I knew from Ryzen, William had been the one to find me. He'd rushed into the burning house, violating so many protocols by not waiting for his men, simply to get to me. Something the doctors had said was most likely what saved my life that day. William was entitled to be worried and overprotective of me and I was perfectly fine with it. Eventually, I knew he would process everything that had happened and calm back down, become less overprotective, and I could more than wait until he was ready.

"I know, I know," he said, and I could tell he was trying to get his mind wrapped around the fact that I was leaving without him today. Whenever we went out, we always went together. He didn't like leaving me alone, too afraid that something was going to happen while he was gone, I guess. Today, I was going to be going to work, a place he couldn't follow.

"You'll be at work when I get done. Are we still going to video chat later, Daddy?" I asked, flashing him a playful smirk. I was hoping the change in topic would help to ease his worried mind.

He gave me a warm smile as he spoke. "Yes, we are, my sweet boy. We have to celebrate your first day at your new job. And I am hoping we can celebrate one other thing tonight as well."

"What thing would that be, Daddy?"

I saw his reflection reach into his pocket and pull out a key. He held it up to me as he spoke. "I know we haven't discussed this, but with you now working and getting things ready to move down here, you are going to need a place to live. I know you said you were going to start looking, but I'm hoping you already found the place you'd like to call home here."

"Are you asking me to move in with you?" I asked, surprised.

I hadn't thought he would want to live

with me yet. I knew the past two months had been amazing, but it could have only been amazing because he knew it would only last for so long. Moving in with him permanently was a huge step and I had no idea he was even ready for it.

I hadn't even told him I loved him yet, because I knew it was too soon, that I shouldn't feel that way about him already, and I didn't want to scare him away. I had been letting him set the pace, but I had no idea he was already at that stage.

"I'd like to order you to live here with me, but I know I can't. The choice is yours, Sweetness, but yes, I would love for you to live with me. I would love to fall asleep every night with you in my arms. I would love to wake up every morning with you pressed against me and on occasion, with my dick buried inside of you," he said, flashing me a smirk in the mirror.

I turned around so I could face him and not his reflection. "I have a condition."

"And what would that be?" he asked, but I could tell he was a bit worried about the stipulation that I was going to be putting into place.

"I will move in with you, but I have to

fall asleep every night that you are here with your dick inside of me. If you can agree to that, then yes, I'll move in with you, Daddy."

An instant smile spread across his face as my words registered. I knew he would agree to my condition, it was a rather simple one to agree to. I knew we wouldn't get to spend every night together, he often had to work two weeks out of the month on the night shift, but when we did get to sleep next to each other, I had every intention of him making up for lost time.

"You drive a hard bargain, my sweet boy, but I think that is something I can easily agree with," he said with a huge smile tugging at the corners of his lips and making his eyes sparkle.

"Then, yes, I will move in with you, Daddy."

He pulled me in for a kiss, one he quickly dominated and left me feeling breathless. The way this man could kiss was unbelievable. He made my whole body feel like it was on fire and that was just from a single kiss. I was truly, madly, and deeply in love with this man.

All too soon, he was pulling back and he gave me the richest smile I had ever seen.

"I love you, Noah," he said with pure passion and love in his voice. It was so strong it caught me off guard.

I had no idea he felt that way about me. I thought maybe it was just me. I wasn't expecting that and I knew I had to say something before he took my shock as something completely different. The last thing I wanted was for him to think I didn't feel the same or I was just saying it back to make things less awkward.

"I love you, too."

He was instantly pulling me in for another kiss and I hungrily kissed him back. I was never going to get tired of this man. He had stolen my heart almost instantly and I never wanted it back. I wanted to spend the rest of my life with this man and I couldn't wait to get started. I was going to live with him. We would get to spend our free time together and I would be able to sleep with him against me.

For the first time in years, I felt like I finally didn't have to swim so hard to keep my head above the water. William had thrown me a life jacket and now, with him in my life, by my side, I was going to be able to make it to shore.

For the first time in years, the future looked bright and I was looking forward to every second of it.

Thank you for reading!

If you enjoyed Noah, do me a solid and go leave a review?

Even a few words can make my day and give me the motivation to keep on plugging away at the stories you love.

Thank you.

Next up is Damien!

And he is joined by Travis and Max.

This story is a ménage, my first foray into more than one partner, so I hope you enjoy it.

Turn the page now to read Damien's story!

DAMIEN

FEDERAL PROTECTION AGENCY

BOOK SIX

BY EVIE RILEY

DAMIEN

It takes three to make life go right...

Private Investigator Damien Anderson and his younger brother watched in horror as their parents were killed in cold blood by the head of the mafia. Eye witnesses to a crime boss suspected in multiple homicides and a major gun trafficker, they have spent the last fifteen years in the Witness Protection program.

A teddy bear at heart, Damien can be sweet and kind but the moment anyone puts the people he loves at risk, he has no problem becoming lethal. Working with the FPA, the brothers find themselves at a crossroads when their past starts to catch up to them. Do they tell the men in the Agency the truth, or run once more and leave behind everyone they've come to think of as family?

Ex FBI Agent Max Morris is a man with a darker personality and a deadly skill set, who just happens to be the very definition of vigilante justice... and he has no issue with admitting it. Fed up with tracking down some of the worst repeat offenders only for the court to let them go on technicalities, Max quit the FBI and took matters into his own hands. He doesn't regret a moment of it. Someone has to take the predators like his father off the street.

Travis Manning is a social worker and the newest member of the FPA task force. He is in his element helping to find safe haven homes for the children in need. The shy, secretive, non-social man suffers from low self-esteem, which isn't helped when he seems to always end up dating men who are in the closet and keep him as their dirty secret. Travis always feels like he isn't good enough, until he's caught between Max and Damien. Literally.

When Travis' abusive ex shows up in Baton Rouge and proves he's a risk to the sweet man they love, what lengths will Max and Damien go to in order to keep Travis safe forever?

CHAPTER ONE

Travis

I WAS LATE. I knew he was going to be mad, but there was nothing I could do about it. Isaiah had to talk to me about the Agency needing one of us in Baton Rouge. He didn't order me, he couldn't, but I knew he was hoping that I would volunteer to leave. To move away from Gaithersburg and go to Baton Rouge.

I had never lived in a large city. I'd never had much of a desire to do it. When I got my degree in Social Work, I wanted to work in a smaller town so I could build stronger connections with the children who were in my caseload. I didn't want to have a caseload of a hundred children and have to try and keep track of that many. I knew that Social Workers with a lot of children in their caseload, well, they lose track of children. They can't spend the time needed with each child to ensure they are safe and happy. That's when things can fall through the cracks, children can fall through the cracks, and that wasn't something I ever wanted to have happen on my watch.

I knew it would be between Isaiah and myself when it came down to who made the transfer, but I also knew that Isaiah had his own life in Gaithersburg. He had his boyfriend and other responsibilities so he couldn't move. It made the most sense for me to move, but what Isaiah didn't know, what everyone didn't know, was that I had a boyfriend. He was in the closet and he held zero interest in coming out of it. I had to respect that. I wasn't in a position to try and give him an ultimatum. Even if I told him he had to come out or I leave him, I knew I would be leaving him. He would never choose me over his reputation. That was something I had accepted, begrudgingly, sure, but I had accepted it years ago.

We had been dating for three years now, and in the beginning, it was all really great. We had met at a gay bar a couple of towns away. I knew he was from Gaithersburg, I had seen him around town. I had no idea he was gay and living in the closet, not until I saw him that night.

I'd never expected to see Detective Joe Baxter in a gay bar. He always came across as an old fashioned man with old fashioned beliefs. He certainly never gave any indication in the few dealings we'd had when I was working with a child in the system. Even when I was brought in because a twelve year old boy's parents were abusing him because he was gay, Baxter never gave any indication that he sympathized with the boy. He very much saw the parents' point of view and he didn't believe in being gentle with the boy.

There were simply no tells. He never let anyone know he was gay. Ever.

I knew Dr. Howard would tell me that Baxter hated himself because he was gay and until he loved and accepted himself fully, he would never be able to have a true and meaningful relationship. At the time, though, I didn't believe that. I believed, foolishly, that I could change him. And now, after three years of dating in secret, my life was no longer my own.

"You're late. Where the fuck have you been?" Baxter demanded the second I walked through the door.

We didn't live together, but he was always over at my place. He would use the fire escape around the back and sneak in that way so no one would see him coming through the front door. It was one of his rules.

He had a lot of rules.

The most important one was that no one in the town could know he was gay. He didn't acknowledge me in public. Even when we were in a different town for a date, there were no public displays of affection. No hand holding, no pet names, nothing. As far as any of the onlookers were concerned, we were friends out for a meal or we were having a business meeting.

At first, I was okay with it. I was younger and had never had a serious relationship before. And with my parents not being affectionate, I wasn't really used to being hugged or shown any affection to begin with. Not having any from Baxter was just normal for me. Now after three years, I was getting very tired. I was lonely and considering I didn't go to bed alone, that screamed volumes.

Baxter, he was rough in the bedroom and outside of it. Even our sex was hard and controlling. He never gave me oral sex. In fact, he almost never touched me. We always had sex in one position, doggy style, because he didn't want to see me. His actual words. He needed to be able to pretend that he wasn't having sex with a guy. His self-hatred was far deeper than I thought it was and it wasn't until I already had feelings invested into him and our relationship did I discover how deep it went.

I also discovered he had anger issues that could result in him hitting me. I should have left after the first time he hit me, but I had believed his lies when he said it wouldn't happen again. When he told me he didn't mean to, he had been drinking too much, that he was under a lot of pressure at work, I shouldn't have believed him, but I was a fool and forgave him.

Now, I had to wear long sleeved shirts

and pants every day to make sure no one noticed the bruises that littered my body from him. He would even hit me now during sex if his anger started to boil over. He wasn't angry at me, but at himself. I was just his punching bag.

I knew I had to get out, but I honestly didn't know how. He had already told me he would kill me if I left him. I wasn't certain if he would, but with a town this small, he could easily do it. Plus he was a detective. He could make it look like an accident or that I killed myself. I didn't really have friends in town and my parents had checked out a long time ago, so I knew no one would even think twice about my death.

"I'm sorry, Isaiah needed to speak with me after work about the new group home project that we are working on," I said as I went and hung up my coat.

I was really hoping he would be okay with my excuse. I knew he was getting annoyed by all of the hours I had been working. It had been a problem since I had agreed to work with the Federal Protection Agency. Baxter didn't like that I had to travel now and that I wasn't there to fulfill his needs on demand.

Before the Agency, I was home every night to make dinner and make sure my place was clean before he came over. Now, I had been so busy that things had slipped. I wasn't always here with dinner cooked when he arrived. I wasn't always in the mood to have sex, either. He wasn't pleased with that.

I had a protein deficiency that made me tire easily. It also made me bruise easier and I had a harder time gaining weight. It's why I was so thin, something that I knew could be a turn off. It wasn't that I didn't eat, I just couldn't gain weight like everyone else so I was thin. I was only a hundred and twenty pounds and at five foot eight, that meant my ribs were easy to feel.

I knew some guys liked spinners, but I also knew that a lot of guys were turned off by someone being so thin. I couldn't help it, though, just like I couldn't help being tired most of the time, or the random bruises that I would get. It also made me have a weaker immune system and with being around kids, I tended to get sick often. It was just another thing that made it harder for me to have a real relationship. No one wanted to date the sick guy. My own parents didn't want to deal with my health. I couldn't exactly expect that there would be a man out there who would tolerate it.

The sudden blow to my stomach was unexpected and strong enough to knock me down to my knees and take my breath away.

"How many times do I really have to tell you that I don't give a shit about your excuses. When you are not out of town, you are home with dinner ready for when I get here. Your only job is to please me and recently, all you have done is prove to me what a worthless piece of shit you truly are. It's no surprise that your own parents don't love you."

His words hurt more than any punch could ever hurt. Baxter knew that, though. He knew how to hurt me, how to truly hurt me. He knew that I felt insecure and had low self-esteem from growing up, and he always made sure to let me know how worthless I was.

As if I needed someone to remind me.

"I'm sorry, I didn't realize how late it had gotten," I instantly apologized. I knew it wouldn't matter, though. He would only see it as me giving him excuses.

His right hand was instantly in my hair and pulling a chunk of it as hard as he could. He then wrapped his left hand around my throat, choking me. He pulled me up and slammed my back against the wall.

I brought my hands up to clutch at his arm, to try and get his hand off my neck. He was gripping it so tight, I wasn't able to breathe. He had never choked me before. In the bedroom from behind while he drove his cock into my ass, yes, but it was never anything like this. Never to the point where I was unable to breathe. The look in his eyes was pure darkness, pure hatred and anger. Something must have happened at work to push him over the edge today, and I was the one who would be paying for it.

"How many times do I have to tell you that I don't want to hear any excuses coming from your mouth? Your excuses mean nothing to me. You mean nothing to me. Your job is to cook, clean, and be there for when I need to fuck someone. That is all you are good for. You don't get to talk, all you get to do is apologize for being a disappointment." Another blow to my side, landing right where my healing bruises from the last fight we had were. "Now, take your punishment like the good worthless whore that you are," he seethed.

Before my brain could even register what was happening, Baxter had thrown me to the floor and had started to pull my pants down.

***

Two Weeks Later....

I placed the last box down on the floor in my new bedroom.

This was still so surreal to me. I had never expected that I would be moving to Baton Rouge, but this was where my job had brought me. I had been working in Social Services in Gaithersburg since right after I graduated College, close to five years now. I enjoyed working there. I liked being in a smaller town, getting to know the people and building connections with the kids that I had in my charge.

Now, unbelievably, I was going to work in Baton Rouge.

A city with over two hundred thousand people and a crime rate that could give New York City a run for its money.

Daunting didn't even begin to explain how it felt. I was excited, though. I'd desperately needed the change.

When the Federal Protection Agency had moved here, I'd understood why. It made complete sense for them to be in a larger city that could accommodate all of the new Agents. Plus, the city was very high in the sex trade and most were underage children who were either runaways or kidnapped victims. The Agency was very much needed there.

With the move of the Agency though, Isaiah and myself had been very busy with having to travel all around the country with them. It was getting to be a lot and we were having a very difficult time with trying to find safe places for the victims that were rescued to go to. Isaiah had been working with Dominic to build a group home that we could use for the victims that we couldn't find a safe home for right away, but it was slow going.

When Mason had informed us that he needed one of us to be down here, to move down here, I knew it would be me. Isaiah was madly in love with his boyfriend, Sol, and Sol's younger brother, River. They all lived together and River was attending a private school for exceptionally gifted children. They had a whole life together in Gaithersburg now, a family, and it wouldn't be fair to make them all uproot their lives. Besides, it was the excuse that I needed to get away. The justification I had been waiting for to finally leave Baxter. He had made the decision for me after that horrible night, and it truly was a night I would never forget.

The bruises still littered my body from what he had done to me that night. When he'd finished the many rounds of sex with me, he'd finally left. We'd had had rough sex plenty of times in the past, hell, it was the only type of sex that we had.

That night, though, that night was different.

Normally, he would stretch me a bit first and he would use lube, but that night he didn't. He'd forced his way into me and he didn't care that he had made me bleed. That he'd really hurt me.

Afterward, I couldn't fool myself into believing that it was sex anymore. No matter how hard I tried, my mind refused to allow me to accept that it was just sex. Looking back now, that was probably a good thing. It made me finally realize the truth.

He had raped me.

My own boyfriend had raped me. He'd beaten me and raped me. And then, he left me there in a mess of blood and cum, lying on the floor like I was nothing. I knew I couldn't do it anymore. I had taken a shower and called Isaiah and told him I would be happy to make the move to Baton Rouge.

From there, I spent the next two weeks trying to avoid Baxter and getting my apartment packed up. I couldn't pack it until I was ready to leave. I had to make sure Baxter didn't know I was leaving, because I truly believed he would kill me to keep me quiet. That he wasn't going to risk me talking about him being in the closet.

I had boxes stored under my bed and hidden in the back of the closet so Baxter wouldn't see them. Then the night before I left, I was up all night packing everything up and loading it in a rented U-Haul truck and I left for Baton Rouge in the very early morning hours.

I had gotten a whole new phone with a new number and made sure to give it to

Isaiah so he would have it. I had to disappear as far as Baxter was concerned. If he didn't know where I was, then I wouldn't have to worry about him trying to find me. He would have no reason to ask about me at work or ask Isaiah where I was. At least, not without him risking people wondering why he cared about my whereabouts.

Baton Rouge was going to be my fresh start. It was going to be the time that I needed to try and recover from Baxter and the abuse, and from my parents. I was twenty-seven, I shouldn't feel like this. I shouldn't feel like I was worthless and unimportant. I had to figure out how to heal, otherwise I was never going to be able to not only love myself, but someone else.

I wanted to have a real relationship someday. I wanted to know what it felt like to truly be loved and cherished, but that was never going to be possible if I couldn't love myself first. If I wasn't able to see my own self-worth.

I had a lot that I needed to work on internally, emotionally and psychologically, but I was hoping that being in Baton Rouge and having my own space again, I would be able to start to mend from everything. This was my new life, my new home, and I was determined to make the most of it.

CHAPTER TWO

Damien

"RACHEL'S STALKING CASE has been closed. The guy is sitting pretty in jail now," Sebastian said as he walked into my office and plopped down in the chair across from my desk.

"Did he give you any trouble?"

Rachel had been a new client of our private investigation agency. I knew Mason wanted us to work exclusively for him and the Federal Protection Agency, but I was not about to let the company that Sebastian and I had built dissolve. We had men who worked for us and they were relying on the work to feed themselves and their families.

We used to be located in Gaithersburg, but with the FPA utilizing our skills so often, it made sense for us to move down to Baton Rouge. We had clients all over the country and with being in a larger city now, we were getting more local clients.

Rachel had been dealing with a stalker for two years now, but the police hadn't done anything about it. It wasn't their fault per say, they could only do so much, and Rachel's stalker had made sure to stay within the terms of the restraining order. That didn't change the fact that he was still stalking her and terrorizing her.

"Nope, he fell right into the trap and he is now facing ten years in prison. Rachel is going to use this opportunity to relocate to California where her sister lives. You got something else for me?"

"Not yet. Mason is on his way over here to talk about something with me. They might have something that they need help with."

"He didn't say what it was?"

"Nope."

We had done plenty of cases with the FPA since it was created. Both Sebastian and I enjoyed the work and we were always willing to help someone, should they need it. We wanted to help make this world a safer place for the current generation and the future ones. If it involved children, there was nothing we wouldn't do, and I do mean *nothing*.

We had both killed someone before and hidden the body. Hell, I had done that within the past six months when Isaiah called me when his boyfriend Sol's younger brother had been kidnapped. I arrived on scene to find the kidnapper dead, by his own son's doing.

Max Morris was just standing there completely calm, as if he didn't just shoot his father to death. We had buried the body and had covered it all up with the help of Mason.

It had helped to know that Max's father, Phillip, was a pedophile who had not only molested and raped children, but he had killed them as well. He deserved to be killed and it was one time I'd had no problem covering it up.

"Any news on Russo?" Sebastian asked.

David Russo.

That man had been a thorn in both of

our sides for fifteen years now. People knew that Sebastian and I were best friends. That we grew up together and started this company together. We kept our personal lives pretty quiet and only told people what they needed to know.

What people didn't know, though, was that it was mostly all a lie.

We did grow up together and we were best friends, but we were also brothers. Sebastian was my kid brother. We had always been close growing up. We grew up in New Jersey with a big loving family. We were full blooded Italians so there was always a family gathering with close to a hundred people there for it. Every month, someone in the family held a family dinner for everyone. Our mother didn't work, but our father was an accountant for a major corporation. At least, that's what we were told.

We grew up rich, we never went without, and anything we wanted, we got. On our sixteenth birthday, we were both given a brand new Dodge Charger. Birthdays we had a huge celebration and would receive easily five thousand dollars worth of gifts. Christmas was even worse.

For two decades, I thought my family

was perfect, that we were always going to have each other. That was, until I was twenty. Sebastian and I had been off on a vacation in Europe. We were not set to come home for a few more days, but there was a major storm coming into New Jersey and we had been worried about our parents. We wanted to be home to make sure they were safe and if they needed to be evacuated, we would be there to make sure they went.

When we had arrived no one was home, but we were exhausted from jetlag so we headed up to our rooms and crashed for a few hours. I woke up to Sebastian shaking me four hours later. I figured our parents had finally gotten home, and they had, but they were also with David Russo and some of his thugs.

Everyone in New Jersey knew who David Russo was. He was the head of the Italian mob in the State. He was a fifty year old man who was known for being cruel and deadly. No one crossed him and if they did, they did so knowing that it would result in their death.

At the time, we had no idea why Russo would be speaking with our parents. Just as we were about to go downstairs to ask what was going on, Russo's thugs pulled out their guns and shot both of our parents. Killing them execution style.

I'd had just enough reflex within me to grab Sebastian, cover his mouth with my hand and pull him back into my bedroom.

Even thinking about it now, I could feel my heart racing. That was the night that I first felt true fear. We both did. Up until that point, we had never felt terror; we never had the need to. Seeing our own parents being executed was not something either one of us could forget.

I had taken Sebastian into my room and we hid in the closet. It would have been funny considering we had always been out and proud; if it hadn't been for the fact that we had to hide from the men who killed our parents. We hid for close to an hour, waiting to see if someone knew we were here, but when no one came looking for us, we ventured out.

We found them right where they had died in the living room and Russo and his guys were gone. We had called the police and the Feds came. We both agreed to testify and we were immediately placed in witness protection. We testified against Russo and he went away for a double homicide. He was sentenced to life, and Sebastian and I were sentenced to a life of being hidden.

We had foolishly thought that when Russo was sentenced to life in prison that meant we would get to be free from the witness protection program. That we could go back to our lives like it never even happened.

We were sorely mistaken.

The threat against our lives didn't stop with Russo in jail, it got worse.

We were taken back into WitSec and spent the next five years moving around. The Agent who had been put on as our protector was killed five years in.

We had always suspected that Russo had someone working for the Feds and that mole gave up our location. After that, we spent the next ten years relocating ourselves and constantly changing our names and appearances. Gaithersburg was supposed to be a quick stop, but we ended up liking the place and the people that we came across. Now, we were in our first major city in fifteen years and we were on even more of a high alert than usual.

We both wanted this to end. We both

wanted to be able to feel safe and not have to look over our shoulders. We had been investigating ourselves. Trying to figure out who Russo's hit men were so we could take them out before they got to us. It wasn't an easy process, though, and so far, we had only managed to take out two. We knew there were at least a dozen, if not more, but with each one that we took out they got smarter and it got harder to find them. We would get them, but I wasn't confident that would be before they found us again.

"Nothing yet. We got feelers out, all we can do is wait and see what comes up," I answered.

"Maybe no news is good news in this case. Do any of the guys need any help with what they are working on?"

"Nothing has come up yet."

"And our newest member, where is he?"

Max Morris.

There was a new pain in my ass. I had not been planning on hiring him, especially after that whole Phillip fiasco, but against my better judgment, I did. I was hoping that maybe he just needed a place where he could call home, have brothers around him.

I did look into him. I knew he used to be a Federal Agent before he left to hunt down his father. With his father now dead, I figured he would calm back down.

Turns out, the man preferred vigilante work over letting the justice system handle it.

He was careful, very careful, I had to give him that. But I knew, eventually, his luck was going to run out and it was either going to be a bullet or a prison cell that got him. Both options bothered me and I wasn't truly certain why.

We were polar opposites in a lot of ways. He had no problem killing in cold blood, as long as the one on the other end was a criminal. I only killed if lives were on the line. There was a difference and Max didn't seem to have that moral compass like most human beings do.

"Fuck if I know, which isn't a good thing."

"I'm surprised you have been keeping him around. You don't like wild cards, and Max is the very definition of a wild card."

"I keep hoping he calms down. We've both come across guys who are like him and all they needed was someone to show them the right way. To give them a family. Maybe Max needs the same."

"Maybe, but I would keep a close eye on him, if I were you," Sebastian warned before he stood up.

Just as he made it to the door, Mason strode in. Mason offered us both a small smile as Sebastian nodded at him and headed out.

"I hope I'm not interrupting anything," Mason said as he slipped into the chair that Sebastian had just vacated.

"Not at all. Sebastian just wrapped up a case. What can I do for you?"

"I am hoping you will be able to take on a security assessment gig. It's local and there aren't any immediate threats. You would be assessing a situation to see about any potential threats and then helping to prevent them from happening."

"Okay, I'm gonna need more information than that." I chuckled.

We had run threat assessments before and it was easy work. Mason paid well so this would be an easy payday for me. We all worked our own cases and we got the pay associated with that case. Sebastian and I used some of our pay to keep the lights on, but my guys didn't have to worry about any overhead expenses. It also helped to give my guys the incentive to bring in new clients. It was working and since we had been helping with the Agency, we had both been able to make pretty decent money. Money that would come in handy should we have to leave at a moment's notice once again.

"As you know, the safe havens in the foster home system are being restructured. Travis is reworking the whole system. He is going to have new safe havens constructed from older homes. It would help to have someone within the security world to go with him and run the threat assessment so the city can implement the needed changes to the structures. You would go with him to the different homes and run the threat assessment. At the same time, though, you would also be working as protection. Some of the areas that Travis is going into are dangerous and they might not take it too kindly to a Social Worker poking around."

To say the least.

Most of the gangs in town didn't like Social Workers or first responders of any kind. It was part of their society and that was something we all had to accept. They didn't care for my guys either, because we worked with the Agency. If some of them knew that Travis was poking around to get ideas for the new safe havens, they might take matters into their own hands to stop him. A lot of gang members weren't happy about the safe havens because the children who were being kept safe within them were snitches against them.

"That's fine. I'll handle it. When is he going to get started?"

"On Monday. I can have him text you the information."

"Works for me."

"Thank you. I really appreciate it. My guys are spread thin right now. We got case requests coming out of our ass."

"Better than nothing coming in. We're happy to help, you know that."

I knew they were getting busier. Mason had to bring on more guys for the field and for the computer tech stuff. It was good, though, it meant they were solving more cases and helping more children. That in and of itself was worth all of the long hours.

"I appreciate it. You guys have been saving my ass for a while now. Couldn't do it without you," he said, flashing a warm smile as he stood.

"Sounds good. Be safe," I said.

"Same for you and your brother," he said with a smirk.

"He's not my brother," I instantly countered.

"Sure," he said with a knowing smile as he headed out.

"Son of a bitch," I said softly to myself once I was alone.

I knew Mason was smart. Both him and his brother, Roland. Neither of them had believed us when we said we were just best friends. They both knew it was a lie.

Sebastian and I don't look identical, but you could clearly tell we had the same facial characteristics. Most of the time, we could play it off as a weird coincidence, but every now and then, we came across someone who didn't buy our story. It would appear that Mason and Roland really didn't believe us, and they obviously knew that something more was going on. Thankfully, they both seemed perfectly happy to live in our lie and not demand answers. Though, that could be because they both knew we wouldn't be able to give them. Still, Mason letting me know that he knew was his way of making sure I knew that he had our back. That should there ever come a day when we needed their help, he would be there.

That was something that Sebastian and I had this time around compared to the other towns over the past fifteen years. We had friends who were more than capable of handling themselves in a dangerous situation. I just hoped we would never have to ask them for help. That we would never have to ask them to put their lives on the line for us. With some luck, that day might never come and Sebastian and I could finally live our lives in peace without having to constantly look over our shoulders waiting for the next attack to happen. We could have a boyfriend and settle down without having to be ready to pack up and leave at a moment's notice. Maybe one day. Hopefully.

CHAPTER THREE

Max

"COME ON, YOU son of a bitch," I said as I peered through my scope.

I had been trying to get this bastard for a couple of days now, but so far he hadn't moved into a position that would give me a clean shot. This had to be clean. I was only going to get one shot at this without anyone noticing.

Matt Wentworth, an unconvicted child molester.

His latest victim was a six year old little boy that he'd raped. The boy was so traumatized that he had stopped speaking, and by the time he was found in an abandoned warehouse, the evidence was completely gone. It fit Wentworth's MO, though, and the police had him on camera speaking with the boy, but they never had anything concrete that they could use to convict him. The other times he was arrested for child molestation, the cases had been dropped because the children refused to testify and the parents couldn't bring themselves to force them.

It was a common occurrence in the justice system. Victims being too afraid to speak up and testify. To sit in an open court filled with strangers and tell them what had happened to them. To talk about being violated with the person that had done it to you sitting right there not even ten feet from you. Nope. The kids were simply too afraid. The justice system was seriously flawed and we would have more victims willing to speak up and testify if they didn't have to go through something so public and humiliating. And that was before you factored in the defense attorney who loved nothing more than to make the defendant feel like the victim. To turn it all around on the victim and have everyone believe that they asked for it or they were having second thoughts afterward and thought they should try and cover it up. Or it was a custody battle and mom was just crying child molestation to keep dad away from the kids. It was all bullshit and often the offender got to walk away and attack the next person.

Pedophiles and rapists, they don't just stop at one. They liked to keep going until they got caught, and even if they did get jail time, when they got out they went right back to it. There is no cure for that kind of scum. There is no set amount of time where they could be locked up and rehabilitated that would make an honest to goodness change in them. There was no changing them, period. They were hard wired to violence, to those sexual urges. They didn't have that little voice in their head telling them not to touch that child. They didn't have any impulse control and they would always act on their urges. If the justice system wasn't going to lock them up for life, then someone had to be there to make sure they didn't get to keep violating people.

And I was more than happy to be that person.

I knew from personal experience that pedophiles never changed. I grew up with one in my home. I was just a kid when my own father started to touch me, started to rape me. By the time I was sixteen, I had grown too old for him and he left me alone. I should have been thankful, I guess, but the damage had already been done. I knew, though, that I wanted to be a Federal Agent, that I wanted to help put people like him behind bars, even if I couldn't bring myself to put *him* in jail. I became an FBI Agent and spent years chasing down criminals. Doing everything I could to make sure the bad guys ended up in prison where they belonged. I had also been keeping track of my father, making sure nothing was going on with him.

Even when I discovered that he was a foster parent, I didn't do anything. I should have, I knew that, but my own trauma kept me afraid of him. It kept me from being able to move on and take action. I hated myself for it.

I had discovered that I was gay when I was eighteen and in the FBI Academy. I hadn't even noticed up until that point, and discovering that I was attracted to men after being raped by my own father for years, had caused a serious identity issue inside me.

It took a long time before I was able to accept that I was gay and that even though I was attracted to men, that didn't mean I wanted my father to do those things, that I enjoyed it. It took even longer before I was able to allow another man to touch me. Still, it was always there. He always stood in the way of me being able to find peace and move on from what he had done to me. I knew I was never going to be able to start to heal until I finally got justice for myself.

It was in that moment of clarity that I knew what I needed to do. I left the FBI and I started to follow my father around the country. He moved around a lot so he could continue to be a foster parent and abuse the children without it getting out. There were only so many times a single male could take in young pre-pubescent boys before it started to look suspicious. The trick with my father was, though, he didn't beat them or neglect them. He took very good care of them. He made them feel like they had everything to lose if they told anyone about what he was doing.

That's what he'd done with Sol and River.

He never touched River, he was too young at the time, but he did with Sol. He made sure Sol knew just how lucky they were to be with him. He made sure River had everything he could ever want and as long as Sol continued to allow my father to rape him, River would never know what it felt like to be hurt. My father knew exactly how to play things.

It wasn't until a couple of years after I started tracking him did I discover that he was also going after runaways and killing them. I didn't know that he could be violent. He had never been violent with me or with any of his other victims after me. He seemed to have everything figured out and had a perfect system to not get caught. It was a shock to discover he had been killing his victims. The ones that he couldn't ensure would never talk. Runaways were easy targets but they were also impossible to control. They didn't live under his roof, they could easily tell someone what had happened to them. It didn't have to be a cop or a doctor, it could be a friend, a priest, someone working in a soup kitchen.

There was no telling who that person could tell. The only way my father would be able to ensure that his victim didn't talk would be to kill them afterward. After all, if a runaway doesn't get found, police just assume they fled to a different town or were good at hiding. They didn't look too hard for them.

I had every intention of killing my father when Sol and River were in his care, but before I could, all three disappeared. I knew Sol and River had run away and my father was trying to find them. I started to follow them as well, knowing that eventually, my father would pop up. He wasn't going to tolerate them getting away from him. He couldn't report them missing either, because that would lead to too many questions once they were found. My father couldn't risk Sol talking to the police.

I had followed them for years with the hope that my father would show up. I was still trying to keep track of his movements, but they were harder to follow. He was no longer getting children from the foster care and relying on runaways to fulfill his sick needs. When I had overheard that Sol and River would be heading into Gaithersburg, I headed there myself, never expecting that it would change all three of our lives.

When my father had kidnapped River, I knew what he was planning to do to him. I was not going to let the opportunity to finally get my own justice slip through my fingers. Not again. Getting to that motel, being able to look him in the eyes as I held that gun on him, getting to pull the trigger and watch as his life left his body...

There was no greater feeling.

I was finally able to feel peace.

It didn't even matter that I had killed him in front of witnesses or in broad daylight. It didn't matter that I could be going to jail for murder, it would all have been worth it. Every single second would have been worth the level of peace his death had finally brought to me.

Surprisingly enough, I didn't end up in jail. Damien had come into my life and he had helped me to cover it all up. He had managed to convince Mason to let it go and grant me immunity for the kill. I figured that would be it. I never figured that Damien would also make an offer for me to work in his private investigation business.

I had worked a few jobs for him and for the Agency when they needed it. When I didn't have a lead that was. Killing my father only helped me to realize that there were more like him out in the world. More pedophiles who were able to continue to rape and molest children because the justice system was failing them. I was in a position to be able to do something to stop them.

To give their victims some justice.

So whenever I got a lead and it was solid, I would go and take care of it. I would kill them and bring justice and peace to their victims and protect any future ones from being harmed by them. I had zero regrets about it. Someone had to protect the children and I would step up and do what had to be done without a single ounce of reluctance or feelings of guilt.

Every. Single. Time.

My phone vibrated in my pocket and I moved carefully to grasp it without jiggling my rifle around.

Where are you?

I couldn't contain the eye roll at seeing Damien's text. I didn't work full-time for him. I was free to come and go whenever I'd like as long as I wasn't working a case or helping with the Agency. I didn't think that meant he would be trying to keep tabs on me all of the time. I was free to do whatever I wanted and I didn't have to run it by him first.

He knew that I went after people on my own. He called me a vigilante, but that wasn't what I considered myself to be. I was just a guy utilizing his skills to get predators off of the streets. To help give justice to some victims and prevent additional victims in the future.

I sent him a text back telling him that I would be back in a couple of days. I was confident that I would be able to get my mark by then and I would head right back to Baton Rouge. I was going to need the money from another case if I wanted to keep paying my rent. I wasn't charging anyone for my services. I wasn't a hit man. I was simply doing this world a civic duty.

Once I got back to town, I could go and see Damien and find out what he wanted. Until then, I didn't have to worry about what he wanted or having to answer to him. He wasn't my boss and he wasn't about to be. I didn't need anyone in my corner. I didn't need to be a part of some misfit family like he had going over there, or like the guys in the Agency. I was perfectly fine on my own and that was how I was going to keep it. That's how I liked it.

CHAPTER FOUR

Travis

I MADE MY way toward the first house that I was going to be checking out today. I had received the list of abandoned properties that the city owned and I was planning on checking out the houses that would be outside of the gang-infested areas.

I had no idea what condition some of these properties would be in. Unfortunately, the listing only had the address and that was it. There were no photos or much detail about the property itself. I tried to do some research on the properties last night, but there wasn't much coming back on them. All I was able to pick up was what type of property it was, such as a house or an apartment complex. I wanted to avoid apartments or homes that had been turned into different apartments. I wanted the children to be able to have their own home. It would be easier for security purposes as well if we didn't have to try and worry about who else could be renting the same house.

What I wasn't made aware of until late last night, was that Damien was going to be accompanying me to each of the properties. He was going to be running a threat assessment on each home to see if it would be a viable option for a safe haven. I also knew that he would be there to ensure I didn't cross paths with anyone dangerous while I went into abandoned buildings.

There was nothing stopping the homeless or drug users from squatting in the properties. As a result, it could be dangerous for me to go into them completely unarmed and alone. I was a Social Worker, so I was not about to start carrying a gun with me. I didn't like them to begin with and I didn't even know how to shoot one. Having a bit of added protection would be nice.

I didn't know Damien on a personal level. I had heard of him from other Agents in the Agency and from Isaiah. I had never met him, though, nor had I ever shared a conversation with the man. From everything that I had heard, he sounded like a decent man who was serious about his work and passionate about his business. I couldn't fault a man for any of that.

I was hoping he would keep everything professional and not want to engage in small talk all day. That could be exhausting. It wasn't that I didn't enjoy a good conversation, it was that I didn't care to share personal information about myself. Isaiah had been trying for years now to come over to my place and I always had an excuse as to why he couldn't. Baxter never wanted anyone over at the apartment in case he decided to come by. He wasn't going to risk anyone even seeing him with me in case they thought we were together.

To Baxter, being gay was the ultimate sin. He hated gay people and found them disgusting. However, if he ever wanted to feel true pleasure, he had to give in to his urges and have sex with a man. It was what made our interactions so violent and hostile. He had all of this self-hatred and self-disgust within him that he had to take it out on someone, and I was the only one he could take it out on.

I had grown used to keeping everything a secret. I had gotten used to making sure I chose my words carefully when I was around people so nothing ever slipped. It made conversations exhausting and I often found that they weren't worth all of the work and energy needed to bother. So with any luck, Damien would only want to focus on the job and nothing personal.

I pulled up to the first house and turned my car off after parking. The area wasn't too bad. There were some older homes in the neighborhood that needed work, but people were living in them. The house that we were going to be looking at was very rundown and I suspected the outside didn't do the inside any justice at all. Honestly, I was surprised it was even still standing. It looked like a good gust of wind would knock it right over. I knew they were going to be in rough shape, they were homes that were abandoned and had gotten picked up by the city with the hope that one day they would do something with them. So far, no one had been interested in purchasing them and the city held zero interest in renovating them or turning them into a business to sell. They could be perfect for safe havens if we were able to renovate them so they would be safe and livable.

I saw Damien pull up and park. I climbed out of my car and made my way toward him. I couldn't help but look around to make sure I hadn't been followed. I knew it was silly. Baxter wouldn't know I was out this way and he would never ask about me. That would attract too much unwanted attention to him and he wouldn't risk people questioning if he was friends with me. I was safe, but I still felt like I was being watched. I was hoping that feeling would fade with time.

"Hey. Damien, right?" I said, once I was close enough.

"Morning, it's nice to finally meet you properly," he said as he held his hand out for me.

I easily took it and I couldn't help but notice the warmth that I felt with just a single touch from him.

"It's nice to meet you," I said, doing my best to not stutter.

I pulled my hand back and started to head toward the house. He easily followed behind me and I could see him looking around. I knew he had to work security and a big part of that was taking in the neighborhood and area of the potential safe haven. We had to make sure it would be safe from outside threats for everyone living in it.

"So, what made you decide to move to Baton Rouge?" he asked as we headed inside.

"Isaiah wasn't in a position to move, so I offered to," I answered, trying to keep it short and simple. It also wasn't a lie, so it would be easier to keep track.

I didn't want everyone knowing about Baxter or that I had been in an abusive relationship. I didn't want to be seen as a victim. As the guy who everyone had to walk on eggshells around. I didn't want to be seen that way and I wasn't about to start fresh by having to carry around that baggage.

"How are you liking it so far?" he asked next.

"Um, it's good. You?" I asked, trying to get the attention off me.

"Yeah, it's a nice enough town. Bigger than what I'm used to. It's been a long time since I've lived in a town this size. Makes it easier to find clients, though."

I just gave a nod as I moved around the house and started to take notes on what would need to be fixed up. I would have to submit a rough estimate of what would be needed by the city to make these homes livable. That was going to be the trick. I knew the city wasn't going to want to hand over a great deal of money just to make foster homes. However, they were going to have to do something if they didn't want a repeat of what recently happened. At least I had the most recent tragedy on my side. That wasn't a good thing morally, but for getting the city to agree to hand over thousands of dollars, it helped to have the media still up in arms over the death of nine innocent children. If we were going to make this happen, we had to move fast to get the support money.

"What about your family? Any siblings, your parents still alive?" He asked after a few minutes.

"No siblings and my parents are alive."

Typically I would ask him the same question, but I didn't want to make small talk. I didn't want to do the first date questions. I wanted to keep this strictly professional.

"Did you move here alone? Or do you have a boyfriend?" he asked next.

"No," I said, perhaps too tightly.

I really didn't want to talk about my past relationships. Not that it was any of his business to begin with. We didn't know each other and it wasn't like I was trying to be his friend. I didn't need friends. At least, not right now. I had to settle into my new life first, and start to work on myself before I tried to bring other people into my life. Hopefully, he would be able to accept that.

He must have gotten the picture that I wasn't about to keep talking, because the questions stopped. I finished making my way around the house and I could see that Damien had explored the house as well and had noted a few things down on his pad of paper. I suspected it was entry points that could be weak spots. The trick was we had to make the place look like a normal home so it wouldn't attract unwanted attention. If we put bars on the windows, people would talk about it and wonder what the kids had done to be in a house this secure. A crucial part of safe havens was their anonymity. No one knew where they were located, so they couldn't hire someone to go in and kill one of the witnesses.

"Is it viable?" I asked Damien once we both returned to what I assumed was the living room area.

"Construction wise, it seems like it's got solid bones. It needs a lot of work done on the inside. I think if we get bulletproof glass on all of the windows and add some locks to them they will be safe. The trick will be the front and rear doors. We will need to find some type of security door that doesn't come across as a security door. The neighborhood seems to be in decent shape. I'll run their names when I get back to the office and make sure there aren't any criminal connections in the surrounding homes. Pending that, I think it's viable."

"Perfect. I have two more places that I can see today and then more tomorrow. Is that good for you?"

"Lead the way," he said with a nod.

We both made our way out of the house and I locked it up before I got to my car. He was going to follow me in his. I was happy to hear that it would be a viable option if we could get the money to renovate the house. I would need his threat assessment and his approval for it, but if everyone in the area came back clean, I was confident I would have it.

Ideally, we needed five homes to start with to make sure everyone had a safe place to be and we didn't have too many children in one home. That was the problem with the current safe haven homes. There were anywhere between seven to a dozen children in each home. And with only one person watching and caring for that many children, it was too much. We needed to have enough homes so that we could get the numbers down to five children maximum, with two adults in the home. It was going to be a lot of work, but I knew it would all be worth it in the end. For now, we had one house pending and I needed to find four more.

CHAPTER FIVE

Damien

WALKING AWAY FROM Travis didn't feel right. I couldn't help but feel like I was missing something vital about him.

All day long, he had been a bit jumpy and he seemed to be waiting for something to happen. He was trying to hide it, but my trained eyes could see the internal struggle he was going through. It could have easily been a side effect of his job. He did go into people's homes and remove children that were not safe. It wasn't just the cases that he worked on for the Agency, he had his own cases that he needed to work for the city and there was no telling how violent some of those cases could be.

When someone was dealing with children and having to remove them from their parents, emotions ran hot. The parents could take their anger out on him. Travis would be an easy target for their anger at themselves or the situation. He also wasn't a very large guy, he was definitely on the smaller side, and that would make him an easier target for their rage.

He was thin and I couldn't help but wonder if he was eating properly or if his job was getting to him. I knew it could be hard to be a social worker who worked with children. I knew that Travis had been involved in multiple cases for the Agency and had seen some of the worst that humanity had to offer. Seeing children being abused and injured day in and day out would take a toll on anyone. It wouldn't be surprising if he had trouble sleeping or eating at times.

It did concern me, though, that he was so thin. It shouldn't have mattered to me, but I couldn't help it. He didn't come across as healthy. He seemed very nervous, anxious, and stressed, and it wasn't good for someone to live that way. I had tried to talk to him, but every attempt to get any type of personal details from him was shot down. He kept everything professional and it was clear he didn't trust me on any level.

I was used to not being trusted, though. There had been plenty of times when I met with someone and they were uncertain about me. Whether it was due to my appearance, or the fact that I was the new guy in a job.

I would eventually earn Travis' trust. It would take time, but I also knew that working together had a way of forging bonds with people. I would earn his trust and, hopefully, he would feel like he could talk to me about anything that he was feeling or what was going on with him.

I was oddly fascinated by him. He was a good looking man, even if he looked like he needed a few good meals into him. He seemed to care a great deal about children and he took his job very seriously. He came across as a man with a good heart and that only made him more attractive.

I arrived back at the office for the

detective agency and I trudged down the hall toward my office, intending to get started running the names of the neighbors for the one potential safe home location. I figured since I was aware some of the guys were already out working on a case and I knew that Sebastian had gone over to the FPA to see if there was something he could help out with, I'd have some time alone to work on this case. I loved my brother, but Sebastian always got antsy when he didn't have anything to do and sometimes he got under my skin in his boredom so I was glad he'd gone over to the Agency today.

The second I walked into my personal office, I was instantly annoyed. Max was back from whatever he was doing. He was sitting in the extra chair in my office with his boots up on my desk as he sat back in the chair. He knew that it drove me insane when he put his dirty boots on my desk, when anyone did it. This man was driving my tolerance and he knew it.

I tried my best to be understanding with him, to be patient and open minded where his quirks were concerned. He was very rough around the edges and I was trying to calmly help to smooth them out.

To get to know who he was at his core, but this man could make a nun swear.

I went over and pushed his boots off from my desk as I spoke. "Where the hell have you been?"

He actually rolled his eyes at me, like he was twelve, as he put his legs up on the chair next to him. "You're not my father. He's in the ground getting eaten by worms. You seem very confused by that."

It was a good thing I wasn't his father, because when I punched him in his pretty face it wouldn't be child abuse. This man was the definition of guarded, and I knew that, I did, but some days it was very hard to remember that his attitude was his armor and not just his shitty personality.

I knew he had been through a lot growing up. I knew he had seen horrific things from his time in the FBI and while he followed his father around the country. His own father had raped him repeatedly, and he had been through horrible things at a very young age and I knew that could screw anyone up. I knew he had problems. What happened to him growing up didn't magically disappear because he was an adult. It had to be dealt with before the trauma would be able to be healed.

Max's way of protecting himself, from keeping the world from getting too close to him, was his attitude. He wore it like an armor and it screamed leave me the fuck alone. He wasn't arrogant or cocky. He was just unapproachable. He constantly wore this *fuck you* face that made everyone want to avoid any type of conversation with him. Being close to Max was the equivalent of dry humping a cactus naked.

I was trying to remember that he had been traumatized. I was trying to work on getting through some of the walls that he had placed around himself. The problem was, they were reinforced steel that was about six inches thick. Nothing short of a bomb would make a dent in his walls. I had yet to find anything that we could connect with outside of possible work cases. Something that would be a starting point for us to have a normal conversation or normal interactions on a more personal level.

I didn't want him to feel like I was lecturing him all the time. I didn't want him to feel like he couldn't come to me if he needed to talk or needed help. I would love for him to be *one of the guys* here. To see the guys that he works around most days of the week as friends, as brothers. I wanted all of our guys to feel like they had a family and a home here. And that was something that Max desperately needed, even if he didn't think so.

"I employ you, I have the right to know when one of my employees takes off to without any notice," I countered as I sat down.

"I work for you part-time when you need the extra hands. Not really the same thing. I'm basically a contract worker, so I can come and go whenever I want. But you will be happy to hear that I am back in town and open for work."

"Open for money, you mean," I pointed out.

I knew what he was doing. He was only working when he needed money to keep paying his bills and to cover travel expenses. Once he had enough, he went off to hunt down his next target on his personal list. I wasn't legally an accessory to murder, but I knew if Mason discovered that I knew what Max was doing, he would stop utilizing me and my guys for their cases. If it had just been me and

Sebastian, I wouldn't have thought much about it, but our guys relied on the money coming in from the FPA cases and I was not about to screw them out of something they needed for their families.

"Why else do people work?" he countered with a smirk.

"Some people do it because they want to make a difference in the world. You do know that you could be making a bigger difference if you worked full-time here or at the FPA. Compared to going out there and being a vigilante, at least."

It wasn't that I didn't understand why he did it. I truly did comprehend his reasons and the younger version of me would have been right there with him. I completely agreed that there were too many times when the justice system failed and dangerous criminals got to walk away scot free without suffering any punishment or injury. I completely agreed that those criminals deserved to be killed. That people who murdered, abused and molested children should automatically be sentenced to death and not allowed to languish on easy street in a jail cell. If anyone destroyed a child's life, they should have to pay for it with their own life. Yes, prison wasn't fun, but they were getting three meals a day, they could still work and make money, crappy money but money nonetheless, and they still had their lives. They could even use computers, get an education, get married, have sex, they could have a lot of luxuries that came with life.

Whereas if they lived through the horrible experiences done to them, some of their victims would never be able to function normally in society again. Some might never be able to tolerate being touched by another human being again. Others might never be able to leave their own home because of the trauma they experienced. It wasn't right that the evil people who did that to them got to live out the rest of their life comfortably.

Still, Max was putting himself in a dangerous position. He could potentially be arrested for murder and spend the rest of his life locked up. And then what would happen to all of the children out there who are waiting for someone to come through the door and save them from their hell. He wanted to make a difference, but he was going about it the wrong way and I had been trying to get him to see that for months now.

"So you have said. Look, I am careful and I cover my tracks. Besides, when the cops find the bodies it's not like they are going to be heartbroken and alert the media to seek justice for their death. No one cares when a monster gets put down."

"Monster or not, the detectives still have to solve their cases, regardless of who the victim is. Every time you go out there to kill someone, you are putting yourself at risk of being thrown in prison. How are you going to help people if that happens? How many children will you save then? You're not thinking about the long-term or seeing the bigger picture. All you can see is your father's face on every child molester, but your father is dead. You killed him, you don't need to keep killing him to help children."

And that was exactly it. The trauma was still too fresh in Max. He wasn't able to see anything but Phillip's face on each of his targets. He was still trying to get justice for himself and he was using surrogates to accomplish it. He needed time to process what happened to him growing up and the fact that he did kill his own father. He wasn't giving himself the time that he needed and I was worried it would get him killed one day.

"What I do with my time is none of your business," he said, with a deadly edge lacing his voice.

I had apparently pushed too hard today and I knew I was going to have to let it go for now. Thankfully, I had something we could talk about.

"We have a new case we're working. Travis, a Social Worker for the Agency, needs to create new safe havens after the last one was set on fire and killed nine children. Mason would like us to run security and threat assessments while the homes are being designed and built. I saw Travis today and we are meeting tomorrow for nine in the morning at a potential location. I'll text you the address."

He just gave a nod before he climbed to his heavily booted feet. I felt slightly surprised at the easy acquiesce. I figured he would have given me some excuse about him not doing a case this simple. It seemed like Max needed money more than I thought he did. It worked well in my favor, though, because now I would be able to keep an eye on him and maybe start to put a dent in his steel armor.

CHAPTER SIX

Max

IT WAS JUST before nine in the morning when I pulled up out front of the address that Damien had texted to me.

I wasn't looking forward to spending the day with Damien. We had worked together in the past before, but that was different. We had been working a case for the Agency so there had been plenty of things for us to focus on. We had been chasing down a criminal. This time, though, there would be no suspects to chase down, no crime scene to investigate. We would be basically walking around checking out buildings and making sure Travis didn't get hurt in the process. There wouldn't be any buffer between us and I wasn't really in the mood to deal with him trying to judge or lecture me about my life choices.

There were only two reasons I was even here. First, I needed the paycheck. Second, and more importantly, it would allow me to see Travis. I didn't know him. I had only seen him in passing and I'd heard little things about him through the grapevine. What struck me the most was the fact that everyone had basically said the same thing. A nice, quiet, shy man who had a good heart. That wasn't the issue. It was all the things they hadn't said about him. There was never any talk about his personal details. Little details that usually came up in conversation with someone. No one knew where exactly he lived. No one had been over to his place. No one knew anything about his personal life outside of him being gay. He didn't appear to go out and hang out with friends or even colleagues at the end of the day. He kept to himself and where most people took it as him being shy and introverted, I couldn't help but wonder if something more was going on. To say the man and his possible secrets intrigued me was an understatement.

Lots of people who were introverted went out and got a job where they would have to deal with the public. I had seen it plenty of times and I knew when they got home at night they didn't want to do anything but crash on their couch and watch some television. All of that was normal, but Travis didn't come across as the type to me. I had a weird feeling it wasn't just that he didn't *want* to share personal details about his life, but rather it was almost as if he wasn't *allowed* to.

In the rare couple of times that I'd seen him interacting with someone, I would hang back and watch. Not in a creepy stalker way, but in a curious way. I wanted to see what I could gather from the man who had caught a lot of people's curiosity. Him not wanting to talk about anything personal had almost become a game with the people Travis worked with. As if they were collecting points every time they got a new piece of intel out of him. Only, it seemed to me like it was a game everyone was going to lose, because Travis was extremely careful with his choice of words. He never let anything slip. It was as if his very life depended on it.

And that very realization was what made me so curious about him, because maybe his life literally did depend on him being quiet. He could have easily been on the run, but my gut said not from the cops, from someone dangerous.

Travis didn't come across as someone who had broken the law. He honestly came across more as a victim with his size and timid personality. He almost appeared scared of life, which was odd considering he wasn't that young. He was twenty-seven. He had enough years behind him to help teach him valuable lessons to make him tougher. Looking at him, I couldn't help but wonder what he might have gone through to make him that way. I was willing to bet his self-confidence was in the shithouse. That either came from a traumatizing childhood, shitty parents, or both. I wasn't sure just yet which category Travis fell under.

I wanted to know, though. The protective side of me was screaming out at me to protect him and try to make him feel safe. I didn't even know what I was supposed to be making him feel safe against, but maybe this was the opportunity that I needed to try and get some information out of him. To finally have a chance to sneak into his fortress and learn something that other people didn't already know about him. I almost felt obsessed with figuring the man out when no one else could.

I could also see the irony in the situation, because I was positive that Damien was trying to do the very same thing with me. Only, I didn't need anyone's protection. I was more than capable of taking care of myself and I didn't want or need anyone in my life.

I enjoyed being home alone. I enjoyed not having a connection to anyone who could either hurt me or leave me. I enjoyed having random one-night stands in the back of the clubs. Everything was simpler that way. Easier. No emotions were involved, no expectations or strings. Both parties knew it was just for sex and that names were irrelevant. Everything was simple and easy and I was not looking to have anyone come into my life and complicate things.

I saw both Damien and Travis pull up so I climbed out of my car. I glanced over and saw the both of them exiting their own vehicles and once again my gaze landed on Travis. He was wearing a long sleeved turtleneck and that instantly tossed up a red flag in my head. It wasn't that cold out. Both Damien and I were wearing t-shirts. There was no need for Travis to be wearing a long sleeved shirt, much less one with a turtleneck. That was overkill and I couldn't help but wonder why he was wearing one.

In the times that I had seen Travis, he was usually always wearing a long sleeve or a sweater or jacket. He never walked around in just a t-shirt, not even when it was a casual dress day for his job. I hadn't thought much of it before because I didn't see him on a regular basis, but now I was starting to question it. It was just another piece to his puzzle and soon enough, I would have enough pieces to be able to figure out what the puzzle was.

"I don't believe we have been officially introduced. I'm Max Morris," I said to Travis as I held my hand out for him.

"Travis Manning," he said as he gently took my hand in his.

I ignored the light bolt of electricity that raced up my arm at the contact of his skin against mine. It wasn't that Travis wasn't my type, he was, it was that we were here for work. But maybe if I could get him to open up to me more, we could have some serious fun later on.

Travis quickly pulled his hand back and I couldn't help but wonder if maybe he felt the same electricity hitting him that I did. He scanned the area as he spoke.

"This is one of the houses we are considering using."

Both Damien and I turned to see the house that was across the street. The house was in rough shape, but I suspected that was by design. Social Services wanted to be able to renovate the older homes that the city owned to turn them into safe havens. It was on us to make sure it would be safe for the children who were seeking shelter. We walked inside and we all started to look around. It was in very rough shape, but it appeared to be all cosmetic work from what I could pick up.

"It's a low crime area," Damien commented.

"There's also not much around. That could be a problem if the kids need help. There's no open businesses and the houses in the area are all rundown and either empty or homeless people live in them," I added.

"Which would be an issue if something happened. There wouldn't be any witnesses or someone who would call the police," Travis said with complete understanding.

When doing a threat assessment we had to focus on other factors than just the initial home. We had to focus on the other factors like who would potentially be around the children and who won't be. We didn't want the kids within the gang areas of the town because most of them needed safety. At the same time, we didn't want them almost isolated because if something did happen there was no one they could go to for help. We had to find a balance. It was why places like the suburbs were good for safe havens. There was safety within a community, even if the people around them didn't know they were helping to protect a child.

"I don't think this would be the best place for a safe haven. We need a more populated area," I said.

"I agree. We run the risk of having a nosy neighbor in a more populated area, but it would be better than not having anyone around. We also aren't that far away from the gang area. If they start to spread out into other territories, it would bring them too close to here," Damien added.

"Okay, then. I'll remove this place from the list of possibilities. Do you have a bit more time? There's another house we can check out."

"We have all day," Damien said, flashing a warm smile at me.

The asshole knew I didn't really want to be doing this. Well, the joke was on him because I was very interested in spending more time with Travis. Even with us being inside the house, Travis didn't seem to loosen up any. He still seemed like he was on edge, waiting for an attack to happen.

I was getting a bad feeling in the pit of my stomach. Whatever was making Travis this hyper vigilant and on edge all of the time, it had to be bad and I suspected it was still fresh within him. He had seemed antsy and anxious other times I'd seen him as well, but I had never seen it at this level. It could just be because he was in a new town and still trying to adjust to it, but I suspected something had happened to force the difference in him. Maybe even had a hand in him deciding to make the move down to Baton Rouge. Whatever was going on, I was going to find out. I was going to be keeping a very close eye on Travis and I wasn't going to stop until I finally had the whole puzzle completed.

And if he was in trouble, I would be there to make sure he was safe. If there was a threat out there looking to cause him harm, I would eliminate it. I wasn't going to allow anyone to hurt him, not while there was still breath in my body.

CHAPTER SEVEN

Travis

I SHOULDN'T BE here. I knew I shouldn't be here, but I felt like this was something I *needed* to do.

I wanted to wash away Baxter and everything that he put me through in order to start fresh. I needed a rebound, a one-night stand that meant nothing to me to cleanse my body and my mind from Baxter. More importantly, I needed to remind myself what good sex felt like. I wanted to remind myself what an orgasm felt like. I needed this tonight, more than anything else. I had to be able to be myself. I had to be able to be out and proud again. I had to be able to have sex and enjoy it, to crave it like I used to do before Baxter came into my life. I needed to be able to feel free and that was what tonight was all about.

The club was packed and from what I had heard from the locals, this place was the number one spot in Baton Rouge for meaningless sex. It was also the hottest gay club in town and it showed. Even though it was only the beginning of the week, the place was full to capacity. Apparently, I wasn't the only one in need of a random hook up.

I made my way through the crowd to reach the bar. After ordering a drink, I took a moment to scope out the room. The club itself was actually pretty nice and well kept. There was a massive dance floor, unsurprisingly, that took up the majority of the room. Along the walls, though, there were booths that were lined red with a black table.

Even though it was a club, all of the dance floor lights made it possible for me to be able to see all around the room without someone hiding in the shadows. I really liked that. At least this way I would be able to see the people around me without having to try and guess what I was seeing.

The patrons were all very different from each other. I could see some clear manly gay men, the flamboyant gays, the cross dressers, the bears, and the spinners. There was a healthy mix in the crowd.

I myself preferred the manly gay type. I liked a man who worked with his hands, had muscles, wasn't too old, but old enough that games weren't involved. A man who didn't cling and could understand it was a one time deal.

That was supposed to be Baxter. When we met in that club, it was only supposed to be a one time deal. It wasn't supposed to go anywhere and that was something we'd both wanted. But then one time turned into two, and before I even knew it, he was practically living with me.

That wasn't going to happen tonight. I wasn't going to allow that to happen tonight or any other night. I wasn't going to be in a relationship for a very long time and I doubted I was ever going to allow another man to invade my home and live with me again. I had already done that and it turned out to be the worst few years of my life. I was determined that I wasn't going to be a victim ever again.

"Well now, isn't this a surprise," a voice said from behind me.

I knew that voice. I had only just met him earlier today, but I knew that voice. I turned to see Max standing behind me holding a drink in his hand. I had no idea he was even gay, so I was very shocked to see him there out of all places.

Most people saw me, they knew I was gay. It hadn't been anything that I kept hidden and my size didn't do me any favors. I was surprised that he was gay, though. I didn't expect that curveball.

I knew he had done some work for Mason with the Agency and helped Damien out with his business. I never expected for him to be into men, though. I didn't get that vibe from him. My gaydar wasn't perfect, but it was pretty close. I knew Damien was gay from what I had heard and seeing him yesterday had only confirmed it. Max had slipped underneath my radar, though.

"I'm surprised to see you here," I said as he moved closer to stand beside me.

"In a gay club or a club in general?" he

asked, flashing me a warm smirk.

"A gay club. I didn't know you were gay."

"I am and it's not something I hide, either. What about you?"

"Oh no, I'm out. I've been out practically my whole life." Not that my parents ever cared or noticed.

"Good, I never got the whole closet thing. People are happier when they are being their true self. People shouldn't have to feel like they need to hide a huge part of themselves from the world."

"I couldn't agree more," I said, flashing him a warm smile. It was refreshing to speak to someone who felt the same way that I did. I never saw the point in hiding that I was gay. It was a serious piece of me and I never felt like I should have to be ashamed of it or try and hide it away.

"So, what brings you here tonight? Looking for a boyfriend to kick off your new life?" he said, and then took a swig of his drink.

"No, not a boyfriend. Just looking for a quick rebound to cleanse my palette. You?" I didn't want to talk about Baxter. I didn't want to have to think about him. Tonight was all about me and my own pleasure. Baxter had no place in my life anymore.

"Looking to scratch an itch. I've been pretty busy recently. If it's a rebound you are after, maybe we could help each other out," he said with a flirty smile and a wink that made heat wash over my body.

I would be crazy and blind to not notice how sexy Max was. He was exactly my type and under normal circumstances, I would have easily jumped at the opportunity to have sex with him. But we wouldn't be two strangers meeting in a club, and that posed a problem. I would have to see him tomorrow morning at work. I would end up seeing him around on different cases even once the current case he was helping me with was wrapped up. Hooking up with Max wouldn't be something that could stay here at the club. It would be reckless for me to sleep with him, so why wasn't I instantly saying no?

He held his hand out to me as he spoke. "Dance with me?"

It was a terrible idea and yet, I placed my hand in his and allowed him to guide me over to the dance floor. He turned me around so my back was pressed against his chest and his hands went to my hips, grasping me firmly. I couldn't help but tense up at his closeness. I knew I'd come here for some fun times, but now that I was going through with it, I couldn't help but be tense. Questions raced through my mind at warp speed.

What if it didn't feel good?

What if Max was just like Baxter and didn't even touch me?

What if he only cared about his own pleasure?

What if he didn't care that I didn't get off?

What if he was too rough or abusive?

I wanted to enjoy sex again. I wanted to embrace who I was, but now I was seriously starting to second-guess if this evening was even a good idea at all.

And what about my bruises?

There was a chance he would notice them. I was wearing a long sleeved shirt and I really only needed to drop my pants a bit, but if he wanted me fully naked, he was going to see the bruises.

Shit.

This was a mistake.

I shouldn't be here.

"Hey, relax. We're just dancing.

Nothing has to happen tonight, we're just dancing and having a good time. Stop thinking, stop worrying, and just allow your body to feel," Max whispered, into my ear, his voice all sorts of growly and sending shivers down my spine.

I closed my eyes and tried to relax. Max was right, I just needed to relax and allow myself to feel good. I needed to stop thinking and worrying about what could happen. I could easily say no at any point, should I change my mind.

I felt Max gently move my hips in time to the bass of the music and I allowed myself to feel the beat. I swayed my hips along with Max as he pressed up against me. He felt amazing against my body and I couldn't help but wonder how incredible his skin would feel against mine.

As the songs changed, our movements got bolder. I started to get bolder. His hands against my hips started to trail up my torso and lightly ghost over the skin underneath my shirt. As his fingers touched my skin, they left a trail of electricity behind. I wanted him and I could feel he wanted me. His hardness felt very impressive pressed up against my ass and low back, and I wanted nothing more than to see it.

"We could go into the bathroom, if you want," he whispered into my ear.

I had never had a bathroom hookup before and it wasn't something I ever thought I would do, so all of this was new to me, but at that very moment it was the only thing I wanted. I had come here for this exact thing tonight and I would be a fool to turn it down. I could worry about the rest of it tomorrow.

"Lead the way," I said with a nod.

Max simply grabbed a hold of my hand and led me to the back of the club where the bathrooms were. I hadn't been here before, so I wasn't really certain what to expect. The second we walked into the bathroom, I noticed that it was empty, thankfully. I also noticed that it looked like a normal public washroom, only the bathroom stall doors had one hole in the middle of the door. It wasn't very big, but I was confused as to why it would be there. Max brought me over to the last stall and once inside, he closed and locked the door before his hungry mouth slanted over mine.

I instantly moaned at the sudden kiss and easily allowed Max to have full control over it. I didn't mind when the man that I was with took a bit of the control. I didn't need to be in control all of the time and I was good with letting the moment dictate who the aggressor was. I wasn't looking to be manhandled or dominated, I'd had enough of that from Baxter. I was looking for passion and someone who would show me pleasure to all new heights.

When the need for air became too great, Max pulled back a bit and spoke, his voice breathy as he panted. "Tell me you like to bottom."

"I only bottom." No truer words could have left my mouth. That was something I could confidently say and admit. I loved being gay and I loved to bottom. I held zero interest in even trying to top. When done right, the pleasure was indescribable being on the bottom.

"Fucking perfect."

I found myself being turned around very quickly and I heard the sound of Max removing his belt. I moved my hands down to undo my own pants, not all that surprised that Max wanted to skip foreplay. I was good with that, because in the end, I just wanted to feel pleasure and come with a guy inside of me again. I didn't need to have any foreplay as long as Max could make me feel pleasure again.

Max placed his hands on my hips and I easily allowed him to move me into whatever position that he wanted. I spread my legs as best as I could to give Max proper access to my ass with my pants and boxers around my ankles. The next thing I felt was a cold and wet finger being pushed inside of me.

"Fuck, you're tight," Max moaned.

I knew that all too well. Baxter used to tell me it all the time, but he had never bothered with stretching me before. It had been a long time since someone had stretched me first and the fact that Max cared enough to do it almost brought tears to my eyes. I had to blink a few times to fight them back. This wasn't about Baxter or any feeling associated with him. This was about me feeling good again and getting to feel true pleasure.

I started to moan as I felt Max add a second finger and start to scissor me, pressing against the tight ring of muscle to stretch me out. I was hoping that he wouldn't take too long, though. I needed his dick inside of me and I needed it now.

When I felt Max add a third finger and that finger hit my sweet spot, I couldn't hold back the loud moan that escaped my lips. It had been so long since I had felt that rush of pleasure and with just that one touch, I knew I had made the right choice by doing this tonight.

"I love that sound," Max said as he started to pick up the pace with his fingers.

"I'm ready, I want your dick," I moaned. I knew I wasn't fully stretched, but it was good enough. It wouldn't hurt anywhere near the amount I was used to.

"As you wish," Max said,

Max slipped his fingers out of me and I could hear him opening a condom and sliding it on. I couldn't wait until I could feel him inside of my needy hole. When I felt the tip of Max's dick against my pucker, I knew that Max was big; he was bigger than I imagined when we were dancing against each other.

Max kissed the back of my neck as we both breathed heavily.

"This isn't going to be sweet and gentle," he warned.

"Good, I want it hard and deep," I said

with a heavy breath. I didn't want it sweet and gentle right now. I wanted to be taken on a rollercoaster of pleasure.

I let out a deep moan as I felt his tip slip inside of me and I reveled in the burn as he stretched me even more. Max didn't disappoint. He didn't stop the forward motion, the intense pressure, until he was balls deep inside of me. I loved that he didn't stop or go slow. I loved that Max buried himself deep inside of me in one go. He knew what he wanted and he went for it.

Max didn't hold back after that. I felt him pull all the way out before he slammed right back in. I groaned at the slight shock of pain that raced up my spine, but I wasn't bothered by it, I knew it would turn into a deep pleasure soon enough.

Max's pace was hard and fast and the next time he slammed back into me, I felt nothing but pure pleasure. I had to fight to keep my moans from echoing off of the walls.

The sound of the door opening and footsteps told me that someone else was here, but it was only one person and not another couple. At the next powerful thrust, I had to bite my lip to keep the moan from coming out. I didn't mind someone else being in the bathroom, but I didn't exactly want to put on a show for them, either.

I felt Max's hot breath against my ear as he whispered, "Let it out. Let him hear how much you love having a dick pounding into your ass."

A sharp thrust from Max caused me to let out a very loud moan that anyone in the bathroom could easily hear. I figured there was no point in staying quiet now, the man obviously knew we were there and having sex.

Max continued to hammer deep into me and I wished that he would touch my aching dick. I would have loved to feel his rough hand clasped around my dick. If he didn't do it soon, I knew I would have to do it. I wanted to feel his skin on me, though, and not my own hand.

"Oh fuck," I moaned out on a strangled breath as a strong thrust just skimmed my sweet spot.

I heard the man's footsteps moving over to the bathroom stall and for a second, I felt a jolt of excitement shoot through my body. I had never had someone on the other side of the door standing there listening in before, I couldn't help but wonder if the man was jerking off at the sounds of our sex. There was a sudden knock at the door and I was not sure what the man wanted.

"He wants to suck your dick," Max whispered to me.

Those words caused my dick to pulse and some precum dripped out, sliding down to coat my balls. "I've never done that before," I admitted.

"Let him, it's exhilarating," Max growled into my ear as he guided me, pushing my hips closer to the door.

I'd just realized what the holes in the doors were for and the thought ricocheted through my mind.

They were glory holes.

I felt Max guiding my hips forward and when he put his hand on my dick, I couldn't help but whimper at the sensation. I allowed Max to guide my dick through the hole and a second later, I felt a man's tongue run along the tip of my dick. I couldn't help but moan at the contact of his hot tongue in my slit, his heated breath washing over my hardness. The fact that I had no idea who this man was only made the pleasure more intense. The man then sucked my tip into the heat of his mouth and I saw stars dance in front of my eyes. I had never been with more than one man at the same time before, and this experience was already blowing my mind.

Fuck," I mewled at the pleasure that was coursing through me as one man fucked me and the other sucked me.

"So fucking tight. Your ass feels amazing around my dick," Max said loud enough for everyone in the bathroom to hear him.

"Fuck, right there. Don't stop," I cried out when Max hit my prostate dead on. I gave up all hope of staying quiet at that moment. If either guy was bothered by my sounds, I didn't care. My whole body was singing with pleasure. Between Max's harsh thrusts hitting my sweet spot over and over again, and the mystery man's mouth, I was barely able to stand upright. My knees were weak, my legs shaky from the pleasure taking over my body. Not only was this mystery man incredible at giving head, he was able to take all of me in his mouth. I could not explain the amount of pleasure I was in every time the tip of my dick hit the back of this man's throat.

I was a moaning mess and as Max picked up his pace even faster, I knew I wasn't going to last much longer. After a few more thrusts, I felt my balls pull up tight and electricity raced up my spine as my orgasm hit. I let a loud and deep groan as my cock thickened and I came right down the mystery man's throat.

Max followed a few moments later and I moaned at feeling his dick pulse inside of me. I wished I could have felt Max's dick without the condom so I could have felt his hot cum searing my insides. I could feel each pulse of cum shooting out of him and my walls clamped around his girth with each one.

Once he stopped pulsing, Max pulled back, slipping from my ass, and I felt the loss of his dick inside of me instantly. The mouth on my cock had let go and I stood back up. As I started to get myself redressed, I realized the other man hadn't moved away from the door, and I couldn't help but wonder why. I assumed most would've walk away right when everyone finished.

My curiosity got the best of me,

though. I had to know who had just given me quite possibly the best blowjob I had ever received before in my life. I reached out and unlocked the door and opened it. I couldn't believe who stood on the other side looking pleased with himself, and as the shock hit me, my jaw dropped open and heat climbed up my cheeks.

CHAPTER EIGHT

Damien

I HAD NO idea why I'd come to the club tonight. I had been so stressed and tense these past few months, I just needed something to take my mind off of it all. Something that would let me have some fun and forget about everything else that had been going on.

I had been to this club a few times since I had been in Baton Rouge. It was a decent club and the guys here had a wide variety of types to choose from. I wasn't really picky. I liked guys that had some muscles, but I also liked the spinner type.

I was more about personality than a set type. Tonight, though, no one was really catching my eye.

No one seemed to be interesting enough.

I had been hoping that I could find someone who would pique my interests. I was striking out, though, so I figured I would head out. I just needed to make a quick pit stop to the bathroom first.

I headed into the bathroom and saw that it was empty. The night was still young and I knew soon enough, there would be guys all over the place having sex and giving head wherever they could.

As I stood there taking a leak, I heard quite possibly the most amazing sound I had ever heard. A guy was moaning from one of the stalls and I could hear the telltale sounds of sex coming from the cubicle. I had heard moaning before, but for some reason this guy's voice was sending shocks of electricity down my spine.

I had fully intended to ignore it, to just let the couple have their fun in peace, but I just couldn't seem to help my curiosity and excitement. Instead of leaving after tucking my half hard cock back into my pants and washing my hands, I stood there listening to the sounds coming from the two men in the stall. Just hearing the loud, pleasurable moans of the one man was enough to make me rock hard in a heartbeat, something that normally never happened.

I couldn't just stand here and listen to them. I turned and strode over to the bathroom door, flicking the lock, and then I went over to the last stall. I was about to do something I had never done before. I was going to suck a guy off when I had no idea who he was or what he even looked like. I had never utilized the glory holes in the bathroom at the club, but my body was screaming at me to do it.

I gave in to the demand.

I knocked on the door and I assumed both men on the other side knew what that meant. I had no idea if they would even be up for it. Some guys wanted to just get off in the stall and be left alone, while others were all too happy to have the added sensation of a third person from outside.

A second later, I was on my knees as a beautiful hard dick was pushed through the hole. It was thick and large, easily eight inches with precum already dripping off of its tip.

I ran my tongue along the tip, probing the slit and loving the flavor dribbling down the man's cock. The man let out a deep moan at the contact and it only turned me on even more, making my cock throb as it pressed against my zipper.

I sucked on the man's tip, and moaned in appreciation as another trickle of salty fluid flooded over my tongue. I could not believe how amazing this man tasted. He was sweet, like honey, and it was a new flavor for me. One I could get used to, I decided.

He was simply delicious.

I used my free hand and unzipped my pants. Pulling my own rigid dick out, I started to stroke myself as I took as much of the man's dick as I could before my lips pressed against the edges of the hole in the door.

"Fuck," the man let out a throaty mewl, and I hummed around his length, pleasure coursing through me as I felt his cock twitch against the back of my throat.

"So fucking tight. Your ass feels amazing around my cock," the third man growled out and I could almost see his actions as he continued to pound even harder into the man whose cock was lodged deep in my throat.

"Fuck, right there. Don't stop," the man screamed in pleasure, his cock thickening as it slid in and out over my tongue.

They were no longer being quiet and I was loving every moment of it. Their sounds were driving me insane and my own cock throbbed and twitched in my hand, precum leaking heavily from its tip. I had never been this turned on before and neither of them had even touched me. I was so close to coming, I couldn't believe it.

I could feel the man's dick getting harder and harder in my mouth as I sucked him deep again. He was so obviously close to falling over that edge, too. For the first time in my life, I wanted to taste this man's cum so badly. The need for it was so strong that I thought it would break me.

After a few more deep moans and erratic thrusts into my mouth as the other man obviously powered into him, the man was coming hard down my throat. I moaned as the taste of him flooded my mouth. It was the sweetest taste I had ever had in my entire life. The taste of this man on my tongue was enough to push me over the edge.

My balls pulled up tight and fire raced up my spine as I erupted over my fist with a deep moan, one that was followed by another long, low groan as the third man in the room came as well. I could feel myself pulsing as I shot rope after rope of thick, white cum onto the floor.

I sucked on the man's tip, making sure I lapped up every last drop of his sweet cum before I reluctantly removed my mouth from his still hard dick. I stood, tucking my deflating shaft back into my pants.

I knew I should technically be leaving; they were done and would be coming out soon. My part in this escapade was over and I should leave them to theirs. I knew that was the typical expected etiquette in these situations, but I couldn't help myself. I had to know who the other men were, especially the one that I had just sucked off. The one whose taste called to me on so many levels.

I decided the need to know who was on the other side of that door was too great and it was worth the risk of being told off by the obvious couple. Apparently, one of the men on the other side of the door was thinking the same thing, because I didn't even have to knock before it was quickly unlocked.

The door opened and there standing on the other side were two people I never expected to see. Max stood behind the man that I had just given head to and that man was none other than Travis Manning.

Both stood there with their pants still undone and their dicks tucked away. They were both just as shocked as I was, if Travis' jaw drop and Max's shocked expression were any indication. I couldn't say I'd ever expected to see either of them in a place like that, let alone on the other side of a bathroom door. I knew they were both gay, so the possibility was always there, I guess, but they never came across as the club going types.

I couldn't believe it was them standing there in front of me. That we had just done *that*. I should probably be freaking out and I was fairly confident that would come later when the high wore off from my orgasm. Instead, I simply flashed them a cocky grin.

"Imagine meeting you guys here," I quipped.

Max was the first to snap out of it. He reached over, with Travis still in front of him, and grabbed me by my shirt, pulling me toward him as he spoke.

"I wanna taste him."

That was all I needed to hear. I grabbed Max by the back of his neck and pulled him in for a kiss, pressing my tongue into his mouth. Max moaned at the taste of Travis on my tongue. Our kiss turned heated very quickly, both of us fighting for dominance that I eventually won.

Kissing Max was not something I ever thought I would be doing, but I liked.

I liked it a lot.

When the need to breathe became too much, I pulled back and then looked over at Travis. I could see the heat in his eyes. He was turned on by watching us kiss. I saw Travis' gaze travel down to my mouth and that was all I needed.

Throwing all logic out the window, I gently grabbed Travis by his jaw and pulled him in for a kiss. I quickly dominated the kiss, shoving my tongue into Travis' mouth. He moaned and quickly submitted to me, causing a hum of approval to escape my own mouth. Travis shivered, leaning into the kiss, and I could feel myself getting harder knowing that Travis was turned on by me, by us. By the time I pulled back, we were both breathing heavily.

"We should take this party somewhere more private," Max suggested, but he kept his gaze on me.

I had a feeling if I said no, they might go off on their own and continue for another round. They were both still horny and Travis, he seemed hungry, very hungry. If I said yes, though, that could change everything. Right now, we were just three guys that hooked up in a bar unexpectedly. We could pass it off as an encounter in a dark club and call it a night.

We couldn't unring a bell, but we could ignore the chime.

The trick was, though, I didn't want to ignore it. As horny as they were, I was just as much. I wanted to feel their skin against mine. I wanted to keep kissing them and hearing their moans.

Just one taste wasn't enough.

"Where?" I finally asked.

"My place is ten minutes away," Max answered.

I glanced over at Travis and I could see he was all in for another round. Screw it. "Let's go."

Max and Travis quickly set their clothing to rights and once they were ready, we headed out. Max gave us both his address and we all climbed into our respective vehicles and made our way over to Max's place.

I still couldn't believe I was about to do this, but my whole body hummed with excitement. I had been with plenty of guys, but I had never done something like this before. I had never had a threesome and I was more than ready for it.

Could this be a colossal mistake?

Absolutely, but that was going to be tomorrow's problem. Tonight, I was going to have some fun.

***

Once we arrived at Max's place, we were instantly heading inside and up to his bedroom. I was so distracted by them that I didn't even bother with looking around.

The second we were in his bedroom,

Max was pulling Travis in for a heated kiss as they both worked on removing the other's clothing. I still couldn't believe I was about to do this, but at the same time, I was already through the looking glass.

I removed my clothes and made my way over to them. I placed a kiss to the back of Max's neck as my eyes landed on Travis, who was now naked.

"Whoa, hold up," I instantly said as my gaze scanned Travis' naked body.

Max pulled back from the kiss and I could tell he was a bit annoyed. That changed into anger as he saw why I'd said stop. Travis was covered in bruises, including one around his neck. They didn't look too old, a couple of weeks at most.

"Who did that to you?" Max asked with a deadly edge to his voice.

Travis simply rolled his eyes as he spoke. "It's from work. A father was upset that I was taking his son from him. His anger got the best of him, it's not a big deal."

"He choked you, that's a big deal," Max stated.

I had to agree with him on that one.

The bruises weren't from an angry father who lost control for a minute. Nope. Not a chance. This was serious. The bruising around his neck was deep enough to tell me that whoever put it there, didn't let go until damage was caused. It wouldn't have surprised me if Travis had lost consciousness from it. I hadn't heard of a problem from one of the cases, but I would be asking Mason about it tomorrow.

"Okay, we could talk about past cases if you want. Or, we could do something else," Travis commented as he got down on his knees and ran his tongue over the tip of my dick, causing me to moan at the contact.

"We could do something else," I relented as I looked down and watched as he sucked my tip, his gaze meeting mine through his lashes. Travis let out a hum of appreciation as he took me all the way down to my base, something that wasn't an easy task. I was on the larger size and most of the guys I had been with could never deep throat me.

"Holy fuck, he can deep throat," Max moaned at the sight of it.

I threaded my hand into Travis' hair

and pulled it a bit, causing him to whimper. Max came over to me and started to kiss me. As our tongues danced, I thrust my hips slightly, pushing myself even deeper in Travis' mouth. The sounds that were coming from Travis were driving me crazy and I knew that if he didn't stop soon, then I would be coming down his throat. Which would have been glorious, but I wanted to be coming with Travis' ass wrapped around my dick. Grasping his hair in my fist, I pulled Travis' head away from my dick as I broke the kiss with Max and spoke.

"Where's your stuff?"

Max just smirked as he went over to his bedside drawer and grabbed what we needed.

"I want your ass up. I'm gonna pound into you while you suck his dick," I ordered Travis.

That sentence caused both Max and Travis to moan, Travis' eyes lighting with excitement. Max quickly grabbed the lube and a condom as Travis climbed up and onto the bed on his hands and knees. He spread his legs wide to give me proper access. Max placed the lube and condom on the bed, before he got on the bed to kneel in front of Travis.

"Wrap that pretty mouth of yours around my dick," Max ordered.

Travis hummed as he instantly took Max in his mouth. Watching them was driving me crazy and I knew if I didn't get to be inside of Travis soon, I was going to explode.

I smeared some lube onto two fingers before I slowly inserted them into Travis' ass. He let out a deep moan at the pleasure coursing through him as I made quick work of stretching him. I knew he had already had sex, so it was really just about adding some more lube so I wouldn't hurt him.

Once he was ready, I rolled the condom over my hardness and, without waiting a beat, pushed my tip inside of him. Even though he had been stretched a bit more, I couldn't believe how tight his ass was. It felt amazing as his muscles clamped around my dick. I pushed my dick all the way inside of his ass and once I was balls deep, I stopped, allowing him a moment to accommodate to the intrusion.

I couldn't believe how amazing this felt. I had been with plenty of men in the past, but none had ever felt this good before. His ass was hugging my dick like a glove and I feared I could easily become addicted to the feeling. I glanced up and saw that Travis was devouring Max's dick like it was his last meal and I reveled in the sight.

"Fuck, those moans," Max groaned as he lightly shuttled his hips, his cock pressing into Travis' mouth.

I couldn't take it anymore. I pulled out almost all of the way before I slammed back in. I couldn't go slow even if I wanted to right at that moment. I couldn't believe how fucking amazing it felt to be inside of Travis as I watched him suck on Max. I never wanted it to stop. The intensity of the culmination of physical and visual stimuli was not something I had expected and it was driving me to the edge quickly.

Max reached over and placed his hand on the back of my neck, pulling me in to slant his lips over mine. I easily kissed him back, both of us fighting for dominance in the kiss and neither of us giving it up this time. The result was a very heated melding of mouths as our tongues fought with each other.

Max was the first one to pull back, he was breathing heavily and panting. I knew that meant he was going to come. Max's grip on the back of my neck tightened and he let loose a long, deep moan as his climax hit him.

"Fuck," Max moaned as his hips continued to twitch involuntarily and he emptied himself inside of Travis.

I pulled Max in for another kiss, one I quickly dominated as Max was distracted, still pulsing within Travis' mouth. I could feel myself getting closer to the edge, but I wanted to feel Travis come with my dick buried inside of him. I pulled back and spoke.

"Think we should let him come?"

"I think he's earned it," Max agreed as he pulled his semi-hard dick out of Travis' hungry mouth.

I used my right hand and grabbed Travis by the front of his neck in a very light touch. I didn't want to cause him any pain with the bruising already around his neck. I pulled him up so his back was against my chest, keeping my hand wrapped around his neck to hold him up against me.

Travis moaned at the new position and it made my dick pulse with need. I watched as Max got down onto the bed and ran his tongue over Travis' tip causing him to moan.

"Jesus, you taste so sweet," Max moaned, before he took Travis' tip into his mouth and sucked on it.

Travis moaned and I felt his left hand move over to my thigh, gripping it as the pleasure overtook his body.

I angled my hips and on the next thrust, I hit Travis right on his sweet spot. Travis let out a small scream and I could imagine the electricity the pleasure sent all up his spine.

"Fuck, oh fuck," Travis moaned as he moved his other hand up to my bicep, grasping it tight.

"You're so close. He wants to taste how sweet you are. Give him that sweet cum of yours. Come for us, Baby," I growled in his ear as I picked up my pace even more, hitting his sweet spot every time I pressed myself deep into his hungry hole.

I could feel the walls of Travis' ass tightening around my dick and I knew that he was about to come. In the next heartbeat, Travis let loose a deep, keening cry and then he was coming hard.

Max moaned as Travis' sweet tasting cum filled his mouth.

The tightness of Travis' ass clamped around my cock pushed me over the edge. I slammed into him as deep as I could and let out a deep groan as I shot my load into the condom.

I couldn't believe how hard I was coming. I had had mind-blowing sex many times before, and yet tonight had been even better than all of them combined. I couldn't believe how many times I was pulsing, still coming as Travis' ass kept a tight grip on my dick.

Max pulled his mouth off of Travis' dick and instantly moved to pull Travis in for a heated kiss. He shoved his tongue into Travis' mouth, sharing his own essence with him, causing them to both moan.

"See how sweet you taste?" I said into Travis' ear, causing him to shiver.

When Max pulled back, I used my hand that was still lightly around Travis' throat and I turned his head so I could claim his mouth for myself. I didn't think I would ever get tired of the taste of him. I felt Travis move his left hand up to the back of my neck as I deepened the kiss. I loved the faint taste of Travis' cum on his own tongue. He truly was sweet and I couldn't help but wonder what the hell he ate to get that sweet tasting.

When I finally pulled back, I removed my hand from his neck. Slowly, I pulled out of Travis' ass and got up so I could dispose of the condom.

Travis instantly collapsed down onto the bed as he breathed heavily. Max sat back on the bed and we both smirked at each other. We both knew it wouldn't be long before Travis was completely passed out.

CHAPTER NINE

Max

MY WHOLE BODY was tingling. I had had some pretty epic sex in my life, but I had never had sex that left me feeling this good. *Good* didn't even cut it; *amazing* didn't even cut it. I felt like I had just had the world's longest sex marathon and every inch of my body was feeling the pleasure from it. I had no idea sex could even feel this good.

People talked about threesomes all the time, but they never described it as that. They never said it could leave you ruined for regular sex. I had no idea that a case could turn out to be this interesting. I figured I would walk around the city with Travis and Damien and at the end of it, have a nice paycheck from it. I didn't think I would be having sex with them. Hell, I never would have thought I would ever have sex with Damien, of all people. Now technically, we didn't have sex with each other. We didn't even touch the other really. It was all about Travis.

Still, I couldn't help but wonder what his dick would feel like inside of me or down my throat. That man was very blessed in the manhood department. Typically, I was a top, but I had bottomed before. It was not something that I did often and I really had to trust the other person before I did it.

Damien had strolled out of the bedroom a few moments after we'd finished, to use my bathroom I figured. I looked over to see Travis completely passed out. I doubted he was going to be waking up any time soon. That was fine with me. I wasn't usually one for cuddling, but every now and then, I enjoyed not sleeping alone.

With the need for sex tamed, I could now focus on the bruising that seemed to cover Travis' body. I wasn't certain I believed him when he said they came from an upset parent. It was possible, sure, but I had a feeling it was something more.

Damien walked back into the room and I could see his gaze instantly going to Travis' sleeping form. I had a feeling he also didn't believe the story. I got up and grabbed my boxers, slipping them on as I spoke.

"Beer?"

"Sure," he said, nodding as he grabbed his own boxers and slipped them up his hips.

I tossed a blanket over Travis so he wouldn't get cold before I strolled out of the bedroom. I made my way down to my kitchen and grabbed two beers from the fridge as Damien wandered out to my back deck. I stepped out onto the deck and breathed a contented sigh. The coolness of the night felt good against my heated skin.

When I decided to move down here, I had looked for a house that would suit my needs. I didn't care too much about what it looked like as long as it was in a good area of the city and had what I needed within walking distance. If I was going to live in a larger city, I wanted to be able to have what I needed within a reasonable distance. There was a cafe that served decent coffee just down on the corner. A Chinese restaurant and a pizza joint were on the opposite corner. There were three bars and a gym all within a block from me. I had neighbors, but they weren't too close. We didn't share a fence and I liked that.

The house itself had three bedrooms and two bathrooms. It was roughly eighteen hundred square feet. I didn't care about having a big house or what it looked like. This was the only house for sale in an area that matched my needs, so I picked it up. It was an older home, but the bones were good. I figured I could always renovate it when the need or want hit me. I would rather use my money to take out my next target than to redo the kitchen, though.

I handed a beer over to Damien as I opened my bottle and leaned my arms against the railing of my deck.

"So, how's your night going?" I said with a smirk.

"Jesus," he said, before he took a

drink. "This never happens again and we don't talk about it," he added once he swallowed.

"Don't worry, I won't tell your little brother about the threesome you just had."

"I don't have a brother," he said with an edge to his voice and I couldn't help but roll my eyes.

"You know, if you don't want people figuring out that you're both lying, you shouldn't be around intelligent people that investigate for a living. Neither one of you is fooling anyone. We know you are brothers. It's pretty obvious given how close you are. Not to mention you have similar facial characteristics. The question is, are you on the run because you *committed* a crime or because you *witnessed* a crime. I'm willing to bet it's the second one. Not because I don't think you're capable of killing someone, but more about those morals of yours. If you were a criminal mastermind on the run, then you wouldn't care about me killing pedophiles. But you do, because to you that's not justice, which tells me you are hiding from some criminal organization that you helped to get justice for."

He could tell people all he wanted that him and Sebastian were best friends, and I'm sure they were, but they were also brothers. There was no doubt in my mind that they were hiding because they'd witnessed a crime. And from what I knew of both of the brothers, they weren't the running away type. They were forced away because they'd testified.

I hadn't seen a US Marshal around them, so that likely meant they were completely on their own. Most likely the Marshal had been killed and they had to run. There was probably a leak within the Marshals and it would have been safer for them to go at it alone.

They were smart about not splitting up. Most would have assumed it would be better for them to go separate ways so they wouldn't stand out. The trick with that, though, was they would inevitably call each other or send emails and that could be easily traced. It would have been safer to stay together in the same town.

"I suspect that story that Travis told is a lie," he said, not even acknowledging what I had said.

I didn't know what I was expecting. I guess I wasn't really expecting for him to tell me the story, though. To trust me with that information. It would have been nice to have it, to know what had happened to them and how long they had been in hiding. To know if the threat was truly still active or not. He didn't trust me on that level and I doubted he ever would. Him and Sebastian had been doing this for a while. I was willing to bet they had been on their own for a few years at least. I knew they had moved to Gaithersburg three years ago, so they had been in hiding for at least three years. He wasn't ready to let anyone else in and he had no reason to let me in. We didn't even really like each other.

"Of course it's a lie. He has bruises healing at different stages. He's anxious, always on edge, looking around, like he's waiting for someone to show up. He's been like that since the moment I met him. He's always wearing long sleeved shirts, sometimes turtlenecks. He doesn't release any personal information, doesn't let anyone over at his place," I listed off.

"He's being abused," Damien stated.

"Not anymore. His anxiety has picked up since I've known him. Whoever it was, he didn't move with him. And last night, he said he was looking for a rebound. He's trying to get over what happened."

It made sense why he was looking for a rebound. He had been abused and chances were his sex life had taken a dark turn and the common decency of mutual pleasure went out the window. Last night was about him taking his life back. It was about him having pleasure again and feeling like he mattered. He needed it more than Damien and me.

"Abusers don't always let their victim go," Damien stated and I knew that was all too true.

"Depends on how long they were together. Who his abuser was and if he is the letting go type."

There were two types of abusers. The first was the less dangerous kind, as hilarious as that sounded. They abused, but if their victim ran or left them, they wouldn't risk going to jail by stalking their ass and trying to kill them. They put their time and effort into finding a new victim instead.

The second type, though, were the dangerous ones, because they were the ones who didn't think they would ever go to jail. They were the ones that would stalk a victim across the county because the thrill of tormenting their victim was too great to turn away. They believed the victim belonged to them and they could do whatever they wanted with them. That the only freedom their victim would have is when they killed them. Whoever this man was that Travis had been dating, my gut said there was a fifty/fifty chance that he would follow him to Baton Rouge. And if that happened, if he got his hands on Travis again, Travis wouldn't be walking away. His abuser would kill him to make him pay for leaving in the first place.

"In my experience an abuser that chokes his victim that badly, they don't let them go."

"Personal or work experience?"

I highly doubted it would be personal, the man was huge, but he could have had a sister or his own mother could have been abused growing up.

"Work. I've never been abused," he gently answered.

"Loving parents,huh? What's that like?" I said sarcastically.

I had stopped playing the *what if* game a long time ago. The one where I created this whole world where I had two loving parents and my father didn't rape me for years. I'd lived within that world a lot growing up. I would tell myself that my mother was going to come in and rescue me from the life. And each day that it didn't happen, a small piece of me died until, eventually, there was nothing left. That's what people didn't understand. I'd died a long time ago.

"What about your mom? Where was she when you were growing up?" he asked, gently.

"Gone. She didn't want to be a mom. I found her six years ago, still working as a stripper and giving out blowjobs in the backroom for fifty bucks. My parents were never married. Phillip had been a regular customer at her strip club and one night she got knocked up. I guess I should be thankful that she stopped using cocaine when she discovered she was pregnant. So at least I wasn't born addicted to drugs."

"I'm sorry."

"Don't be. She was at least honest with herself. Too many parents who never should have been allowed to raise children, keep them because they think they have to. At least she knew she didn't want to have children and wasn't capable of being a parent. The best thing a shitty parent can do is step out of their child's life and let them be raised by someone who wants to be there. If Phillip had done the same, my life might have been completely different."

"Do you want kids?"

"Why, you want to adopt together?" I asked with a smirk.

"Some people like kids, some don't. I'm not burning to have a child, but I wouldn't say no if it was important to my partner."

I gave a shrug as I spoke. "I'm indifferent, I guess. Tomorrow should be interesting at work."

"We're three grown men, I'm sure we can be professional after a one-night stand. You good if I crash here?"

"You looking for round two?" I asked, flashing him a cocky grin as I looked at him.

He stepped closer to me, grasped my waist, and then turned me so my back pressed against the deck railing. He then placed a hand on either side of me, boxing me in before he spoke.

"There's that smirk. You're always

smirking. I have yet to see a real smile on your face. You want to lecture me about being friends with intelligent investigators, but you have your own secrets. You see mine, but I see yours, too. I see your armor, the steel walls you have built up around yourself so you don't have to be hurt again. You never allow anyone to see any form of weakness. You never allow anyone to see your strength waiver. You're afraid to let anyone get close because you can't be hurt again like you have. You want to belong somewhere, but you're afraid people will see that you have demons. That it takes a lot for you to get through each day without the pain and sadness creeping in. You don't have to be afraid of me, Max."

My heart was hammering against my chest. No one had ever been able to read me like he had before and that scared the hell out of me. I didn't want anyone to get close. I'd built the walls up around me for a reason and I was not about to let anyone tear them down. Everyone was a threat and danger to me. The walls kept me safe. It kept people from getting too close, from seeing the pain that surrounded me all the time. I didn't want people to see the pain, to see that I was weak, because that was when they'd move in and take advantage of me. I was never going to be a victim again. I refused to be.

Before I had a chance to even form words, he leaned in and gently pressed his lips against mine. The kiss was brief and I barely had the time to respond before he was pulling back.

"See you in bed," he said, before he turned on his heel and headed back inside.

I needed to get my heart to stop racing. A single kiss shouldn't have me feeling this way, not when it was just a simple kiss. He was putting a dent in my armor and I wasn't sure how I felt about any of it. I needed to repair the dent and keep my distance from Damien. Starting tomorrow, things had to go back to being strictly professional between us.

Tomorrow.

I headed inside and made my way up to my bedroom. The second I walked through the doorway, I could see both Damien and Travis tucked snuggly under the covers in my bed. Thankfully, I had a queen size bed so we could all fit on it, barely. After turning off the lights, I made my way over to the left side of the bed and climbed under the blankets with my men.

Tomorrow.

I would repair the dent tomorrow.

CHAPTER TEN

Travis

THE FIRST THING I noticed when I woke up was that I felt warm and safe. It was an unusual feeling because I hadn't felt like that before in my life.

Ever.

I wasn't sure if that was more depressing or pathetic, but it was the truth. I had never felt safe before, not truly safe. I should have known what that felt like from growing up. I should have known what it felt like to be safe from my parents, but I didn't. Then the boyfriends that I had dated in the past never had me feeling that way, especially not Baxter. I wasn't sure why I had such bad luck with boyfriends. It was as if I had a sign on me that I couldn't find that screamed, *treat me like shit.* I really should stop dating. I should buy a cat and accept my fate.

I knew I wasn't much of a catch. I was thin, I bruised easily, and I was often tired no matter how much I slept. I also didn't know what real love felt like and I had never known real affection. I had a shit load of emotional baggage from my parents and past relationships. I wasn't exactly the type of person you lined up for just to be able to date. There was nothing special or memorable about me.

I slowly opened my eyes as I yawned and stretched. The first thing I noticed was that I was sandwiched in between two gorgeous men.

Damien and Max.

We were all in Max's bed.

We'd all slept in Max's bed together.

I don't know why, but it surprised me that we were still there. I knew I had fallen asleep, something that always happened with me after good sex. My body gets tired easily. It was why I couldn't work out or do anything too physical for long. I just didn't have the strength or the endurance, thanks to my protein deficiency. I would have figured Max would have woken me up to kick me out, though. I didn't expect for the both of them to curl up on either side of me.

We were all spooning each other. Damien was in front of me, with his back to me, while Max had his chest against my back. No wonder I'd woken to feeling like I was safely tucked into a cocoon. Technically, I was.

I would have loved to feel both of their arms around me while I was sleeping, but as it stood, they weren't touching me with the exception of their torsos. It would likely be easy for me to sneak out, assuming I could avoid waking up the two trained law enforcement investigators.

I was surprised to discover that I didn't want to leave. As a rule, I usually ran out the next morning after a one-night stand, but this morning I just wanted to close my eyes and go back to sleep cuddled up between these two hunky men.

To keep feeling safe and warm.

I knew I couldn't, though. This was a one-night stand. This was something that happened after a fun night out. This wasn't an actual relationship. No one was going to be making breakfast in the morning. We weren't going to be having a sexy shower together. We were just three guys who hooked up in the bathroom of a club.

The sex, though... oh god, the sex.

I'd wanted to feel pleasure again, I'd *needed* to, and they didn't disappoint. I had never felt that remarkable before in my life. I had no idea that my body was even capable of feeling that level of pleasure. It was the stuff that dreams were made of and I actually got to live it. I was actually able to have two guys pleasure me in earth shattering ways.

Just thinking about it was making my body hungry for them. I wanted to feel the pleasure that they could bring to me. I wanted to watch as they made out and played with each other. I would have loved to feel both of them inside of me. I would have loved to watch as they went down on each other. There was so much I wanted to experience with them that we didn't get the chance to do last night.

Unfortunately for me, it would never get to happen.

This was a one time thing and that

was something I was going to have to accept and move on from.

Letting out a soft sigh, I knew I needed to wiggle my way out of the bed and get out of there. We were supposed to have a professional relationship and now last night was going to make things awkward. As much as I would have loved to stay and see if any additional fun could be had this morning, I had to remember that we worked together. It couldn't happen again, because we needed to keep things professional.

I also wasn't ready to be in any type of a relationship. I had gotten out of an abusive relationship just two weeks ago. I still needed time for myself. Besides, they wouldn't want to be with me. Not only would it be weird to have a relationship with two guys, they wouldn't want to be with someone like me. I wasn't the picture of perfect health and I had too much baggage. I was too much work to be with. That was something I would need to accept for any relationship that I came across, even potential ones. Last night was just a one-night stand, and it was an evening that I would cherish for the rest of my life.

Very slowly, I started to maneuver out of the blanket and scramble off of the bed. I didn't want to wake them up. I didn't want the awkward *morning after* talk. I just wanted to slip away and do the walk of shame all on my own. I was relieved when Max just simply rolled onto his back, but he didn't wake up.

I quickly got dressed before I headed out. I wasn't able to lock the front door as I left, as it was a dead bolt, but the area wasn't dangerous so I figured it would be safe enough to leave it unlocked. It was also daylight, so the chances of someone trying to break in would be slim.

I trotted over to my car and quickly climbed into it. Only once I was in my car did I let out a breath I didn't even know I had been holding in.

I was never really good at the morning after. It was why I tried my best to not have one. I always felt awkward and didn't know what I was supposed to do.

If I left and they didn't want me to leave, did that mean they would think I was a whore for fucking and going?

Would they think I didn't want anything to do with them?

Or would they be happy that I wasn't

around because they didn't want anything more from me or they didn't enjoy the sex?

It was all very complicated and I never knew how to properly handle it. I turned my car on, shifted it into gear, and started to make the drive back to my place. I had work I needed to start and it would at least help to distract me.

****

The first thing I did when I got home was head into my bathroom for a shower. I didn't want to wash their scents off me, but I had to shower at some point.

I started the water before I removed my clothes. I didn't get in right away, though. I could feel the tingling all along my body and I knew what it wanted. Waking up with two guys around me had made me horny. I had two options, I could ignore it and focus on what I needed to do, or I could go into my bedroom and grab the sex toy and play with myself. Most of the time option one always won, but this morning my body was craving it too much.

"Screw it," I said as I pushed away from the sink and headed into my bedroom.

I grabbed the silicone dildo that I had, the only sex toy that I owned, and headed back into the bathroom. There was a suction cup on the bottom of it and once I got into the shower, I pressed it against the wall at the right height.

The hot water hit my body as I grabbed the body wash and added some onto the dildo. I turned around and bent forward, placing my foot up on the side of the tub and my hand on the wall right across from me.

Slowly, I pushed down and allowed the tip of the dildo to slip into my ass. I didn't stretch myself, but I wasn't that tight from having sex twice last night. I was instantly moaning as the dildo breached my hole. It wasn't a real dick, but it was close enough. At least for now.

I pushed back until it was all the way inside of me before I started to move up and down it. A deep moan echoed in my bathroom as I hit my sweet spot dead on.

I wrapped my hand around my hard dick and started to lightly stroke myself. I didn't want it to be fast. I wanted to build it up until I couldn't handle it anymore and then let it all explode.

I closed my eyes and started to think about last night. I started to dream that it was Damien and Max inside of me. I allowed my mind to think about how good it would feel to suck both of their dicks. I imagined their hands all over my body. The way their mouths would feel wrapped around my dick. How amazing it would have felt this morning to wake up with one of them inside my ass and another in my mouth. The pleasure they would have brought me. I wanted to feel them deep inside of me. I wanted to feel their dicks down my throat, to feel them pulsing over my tongue and their hot cum shooting into me.

I wanted it all.

I let out a loud moan that I was certain my neighbors would be able to hear as I came hard. I stopped moaning as rope after rope of cum shot onto the shower floor where it was quickly washed away, swirling down the drain with the water.

I was breathing heavily by the time I stopped pulsing and I knew I was going to be tired once the pleasure wore off, but I didn't care. It was completely worth it. I looked down and saw that I was still hard; my body wanted more. I had no idea what was happening to me. It was like I was some horny teenager again. It was as if they had awoken something inside of me and the beast was starving. Insatiable.

I slowly moved my hand along my shaft and I hissed at how sensitive I was. It felt even better, though, and I knew this shower had just gotten a lot longer.

***

It was nearing three in the afternoon by the time I woke up. I had immediately gone to bed after my shower.

I had come four times before I was too exhausted to stand up anymore. It had been years since I had come that much and my body was not used to it.

I slowly rolled over onto my back and looked up at my ceiling. There was an old water stain on it and I worried that whenever it rained it would leak onto my bed. The problem was there was nowhere else in the room I could put my bed. The place I was renting was a very old and small apartment. It wasn't anything fancy, because I couldn't afford anything fancy.

I didn't make much as a Social Worker, but what I did earn Baxter had practically taken it all. He would run up charges on my credit card, and once he even took a loan out in my name. A loan that I was still paying off. Three quarters of my paycheck every month went to bills. It didn't leave me very much wiggle room for anything extra like groceries or a decent place to live.

Rent in Gaithersburg was a lot cheaper than it was here. Even in this one bedroom apartment I was paying twelve hundred in rent plus heat and electricity. And with me only making three grand a month, I was losing over half of it to my rent and utilities. Then I had a grand a month that I had to pay for the credit card and loan payments. Leaving me less than five hundred for my cell phone, a car payment, insurance and groceries. It was always tight and even right now I had no food. I only had twelve dollars in my bank account until next Friday. I was living off of canned food and frozen waffles.

It was part of the reason I was so thin. I couldn't afford proper food. Certainly not the meat that my body needed to help get protein into it. I was thinking I was going to need to look into getting a part-time job. Something I could do on evenings and weekends. It would be a lot of work I would have to balance, but it might be the only way I'd be able to pay all of my bills and be able to eat. It was something I was going to have to seriously start to figure out because I couldn't keep going this way. I was going to get sick and I was already at a high enough risk of illnesses, I didn't need to give my body any more reason to get sick.

Letting out a sigh, I reached over and grabbed my phone from the bedside table. I saw that I had a text message from an unknown number.

It wasn't uncommon for me to get a text message from a number I didn't have saved in my phone. Lots of people had my number. Different law enforcement officers, Social Workers, and even some of the children that I had on my caseload. They all had my number so they could reach out to me if they should need help. I opened the message and instantly my blood turned cold.

You think you can run from me? I'll be seeing you real soon, whore.

He found me.

I don't know how, but Baxter had found me. I didn't think he ever would. I didn't think he would be trying to find me. I wasn't anything special to him. There was no reason for him to want to chase after me. He could have found someone else to have sex with. It wasn't like he loved me. I didn't think he would even try and find my new number. He never wanted anyone to know that we even knew each other. I couldn't imagine him trying to look me up or asking someone for my number. But he had obviously done something to find me. And he was pissed. I knew he would be mad when he discovered that I had left, but I foolishly believed he would find someone else to be with. I didn't think he would track me down.

I didn't know what to do. I couldn't change my number, that would look suspicious. I also couldn't up and move to a new town because I had a job here. I had responsibilities and cases I was working. I couldn't abandon these children that were in need. I had to be there for them, even if that meant I risked Baxter coming down here to see me. I just hoped that he was simply threatening me and he would get bored and leave me alone soon. It was a stark reminder, though, that I would never be free from him and I would never be safe.

CHAPTER ELEVEN

Damien

"WELL, WELL, WELL, look what the cat dragged in," Sebastian said the second I opened the front door.

We lived together, had been for the past fifteen years. We couldn't live alone just in case something happened and we needed to leave in a hurry. Living together for fifteen years had been difficult at times. There had been moments when having our separate places would have come in handy. It got hard to bring guys back to the house when your brother was sleeping in the room next to you.

Both of us were gay. It was weird how we ended up both being gay. One wouldn't think two brothers from the same parents would both end up being gay.

But as sure as the sun rises daily, we did.

Our parents were really good about it, though. Our father never made us feel like we were less of a man. He never gave us any shit about not wanting to be with a woman. He had even made sure that we brought our boyfriends home so he could meet them. Our mom, oh man, she was all for it. She never made a complaint about never getting grandchildren. Instead, she would go on and on about how we would be able to adopt a baby and that we could choose if we wanted a boy or a girl. She made us swear that we would give her one of each. Said for us to duke it out on who got the boy.

At the time, we both wanted to have children one day. Now, if we didn't get this organization eliminated, we would never have children. We couldn't bring them into this life. We couldn't risk their safety and welfare.

A child shouldn't have to fear going to

bed at night. They shouldn't have to wonder what would happen when they woke up or if they would be woken up in the middle of the night and have to leave everything they owned behind. They shouldn't have to stop and think about what name they were supposed to give to someone, or having to leave school and their friends only to have to start all over again. It wasn't fair to them and neither one of us were going to be putting a child in that situation.

"You just been sitting there waiting for me to walk in?" I asked as I walked over to the coffee maker.

"No, but it *is* eleven in the morning and you are clearly doing the walk of shame," Sebastian said, flashing me a teasing smile.

I hadn't even woken up until thirty minutes ago. I still couldn't believe I slept that long. Normally, I'm up at six am regardless of when I fell asleep or what I was doing. Sleeping with Travis and Max had felt good, though, and I hadn't been in a hurry to get up and face the day.

At some point, Travis had left and I hadn't even noticed. I always woke up at the first sound or any movement and yet,

I hadn't even noticed when the person sleeping next to me had gotten out of bed.

Very weird.

I didn't know what it was about either man, but when I was around them it made me feel lighter. Even as annoying as Max was. The whole situation was screwed up, because I shouldn't be feeling like this with both men. I should only be feeling like this with one of them. I was attracted to both of them, which was natural, but I wasn't more attracted to one over the other. I liked them both equally, which was surprising considering how often Max drove me insane. The whole situation was different and left me on uncertain ground. All I could do was wait and see how it would play out.

"There's no shame. It was a good night and I slept in. There's no mystery here, brother. What have you been up to?"

"Been helping out on a case for the Agency. Nothing crazy. I think Mason and Roland know that we're hiding something." Sebastian frowned.

"They know we're brothers and so does Max. They have all mentioned something to me."

"Shit, what the hell are we going to

do?" He shook his head.

That was the question. We had never been in this position before. The people we were around had never discovered our secrets. Usually, our story of us being best friends worked without issue. People didn't need to look into it because we never let anyone get truly close enough to see through the carefully constructed illusion that we had to live with. Though, it wasn't all that surprising either, because normally, we only had acquaintances. We didn't have *friends* and we didn't associate with people in law enforcement.

Our business was typically kept small when we did private investigations. When we didn't, we were working on a ranch or for cash in a factory. We had decided to open our own business so we could have more steady cash and be able to take it anywhere we wanted.

Since being in Gaithersburg, though, we had been getting too close with law enforcement officials. At first, it was just Roland and then everything with the Agency started and now, federal agents and cops almost constantly surrounded us. It truly was only a matter of time before people started to figure it out.

Normally, when someone got close to discovering our truth we would pack up and leave, however, I wasn't certain that would be the right call to make this time.

All of the other times we'd been on our own. We hadn't had anyone that we could turn to for help or support. There had been no one who could help protect us, help us fight. That wasn't the case this time around, though, because we had an Agency filled with good men who would be there for us. Men who would help us fight against the organization and maybe, just maybe with their help we would be able to stop it once and for all. Leaving this time around, I didn't think it would be very smart and definitely not in our best interest.

It was time to stop running and fight back.

"We stay. We roll the dice and we stay. If they are able to find us, then maybe it's time we tell some people the truth. We're not working with factory workers or ranch hands this time around. The people we work with, the people that have become our friends, they are cops and feds. Men who can protect themselves and help us investigate. I think leaving this time around would be a huge mistake."

"We could be putting them at risk, though," Sebastian pointed out.

"Do you want to leave?" I asked, gently.

When it was time for us to leave, we always discussed it first. Unless we were attacked, then the choice was taken away from us. I never wanted to just tell Sebastian what to do with his life or make decisions that affected his life without talking to him about it first. We weren't little kids, we were grown ass men who could make our own decisions.

I would never leave without him and I knew he would never leave without me. If we were going to pack up our lives and move to another town, then it needed to be a decision we both wanted.

I was hoping he didn't want to leave, because I wasn't ready for that yet. I enjoyed having our own company and working for the Federal Protection Agency. I adored helping children when they thought no one would be there to rescue them. I delighted in working with the guys and grabbing a beer with them some nights.

Most importantly, though, I didn't want to leave Max and Travis. I wanted the chance to see what would happen next. Maybe we would go back to keeping everything professional and pretend like last night hadn't happened. But then, maybe something could also come from it. Maybe we could have an unorthodox relationship. I knew the chances of the three of us being together again were slim, but I wasn't ready to give up all hope just yet. If Sebastian wanted to leave then I would go with him, but it would hurt to leave this time.

"No, I don't. I like this town. I like the people. Hell, we have friends for the first time in what, fifteen years? I don't want to leave. I'm so sick and tired of having to start over, aren't you?" Sebastian asked and I could hear the exhaustion in his voice.

It wasn't an exhaustion that came from lack of sleep, but one that came from constantly having to be on point. We both always had to be vigil and on guard, always waiting and watching for an attack. It was exhausting on a mental level. After fifteen years of having to live that way, it was taking a toll on both of us and I knew if we didn't do something to change it, there was no telling what mistake we would make because we were too tired.

"Yeah, yeah, I am. I don't want to leave, either. I think it's time we take a stand. I don't know when the organization is going to come for us, but I don't want to run this time. I like the life that we have built for ourselves. I like our business, but I really like the good we are doing with our work for the Agency. I don't want to lose it, even if that means it could kill me in the end."

"Any job we take could kill us. We're not bookkeepers or bartenders, we help chase down dangerous criminals. At any given time we could be killed, what's one more possibility hanging over our head? If we were ever going to take a stand, this is the time we should do it. How do you want to handle it?" Sebastian asked.

"We can sit the three of them down and tell them our story. Have them over one night for a drink."

I knew it wouldn't be too hard to tell them what happened. They had already figured out that we were brothers so there wouldn't be any real shock. It was just a matter of finding the right time to tell them our story and who we were hiding from. I was glad that Sebastian wanted to tell them, that he wanted to fight. I didn't think I could handle running again. We weren't cowards. We didn't usually run from a fight, but for the past fifteen years that is all we had done where our personal situation was concerned. It was time that we took a stand and refused to change our lives once again because of those people. We had made a family here and it was time we trusted our family to be there for us and to help us end this war, once and for all.

Hopefully, when the battle did end, we would all be left standing. I didn't think I could handle losing any of them, especially Sebastian. Not after all of this time.

Not after fifteen years of fighting beside him.

It would already be weird if this did end and we could have our own places again. We had been in each other's lives for so long that not having Sebastian there every morning would be hard. There would be an adjustment period for the both of us, but it would be a good adjustment period. It would be because we'd won and not because one of us was killed.

"They are on a case right now, but once it's done we can," Sebastian said.

"Sounds like a plan. I need to shower and then head into the office. What are you doing today?"

"I'm gonna head into the Agency and help out. We were working late on this case. Hopefully, Coop has been able to pull something out of his ass for us."

"The man has a gift," I easily said as I headed for the stairs. "See you later tonight. Be safe," I called out.

"Always," Sebastian called back.

We both had to be safe, but I knew he was protected with the guys from the Agency. Today, I had my own work I needed to finish up at the office and then maybe I would be able to relax a bit before tomorrow and the day started all over again.

CHAPTER TWELVE

Max

MY BACK SLAMMED into the wall as Damien's mouth devoured mine. Our tongues fought for control, for dominance, but this time I was not about to submit. I wanted the fight to keep going. I wanted to feel every ounce of passion that he had for me. I wanted to feel him against me, his skin against mine once again.

That one single time wasn't enough for me.

I was worried it would never be enough for me.

Ever since that night, I hadn't been

able to stop thinking about either of them. We had been working together for the past week since we had our one-night stand and it had been torture on me. I was spending all day trying to control myself from jumping either one of them. Whenever I was around them, it felt like my skin was on fire. As if I had tiny bugs underneath my skin crawling all over me. The only time it got any better was when I was touching one of them. The closer to them I got, the stronger the urge to touch them became. I had never felt like this before. I never thought I would ever feel this way. Now that I did, I had no idea what I was supposed to do about it.

I let out a deep moan as I felt Damien's hard dick press up against mine. I *needed* to feel him against me. I needed to feel him inside of me. The need for it was stronger than anything I had ever felt before. Never had I wanted to feel someone inside of me this badly before and I didn't even care that we were in his office. That someone could walk in on us. We were alone in the whole building, but one of his guys could come in after wrapping up a case. I didn't care, though, I needed to feel him so bad it hurt.

Like an addict, this man was my next fix.

My fingers fumbling, I grasped on to the waist of his pants and undid his belt. Damien followed my lead and started to remove my own belt. We moved quickly, both of us being impatient. The need within the room was palpable. Neither one of us could wait much longer.

I kicked off my boots as my pants and boxers were pushed down. We were both already rock hard. I kicked one leg free of my jeans and Damien placed his hand on the back of my right thigh, pulling it around his hips. I moved my hips, grinding against his and rubbing our hard dicks against each other. We both gave a deep moan as the sensation sent a shockwave of pleasure down both of our bodies. Damien pulled away from the kiss and began to mouth his way down my neck, nipping, kissing, licking my skin and driving me wild with lust.

"Fuck, I need you inside me," I moaned out, as I arched my back trying to get more friction from him.

Damien let out a small growl as he ground his hardness against me. I could vaguely hear him rummaging through his pants and I really hoped he had lube in his pocket or something. The last thing I wanted to do was stop or settle for dry humming or a blow job.

I wanted him deep inside me.

Needed.

At the feel of his slicked up finger pushing inside of me, I let out the breath I hadn't realized I was holding. A whimper escaped my lips as I felt his finger going as deep as possible inside of me, pleasantly rewarding me with a faint brush stoke over my prostate. Just enough to tease and tempt, making me want more. Just one finger wasn't enough; it was nowhere near enough for me.

I continued to grind against him as Damien pressed open-mouthed kisses all over my neck before making his way back to my mouth.

Fuck, he tasted so good.

His special taste mixed with the salt of my skin left a heady mixture on my tongue. This time, I allowed him to dominate the kiss. I allowed him to have control, because everything was feeling way too damn good to try and fight against him.

He slipped in a second and a third finger, stretching my hole, and I knew I was going to lose my mind if he didn't put his dick inside of me soon.

"I need you. I'm good," I said as I pulled my lips from his, already breathing heavily. If he didn't fuck me soon, I was going to be coming and I wanted that to happen with him inside of me. I let out a small whine as he pulled his fingers out of me, already feeling bereft.

He searched around in his pockets again, but this time he pulled out a condom. He quickly slipped it down his length before both of his hands were on my ass and lifting me up.

I wrapped my legs around his hips and grabbed onto the mounts that were holding up the shelves he had along this wall. I felt his tip against my hole before he slowly pushed in. The second his tip breached me, I couldn't contain the loud moan that slipped from my lips. He felt glorious, fucking glorious inside of me and I knew it was only going to get better.

It was rare when I did this, when I had sex like this. I was usually the one who was on top and not on the bottom. There generally had to be a lot of trust involved and I had to be insanely attracted to the other guy for me to even consider bottoming. It took a lot for me to be able to have sex this way after growing up being repeatedly abused by my father. To push those memories down while it was happening, to combat the feeling of not being in control, it took so much goddamn energy and effort, and more often than not, it wasn't worth it. Sex was supposed to feel good and if I had to spend all of my energy on not remembering my past then it wasn't worth it.

But Damien, he felt amazing.

Every inch he pushed inside of me made my body feel like it was on fire. The only sound in his office was our heavy breaths as he bottomed out inside of me, his full balls pressed against my hole..

"So good, feels so good," I said softly.

"You're so tight and hot. Fuck, you feel amazing," Damien growled as he fought to not move, letting me accommodate the large intrusion pressed inside my walls.

"Move, I'm good." God, I needed him to move. I needed it more than anything else in this world.

He slowly pulled out before he pushed

back in. He kept his pace slow and careful, allowing my body to adjust to his hefty size, and I appreciated him for that. The second the tip of his dick hit my sweet spot, I let out a loud moan and arched up.

"Faster," I moaned, needing more of him.

Damien didn't need to be told twice. He pulled out all of the way before he slammed right back into me, hitting my prostate dead on. I grunted, cursing loudly, not caring if people outside could hear me.

Damien's pace was brutal and it was exactly what I needed. I didn't need it slow and sweet; I needed it hard and fast. Damien's thrusts were so strong and my ass was banging the wall, sending some of the items from the shelves raining down to the floor. His hands on my hips grasped me so tightly I already knew come this evening there would be bruises there, but I didn't give a damn. My whole body was tingling and feeling amazing. This was the second best sex I had ever had. The first being the night when all three of us got to screw each other.

Damien either got tired of the position

or sick of his shit falling all over the floor. He held me even tighter in his grip, swinging around and bringing me over to his desk. I wrapped my arms around his neck as he bent forward and, with one swipe of his arm, knocked everything off from his desk down to the floor.

He lay me down on his desk and grabbed my legs behind my knees, pulling my legs up to press against his shoulders. The new position allowed him to go even deeper inside of me. His hands were once again back on my hips, pulling me to him as he pounded hard and fast inside of me.

I couldn't stop moaning and I was already feeling lightheaded from all of the panting I was doing. I could feel my orgasm building within my belly. I could feel the heat starting to spread, my balls pulling up tight against my body, and I knew it wasn't going to be long before I fell off that cliff. I was beyond excited for it, because I had never come without my dick being touched and I wanted to know what that would feel like. I needed to feel it just as badly as I needed to feel him throbbing and growing within me.

"Don't stop, I'm close," I moaned, arching back as he hit my sweet spot again.

"Come for me, Baby," Damien growled as his pace picked up even more.

After another three direct hits to my prostate, I couldn't hold off any longer. Black stars started to dance in front of my eyes as the heat completely engulfed my entire body and electricity raced up my spine. My scream echoed in the room as rope after rope of creamy white cum pumped all over my stomach. It felt like I was never going to stop, because each time Damien hit my sweet spot it would start all over again. I had never experienced this level of pleasure before in my life and I never wanted it to end.

Damien let out a deep groan as he snapped his hips forward, driving deeply inside my ass, and then I felt him pulsing inside of me as my walls clamped around his dick, and that only heightened my pleasure. He placed his forehead against mine as we both fought to control our breathing.

My whole body was tingling and I felt like I was floating. It was almost like an out of body experience. Like I could see what was happening, but my mind couldn't process any of it. I was up on cloud nine and I never wanted to come back down to Earth.

Damien lightly slanted his lips over mine and we kissed, luxuriating in the intense feelings as our bodies calmed down from the high. I could have stayed here all day and night long. Hell, I could have gone another ten rounds with him if he wanted.

Sex with Damien was something I knew I would never get tired of or bored over.

All too soon, Damien was pulling back and he was slowly pulling out of me. I went to get up, but he placed his hand on my chest and looked right at me as he bent forward and ran his tongue along my stomach, licking up my cum. I moaned as I watched him.

It was sexy as fuck.

Once it was all cleaned up, he kissed his way up my chest over to my neck and then, he hovered over my lips as he spoke.

"You taste amazing."

"I know," I said with a smirk.

It did exactly what I was expecting it would. He crushed his lips against mine as his tongue invaded my mouth. He made sure I tasted myself on him and I had no problem whatsoever licking it off from his tongue. All too soon for my liking, he was pulling back from the kiss. Maybe it was a good thing that he did, because if we kept kissing there was no way I was going to allow him to leave this office until he fucked me again.

Damien stood up and pulled the condom off with a snap, tying the end and tossing it in the garbage can that sat beside his desk.

I let out a deep breath as I moved and stood up. My legs felt like rubber, my knees weak, but I managed to keep myself standing. It was going to take me some time before I would be able to get my legs working properly again. Not to mention my head was still feeling a bit lightheaded from all the lack of oxygen due to my panting in pleasure.

Shit, it wasn't even noon and this day was already out of this world.

"Sorry, you seem to have fucked my brains out, because now I can't remember what you were lecturing me on before you kissed me," I said as I traipsed over to where my pants were lying forgotten on the floor.

When I had come in this morning to see what the plan was for today, I certainly hadn't expected for any of that to happen. It had been a few days since our time with Travis and ever since, we'd all been professional with each other. We had never crossed any lines or even given any indication that something had happened. It was what needed to be done, but that didn't change that I wanted to be with them.

That I wanted to touch them and kiss them almost every moment of every day.

I seriously didn't know what had come over Damien. One minute he was lecturing me on where my dirty boots belonged, and the next we were making out. It was very romantic.

Hot.

"Dirty boots don't belong on furniture. I like to keep things clean," Damien said as we both pulled our clothing back on.

"Yeah, I can tell you like it really clean by the state of this office," I teased.

"This was all your fault. This mess belongs completely to you."

"Oh, it's my fault? And how do you figure that?"

"You kept making sexy noises and

driving me insane," he pointed out as he started to pick his desk items up off the floor.

"I'm sorry, next time I won't make any sounds," I said as I held my hands up in a mock surrender.

Damien strode over to me and placed his hand firmly on the back of my neck as he spoke. "You better keep making those sounds."

"I guess you're gonna have to give me enough pleasure to be rewarded with sounds, then," I countered with a smirk.

"That sounds like a challenge," he said, before his lips were on me once again.

I melted against him, my body still filled with too much pleasure to do anything else. This man was like heroin and I was going to become addicted to him at this rate.

When the need for air became too much, we pulled back and I was already feeling the loss of him against me.

"So, now what? Was this like a one time thing or do we get to play again?" I asked.

I was really hoping he was going to say that we would get to keep playing. I wanted him so badly and I was worried he didn't want to keep doing this. I also couldn't help but think how it was a bit weird that Travis wasn't here with us. As satisfied as I was, and I was beyond satisfied, I was still missing the Travis's presence.

"I would like to keep going, if that is something you would be interested in."

"Definitely."

We both got dressed and I helped him to clean up the mess we had made. Thankfully, his laptop hadn't been on the desk but still in his drawer. There were a shit load of papers, though, and now they were all in a mixed up order and I knew he was going to be spending the afternoon getting it all back in proper order. The man did like order and I couldn't help but wonder if that was something that had always been a piece of his personality or if it was something new that crept up since whatever he was on the run from affected his life. Once we had everything cleaned up, I asked the question that had been burning my brain this whole time.

"Did you feel like there was something missing when we were having sex?"

He looked at me like he was slightly

confused and I could tell he didn't really understand what I was asking him, or why I was asking it.

"What are you talking about?"

"The sex was off the wall, don't get me wrong, but I kinda felt like we were missing Travis's presence with us."

Complete understanding crossed his face before he spoke. "I know what you mean. It's weird, because I enjoyed being with you, but I did find myself feeling like something was missing without him here. Maybe that's just because the first time we were all together."

"Maybe. I doubt he would be into a redo. He seems pretty adamant about keeping things professional. Not to mention whatever shit he has going on in his personal life."

We still hadn't been able to get anything out of Travis so far about his personal life. He was very good at not answering questions without making it seem like he was avoiding the questions. He had clearly been doing this a long time. Long enough for him to have mastered the art of deflection. He was also still jumpy and always seemed like he was waiting for someone to attack him.

We needed to talk to him soon. We had to help him figure this out, to work it out. We needed to make sure that he was safe and whoever was after him wouldn't be coming back for him. I wasn't about to let anyone hurt him. He was under my protection now, and I was going to make sure he was safe.

"We'll figure it out. We'll make sure he knows he's safe and with a bit of luck, we can get him to talk to us. We have time."

Hopefully, we did have time, because if anyone tried to hurt Travis, I was going to kill them. For now, I would be keeping an eye on him and making sure no one was following him. I wasn't going to let anyone hurt him or Damien. They were my men, even if they didn't know it yet, and no one hurts anyone who belongs to me.

CHAPTER THIRTEEN

Travis

EXHAUSTED DIDN'T EVEN seem to cover how I felt. My whole body ached and I felt like my skin was crawling with ants. Nothing I did seemed to calm down my anxiety.

It had been a week since I'd received that text message from an unknown number, a number I was certain belonged to Baxter. For the past week, I had been plagued by endless phone calls at all hours of the day and night. Every time I answered, they would just hang up or breathe heavily on the phone. Whenever I ignored them, they would keep calling until I answered them. I wished it had been as simple as me changing my phone number, but it was connected to all of the children that I had on my roster, so I couldn't change it. And if I placed my phone on do not disturb, I could potentially miss an important or vital phone call from one of those children. I wasn't going to put their lives on the line because I wanted some peace and quiet.

It wasn't just the phone calls that had been keeping me awake, though, it was also the photos. The very next day after that first phone call, I received the first photo from Baxter. It was of me coming out of a potential safe haven with Damien and Max. It was one thing to be getting endless phone calls, but to receive photos of me clearly in Baton Rouge, that told me that Baxter was here and that thought was petrifying. It was either him or he'd hired someone to watch me.

I didn't think he'd hired someone, though.

Baxter didn't have money; at least, not enough to pay someone to follow me around. He spent most of his free time and money on online gambling websites, and he lost most of it. Whenever he lost too much, I had always been on the receiving end of things, which had been often. There was no way he was going to be able to afford to have someone following me.

Which meant he was here and he was watching me. He was biding his time and waiting for the right moment to strike. I knew he wouldn't do it right away. He was enjoying this game too much. He wanted me to be terrified and looking over my shoulder all day and night long. He wanted me exhausted and rundown so I would get sick and be even more vulnerable.

It wasn't good when I did get sick, because my immune system would become weaker from my protein deficiency. I had to be careful with getting sick. A simple cold could turn really bad and put me in the hospital, and that was the last place I wanted to be.

I was worried about Damien and Max as well. I didn't like that Baxter had been following me around, but I really didn't like that he was also following Damien and Max by association. They didn't deserve to be added into this drama and I hated that I was pulling them into it and they didn't even know it.

I knew they hadn't believed me when I'd said that a parent put these bruises on me. They weren't stupid, and I knew they wouldn't believe it, but it was better then the truth at that moment. I wasn't going to ruin the moment by telling them the truth. They wouldn't have wanted me and I'd needed to be with them that night.

I'd needed to feel pleasure again and that night had been remarkable. It had been everything I could have wanted and then some. The memories of it were still flooding my dreams when I did get to sleep. I'd swear when I woke up I could even smell them. I'd keep rolling over expecting for them to be on either side of me. And each morning I was greeted by disappointment when I realized that I was still alone.

Unlocking the door, I headed inside my apartment, coming to a dead stop as horror and fear instantly flooded my body. My whole living room area was trashed. My couch was cut up, deep slices marring the cushions that littered the room. Several photos that had been on the wall were shattered, their glass shimmering on the ground. The coffee table and the small bistro table I had in my makeshift dining room were completely broken, splintered wood everywhere. A quick look to my left showed me the kitchen had suffered the same treatment. There was glass all over the floor, as if someone had taken the time to smash every single dish I owned. The cupboard doors were hanging from their hinges, and some were also on the floor. All of my food had been emptied from my fridge and the condiments were spewed all over the floor and walls in a menagerie of colors. The fake hardwood floor that made up the flooring in my apartment had red paint all over it. As if someone had taken buckets of the shit and just tossed it all over the place. Some had even splattered onto the walls.

I was too afraid to look down the hallway to my right to see what the rest of my apartment looked like. I didn't need to wonder who had done this. I had been waiting for Baxter to come after me once I'd realized he was in town, and this was just him escalating.

He had obviously picked my lock, because I'd unlocked the door to get in. He must have used his police lock pick gun to get in and out without anyone noticing. He'd wanted to send me a message that he could come into my home whenever he felt like it.

Message clearly received.

I pushed my door closed before I made my way down the hallway. The hallway looked about as well as I expected. There was more paint on the floor and the items on my walls were destroyed. The bathroom showed that the mirror had been smashed and my shampoo and body wash was squirted all over the place. I guess I should be thankful that he didn't break the tiles in my shower stall.

I headed into my bedroom, expecting to see the same treatment in the room as the rest of the house. Only, once again shock rocked through my core at what I saw.

Instead of it being destroyed like the rest of my house, it was clean.

There were fake rose petals all over the ground and in a heart on the bed. Candles had been set up all over the room, they weren't on thankfully, but the message was loud and clear. More often than not, if someone walked into their home and saw rose petals all over the ground and candles they would think it was sweet and romantic, but that wasn't what Baxter was telling me with his setup.

He was telling me how I was going to be his again.

How he was going to make sure he hurt me even deeper this time around.

There was a photo on the bed and I moved toward it with dread flooding my body. I expected to see another photo of me alone or with Damien and Max. I sure hadn't expected for it to be anything like what lay there among the petals.

It was of me, but he had photoshopped the image so I looked horribly beat up. The most disturbing part was the position he had placed me in. There was a thick chain, almost like one you would find on a tow truck, around my neck and I was hanging from the ceiling. I was clearly dead in the image and the sight of it turned my stomach.

Baxter was going to kill me and I suspected he planned to do it exactly how this photo was depicting. There would be no forgiveness this time. There would be nothing I could do or say to him when he found me to make up for running. He was too pissed off, too enraged for forgiveness. He was going to kill me and there would be nothing I could do to stop him.

I had to leave. I had to get out of there. I couldn't stay in my apartment now. It wasn't safe. Before he knew where I lived I'd felt at home here, but now I knew he had found me and could easily get inside. I was no longer safe.

With shaky hands, I dropped the photo and raced over to my closet. I grabbed my suitcase and started to throw my clothes into it. I put everything that I could get to fit inside of it, leaving behind anything that wasn't important. I could always come back for the rest. Right now, I needed the things that I couldn't replace should I have to flee town.

With my suitcase packed, I fled out of my apartment, locking the door behind me, which seemed pointless given the state of the apartment.

I headed back out to my car, tossed my suitcase in the backseat, and scrambled into the driver's seat, turning the ignition before I'd even slid my belt on.

I rammed the shifter into gear, peeling out of the driveway, and started to drive down the road forcing myself to keep to a sedate speed despite the anxiety and high emotions flooding my system.

I didn't know exactly where I was going. I needed to find a hotel, a real hotel with a key card and someone sitting at a front desk all night long. If there was one thing that Baton Rouge had, it was hotels. I just needed to find one that would keep me safe until I could figure out what to do about Baxter.

The problem with that, though, was I had no idea what to do about Baxter. I knew I could tell Damien or Max. Hell, I could tell the Agency and they would do something about it. But I wasn't ready to admit it out loud to anyone. I wasn't ready to reveal my shameful secret to anyone, but especially not Damien and Max.

I really didn't want to be seen as the domestic abuse victim that they had to treat like glass. I didn't want them to remember me as a victim or to remember me as the guy who was sick and tired a lot. I wanted them to remember me as the guy they had an epic threesome with. Someone who was fun and strong. Someone who they could remember without seeing all of the things that were wrong with me first.

No, I couldn't tell them, even if I really wanted to be with them again. I wanted to fall asleep between them. I wanted to feel their hands on my body. I didn't want one more than the other, I wanted them both equally, which was exciting and terrifying all at the same time.

It couldn't happen, though, because I *was* the domestic abuse survivor. I *was* the guy who was thin and sick and tired most of the time. I wasn't the sexy, free spirited guy that they'd slept with. And if they knew the truth, they wouldn't want me. It was better to leave it to my fantasies, because that's all it would ever be.

That thought alone hurt so much more than everything Baxter had done to me.

CHAPTER FOURTEEN

Damien

I COULDN'T HELP but pace around our living room as I waited for the others to arrive. Today, we were going to be meeting with Mason, Roland, and Max to tell them our story.

I was nervous about that, not because I was worried they wouldn't believe us, but because it was going to bring more people into the situation. I didn't want anyone to get hurt, especially because of something that we had brought to them.

It was one thing to be hurt while on a case, but this was something completely different. This was a personal experience that Sebastian and I had gone through and it had nothing to do with a case that the Agency was working. We had made the decision to testify together. We had made the decision to go into Witness Protection. We had made the decision to keep going and live in hiding. They were all decisions that we had made ourselves and we had done it knowing full well that our lives were on the line.

What we were doing today, that was us bringing in people who weren't connected to the initial decision and that could get them hurt or killed.

"Relax, it'll be fine," Sebastian said as he sat down in the chair.

"Hopefully," I said, less sure about that fact.

"You're the one who suggested we stay here and bring them into the fold. That they already knew we were hiding something. This was your idea, so why are you having second thoughts now?" Sebastian asked, calmly.

"I'm not having second thoughts. I just don't like that they will be getting involved in it. The risk. I know it was my idea and I'm standing by it. They need to know if we are going to be around them and they already know we're not just best friends. The last thing we need is them looking into us and triggering a landmine they don't know they're supposed to avoid. I just hate that we are bringing them into it and it could get them hurt, that's all."

I really hated that Max was going to be involved in this. I didn't want him to get hurt. I didn't want anything bad to happen to him. I had no idea what was happening between us, but I was enjoying our time together. I knew we were just having fun. That we weren't anything serious. I doubted that he would want anything serious to happen between us.

Still, though, I was enjoying it and I was hoping that maybe we could have fun again with Travis. Being with Max those few times had been amazing, but I didn't feel complete like I had when Travis was with us. It felt like we were missing someone important and I was really hoping we could all enjoy each other once again.

It was a few minutes later when there was a knock at my door. Letting out a soft breath, I made my way over to let the others in. I was really hoping this would go over well. I knew they had already figured out that we were brothers, that we were in hiding, but I wasn't certain they would be okay with what they were stepping into. Unfortunately, there was nothing I could do to take it back. Once they knew, they knew, and they would have to live with it.

"Hey, appreciate you coming," I said as I moved back to allow them to enter my home.

I could tell that they were already expecting what the meeting was going to be about. They had all been patient with both Sebastian and I. They had never pushed to learn more. They had never tried to get either of us to speak about what had happened in our past. I knew they had been itching to ask more questions, that they were curious to know what our story was and now, they were finally going to get answers. We all made our way over to the living room and took our seats.

"I'm not going to waste anyone's time by pretending like you three don't know that Sebastian and I have been keeping a secret. We are brothers and from New Jersey. For the past fifteen years, we have been in hiding; we've been running. Our father was an accountant for a major corporation. What we didn't know, was that one of those corporations was connected to an Italian mob boss named David Russo. There was some type of falling out between them and we witnessed Russo and his men kill both of our parents. They didn't know we were there; we hid upstairs until it got quiet. We called the police and we testified against him," I started.

"We didn't know that we would be in constant danger when we did. The police made it seem like we would be in witness protection with a Marshal until the trial. Then afterward, we would be safe to go back to our lives. Only when the trial was over, the threats kept coming in and we were told we could never go back to our lives. We were placed back in witness protection and five years in the Marshal who was watching us was killed. We suspected there was a mole within the Marshals, so we decided to go it alone. Moving all around the country, never staying in the same place for long. We managed. We didn't know that things would change when we hit Gaithersburg,"

Sebastian finished.

I could see in their eyes that they weren't surprised. They had already figured that something had happened to make us run. That someone was chasing us. I was happy and relieved to see that they weren't taken aback. I would have been more concerned if they were, because then it meant that they weren't certain *we* weren't the criminals in this story. It was good to know that they didn't think the worst of us. That they were truly on our side even when they hadn't known our side of the story.

"Is Russo still alive?" Roland asked.

"He is. We've been keeping track of him. He's almost seventy now, and we figured when he died they would leave us alone," I answered.

"We thought they would calm down after a while, but they kept chasing after us," Sebastian added.

"How do you know?" Max asked.

"There's been a few times when we've been able to get a head's up that they were on their way. We were able to get out. But there have also been times where they've gotten the jump on us. We've been keeping an eye on them and their movements, and so far we're still in the clear," I answered.

"How often do you usually move around?" Mason asked this time.

"Depends on the area and how active the organization is at the time. We've been able to stay in one spot for a couple of years and other times only a few weeks. Gaithersburg had been the longest so far. From what we have been able to gather, the organization doesn't know we're here in Baton Rouge, either," I answered.

"What do you want to do?" Mason asked the million dollar question.

I knew if we told them that we were already packed and ready to leave at a moment's notice, they would completely understand. They wouldn't pressure us to stay or try to change our minds. I also knew that if we told them that we weren't going to run any longer, they would step up to help us.

I knew it was my idea to tell them about it. That we had both agreed it would be better for them to know what was going on then for them to go poking around in the dark. Still, that didn't mean I was fully comfortable with them getting involved. With them potentially risking their lives for us. It wasn't their fight and they didn't deserve to be dragged into this mess. The trick was, we were already through the looking glass at this point.

"We've decided that we're done with running, no matter what happens. We wanted to let you know, because we didn't want to drag you into this mess unintentionally, and without you knowing the facts, the risks," I answered.

"We're not asking you guys to help kill them or anything like that. We just didn't want you to go digging one day and stumble across something that could get you hurt," Sebastian added.

"I can speak for all of us when I tell you that we're not going to sit around and let you both fight without backup. We knew someone was after you, just like we knew, eventually, there could come a day where you would need us. We're always going to be there for you both. Just like you both have always been there for us," Mason said.

It was a huge relief to know that we had their support. That we would be able to rely on them should shit turn up. Hearing them confirm it only made me feel so much better.

And I knew it made Sebastian feel better as well.

That didn't mean we were going to be stupid. We were going to keep being vigilant and making sure that our asses were covered. If an attack was going to happen, we would at least know about it beforehand and have backup. The whole thing had to end at some point, but I just wasn't sure when that would happen.

"We appreciate that," I said, flashing them all a warm smile.

"Do you have someone looking into their movements? Someone who can track them?" Max asked.

"We've been handling that ourselves. We didn't really know who we could trust and we didn't want to put anyone in danger," Sebastian answered.

"We can have Coop keep an eye on them, track their movements. We don't have to tell him what it's for. He'll do it as a personal favor to me, I'm sure. That okay with you both?" Mason asked.

I wasn't too sure how comfortable I was with that. I knew Cooper could sneak around online better than anyone. The man was gifted at hacking and computers. However, I also didn't want to put someone else's life on the line. It was bad enough we were already putting three others on the line and one of them was someone that I cared for.

Someone that I was sleeping with.

The last thing I wanted was for Max to get hurt because of me or something connected to my past. He was tough and could handle himself, I would never deny that, but I also knew underneath that tough exterior was a traumatized man. And the last thing he needed in his life was more pain. I looked over at my brother and he merely gave me a shrug, letting me know that it was my call to make.

Sebastian had always been easy going that way. He was always willing to allow me to take control and follow my lead. He used to do it when we were kids, back when everything was so much simpler. When this nightmare had first started, he often relied on me to make the decisions. Especially, once the Marshal protecting us was killed.

It had suddenly all fallen onto my shoulders.

I was the one choosing the towns and deciding when we needed to leave. I was the one who came up with the rules, the most important being we didn't tell anyone. Followed by, we didn't allow ourselves to fall in love.

No relationships.

Sex was one thing, but we never brought them home. We never got attached and we never allowed them to get attached. At the time, that rule seemed so simple. Neither one of us could imagine that we would fall in love with someone. We both believed we were too broken for that. We had made peace with the fact that we would never have a family and a stable life.

Now, fifteen years later, that rule felt like a dead weight hanging over our heads. It was getting harder to push down the craving and need for love, long term companionship. One-night stands were no longer doing anything for either of us. I figured that Sebastian would be the first one to break the rule but now, it looked like I was going to be.

"As long as he's safe," I said.

"He knows how to cover his tracks. He'll be fine. Are you both going to be okay?" Roland asked with concern edging his voice.

"It's just another day," Sebastian said with a nonchalant shrug.

They all seemed to understand and it didn't take long before they were heading out. I walked them to the door but Max stayed behind with me on my front porch. I knew there was going to be a conversation about all of this. Whatever he had been expecting, I knew he hadn't been expecting it to involve the Italian Mob.

I went over to the far side away from the door and leaned against the railing with my forearms against it. Max mimicked my position.

"And here I thought I was the problem child," he lightly teased, and I couldn't help but chuckle at that.

"Oh no, you are definitely the problem child," I said, flashing him cocky grin.

"You gotta be getting tired by now. Running, always looking over your shoulder, that's a lot for someone to deal with," Max said with complete understanding to his voice.

"It wasn't easy at first. I was twenty, and Sebastian was only eighteen. His birthday had been just a couple of weeks before. I was in College studying business courses and he was all set to be taking the year off to travel around Europe. Life was so simple and then this shit happened and we were terrified. We had never been around violence before. Our parents were good people. We lived in the rich area and went to private schools. Everything was simple in life. We were terrified when we were first placed in WitSec and then, after a few years, that just became our life. It's funny, though, because after that first year there was a bit of excitement. There was something freeing about being someone completely different, moving around and starting fresh. We used to joke around about being spies."

Fuck, we were so stupid when we were younger. We had no idea just how dangerous all of that would be. Just how exhausting it would become. At first there was that bit of excitement and we tried to make the best out of the whole situation. That lasted until the Marshal was killed and we got another healthy dose of reality. We were bitch slapped by the reminder of the danger we were always going to be living in.

"I think it's natural that you would feel

that way. When things get hard, your mind has to adapt and sometimes the best way to do that is by making up a different world. I used to tell myself that Phillip wasn't my real father. That he had kidnapped me, and my real father was going to storm through that door, kill him and save me any minute. I used to read different fiction books and pretend like I was living in them. I think it's how people's brains cope with the shit that happens to them. The shit that they aren't ready to process. Doesn't change that it's gotta be exhausting by now for you. It's been fifteen years. That's a long ass time to be on the run."

I couldn't imagine what he had gone through growing up. The world he had to have created just to be able to get through the day. I might have been living in a rough world, but he grew up in a cycle of Hell. A cycle I didn't think I would ever be able to survive.

"I'm so sorry for what you went through growing up. I couldn't imagine surviving like you have. I wouldn't have been able to do it. Look, you don't have to be involved in this. You've been through enough in your life, you don't need to take on my shit, too." I shook my head, waiting and expecting for him to agree he wasn't into that kind of life.

The very last thing I wanted was to get Max involved in any of this. I didn't want him to get hurt and I couldn't stand the thought of him being hurt because of me. He deserved to have a good life, one free from all of the pain and potential disaster.

"I'm not going anywhere. I'm already invested and I don't run away from something that is difficult or complicated. I like you, Damien. I'm here for you no matter what," he said, complete determination lacing his voice.

"I like you, too," I said warmly, my gaze meeting his.

He leaned in and placed a quick kiss on my lips. I couldn't believe how good it felt to feel his lips on mine. I never thought I would feel this way about anyone and yet now, I felt this way about two men. It was insane, but I was tired of denying my feelings for both men. I was tired of not living my life because of fear.

The fear of the unknown.

The fear of being discovered one day.

The fear of losing someone.

I couldn't do that anymore, I had to

start living so Sebastian would see that it was okay to start living. I had to do this for both of us, but especially for my little brother. After a moment, Max pulled back and I spoke.

"I don't want Travis to know. It's safer to keep him out of this."

"I agree. He has his own issues, and we still need to figure out what those issues are, too. My gut says he's not safe yet." Max stepped back but kept a hand on my waist.

I knew what he said to be the truth. Something was going on with Travis, and whoever was after him, I had a feeling he wasn't going to just let Travis go. We had to work on him and get him to open up to us. We needed to know who was after him so we could be prepared to stop him from hurting Travis again. It was something we were both determined to do.

"We'll keep working with him on it and make sure he knows he can trust us. We'll get it out of him and make sure he's safe. We won't let anything happen to him," I promised.

"I'm not going to let anything happen to either of you," Max promised, flashing me a warm smile.

Together we would make sure that Travis was safe and with a bit of luck, or rather a shit load of it, we would all be safe and maybe get the chance to be together.

I had no idea what a three-way relationship would look like, but I was willing to give it a chance if that meant that the three of us could be together and be happy. It was worth the risk and it would be worth the aggravation as we tried to navigate this new path in our lives.

We just needed to get Travis to trust us enough first and that was going to be a challenge.

CHAPTER FIFTEEN

Max

IT HAD BEEN three weeks since Travis, Damien, and I had begun working together on this large project. Three weeks since we had slept together. In the past three weeks Damien and I had slept together frequently, but each time it felt like something, *someone* was missing. Each time left me feeling incomplete with Travis not there with us. It was insane, because we had only slept together that one time.

It shouldn't feel like that.

It shouldn't feel like I was cheating on

Travis by sleeping with Damien. Something had to give. We had to do something because I wasn't certain how much longer either Damien or myself could last.

Travis had also been weird for weeks now. He was getting worse, more paranoid and anxious. Each day we saw him he was worse than the one before. I thought he would calm down once he got used to living here, but he hadn't. Typically, someone who had gotten away from someone who was abusing them they were anxious and worried for the first little bit, but as each day passed by without any incidents they grew more comfortable. It had been over a month since Travis had arrived in town and he should have started to relax a bit, but the opposite was happening. I was worried that something more was going on with him. That maybe he wasn't as safe as I had thought. That thought alone was enough to put me on edge. I didn't want anything to happen to either Travis or Damien, and I felt like I wasn't on top of things on either front. I didn't know what was going on with Travis and there was nothing I could do about Damien's situation. All we could do was wait and see if someone came for him. Not an ideal situation on any front.

I was trying not to let it change how I lived my life. I was trying not to let it taint our time together, but I was worried about Damien being attacked and I wouldn't be there to protect him, either. I wouldn't be there to help keep him and his brother safe. I had never allowed myself to care for anyone that I had been with, and this was a good part of the reason. Even friends, I kept them at arm's length because I didn't want to have to bury someone that I cared for.

And yet, Damien and Travis seemed to be ruining me and my rules.

Coop was keeping an eye out on any possible actions by the Italian Mob, something I never thought we would need to do. When it came to the mob, the Italian one wasn't really that high on the danger list. Most of the time it was the Russians that you needed to worry about. However, the Italians were not afraid to get their hands dirty, as was evident with what had happened in Damien and Sebastian's lives.

Still, I figured after fifteen years

someone other than Russo would be running things. Sure, when the boss ends up in jail they run it for a little while, but most of the time the vice president is jumping at the chance to run things on his own. They don't tend to keep playing second fiddle for this long. Russo must have something on his men that he is using against them to keep control of the organization. Maybe if we could figure out what that was, then they would leave Russo to rot in jail and we could get the target off of Damien and Sebastian's back.

All of that was going to take time, though, and I was going to have to accept that I wouldn't always be there for him in case he needed me. I was going to have to accept that Damien had been able to keep himself alive this long and that he knew what he was doing. At least this time around, he wasn't going to be doing it alone. He had the Agency standing behind him, too. If something did happen, we would be ready and hopefully, we would be able to end it once and for all.

Today, we were going to check out another potential location for the safe havens. We had been looking at a lot of properties, but we were trying to find the right options that would put the children in the safest home. The trick was we couldn't put a safe haven up in suburbia either, because then they would stand out too much, and just because they were rich people, that didn't mean they were good people. Some of the most dangerous criminals were white collar guys who knew how to fly completely under the radar.

We'd been checking out a lot of places, but only a few were viable because of the location and the people within the neighborhoods. We couldn't have the children around criminals because they could cash in on a serious payday. It was looking to be a longer process than we had expected for it to be.

I pulled up to the address and saw that Damien and Travis were already there waiting for me. We all got out of our cars and headed toward the house. This area wasn't the best, but I had seen worse. It was a solid middle ground and that was perfect for a safe haven. If we could make sure everyone in the area didn't have any criminal connections, this could be a viable option.

I kept my eyes on Travis and I could

see him looking all around. His eyes were taking everything in and I could see he was scanning for any potential threats that could be hiding in the homes or around them. He reminded me of one of the Agents that I'd worked with who had to be medically discharged for PTSD. He was constantly on edge and wired so tightly that he couldn't even sit down. The hyper-vigilant attitude was a clear sign that something was bothering him and that he was expecting an immediate threat. Which told me that he had a reason to believe that his abuser was either here or watching him.

"Morning," Damien said to us.

"This the place?" I asked with a nod to the one house that Travis was parked in front of.

The house looked rough, but every place we had seen was in rough shape, in one way or another. That's why the city was willing to give them to Social Services for free. It was going to take a good amount of money to repair the safe havens and I knew Travis had been working on some ideas to help raise the funds, because the city was only going to give them so much and it wouldn't be enough to repair the ten houses that they needed for the safe havens. The whole process was going to easily take a year by the time we secured the ten homes, generated the funds to repair them, made the repairs and found the adults to run the homes. It was a long process that we were just barely starting. Both Damien and I had offered to keep helping Travis with the process until it was complete, though. He shouldn't have to go through all of this on his own and we were not about to let him.

"Yes," Travis said as he unlocked the door and we made our way inside.

It looked just about as good as the other places and there really wasn't anything special about it. The houses themselves were pretty basic and simple to set up for security. Houses like these were all the same in terms of security, they had windows, and front and back doors to secure. Other than that we couldn't do much of anything for them. Anything drastic and it would call attention to the house and that was the very thing we were trying to avoid.

Damien and I went all over the house making any notes of anything that could be an issue, but nothing stood out. I headed back down to the living room and kept my gaze on Travis. I could see there was a slight tremble to his body. There were dark bags under his eyes; he clearly hadn't been sleeping. The tremble in his body could be from lack of sleep or from anxiety.

Either way, the shit had to stop.

Some people could handle being on the run and never knowing when an attack was going to happen, but most couldn't. Travis wasn't one of those people who could live their life never knowing if someone was going to attack him. His mind didn't work that way, and that wasn't a knock against him, most couldn't. The human brain wasn't designed to constantly be on high alert; it was why soldiers had so many issues. The brain needed the chance to relax and to no longer have to process every single thing they saw. That became impossible to do if someone was paranoid and on edge waiting for someone to jump out at you from behind a bush or when they were sleeping. Travis needed to talk to someone and I was done waiting for him to decide he was ready. It was time it got forced out of him.

"Okay, that's it, I'm done. We're all going to my place," I ordered.

"What?" Damien asked, confused.

"My place, now," I demanded, then I turned and headed out without further explanation.

I knew they would follow, Damien would be pissed about it, but he would follow. Travis would do it because he wouldn't know why I wanted to talk to him and he was more timid than either of us.

I knew I was supposed to wait until Travis felt comfortable enough to come to one of us, but that wasn't possible anymore. I wasn't going to sit around with my thumb up my ass just waiting for Travis to feel like he could talk to us when he was clearly risking his health. That had to stop. He needed help and he needed it now. He couldn't keep going on the way he was. With not sleeping and barely eating. Fuck, the man looked like he was going to disappear if he turned sideways. We had to do something and the option of waiting was now officially off the table.

As I made the drive to my house I saw

their cars following me. I knew Travis was going to be a ball of nerves and Damien was going to be annoyed and pissed that I had given him an order like that, but he'd get over it.

The second I pulled into my driveway, I climbed out and strolled inside, leaving my door open for the others to follow me. I immediately headed over to my living room where we could sit and have this discussion, hopefully calmly. They both walked inside and Travis closed my front door as I spoke.

"Come sit down."

I took a seat on the couch and Travis sat next to me, but Damien went and plopped down in the chair so he could face the both of us. I could see the anger in his eyes; he wasn't happy about any of this, but he would be fine once I got Travis speaking. It needed to happen, Travis was getting worse and I couldn't stand around and wait for him to eventually trust us enough to open up, because he might never open up to us. He might never feel like we would care to know what had happened. Abuse victims didn't always talk about it. A lot of them kept their mouths shut for the rest of their life and suffered in silence. That wasn't something that I wanted for him. He deserved better and he didn't deserve to carry this with him for the rest of his life.

"What's going on, Sweetheart?" I asked Travis, gently.

I wanted him to know that I wasn't attacking him, that *we* weren't attacking him. That he could open up to us and we weren't going to lecture or judge him. A quick glance over at Damien and I could see that he now understood why I had us all come here. He leaned forward and did his best to relax his body and try to appear less intimidating, which was funny considering how big he was.

"Nothing," Travis instantly said, but it fell short of being convincing.

"We know something is going on. We know those bruises didn't come from a fight with an upset parent. We can help you, but we can't do that if we don't know what is going on, Sweetheart," I tried.

"Max is right, you gotta talk to us. We can help," Damien added.

"There's no fixing this," Travis whispered as the tears started to build in his eyes. His shoulders slumped.

Damien got up and moved so he was sitting next to Travis. I reached over and placed my hand on his thigh as I spoke. "There's always something that can be done to fix something. We can help, but you gotta tell us, Sweetheart."

"We know someone hurt you and we know that they were most likely someone you were dating. If he's reaching out to you, or harassing you, we can stop him. But we can't do anything until you tell us your story," Damien added.

I could see the conflict flickering through Travis' eyes. He *wanted* to tell us his story. He didn't want to have to carry this all on his own anymore and he shouldn't have to. He just needed to tell us and then we could help him carry the weight. Travis sniffed and a few tears started to track down his cheeks before he spoke.

"Joe Baxter."

"The asshole cop?" Damien asked, confused.

I didn't have any personal experience with Detective Baxter, but I had heard enough from Damien, Roland, Jarod, and Mason. They had plenty of run-ins with him, and from what I had been told,

Baxter was a piece of shit cop who was homophobic and had been Jarod's old partner that treated him like shit. He wasn't a good man and it was both surprising and not surprising that he was gay. It was a typical closeted move. Show off to the world that you hated gays and are a man's man, when behind closed doors you were either getting it up the ass or putting it up some guy's ass.

Also it wasn't surprising that he was violent. All of that self-hatred had to turn onto someone. He had to take it out on someone, because he couldn't take it out on himself. Travis was small, had a timid personality, and didn't have much self-confidence. It only made sense that Baxter would target him to be his secret lover.

"It started three years ago. We'd always kept it a secret because he didn't want anyone to know that he was gay. I thought it wouldn't last that long, that he would only want to keep things hidden until he was certain we were going to work out. But as time went on, he got worse. We would go on dates, but in different towns an hour away, and even then, he made it seem like we were just friends. When we were around each other at work or in town, he wouldn't talk to me or even look at me," Travis said in a shaky voice.

"When did it first turn violent?" I asked, gently.

"Not long after we started dating. I dismissed it at first, believed him when he said he was sorry. I made excuses for it. He was stressed at work or he had been drinking, that I shouldn't have said what I said. Before I even knew what was happening, he was staying with me most nights and there wasn't a day that went by where I had a new bruise from him. Sometimes, it was from him beating me and other times him being too rough during sex. I thought maybe it would get better, that maybe he would accept who he was, but he just got more angry."

I could feel the fear radiating off of him and I hated that it was still fresh and raw within him. He was in a different town from that asshole and he was still scared of him. We needed to do something to help him, something to make him feel safe and not anxious and worried all of the time. He needed to start to heal from the trauma.

"He's the one that put those bruises on you," Damien gently stated.

Travis gave a shaky nod before he spoke. "He just got so angry. I was late getting home from work. He always expected to have dinner ready for when he got there. Isaiah needed to talk to me about the possibility of me moving out here. I wasn't going to take the job, but after Joe attacked me that night, I knew I couldn't stay. I avoided him for two weeks as much as I could and the night I left, I packed up everything and drove down here. I thought he would let me go."

"But he hasn't," I stated this time.

I'd suspected that Travis was getting worse and not better with the distance because whatever asshole he was running from had been reaching out. Turned out, I was right.

And of course Baxter was reaching out.

He wasn't just some random asshole, he was a fucking detective. If Travis told someone about the abuse, Baxter would lose everything. His career, his respect, his pension, plus if he went to jail as a cop, he would never get out alive. He needed Travis either terrified or dead.

"It started a few weeks ago. I got a text from an unknown number and it was him telling me that I couldn't run and he knew I was in Baton Rouge. Then the phone calls started to happen, just hang-ups or heavy breathing at all hours of the day and night. Then, I started to get photos of me and you guys leaving the different houses. Last night, I walked into my apartment and it was destroyed. There was a photo sitting on my bed. It was of me, but it was photoshopped. In the photo, I was badly beaten and hanging by a chain from some ceiling somewhere. It had a note written on the back about how he couldn't wait to spend the night with me. I packed up my stuff and went to a hotel."

"Jesus Christ," I said.

Baxter was in Baton Rouge and he wasn't going to leave until Travis was dead. He wasn't going to risk Travis talking to the police or the Agency. He wasn't going to risk his life and career. He needed to silence Travis for good and the only way to ensure that would be to kill him. If we didn't do something soon, Baxter was going to get his wish.

"I don't know what to do," Travis said

as the tears started to flow over his cheeks.

I instantly wrapped my arms around him and pulled him in for a hug. I saw Damien place one hand on Travis' back and the other on his knee. We were trying our best to offer him whatever comfort we could, but the only true comfort we could give him was Baxter dead. That was the only way Travis was going to be able to move on. I just hoped that Damien wouldn't fight me on it.

"It's going to be okay. We're going to protect you. He's never going to touch you again," Damien promised, a deep anger edging his voice.

Maybe I wouldn't have to fight him on it as much as I thought.

I placed a kiss on the side of Travis' head as we both continued to hold onto him and allow him to get the tears out. To cry out all of the pain and fear that he had been feeling and holding in for the past few years now. He needed this in order to start cleansing his body and soul from Baxter and the abuse.

After a moment, when his tears had quieted down, he pulled back slightly. I wiped the tears from his cheeks. I couldn't help but notice how beautiful he looked. His eyes, they were so expressive. I could see everything he was feeling. All of the pain, the fear, the vulnerability, it all lived and played out in his eyes. I hated seeing it. I wanted to see his eyes light up with joy, with pleasure. I wanted to see what he would look like when he was free from all of the pain. And I would see it, no matter what. I was going to make sure Baxter never caused him any problems ever again.

"You're gonna stay here with me until Baxter is dealt with and it's safe again," I said.

There was no way I was going to allow Travis to stay anywhere but here. He might feel safe in a hotel, but I knew from personal experience that anyone could walk through the front door and get someone's room number.

Shit, I'd killed ten people that way.

All Baxter would have to do is flash his badge and they would give him a goddamn room key. If Travis was here, then I would be able to have eyes on him at all times and know that he was safe.

"Are you sure? I don't want to put anyone at risk."

"I'm not going to have you un-secure in a hotel room. You'll be safer here than any hotel room. We can go and grab your stuff and check you out."

"Max is right. Baxter has a badge, it's child play for him to get into your room. You'll be safe here with us," Damien said and I was surprised by the *us* part of his comment.

"Us?" I asked.

"I'm not about to leave either one of you alone to deal with this. We deal with it together. We stay safe together," Damien said with a deep strength to his voice.

He was right, we were safer together, especially Travis. I had no problem with the three of us staying here, and I would be lying if I didn't admit that I wasn't half-hard at the thought of possibly getting to share my bed with both men once again.

CHAPTER SIXTEEN

Travis

I COULDN'T BELIEVE everything that was happening. I never thought I would tell anyone what had been going on. I wanted to deal with it on my own, but then Max and Damien had shown me the affection and care that I had been craving.

They wanted to keep me safe. They wanted to make it better and I couldn't keep it in any longer. I couldn't hold the secrets anymore. It was eating me up inside to keep everything to myself and deal with it all alone.

I had been barely sleeping and it had

only gotten worse. I needed Baxter to leave me alone. I needed to feel safe and to finally get some real sleep. I was already constantly dealing with headaches and my entire body was sore from being so tense all day and night long.

They were offering me the chance to be safe and I had to take it. I had to get their help. It was the only way I was going to ever be able to be free from Baxter and start to heal from everything he had done to me.

Staying here with them both sounded like heaven to me and I was all too happy to spend more time with them. And I also knew they would keep me safe. Baxter wouldn't be dumb enough to attack me when I was around them. They were my guardians, my protectors, and I couldn't have been more thankful to them.

I could see the love that Max had within his eyes. He truly did care for me. Both of them did. It might be a mistake, it was going to potentially be messy, but I wanted to be with them. I wanted them both in my life and not just for sex. How it would work, I had no idea. I could barely handle a two person relationship, let alone a three-way relationship. I had no idea how that was even going to work, but I wanted to try and figure it out. Hopefully, they did as well.

But I didn't need to ask them about that tonight.

Tonight, I just wanted them close.

I looked at Max for a moment before I leaned in and captured his lips with mine. Max didn't even hesitate to kiss me back and he was instantly licking at my lips asking for permission to enter. I opened my mouth and welcomed his tongue, letting out a soft moan as his tongue touched mine.

Max placed his hand on the side of my face, cupping my cheek and running his thumb over my five o'clock shadow as he deepened the kiss.

I loved kissing, for some reason it was my favorite part. Baxter was never really into it, he said it was too immature. That there was no need to kiss when we could have sex. To me, though, I loved the intimacy involved with kissing. I loved how it made me feel closer to my partner. It was one of the best parts and I never wanted it to end.

When the need for air became too

much for the both of us, Max pulled back. I could see the heat and love in his eyes and I knew he was more than happy to continue this.

I turned to see Damien, who had been watching us. I could see the heat within his eyes, but I could also see the uncertainty in them. I could tell he wasn't sure if I wanted him there or not. He wasn't sure if he should be sitting there watching us or not. Traversing this relationship was all new to the three of us, but I wanted to make sure they both knew how important they were to me. How much I wanted them both.

Damien went to get off the couch, most likely thinking I wanted him to leave, but that was the last thing I wanted. I decided I needed to take a chance, so I reached over and placed my hand on the back of his neck before he stood up. I gently pulled him in for a kiss.

He easily took control of the kiss and I was once again moaning and whimpering as his tongue tangled with mine. I heard Max let out a deep moan as he watched us making out.

I felt Max's lips feathering all along my neck as Damien and I made out. Max leisurely trailed his hand down my chest to my pants. He easily undid the button and zipper, freeing my erection as Damien devoured my mouth. I groaned as Max's gripped my dick in his fist, rubbing his thumb up over the head to snag the slick pearl of precum that had gathered. I hummed into Damian's mouth as Max spread the moisture down my engorged shaft.

"That's it, Sweetheart, we have you," Max said. He nibbled on my ear lobe, then used the tip of his warm tongue to trace the shell of my ear, sending shivers skating down my spine.

My whole body was already tingling and we had barely done anything. I wanted them both so badly. No one had ever made me feel this good before and all I wanted was to spend the next week in bed with the both of them.

I let out a whine as they both pulled back almost in unison, but then Max placed one last kiss to my neck as he spoke.

"Get him in bed, I'll lock up," he instructed to Damien.

"You want to go to bed, Sweetheart?" Damien, flashing me a warm smirk.

"Fuck yes." I wanted nothing more.

I felt Max stand and before I could even climb to my feet, Damien was scooping me up against the warmth of his massive chest. I wrapped my legs around his hips and started to kiss and suck on his neck as he took us upstairs. He got us to Max's bedroom and with the ease of him knowing the layout of Max's house, I instinctively knew he had been here since our one night stand together. The fact that him and Max had been together without me left me feeling sad. I felt like I had been left out. I didn't want to be left out. I wanted to be able to experience the pleasure with them. I was going to push that feeling away for tonight, but maybe tomorrow we would need to have an actual conversation about what was going on between the three of us.

Once we were in the room, Damien lowered me down. The second my feet touched the floor, we started to work on the other's clothing. Damien's mouth captured my own once our shirts had been removed. I moaned as I felt his tongue against mine as he fumbled with my button and zipper before he yanked down my pants and boxers. I was already hard and felt an overwhelming desperate need to feel them inside of me. Both of them.

"Fuck, you two are so sexy," Max said as he walked into the room.

Damien pulled back from the kiss and we both turned to look at Max and saw that he was removing his clothes, haphazardly tossing them to the floor in the corner. Once he was naked, he spoke as he joined us.

"How do you want to do this?"

"I want you both inside of me," I said.

I knew it would take more prep work, but they would both fit inside of me. I wanted to feel them both at the same time and not one after the other. I wanted to feel connected to them and for them to feel connected to each other.

I could see the heat in both of their eyes as my words sunk in. They were very interested and I knew this was something they hadn't done before. I got down onto my knees and took both of their hard dicks in my hands. I brought them closer together as I ran my tongue along both of their tips, causing them both to moan.

"Oh fuck," Max let the curse slip from his lips as I tongued his slit.

I looked up at them as I continued to lick and suck at their tips. Damien pulled Max in for a rough and all consuming kiss. Seeing their tongues battling it out with each other only turned me on even more.

I wrapped my hand firmly around Max's long dick, pumping him as I took Damien's thick member into my mouth. I went back and forth between the two cocks, making sure to give them both equal time in my mouth. I had both of their combined tastes on my tongue and it was enough to make my own engorged dick throb. They tasted amazing, especially mixed together.

"Fuck, Sweetheart," Damien moaned.

I knew they were both enjoying getting to watch me suck them both off at the same time. They weren't the only ones loving it. I loved having them both at my mercy. I was able to give them pleasure and I knew they were in desperate need of coming.

"Your mouth feels so good," Max moaned. "Make us come, Sweetheart, then we can fuck you. Make you ours."

I let out a groan and then a whimper as I felt my dick swell even more at the idea. I wanted to feel them both inside of me at the same time and knowing that they both wanted it as well was only turning me on even more.

I took Max down to his base, his head hitting the back of my throat. Up and down, I sucked him harder and faster as his precum continued to trickle over my tongue. I continued to jerk Damien off at the same time, making them both pant heavily and hiss out noises that sent my senses reeling.

I kept moving back and forth between the two of them. Taking turns to take one into my mouth for a few moments before moving to the other. Max was the first one to come deep inside of my mouth and I happily sucked and swallowed everything he had for me.

Once Max had finished providing his musky offering, I moved over and quickly took Damien into my mouth down to his base. I knew he was close and it didn't take long before he was letting a deep moan escape from his lips as he shot his essence down my throat next.

His climax complete and his balls emptied into my mouth, Damien pulled back. Cupping my cheek, he pulled me in for a deep, soul-consuming kiss. I moaned as I felt his tongue licking my own, sucking it, tasting the combination of himself and Max from my mouth

I could vaguely hear Max digging around in his drawer to find lube and most likely a condom, but I didn't want condoms. I wanted to feel them both inside of me. I wanted to feel the heat of their cum scorching my insides. Damien continued to kiss me as he lay me down onto the bed and I opened my legs as he fit himself between them. We continued to kiss for a moment before he finally broke the kiss.

"You sure?" he asked.

"Make me yours," I moaned, nodding. I wanted them so badly. Nothing else mattered more than feeling them inside of me at that very moment.

"We need to really stretch you to make sure you can take both of us deep inside of you," Damien said as he grabbed the lube and squeezed some out onto his fingers. "Turn over, it'll be easier with your sweet ass in the air."

I rolled over and shifted up onto my hands and knees. I lowered myself so my elbows were against the bed, making my ass stick out. I could feel Damien's index finger circling my puckered hole, getting it wet before he slowly pushed the digit inside of me. I relaxed with little difficulty; I knew it would feel good in a minute.

Max bent and took my dick onto his mouth, causing me to let out moan at the sudden pleasure that shot up my spine. Damien continued to finger fuck me with his index finger for a moment before he slowly added his next finger.

The pressure of his fingers made their way around the tight muscles, and the combined slurping and tugging on my dick by Max made my head swirl. I let out a grunt and then a whimper as Damien split his fingers wider inside me.

"I can't wait to get inside of you. I've been wanting to feel you wrapped around my dick again ever since that night. You are going to feel so good with both of our dicks inside of you, Sweetheart," Damien promised, his voice gravelly, as he started to truly stretch my ass and search for my sweet spot.

I moaned and gripped the bed sheets as the pleasure from both Damien and Max began to skyrocket. I arched my back and a long, profound groan bubbled from my lips as Damien's fingers hit my sweet spot and I saw stars. He made sure to continue to aim for the bundle of nerves as he added a third finger to my hole.

Max continued to work my dick with his mouth, his tongue flicking repeatedly over that sensitive spot below the swollen head of my cock, causing my hips to jerk in response. He was unhurried, teasing me and trying to prolong my pleasure. It seemed like both of my boys were trying to milk me and it was driving me crazy, but the very last thing I wanted was for them to stop.

I felt Damien add a fourth finger so I could be properly stretched to be able to handle them both inside of me. I knew it was going to be painful at first, but I didn't care. The need to feel them both inside of me was too much.

Damien picked up his pace with his fingers, making sure to hit my sweet spot repeatedly each time. The feel of multiple fingers pressing against my prostate and the pleasure I was getting from the sweet heat of Max's mouth was driving me crazy. My legs were shaking and my hips bucked to and fro as my mind whirled, trying to keep up with the dual assault.

They were keeping me right on the edge, but not allowing me to tumble off of it.

"He's ready, Baby," Damien said to Max.

It was that moment when Max stopped teasing me and gave the head of my dick a deep and hard suck as Damien rubbed his finger rapidly over my sweet spot. The combination of the two was exactly what I needed to fall off the cliff. I gave a small scream as I came hard and deep inside of Max's hot mouth. Feeling his throat constrict around me with each swallow only milked my dick for more cum. When I finally stopped pulsing, both Damien and Max pulled back, identical satisfied looks on their faces.

"How do we do this?" Max asked Damien.

"He'll be on his side. I'll face him and you will be behind him. I'll enter first as I'm bigger, and then you will." Damien turned to grab condoms and lube.

"I'm negative. We don't have to, but I'm negative." I let the words rush out as I moved so I was lying on my side like Damien wanted me to be.

"So am I," Max said, as he glanced at Damien.

"Me too. You both sure?" Damien asked.

"I am if you both are," Max agreed, nodding.

"Definitely. I want to feel you both." And there was nothing I wanted more than that right now.

Damien gave a nod and squirted some lube into his palm. He grasped his hardness and slicked himself up before he reached over and did the same to Max, who hissed at the pleasure. Damien laid down on his right side in front of me while Max climbed in behind me. Damien moved my legs so one was underneath him and the other fell over his hips so I was at the right angle for the both of them. Max began to trail open-mouthed, heated kisses all along the back and side of my neck as Damien spoke.

"You ready for us, Sweetheart?"

"Fuck yes," I agreed, nodding eagerly.

Damien lined himself up with my stretched hole and gradually pushed himself inside me, past the loosened ring of muscles. It wasn't too bad, because I had really been stretched out. He took it slow and I couldn't help but groan and pant at the pleasure of feeling his large size inside of me. Once he was all the way in, he gave a nod to Max so he could start to push himself inside of me as well.

"I'll go slow and if it hurts too much just say stop," Max said as he notched his tip against my hole beside Damien's cock.

"Okay," I panted, anticipation turning my mind to mush at that moment and making any other words impossible. I turned my head and started to kiss him to reassure him that I was all right with it.

He slowly started to push himself inside of me as he gently kissed me back. It was tight, it was really tight now, but Max had been able to press his tip inside of me and that instantly had the three of us groaning.

I broke from the kiss as I couldn't help but pant harder as Max slowly pushed himself inside of me, inch by glorious burning inch, stretching my hole beyond my imagination. He went slow, but he didn't stop until his hips pressed against my back and he was completely buried inside of me. I felt like any more than that and they'd split me in two.

I alternated between hissing out my breath and sucking another in as they both paused for a moment and my hole accommodated both men. By the time they were both balls deep inside of my ass, we were all panting and trembling with the need. It was more than just a need for pleasure, though. I could see it in both of their eyes. They felt that connection just like I did. As if our souls were connecting with each other for the very first time. The power of it was exhilarating and almost strong enough to make me come.

"Holy shit. So tight," Damien moaned as he licked at the sweat trickling along my neck. I moaned and threw my head back to give him even better access.

"Let us know when you are ready for us to move," Max said, clearly not wanting to rush anything, but I could hear in the quiver of his voice how desperate he was for me to give them the go ahead.

"I'm good move. Please, move," I begged.

I needed to feel them inside of me as they chased their pleasure. I needed to feel them pulsing within me more than anything I had ever needed in my life. I felt like I needed it more at that moment than I needed oxygen.

Max was the first one to gradually start to pull himself out. Once he was almost all of the way out, Damien began to slowly move in the opposite direction as Max pushed back inside of me. It took them a few tries to get the right timing down, but soon they had it so that one of them was pushing inside of me at all times. They were both aiming for my sweet spot and managed to hit it each time dead on, amping up my pleasure to extreme proportions. I couldn't stop moaning. My whole body felt like it was on fire and they were gasoline. With each thrust my body was getting hotter and hotter. The pleasure was on a whole new level, a level I didn't even realize was possible to achieve. The last time we had sex together it had been earth shattering, but this, I didn't even know how to describe it. There were no words to the level of pleasure that these men were bringing to me. I had never felt anything so incredible in all my life.

"Shit, this feels so good," Damien moaned as he picked up his pace, which only encouraged Max to do the same.

"So tight. So fucking hot," Max moaned, punching his hips even faster.

The pace of both men pounding into me was brutal and I was loving every second of it. I couldn't even form words, all I could do was moan and pant as the pleasure filled every cell in my body. With their brutal pace and the constant pleasurable assault on my sweet spot, I was soon seeing stars and coming with a loud scream. My whole body went rigid and I arched my back as rope after rope of hot cum shot out of my dick to coat over my belly and Damien's.

"Oh fuck," Max yelled. They both moaned as the tightness of my ass squeezed both of their dicks even more.

"Shit," Damien hissed, his fingers gripping my hips as he thrust deep inside me once more. I knew I would have bruises tomorrow but at that moment I didn't care.

I had no idea who came first, but I let out a deep moan and pulsed even more as I felt both their searing cum soaking my insides. Words could not describe how remarkable it felt to feel their combined liquid inside of me. To feel it painting my walls and knowing that I had been marked by both of them.

I belonged to them.

We all belonged to each other.

The room was filled with our heavy breathing as we all tried to calm our bodies down from the great high. My whole body tingled from the pleasure and lack of oxygen from panting so badly. I didn't care, though, because it had been more than worth it. And that was the last thought on my mind before everything went dark as sleep overtook me.

CHAPTER SEVENTEEN

Damien

MAX LET OUT a deep moan, a verbal indication of the pleasure that shot through him at that moment, that turned me on even more. He was currently buried deep inside of Travis' ass while I was buried deep inside of him. When the three of us woke up this morning, we were all hard and horny, and figured a sex train was the best way for the three of us to be pleasured. We were all perched on our knees on the bed with Travis in front, followed by Max, and then myself.

It was interesting, though, because

Max truly held most of the power and control for all of our pleasure. He had to be the one to move so he could pound into Travis, but as he moved back, he ground himself onto my own dick. The position was not something I ever thought I would be doing, but I was enjoying it a great deal. The physical feelings and pleasure combined with the visual aspect was a new sensation indeed and one I would happily participate in again.

"Oh don't stop. I'm so close, Baby," Travis whimpered, shifting his hips backward.

I reached around to grasp his dick in my fist and started to jerk him off as Max continued his brutal pace, shuttling into Travis' hole. The second my hand touched his rock hard dick, Travis let out a keening cry and I could tell he was going to be flying off of the cliff soon enough.

"You both are so fucking sexy," I said as I pressed my lips along the back of Max's neck, causing him to moan and shift his hips as he powered into Travis and then back onto my cock even harder. Travis' cock swelled in my hand, Max's ass clamped hard around my girth, and my balls pulled up tight. I knew at that moment none of us would last much longer.

I never thought sex could ever feel this amazing. I had never been one for sleeping next to someone before, but waking up this morning with both of my men in my bed, it felt beyond wonderful. Even now, I was getting to pleasure both of my boys at the same time and it was only heightening my own pleasure.

Travis was a moaning mess and we both knew he was just about to come. I picked up my pace as I moved my hand up and down his shaft and after a hard thrust from Max, Travis let out a scream as he came into my fist.

I felt his cum covering my hand and once he finished pulsing, I removed my hand from his length and instantly brought it up to Max's mouth. Max flicked out his tongue and started to lick up Travis' cum without any hesitation. I knew he loved the taste of our sweet boy and I could relate to the enjoyment he was getting out of the action.

Once my hand was clean, I placed both of my hands on Travis' hips and held him in place.

"My turn to be in control," I growled

into Max's ear and it made his body shiver.

I pulled myself out almost all of the way before I slammed right back into Max, causing him to grunt as my dick hit his sweet spot dead on. It also pushed his hard dick deeper inside of Travis' sensitive body. Max made sure he stayed where he was, balls deep in Travis as I started to pound into him at a fast and brutal pace.

We were both on that edge, ready to come, and I was going to be making sure he reached his peak first. With each thrust, I made sure to hit Max's sweet spot dead on, relishing the grunts and groans I drew from his body with each fevered thrust. Both Max and Travis couldn't stop moaning and groaning as the pleasure within their bodies took over and the sounds both thrilled me and pushed me closer to my own climax.

"You feel so good, Baby. So tight, so hot," I moaned as I shuttled my hips even faster and harder. I was so close, but I wanted Max to come first. I wanted to feel the tightening of his walls as he clamped down around my dick. I *needed* to feel his ass milking me for everything that I had to offer.

"You want him to fill you up, Sweetheart?" I said to Travis.

Travis let out a profound groan before he was able to form any words. "Fuck yes. I want to feel it. Come for us, Baby. Fill my ass with your hot jizz."

I pounded Max's prostate a few more times before he finally let out a long, throaty moan as he came hard and deep inside of Travis. The pleasure from it caused Travis to moan, too, and I knew he was coming once again.

I had managed to milk both of my boys and that pleasure alone was enough to push me over the edge. I snapped my hips forward and kept my dick buried as deep as I could inside of Max's ass as I pulsed and released every drop of cum that I had for him, coating his inner walls with pulse after pulse as my dick throbbed. I knew all of our bodies were screaming out in pleasure in unison and the thought made my head spin.

Once we all finished our respective climaxes while we each held tight to the man in front of us, we all collapsed down onto the bed. We were all breathing heavily and I knew we were going to need a minute before any of our legs would start to work once again. If this was what it was going to be like in the morning waking up to my men, then I never wanted to leave the house. I wanted to keep them both hostage so we could continue to enjoy ourselves in the same way every single morning—what an incredible way to start the day—and all day long for that matter.

"I think we broke him," Max said with a smirk as Travis swiftly fell back to sleep.

Max may have been right about that, but I could admit that these two might also break me if we started every morning like that. The first time we all had sex, I could chalk that up to being an exciting time with my first threesome. It only made sense that the sex would be off the wall amazing. But now, after three times, I still felt like my whole world had been shattered. Everything I knew about myself and expected for my future had changed in the space of a couple of weeks and the thought left me mind blown.

I never thought I would be in this position. I never thought I would be in a relationship, even just a sexual one, with two other men. It was insane and I honestly had no idea how well this was going to end or what would happen, but I wasn't going to allow fear of the future to dictate what happened between us. I wasn't going to allow that uncertainty to control what I did. I was having fun. I was finally enjoying life again, for the first time in many years. I wanted this relationship to continue and I wanted to see where it could go, even if parts of it scared me to death. I knew I had my own uncertainties about the possibility for stability or a future with the organization after me, but hopefully that could be worked out and the end result would allow me to stay there with my boys.

For the first time in forever, I had hope.

I climbed off the bed as I spoke in a whisper. "Almost broke me on that one."

Max gave a soft chuckle as he slowly got up off the bed. I watched as he covered Travis with a blanket before I turned and strolled into the bathroom to get cleaned up. Max came in behind me, sliding past me with a quick caress over my ass, and he started the shower. Without even needing words we both moved into the shower to get cleaned up.

"What do we do about Baxter?" Max asked.

We hadn't had the chance to discuss Baxter and that whole situation yet. We had been having sex and sleeping since learning who was after Travis. I was still surprised that it was Baxter who had been abusing him. I knew of Baxter from the stories that I had heard and I knew he was homophobic. I just hadn't expected for him to be in the closet.

I knew that some guys, who were filled with so much self-hate that they were gay, turned violent toward others. That wasn't new to me. I had seen it, had investigated crimes in the past where it was a hate crime. I just hadn't pegged Baxter as one of those guys. He hid it well. Almost perfectly, in fact. He had it figured out down to the last detail. I knew that likely meant he had done the same type of thing before. Travis was not his first victim. That didn't mean the others were dead, Baxter could have easily abused them and allowed them to leave, but I wouldn't put it past him to have killed people and hidden the bodies, either. The man was dangerous and I wouldn't be neglecting that tidbit of information.

When someone like Baxter first started to date, they didn't always want to hold onto their victim. Abusers tend to build up over time. They start off slow and they see how far they can push things. It was a lot like a serial killer. They start off slow with animals and then they build up.

Abusers typically had previous victims who were able to get away only because the abuse wasn't as bad as their present victims. They may have been controlled and hit a few times, but they got away. Their abuser wasn't trying to keep a death grip on them.

As the abuser becomes more comfortable and gains self-confidence in being able to push their victim to a whole new level, the abuse becomes worse and their grip on their victim will increase and become tighter.

Now Travis was Baxter's most recent victim and had been for several years. He wasn't about to let him go. Baxter following him to Baton Rouge made that very clear. He was calling him, sending him photos, and now, he had destroyed Tavis' apartment and left a death photo. The situation was getting highly dangerous.

I suspected some of that escalation was due to myself and Max entering the picture, too. If there was one thing an abuser hated, it was their victim finding someone else. It didn't matter if Baxter believed we were all sleeping together or not. Just the fact that we were in Travis' life and we saw each other often, that was enough for Baxter to label us as a danger to him. It was probably why he had been going harder on Travis. He needed to prove he was still in control. He needed to break him. He needed Travis to feel like he had to leave town to keep us safe, leaving him alone and defenseless, and that is when Baxter would attack him and most likely kill him. That wasn't something that either Max or I were going to allow to happen. We needed to end this man's toxic, stalking behavior, and we had to do it fast before Baxter grew more angry and dangerous.

"We gotta find him. He's in the city so he has to be checked into a hotel somewhere."

"And when we do find him? Then what?" Max asked as we switched spots so I could be under the hot water.

What we did with Baxter, that was the million dollar question. He was a cop, an active cop, so it wasn't like we could just threaten him and move on. Baxter wasn't going to risk his career by allowing Travis to live. He had to kill him to ensure that Travis didn't talk.

I suspected that his previous victims weren't upstanding members of society. If Travis talked, people would listen. He was someone that people respected. He was a Social Worker; he wasn't some drug user or shady person who could be trying to maliciously bring down a good cop. People would listen if he spoke up and Baxter knew that. He wasn't going to risk that happening so he had to kill him. He had to make it look like either Travis fled town, or he was killed in a home invasion. There really was only one thing we could do.

"We kill him."

I could see the shock flash through his eyes at my simple statement. Between the two of us, I was the one always telling Max that he couldn't be a vigilante and kill people. I was the one who was always telling him that he needed to use his skills for good, but in a different way. In a way where it didn't put him at risk of getting killed or going to jail for the rest of his life. I knew he wanted to kill Baxter, but he hadn't been expecting me to agree and to say that we needed to kill an active cop. It would make things messy, I knew that, but I also knew we could cover it up.

Hell, we had done it before.

In a typical situation, I would suggest we needed to get Travis to file a report and press charges against Baxter. However, this wasn't a typical situation. Baxter was a cop and despite the fact that people would more than likely believe Travis' story, that didn't change that Baxter *was* a cop. He had connections that would keep him out of jail.

We had no solid evidence that what had happened in Baton Rouge was him. We also had no evidence that Baxter had ever hurt Travis. We didn't have any photos or scientific evidence that we could use to prove that Baxter was the one who had abused Travis. Everything we had was circumstantial and would leave way too much on the table as 'he said, he said.'

I also knew that having to testify was terrifying and I didn't think Travis would have it in him. That didn't mean I thought he was weak or incapable of being strong. I just knew that it wasn't easy to sit in an open court and look at someone to testify against them.

It had been hard for me and Sebastian to do it, and we hadn't been physically abused for years by the person sitting at that table across from us.

Travis would have to sit in an open court and look at Baxter, feel the man's hate-filled eyes on him the entire time, and tell people about the abuse the man had put him through. And then, he would have to deal with Baxter's lawyer trying to make it seem like he was lying.

It was why most cases for abuse didn't go anywhere. The victim can't handle the trauma of testifying and defense lawyers were all assholes. They only cared about getting their client off from the crime and not what they were doing to destroy the victim.

When Sebastian and I had testified, Russo's lawyers, all five of them, had tried to make it seem like we were mentally unstable. They wanted us to be evaluated by multiple shrinks; they wanted to plead that we were too incompetent for anything we had to say to be taken seriously. It didn't work, but it made a horrible situation even worse. It prolonged our pain, and that was the last thing I wanted for Travis.

"You see the irony in that, right?" Max asked with a smirk.

"Yeah, I know. But you know just as well as I do that he's too dangerous to leave alive. He's not going to stop until Travis is dead. Even if we could get him arrested, you know he's never going to see the inside of a jail cell. He'll use his connections to get out on bail and then he'll do everything he can to make it seem like Travis is unstable. He'll ruin his reputation and his career. The only way to save Travis, to protect him, is to kill Baxter."

"Hey, I'm not saying no. We find where he's staying, I can grab my rifle and take him out."

"Let's find him first before we start making execution plans. First step is finding this asshole."

I wasn't certain assassinating Baxter was the best route to go with this one. I wanted him dead, we needed him dead, but it might be better if it was a mechanical malfunction on his car, versus a bullet between the eyes. A clear hit would have every cop in the city on the hunt for whoever had done it. If he died in a car accident, then it could be ruled as an accident, or mechanical error, and that would be the end of it. We needed to kill him in the right way so it wouldn't come back on either of us or on Travis.

"Fine, just so long as the end result is the same, I'm good," Max said with a shrug before he leaned in and pressed his lips against mine. He kept the kiss quick before he slid out from under the water and climbed out of the shower and I let out a soft sigh.

How the hell had we gotten here?

***

It was nearing one in the afternoon when Travis finally made his way down the stairs. He had been asleep the whole time since our last intimate encounter and I could tell he had desperately needed the rest. He was freshly showered and he looked awake and perky for the first time in a long time.

Max and I had been spending the last few hours trying to track down Baxter. We had been running his name against all hotel and motel registrations in the city. We hadn't found him yet and it was becoming clear we were going to have a real problem figuring out where he was. He could be using a false name for the booking. He could also be at one of the motels that didn't keep their registration list online. Some didn't even care to grab a name if you paid in cash. We were going to have to physically go to the hotels and motels with a photo of him and see if we could find where he was staying. It was going to take longer, and that wasn't something either of us were happy about.

We also had to take into account if he was planning on staying here for longer than a couple of weeks, he could be renting an apartment or a house. There were plenty of short term rentals in the city, and he could have grabbed any of them and we wouldn't know which one. There was no database for short term rentals.

It wasn't like Baxter would need to update his government ID with the new address. He must have a car, but again, we couldn't find any rentals with his name. So, either he was driving his own vehicle, which would make sense, or he was using a false name for the rental. I suspected he was driving his own car so there wouldn't be a need for him to rent one. It would just add to his own complications and it would be hard for him to explain it away if he got arrested.

"He lives," Max quipped with a warm smirk.

"Sorry about falling back asleep," Travis said bashfully, with a shy smile crossing his lips as he looked at the ground.

"It's okay. You obviously needed the sleep. How are you feeling?" I asked.

He still didn't look too good. Not the way I figured he should after getting a good rest. He didn't look as tired as he did last night, but I could tell he was still rundown. He needed some food and some love to get back to being fully healthy.

"I'm okay. I guess I owe you both an explanation," he said slightly awkwardly, toeing the floor.

"You don't owe us anything, Sweetheart. But if you want to share, we will always be there to listen," I said as I held my hand out, indicating he should sit on the couch.

I could see him hesitate for a moment before he went over and plopped down on the couch. We both joined him, once again sitting on either side of him to show our support. We could both tell that Travis needed more support, more displays of affection than either of us needed. He had been abused, but I knew strong and confident people didn't tend to get abused. If they entered an abusive relationship, they left that first time they were hit. People who had lower self-esteem and self-confidence tended to be the ones who hung around and believed the lies and hope that things would turn around.

"What's going on, Sweetheart?" Max asked as he placed his hand on Travis' knee.

Travis sucked in a deep breath before he spoke. "I have a protein deficiency. It's idiopathic, so there's no real reason for my body to not absorb enough protein. But the lack of protein makes me tire easily, and I have a harder time gaining weight and healing. I also tend to get sick often from it."

"Do you take supplements?" I asked.

A protein deficiency wasn't what I had

been expecting, but it did explain why he was so thin and always seems to fall asleep after sex. It also would explain why his bruises were still not fully healed even after a few weeks. I had never heard of a protein deficiency, but I did know that everyone's body needed protein to function properly.

"No. Your body can only absorb so much and with mine not absorbing the proper amount of protein, taking a supplement would be pointless. I basically have to eat healthy to try and keep my immune system up and to make sure my body gets all the nutrients that it needs. I would understand if you didn't want to keep being with me."

What the hell?

"I know I can speak for the both of us when I tell you that you having a medical condition, it's not a deal breaker, Sweetheart," Max said before I even had the chance to speak.

I couldn't believe Travis actually thought we wouldn't want to be with him because he had a medical condition. That would be like Travis and myself not wanting to be with Max because he had PTSD from his childhood trauma. We couldn't help having medical conditions, for fuck's sake; they were out of our control and not something anyone asks for. It was clear, though, that he had truly expected for us to not want to be with him because of it, and that made me believe that for previous boyfriends, even before Baxter, this had been an issue for them. Travis really hasn't dated anyone who was a good man and knew how special he was. How to treat him right, the way he deserved to be treated.

"I get sick a lot and I'm tired most of the day. I can't play sports or do anything crazy active," Travis started, but I cut him off. I was not going to listen to him try and give us reasons as to why he didn't deserve to be with us.

"We don't care about that. We care about *you*, Sweetheart. We're not going anywhere. We all have problems, scars that we'll carry for the rest of our lives. It's part of who we are and I know neither one of you would walk away because of my own issues. Just like we wouldn't walk away from Max's issues. And trust me, he's got a few," I said, flashing a warm smirk at Max.

"Asshole," Max said, flashing a grin

back at me before he looked at Travis again. "He's right. We all have baggage and we all have quirks. Your medical condition, it doesn't change how we feel about you and it never will. If you get sick, we'll take care of you. As for sports, neither one of us plays any and we can always make sure you get enough sleep after sex. We're not walking away, Sweetheart, so you better get used to having people in your corner."

I could see the tears building behind Travis' eyes. He hadn't expected for us to be on his side with this. He was going to need a lot of love and affection before he would be fully healed from all of the pain people in his life had caused him. We were both determined to make sure he was cared for. That he was healed from all of the abuse in his life. He was a good man and he didn't deserve any of this. He deserved the world and we were going to give it to him.

"Why don't I make us all something to eat. Then afterward, you should go with Max to your hotel room and grab your things. I'll keep looking for Baxter," I suggested.

Travis just gave a nod in agreement

and I knew he still needed some time to process everything that had happened. He would be going through a lot of emotions before this was all said and done, but we would get him through it. We would get him safe and then we would get him healthy and happy. We just needed to kill Baxter first.

CHAPTER EIGHTEEN

Max

WE PULLED UP to Travis' apartment building and nudged the car into a parking space.

We had already gone to his hotel room and grabbed his things and checked him out. I wanted to come to his apartment, though, for two reasons. One, I wanted to make sure he got everything that he wanted or needed that he couldn't grab when he ran. And two, I wanted to see the destruction with my own eyes.

Travis had said he hadn't cleaned up that night and he hadn't been back since.

I didn't blame him for not spending the time to clean up. He was terrified and he had no idea if Baxter would come back that night. The smartest thing he could have done was run and worry about the mess later. I was already sure he would be losing his security deposit. I would need to talk to his landlord and see if there was something we could do. Hopefully, he would understand the situation and not use it against Travis. It would all depend on the type of landlord they were.

As I followed Travis up to his apartment, I was already getting a bad feeling about this place. It wasn't a nice place. The apartment building was rundown and dirty. The elevator didn't work, and even if it did I doubted I would be going into it. It looked like it was just one bad jerk away from collapsing.

Travis unlocked his door and we headed inside. Instantly, I could see the destruction that Baxter had caused. He didn't leave a single spot undamaged. Shit, the floor was even covered in paint. There was a great deal of hatred in this apartment. If Travis had been here, it could be his blood all over the floor instead of paint.

It was not lost on me that the apartment itself was a shit hole before the destruction. It was a crack shack, which didn't make sense when he made decent money as a Social Worker. He didn't have a spouse, no kids, and his medical condition didn't require medication or medical treatments.

So where was all of his money going?

"It's pretty bad, I know," Travis said with complete understanding to his voice.

"You were lucky you weren't here," I said, but I could tell that Travis was well aware of that fact.

He turned and headed toward his bedroom and I followed behind him. His room was a whole new level of disturbing. It was set up for a romantic evening, but for Baxter it would be a romantic evening of slowly killing Travis. There would be no love in this room. And once again, I couldn't help but notice the single bed, the old furniture. It screamed someone who didn't have much money.

"I have to ask, and I know it's a personal question so feel free to tell me to fuck off. Where is your money going?"

I could see the understanding in his

face before he answered. "Baxter. He took out loans in my name. He gambles and he loses all the time. I'm still paying off the loans. I don't really have much by the end of the month. Having the hotel for the past couple of days has maxed out my credit card. I was gonna have to come back here today or live in my car. There's one loan left, but it's high, it's really high. The interest rate is killing me. He got it from some loan shark; it's thirty-seven percent interest on a fifty thousand dollar loan. I'm gonna have to find a part-time job just to be able to afford food at this point."

He sounded so defeated and tired, just exhausted. He had been doing this for years now and on top of the abuse and fear, he'd had to deal with the financial strain that Baxter had placed on him. It was no wonder he was living in a place like this; he couldn't afford anything else.

Now I *really* wanted to kill the bastard.

I went over and joined him and placed my hand on the side of his face, cupping his cheek in my palm, my thumb scraping over the barest hint of five o'clock shadow.

"You can stay with me as long as you

want. We'll figure it out, Sweetheart. First, is getting you safe. Afterward, we can figure out the financial aspect of this whole mess. It'll be okay, Sweetheart," I said, flashing him a warm smile and then pressing my mouth to his warm lips in a quick peck.

He offered me a small smile when I pulled back and I knew it was going to take more than a few words to make him feel better. All we could do, though, was take this one step at a time and get him safe. Once we had Baxter in the ground, then we could work on figuring out how to help him with the illegal loan against his name.

I leaned in and placed another soft and quick kiss to his lips, then pressed my forehead to his. I didn't want to push him right now and I didn't want to get too caught up in loving on him. Not in this apartment. We could always have fun later. Right now, we needed to grab whatever he had left behind and then get back to my place where he would be safe.

I pulled back and I was instantly missing the connection to him. A quick look into his eyes told me he was feeling the same way.

"Come on, let's grab what you need and then get back to our man," I said, flashing him another a warm smile.

"I'd like that," he said, with a genuine smile turning up the corners of his lips.

That single legitimate smile told me everything I needed to know. He did like both Damien and myself. He liked being with the both of us, and knowing that had me feeling all bubbly. We would need to have a conversation about that today. If we were going to give it a real try, then we all needed to be on the same page.

I just hoped we could work it out. I knew having a three-way relationship was not going to be easy. We were going to have a lot we needed to figure out, and that was before we factored in how our friends and people in society would handle it. All of that could be worked out later, though. Right now, all that mattered was that we were together and we would all be safe.

***

We arrived back at my house and Damien was there to greet us outside. He helped us unload the car and bring Travis' items into my home. We had another load to bring in and my eyes picked up on the black four door sedan that was parked just down the street from my house. I made sure to not look directly at it, because it had been following us since we left Travis' hotel. I suspected it was Baxter and he had been watching Travis' hotel just waiting for him to leave.

I shot my hand out and placed it on the back of Damien's neck, pulling him in for a quick kiss before I kissed along his neck beside his ear so I could speak to him.

"Black, four door sedan just down the street. He's been tailing us since we left the hotel."

Damien placed his hands on my ass and started to kiss along my neck. I knew he understood what I was doing. He needed to get a look and we needed to come up with a plan.

"That's Baxter, I've seen him around. So he'd obviously been sitting on the hotel and waiting for when Travis would leave. I'm thinking he's done waiting and wants to end this quickly. He must have to get back to Gaithersburg for his job soon."

"We need to end this and we can do it today. He's the angry type, if we piss him off enough, he'll storm right into my house looking for blood. I'd be willing to bet everything I have that he's got a gun."

"You want to use Travis as bait. Use all of us as bait. Get him so pissed off he storms in and tries to kill us. If we do that, we would have to be ready for it. And we have to make sure Travis is on board."

I looked over and saw Travis walking back out. I pulled back slightly as I held my hand out for him. Travis easily took it and I pulled him so he was in between both Damien and me. Damien was instantly kissing along Travis' neck as I spoke.

"Baxter is here. He's in the black sedan just down the street from here. He's been following us since the hotel."

"Oh my god," he whimpered and I could see that he was about to freak out, but we needed to keep him calm so Baxter didn't know we were onto him.

"Stay calm. He can't know that we know he's here," Damien said as he ran his hand down the front of Travis' chest.

"We have a plan on a way to get rid of him. And I'm talking for good, Sweetheart. He could be dead within the hour and you will be free from him forever. But we need to know if that is what you want. Do you want him dead or we can arrest him and press charges against him for domestic abuse and allow the courts to handle it. The choice is yours and we will support you one hundred percent," I explained.

"We don't have enough for court," he said as he did his best to keep the expression on his face even.

With him being a Social Worker, he knew what we needed to make any of it stick within a courtroom and we didn't have anything we needed. And even if we did, Baxter's lawyers would be able to fight against it. There was a very high possibility that Baxter would be back out on the street within forty-eight hours.

"No, we don't. But if you don't want him dead, then that is what we will do," I said.

"I can't do this forever. I can't be afraid all the time. I can't be looking over my shoulder everywhere I go or too scared to fall asleep. I can't live this way," he said, with a deep amount of pain lacing his voice.

"And that's okay. We understand that, Sweetheart. We can end it today, but we need your help. I will handle killing him, but we need your help to piss him off enough so that he breaks into Max's house," Damien said.

"How?" Travis asked, still unsure. At least he was willing to help.

"We need to make him extremely mad so he has no choice but to take action. The best way we can do that is by making him jealous. We stand here and make out for a bit before we head inside. We can go up to my bedroom. We'll have a gun and be ready for when he comes in. All you have to do is play along with us. We'll keep you safe," I promised.

I knew this was asking a lot from him. I hadn't been planning on including Travis in killing Baxter. Neither Damien nor myself wanted him to be involved in any of this, but the best chance we had of killing him and getting away with it was right now. If he broke into my home with a gun, we were well within our legal rights to kill him. It would be simple and we would never have to worry about someone digging into his death. But neither of us were going to put Travis in a position he wasn't comfortable being in. If he said no, then we would come up with a new plan.

Travis let out a shaky breath and we both knew he was thinking about it. We weren't putting him in the best position with this situation. We both would have loved for him to not be connected to any of this, but it truly was our best chance. It was asking him to help lure a man into my house to be killed, though. He would need to lie to the police about some of what happened here. We would have to make it seem like we didn't know Baxter had been following us. The rest could stay the same, but it was still asking him to lie. Now, we could make it so that one of the guys from the Agency came to take the report and to handle the body. That would give us some leeway and it might keep Travis out of this part of it. Still, it was asking a lot for him.

"Okay. I can't do this forever. I need it to end. If this is the best way, then okay. What do I need to do?" Travis asked, sounding more confident that I had a feeling he felt.

"Just play along. Don't look at him and just focus on us," I said, before I went in for a kiss.

We had to make this look very good. We had to piss him off so badly that he threw all logic and common sense right out the window. We needed him to break into my house and try to kill us.

I held Travis close against me as we kissed. I knew Damien would be kissing him and running his hands all over his body. After a moment, I pulled back and got down on my knees. The position we were in and the height of my vehicle would make it so that Baxter wouldn't see what I was doing, but he would know it.

"Pretend he's sucking your dick, Sweetheart," Damien said against Travis' neck.

I felt Travis place his hand on my head and he arched back and gave a long moan. Damien started to grind against Travis' ass and I knew they would both be hard even though we had an audience. I couldn't wait until later on tonight when we could all play together for real. I wanted to feel both of them against me once again.

I was starting to think I needed a bigger bed. My room was big enough to handle a king size bed and it would give us plenty of room to roll around in it.

We kept at the fake blow job for a few more minutes before Travis gave a deep moan and I stood up. I pulled Damien in for a kiss and we both grinded against Travis' body. We needed to make it very clear that the three of us were together. After a moment, we pulled back and then headed inside.

Once we were inside, I closed my door, but I didn't lock it. I wanted to make it easy for Baxter to come into my house. Now that we were inside, I could see the heat within Travis' eyes, but I could also see the worry. This was going to be the scary part, but we would get through this.

"Come on, let's get up into my room," I said as I took Travis' hand in mine.

I brought them both into my room and Damien left the door partway open. I then went over to my bedside table and pulled out my gun. I placed it under the pillow so Damien would be able to grab it easily. He just had to make sure he was on the bed. I wanted to be the one to kill the asshole, but I knew it would be better coming from Damien. He was the one with the connection to Mason and Roland. Plus, if he did have to go down to the station for the kill, it was better that they didn't have me being investigated. I had a lot more kills than Damien did and the last thing any of us needed was one of those kills coming back to bite me in the ass.

The irony was not lost on me.

I knew Damien had said that one day I might live to regret the choice to be a vigilante and it seemed like that day had come. I never thought it would, but here I was afraid of going to jail and being away from my men. After this was over and done with, I would need to re-evaluate my stance on vigilantism.

"Okay, Sweetheart, we're gonna lie on the bed and wait until we can hear Baxter. We'll hear him come up the stairs and then you and Max will kiss and I will take Baxter out," Damien explained to Travis.

"He's not going to hurt you, I promise I won't allow it," I promised him.

"I know you won't. I know either of you won't," he said, fear still shining brightly behind his eyes.

I got him down onto the bed and I lay next to him. Damien was behind me and I knew he had his hand on the gun underneath my pillow.

We didn't have to wait long.

I could hear my front door opening and

I turned and started to kiss Travis who was lying on his back. I could feel that he was anxious and scared, not that I could blame him. I hated that he was here for this, but I was going to protect him and make sure he didn't have to see any of it. I could feel Damien against my back and his body was tense. He was ready to react the second he needed to.

"You fucking whore," Baxter seethed as he pushed the door open so fast it smacked against the wall.

I instantly pulled away from Travis and looked over to see Baxter standing in the doorway, his face crimson in anger, a gun in his hand pointed at the ground. I kept my hand on Travis' chest to keep him down, though. I didn't want him to make any sudden movement that would cause Baxter to fire. We just needed him to talk long enough for Damien to get the gun out from the pillow without Baxter noticing.

"Who the fuck are you and why the fuck are you in my house?" I demanded.

"You dirty whore. You left me for them? You left me so you can be a slut with not one but two men. If I had known you liked to be fucked by two men, I could have put your ass on the street corner and made money from you. At least then you would have been worth something instead of being a worthless piece of shit. Maybe you need two men, though. You always were shit in bed, could barely get me off. At least when you are sick and pathetic in bed all the time they can still get off with each other."

"I don't know who the fuck you are, but the last thing he is is worthless. As for the sex, he has no problem making either of us come. I guess that means it's your dick that doesn't work and not him. Or maybe he just needed a real man to show him what pleasure is. What it feels like to have a real, big, juicy, dick inside of him, compared to your pathetic mini dick that he's had to suffer through. It's no wonder you couldn't even get him hard," I said back with a cocky smirk.

I had no idea if Baxter had been able to make Travis aroused. I was assuming based on how responsive Travis' body was that Baxter hadn't been able to turn him on. The point in my words was to piss Baxter off even more. I wanted his attention on me. I wanted him so furious that he didn't even see the gun coming.

I was also not going to sit here and listen to him talk shit about Travis. He was a good man, a sweet and kind man, and I was not going to allow anyone to talk shit about him. I wasn't going to allow Baxter to use Travis' medical condition against him. It wasn't his fault that he tired easily or that his immune system was weaker. It could happen to anyone and he deserved to be taken care of. He deserved to be cherished and worshipped. Baxter had no idea what a treasure Travis was and he never would.

Baxter did exactly what I thought he would, he turned the gun toward me and before he even had the chance to fire, Damien had pulled the gun out. I grabbed Travis and turned him into me just as Damien fired and killed Baxter with a bullet between the eyes. It was all over in a split second, before the echo of the gun throughout the bedroom had even dissipated.

Baxter lay on the floor, his glassy eyes open and staring off into the abyss, his gun still in his hand.

I didn't want Travis to see the man dead. I had no idea if he had ever seen someone dead before, but if not, I wasn't going to let this be his first time. His whole body was trembling in my arms and I knew he was already going into shock.

"It's okay, Sweetheart. You're okay, we're all okay," I reassured as I held him close to my chest, my hand tracing up and down over his back.

I looked over and saw Damien checking Baxter's pulse, but we both knew he was dead. Fuck, the damn blood was never going to come out of my floor. It might be time to move after all of this. This house was always going to be temporary anyway until I found one that I wanted to spend time in. Now might be the perfect time to start looking for something that could work in the big picture of things.

"I'll call Mason, you get him downstairs," Damien ordered.

I gave a nod and scooped Travis up into my arms. He kept his face buried in my neck and I was thankful that I didn't have to try and maneuver him around the dead body to keep him from seeing it. I could feel a warm wetness against my shoulder and I knew he was crying. All of this was a lot for him to be dealing with so I wasn't all that surprised at the tears. He was finally getting to release all of the pain and fear from the last few years. He was finally free from the abuse of Baxter and it all needed to come out.

I sat down on the couch with him in my lap and I held him against my chest as he cried his heart out. I knew Damien would handle Baxter and Mason when he arrived. It was my job to take care of Travis and that was exactly what I would be doing. Nothing was more important than my man.

***

"Thank you, we appreciate you handling all of this," I said as I shook Mason's hand.

It had taken a couple of hours for Mason and the Coroner to finish up with Baxter's body. He was now out of my house and I was left with a blood stain that was going to be a bitch getting out of the floor.

"It's no problem. I'm glad he's safe. One down, and now one more to go. I'll see you around."

I knew he was talking about the organization hunting Damien and

Sebastian. We would have to handle that next, but for tonight I would be taking care of my men. With Mason gone, I turned to give my two lovers my full attention.

"Okay, we're leaving," I said, and I could instantly see the confusion in both of their eyes.

"You do know we don't need to go on the run, right?" Damien asked, and I wasn't certain if he was being serious or not.

"After what happened here tonight, and with the large blood pool soon to be stained, on my bedroom floor, now is the perfect time to go to a hotel. I vote for one with a hot tub in the room and a king size bed."

"I know just the place," Damien said as he held his hand out for Travis to take.

I could tell Travis was all too happy to get out of this place. We didn't grab anything; we just headed out. None of us looked back at the now dark house. We all climbed into Damien's truck and he took off for the hotel. He gave me the name and I easily pulled it up on my phone and booked us a suite on the penthouse floor with a double king size bed and a hot tub big enough for eight people in the room. It was perfect and exactly what we needed.

The second we arrived, we quickly checked in and made our way to our room. It was just like the photos on the website and truly breathtaking. "Now this is a room," I said as I strolled over and turned on the hot tub.

"Come on, Sweetheart, let's relax and wash the day away," Damien said as he went and helped Travis to get undressed.

I opened the mini-fridge, snagged a few small dark brown colored bottles from the shelf, and made us all a stiff drink. We could all use some whiskey after the hell we'd dealt with today.

Once we were all situated in the hot tub, with Travis between us, I spoke.

"How are you feeling, Sweetheart?"

"I don't know yet. Numb. None of this even feels real just yet."

Travis had been in shock for a good few hours over what happened with Baxter. Both Damien and I hated that he had to be involved in this, but it had been our best chance of killing Baxter and getting away clean from it. I was just hoping that he would be able to process all of this and be okay with it, be okay with us for making that decision.

"It'll take some time, but you will process it. We're sorry that you had to be involved in that," Damien said, trailing his fingertips over Travis' arm.

"I understand why it had to be done that way. I'm not upset that he's dead. Underneath the shock, I do feel relieved and free. I think it's just going to take a little bit for my mind to process everything and get used to a normal life now. What happens to us now?"

"Well, that depends on what we all want, I guess. I would love to be with you both. I know it's unconventional and I am sure there will be problems that come up along the way, but I would like to give this a real shot," I admitted.

I was hoping they both wanted that as well. I knew it wasn't going to be easy for any of us and we were going to have to navigate through a whole new territory for the three of us, but I wanted to try. I wanted to have them both in my life.

"It's not going to be easy, but I can't imagine my life without both of you in it," Damien agreed.

"I want that, too. Though, I'm not

really sure how it will work," Travis added.

"We can figure it out. We have lots of time to figure all of it out. What matters is that we all want to be together," I said, flashing them both a warm smile.

It warmed my heart to hear that they both wanted the same future I did. That they both wanted to see where this thing between us could go. I was worried that they may not have wanted to make our relationship into something serious, that they just wanted to have some fun and nothing more, so the relief I felt in that moment was extraordinary. Knowing that they wanted to give our relationship a real chance, I couldn't have been happier.

"We'll figure it out, but we don't have to do that tonight. Tonight, let's relax and enjoy each other's company. I know of a few ways we can pass the time that will help us all feel so much better," Damien said, flashing a grin and a wink at both of us.

And that was exactly what we were going to do.

EPILOGUE

Four Months Later...

Travis

"ARE YOU GUYS ready? We can't be late."
I called out to my men.

We were getting ready to head out for Finley's and Rafe's wedding. They had gotten engaged close to a year ago and today was their big day. Everyone in the Agency was going to be there for it, and then afterward, we would be going to their home for the reception and party. They were having a simple wedding with just close family and friends. It was a gorgeous summer day and I knew it was going to be a great day for everyone.

I was very happy and excited for both Finley and Rafe, they were truly soulmates and I couldn't have been more in awe of the love they had for each other and for Lilly. Watching them together, as a family, convinced me that was what I, too, wanted some day. A family to call my own.

Lilly was very excited for her flower girl duties today, and I knew she would steal the show. The little girl had adjusted remarkably well since being kidnapped and held in a child sex trafficking ring for almost two years. We couldn't see the fear and trauma in her eyes anymore, and though we all knew she was still going to have problems from time to time, she was back to being a happy and healthy little girl.

Rafe and Fin were still keeping her in therapy, but it was only once a week for an hour. They wanted to make sure nothing snuck up on her. She was doing extremely well with her service dog, Pepper, too. Clearly getting her the dog had been the perfect decision. They were good men and I was so happy for them all.

"We're waiting on you, Sweetheart," Max said as came up behind me and placed a kiss on my cheek.

"I'm ready," I said, flashing a warm smile into the mirror at him as I finished fixing my tie.

Looking back, I still couldn't believe my life had changed as much as it had. Just last year, I never thought I would be free from Baxter and his abuse, but now, I was in a happy and healthy relationship with not just one, but *two* incredible and loving men.

Baxter's death had been ruled as self-defense and I was very relieved that Damien hadn't been charged with his murder. Only the three of us knew what we had done, that we had baited and lured him into the house so Damien could kill him. I knew it had been wrong, but I really couldn't have imagined any another way to handle him. I couldn't have gone through the court system. It wouldn't have worked to begin with. He would never have been arrested and he would have continued to stalk me and eventually, he would have killed me. It was either him or me, and I did what I had to do, what everyone would do, I chose my own life over his.

When Max, Damien and I had decided to give this thing between the three of us a real shot, I wasn't too confident that it would work out. I thought for sure that we would be jealous of each other, or that one of us would inevitably feel left out, but we had made it work. Even when I would walk in on them kissing, I never felt any jealousy, I felt turned on, and they always welcomed me with open arms.

We had come up with a few simple rules, one of which was that we could do anything sexual with each other, but we had to tell each other everything. There were no secrets between us in or out of the bedroom. Ever.

One night, over a bottle of whiskey and pizza, we had all opened up to each other. I told them everything about Baxter and my parents. Max had told me the horror of his childhood with his father. Damien had informed me about the Italian Mob being after him and his brother, and not best friend, Sebastian. It was a lot for me to take in, but I needed to hear it all. I needed to know who these men were just as badly as they needed to know who I was.

That evening had brought us all closer.

We had also decided that we weren't going to hide our relationship from the people in our lives. With my apartment being a wreck, and Max wanting to move due to the blood stain in his bedroom, not to mention the bad memories the place now held, we had all stayed at Damien's place. Sebastian still lived there, but he was good with his brother being happy dating two men, thankfully.

All of our friends were thrilled for us and that was something that still shocked me to no end. I had honestly figured that they would have made disparaging comments and been disgusted with our decision to be in a three-way relationship. It wasn't, after all, a societal norm to date more than one person at the same time. I mean, there were laws against marrying more than one person. I knew we would never be able to get married, at least not legally, but that didn't matter to me. We all loved each other and that was all that truly mattered.

We had moved into a new house together just two weeks ago. Our house. We had invested in a double king size bed and it was more than worth every penny we spent on it. We spent the night breaking it in and it was glorious. We were all having fun and enjoying each other. We had created a real functioning relationship despite all odds that we would never work out. We had created a home and I couldn't have been happier. I had no idea my life could even be this blissful. I didn't think it was possible, but here I was.

I was loving my job. I'd become a huge part of the Social Services department in Baton Rouge and we were helping children by the handful every single week and nothing thrilled me more than seeing the *real* smiles on their faces as I went to the foster homes for my monthly check-ins. My life was good. For the first time in I didn't even know how long, I was happy and excited to start each day.

The safe haven homes had been chosen and the repair funding approved by the city and private investors who were getting a tax write off. Construction had begun and on Monday, I would be starting the process of selecting people to run them. We were getting somewhere with the project, though, and I knew that these homes were going to be a huge step in the right direction for at-risk kids. Hopefully, we would be able to keep them safe this time and we wouldn't have a repeat of the last safe haven home.

"Let's go, you two, we got a wedding to get to," Damien said, interrupting my thoughts with a warm kiss on my cheek.

"You got the wedding gift?" I asked as we headed out of the bedroom.

"I got it, plus Lilly's gift," Max said as he grabbed the two colorful gift bags.

We strolled out and climbed into Damien's truck. He turned the key and the beast started with a roar and a vibrating rumble I could feel in the cushioned seat. He shifted the vehicle smoothly into gear and we started off for the wedding.

We had picked up a gift for Lilly to make her feel like she was a real part of the wedding. Everyone had also been spoiling her because of what she had been through. She was such a sweet little girl it was so hard to imagine anyone trying to hurt her. She had lost her parents, but she now had a lot of overprotective uncles in her life to be there for her.

It was so surreal that I was now a member of that family. That I had all of these strong and powerful men, good-hearted, loving men, in my life. I had come from an extremely small family of just my parents and me. A family with no love. And now, I had this enormous family with all of this real and unconditional love, and it was all because of Damien and Max. They had given me the love of a family and the love of two soulmates. I knew some would argue that you couldn't have two soulmates, but I didn't believe that. I think our souls belonged to each other, that our souls were meant to be connected to each other, and it wasn't anyone's business to dissect it or judge us. We were happy and I wouldn't have my life any other way.

"Maybe one day we will be going to our own wedding," Max said, his voice slightly wistful.

"It wouldn't be legal," Damien pointed out.

"No, but people get married spiritually over a legal one. We could marry that way. I'm not proposing or anything, I'm just saying that one day maybe it'll be us who are getting married," Max explained.

"I'd like that," I said with a big smile turning up the corners of my lips.

I didn't care if it was legal or not. I would love to marry them both one day. I would love to stand in front of our family and friends and share our love with them all. I didn't know what we would do about last names, but that was part of the fun, part of the adventure the three of us were going on.

I hated that the only reason we even got to start this adventure was because of Baxter, though I tried not to let that taint it. If I hadn't been dating him, then I wouldn't have had a reason to make the move down to Baton Rouge. I never would have left Gaithersburg and that meant I would never have met Damien and Max. As much as I hated Baxter, and I was glad he was dead, if I hadn't been with him, I never would have gotten the chance to fall in love with my men.

Now, I never wanted to lose them.

Baxter thought he would be the one to destroy me, that he would kill me, but in the end, because of him, I got to be saved. Because of him, I got to experience what true love felt like and because of that, I had forgiven him for everything he had put me through. I didn't need to live with that kind of hate in my heart. I wanted to spend my life with pure love in my heart and there was no room for Baxter in my life anymore in any way, shape, or form.

"You got your hand sanitizer?" Damien asked as he parked his truck in the lot at the wedding ceremony.

"Yes, it's in my pocket. I swear, you both worry too much," I said, flashing them a loving smile.

They had been very good with my medical condition and the fact that I was often tired and got sick every month. Whenever I got sick, though, they were both there to take care of me. Whenever I got home from a long day at work and fell asleep on the couch, one of them would carry me up to bed. They never got upset with me, they just loved me in every way possible, and it meant the world to me.

"You have to be careful, you just got over pneumonia," Damien said.

"And we would both really like to see how many times we can make you come tonight," Max added with that devilish smirk of his plastered over his mouth.

"Oh well, in that case I will make sure to use it all day," I said with a big smile turning up the corners of my mouth.

I was more than looking forward to spending time with them tonight. I was looking forward to spending time with them *every night* for the rest of our lives. I had found my soulmates and I was finally, truly, happy.

Thank you for reading the Federal Protection Agency Series Omnibus Volume 2.

If you enjoyed this book, please leave me a review, and hey, don't forget to tell all your friends about the FPA!

~Love,

Evie Riley.

Dear Reader,

As you've no doubt figured out, all of my contemporary gay male romance books so far can be read standalone, but they are truly best if read in order if you prefer to know the back story of their family and friends. There are several instances of this kind of cross over in From the Edge and Federal Protection Agency, and that will likely continue through Smokejumpers where we will introduce more delicious men who live for nothing more that to help others, even when it puts them in the way of danger.

My next series, Smokejumpers, may feature some of the men you've already come to know and love from FTE and FPA, so watch for Book One, Hawke, to come this spring!

While you wait, why not check out another one of my series, the Gray Vale Pack, a wolf shifter paranormal romance, with a preview of His Fated Mate on the next page.

Enjoy!

PREVIEW

CONALL

THE FOREST AROUND us radiated life. I drank it in through nose and ears, but there was so more to it than that. My wolf growled inside me, sensing prey.

The feeling was so strong that even my human side itched for action. Any excuse to shift would be fine by me. Patrolling this disputed region between our lands and Stoke Ridge only tossed me a little excitement once in a while, but today felt rich with potential.

Glen came up beside me. The prickling of energy coming off him only got me even more keyed up.

"Deer," I murmured.

"Duh," Glen replied. "You're not the only

one with a fuckin' nose, Connie."

I reached out and slapped the back of his head without even looking. "What've I told you about calling me that?"

Glen let out a low growl. "Used to let me."

"That was when I was also fucking you. You see the connection there, dude?"

Immediately, our attention flew across to the clearing, and the big buck that crept into sight.

Glen slid his rifle down off his shoulder, but I stopped him.

"Uh-uh. We do it like nature intended."

"Ugh, seriously? That's one thing I definitely don't miss about you."

I stripped off in seconds, fending away Glen's lustful glare as I did. We'd had our chance, and it didn't work out. If he couldn't get over it then he was no good as a member of my patrol.

He kept his voice low and deep. "Why do you even come out with us lowly shit-kickers, anyway, Conall? You have options guys like me could never even dream of."

"You call going to fancy-pants shindigs and week-long meetings *options*? That's not me, bro. Besides, in three days, my sister is taking the fall for all of us."

That was the biggest downside to being what amounted to pack royalty. Marriages and matings that were all about strategy. Thankfully, that shit didn't apply to me. Only hetero pairings were recognized, still.

Because of all that, my twin, Fiona, was gonna be all hitched up to the pristine, primped and puckered heir of the Stoke Ridge Pack, Zoltan Valenta. And all for the lamest of reasons.

Peace.

More like death, as I saw it. If we couldn't get into harmless little pissing contests with our snobbish neighbors, then what the hell was the good of being wolves? Life is conflict, and vice versa.

I glanced across at Glen. "You're still dressed."

"C'mon, Con. You know how your father is."

Yeah, I knew. He treated shifting like it was a religious ceremony. Just like the ancient ones had. Tradition was everything in wolf packs.

"Dude, if my father's fancy notions mattered to me, I wouldn't be out here with you lowly shit-kickers, now. Would I? I'd be lying back on a fucking velvet sofa with servant boys feeding me grapes."

Glen made a quiet scoffing sound and worked his clothes off. "Let's just fucking get this done, so I don't have to hear any more shit."

I shook my head with a wry smile. "Do you even shift, bro?"

Before he'd finished rolling his eyes, I

opened myself up to the wolf, letting it ignite within me. Shifting was like sex. No matter how many times I did it, I always wanted more.

My body jolted, my muscles and bones danced around each other, and then it was done. I didn't even wait for Glen. The scent of that buck was too fucking delicious.

I crept forward, keeping low. The buck was spooked already. It was a buzz in the air that brought his scent with it. Twenty feet. Fifteen. His big body quivered and he cast his head around. No need to run this guy down. He was so close I could almost taste him.

As I tensed to spring at my prey, a rifle shot rang out. The assault of noise had me flinching away, and a second later the buck dropped dead.

I'd been so close. Glen was gonna pay for that. Robbing my wolf of his succor. In my rage, I shifted back, ready to tear my cohort a new one.

Before I could turn around, three men in Stoke Ridge uniforms moved into the clearing from the far side. One of them carrying a rifle, all of them pleased with themselves. Obviously new recruits, or they'd be treading a lot more carefully.

I marched forward, more than ready to turn my anger on them. I sensed, rather than saw, Glen moving into position behind me.

"Hey! You fuckin' Stoke Ridge assholes."

All three of the other side's patrolmen tensed as we moved closer. "Back down, Gray Vale. It's our trophy."

"Not when you bag it on our land."

Rifle dude sneered at me. "Well, when we bag one on your land, pal, we'll be sure to let you know. But this here is Stoke Ridge land."

I took a cleansing breath. As much as I'd been looking forward to taking down that buck, that would have been little more than an appetizer. This here was main course and dessert, all rolled into one. There was nothing I liked quite so much as tussling with these hoity-toity Ridgers.

"Is that right?"

"You know it is, grunt. Now, run off back to your kennels." He flicked his eyes down for a split second and then back up. "And tuck that tail of yours between your legs."

I gave the guy a flash of teeth. "Or maybe you want that... *tail*... right between *your* legs, Ridgy. I see how you look at me."

For me, that was just a throwaway comment. But for a Ridgy, it was the ultimate slur. Stoke Ridge society was stuck in the fucking nineteenth century when it came to sexuality.

Okay, a taunt like that one was low-hanging fruit, but all I wanted was for them to make the first move. The fact it worked so well every single time only meant I'd keep using it again and again.

Rifle dude snarled and handed his weapon to his right hand man. I went into a crouch, arms out, waiting.

The guy burst forward, charging straight for me. Like a fucking amateur. I let him slam into me, chest to chest, before spinning on the spot and throwing him halfway across the clearing. He landed in a sprawling mess of limbs.

"Now, you guys stand down," I said, letting all my menace and breeding come bubbling out in my voice. It did no good, though. These guys were young, dumb and full of... themselves.

The rifle guy sprang up to a squat, baring his teeth, which were growing longer.

I raised one eyebrow. "You gonna take this down to wolf level, kid?" That was the other thing with Stoke Ridge. They were even more stuffy about shifting than my father was. "'Cause I spend half my life there. Do you?"

That gentle little reminder seemed to do the trick, and he came back up onto his feet. When he approached me this time, he showed a ton more caution. Still not enough, though.

He threw a wild punch that couldn't have been more telegraphed. It was like a movie punch. He spent so much time pulling his arm back I could have made a coffee while I waited for him to throw it.

I pulled my head back and let his fist fly past, then wrapped my hands around the back of his head and neck, throwing him into the scrub and dirt face first.

No other man had even moved yet. Glen leaned back on a tree, stifling a yawn. The Stoke Ridge guys looked wide eyed and shell shocked. I already knew they were green, but I wouldn't mind betting this was their first ever patrol. That'd explain why they were so cavalier about taking down the buck on disputed lands.

As the main Ridgy came back up onto his feet, I held my hands up for calm. "Give it up, dude. Take your lumps and head back home."

"I'll take my lumps. And my trophy."

"No, you'll be leaving the buck." I crossed my arms and narrowed my eyes. "Understood?"

I could see a thousand different words bubbling up in his head. Some of them were punching so hard at his pride he almost said them.

"All right," he ground out. "But you understand *this*... I'm not backing down."

"No? It kinda looks like you are."

"Well, unlike you peasants, we here in Stoke Ridge value tradition. So, I'm allowing this to pass, for the sake of the upcoming wedding." He took his rifle back from his cohort and curled his lip. "You... do know about the wedding, right?"

"Of course he does," Glen interrupted. "He's—"

"I'm not interested in it. Perky prince Zoltan is lucky we're letting him into our pack at all."

The other guy tensed all over. I wasn't even sure he realized he'd tightened his grip on the weapon. "Let's be clear, you ass. It's your woman who's being elevated here. You and your caretaker Alpha should get on your knees and thank—"

That was as far as he got before my fist hit the side of his face. As much as I loved being wolf, sometimes hands worked better than paws.

The guy dropped like a sack of dirt, and I landed on him just as heavily. My weight on his chest, my hand on his throat.

His two patrolmen froze, their fear filling my nostrils. I'm sure they could sense the battle experience and silent aggression radiating off me, and made the sensible decision to stand down.

"Now it's your turn to listen, sunshine," I growled. "Yeah, Patrick Blair is only a second generation Alpha. If you think that weakens our pack in any way, you're welcome to test your claims."

"Get the hell off me. And for God's sake, cover yourself up."

"You Ridgies are so damn uptight. Never met a bunch of shifters so fuckin' scared of being naked." I rolled my hips just a little. "Or maybe you're scared of how much you're enjoying the view."

"Get off."

As much as I enjoyed roughing up Ridgies, this little scene had passed its sell-by date. There was nothing to be gained anymore. I stood, and offered the guy my hand. He slapped it away and got to his feet at his own speed.

"Lord Valenta will hear of this."

"Lord? You guys are so into this hierarchy shit it's... well, it's fucking embarrassing."

"Whether you accept it or not, every pack is a hierarchy, grunt. And the wrath of your Alpha will come down on you for this."

"It won't be the first time."

They turned and headed back into their territory with a last, narrow-eyed glare at the buck they'd taken down.

As they disappeared into the brush, another of my patrol team came running up from behind.

"Alec," I said. "What's up?"

"Better get dressed, dude. I'm taking your duties from here on. Daddy wants a word with you."

Glen chuckled without any real humor. "Wrath of the Alpha, indeed. News travels fast."

For more of Conall and Zoltan action, snag your copy of His Fated Mate at your favorite online retailer now!

OTHER BOOKS BY EVIE

Federal Protection Agency

Mason

Rafe

Ryzen

Cooper

Noah

Damien

Sebastian

Gabe

Logan

Ruthless Empire

Courting Danger

Chasing Danger

Kissing Danger

Smokejumpers

Hawke

Cyrus

Jase

Gage

Jackson

Xavier

Jasper Springs
Cade
Dawson
Drew
Grayson
Riley
Mitch

From The Edge
Shattered
Runaway
Jaded
Rescue
Hidden
Tormented

Gray Vale Pack
His Fated Mate
His Wounded Warrior
His Healing Heart

ABOUT THE AUTHOR

Evie Riley is a prolific, neurodivergent author known for her captivating MM romance novels. She has gained a significant following and topped the LGBT+ action and adventure bestseller charts with her series.

Evie's writing style often explores dark and gritty themes where her men must overcome difficult obstacles in their search for love, but she has also ventured into sweeter small-town romances, incorporating tropes like enemies-to-lovers, friends-to-lovers, age-gap, and forced proximity. She is known for crafting engaging romantic suspense novels and has a knack for creating interconnected series worlds that keep readers invested.

Interestingly, Ms. Riley has hinted at exploring new genres, such as Alien Omegaverse Romance, in the future.

Outside of writing, she enjoys spending time at the beach and has a quirky personality, described by her partner as ranging from cute to deadly, depending on her blood-chocolate levels.

Evie spends her nights writing bad boys in love, and her days wrangling the sweet boys she loves.